D1196169

STONE OF TYMORA

THE LEGEND OF DRIZZT®

Homeland
Exile
Sojourn
The Crystal Shard
Streams of Silver
The Halfling's Gem
The Legacy

Starless Night
Siege of Darkness
Passage to Dawn
The Silent Blade
The Spine of the World
Sea of Swords

A READER'S GUIDE TO R.A. SALVATORE'S THE LEGEND OF DRIZZT

THE HUNTER'S BLADES
The Thousand Orcs
The Lone Drow
The Two Swords

THE SELLSWORDS
Servant of the Shard
Promise of the
Witch-King
Road of the Patriarch

TRANSITIONS
The Orc King
The Pirate King
The Ghost King

THE NEVERWINTER SAGA
Gauntlgrym
Neverwinter
Charon's Claw
The Last Threshold
(March 2013)

STONE OF TYMORA
R.A. & GENO SALVATORE

STONE OF TYMORA

All characters in this book are fictitious. Any resemblance to actual persons, living or dead, is purely coincidental.

This book is protected under the copyright laws of the United States of America. Any reproduction or unauthorized use of the material or artwork contained herein is prohibited without the express written permission of Wizards of the Coast LLC.

Published by Wizards of the Coast LLC. Hasbro SA, represented by Hasbro Europe, Stockley Park, UB11 1AZ. UK.

FORGOTTEN REALMS, DUNGEONS & DRAGONS, WIZARDS OF THE COAST, D&D, THE LEGEND OF DRIZZT, and their respective logos are trademarks of Wizards of the Coast LLC in the U.S.A. and other countries. All other trademarks are the property of their respective owners.

All Wizards of the Coast characters and their distinctive likenesses are property of Wizards of the Coast LLC.

PRINTED IN THE U.S.A.

Cover art by: Tyler Jacobson
Map by Robert Lazzaretti
First Printing: October 2012

9 8 7 6 5 4 3 2 1

ISBN: 978-0-7869-6224-2
ISBN: 978-0-7869-6138-2 (ebook)
62098403000001 EN

Originally published in hardcover in three volumes: *The Stowaway* (2008), *The Shadowmask* (2009), and *The Sentinels* (2010)

Cataloguing-in-Publication Data is on file with the Library of Congress

For customer service, contact:

U.S., Canada, Asia Pacific, & Latin America: Wizards of the Coast LLC, P.O. Box 707, Renton, WA 98057-0707, +1-800-324-6496, www.wizards.com/customerservice

U.K., Eire, & South Africa: Wizards of the Coast LLC, c/o Hasbro UK Ltd., P.O. Box 43, Newport, NP19 4YD, UK, Tel: +08457 12 55 99, Email: wizards@hasbro.co.uk

Europe: Wizards of the Coast p/a Hasbro Belgium NV/SA, Industrialaan 1, 1702 Groot-Bijgaarden, Belgium, Tel: +32.70.233.277, Email: wizards@hasbro.be

Visit our websites at www.wizards.com
www.DungeonsandDragons.com

DEDICATION

To Diane, always. And this one's for Julian, for reminding me of the "why" of it all.
—R.A.S.

For all the teachers who helped shape my life. And for Mom and Dad.
—G.S.

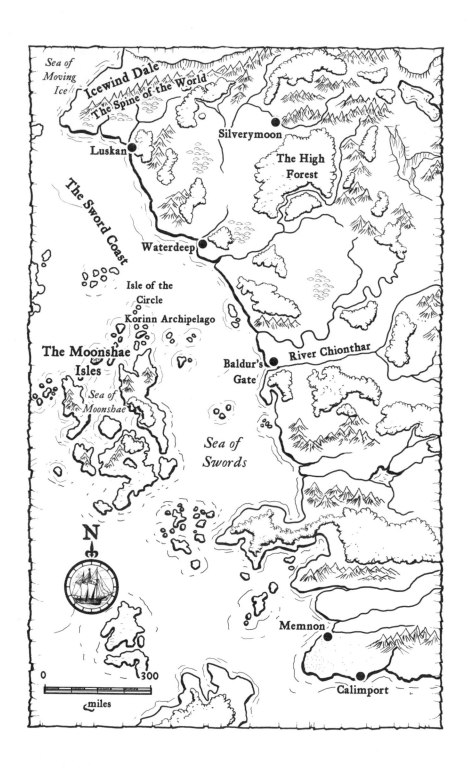

Sea of
Moving
Ice

Icewind Dale
The Spine of the World

Silverymoon

The High
Forest

Luskan

The Sword Coast

Waterdeep

Isle of the
Circle

Korinn Archipelago

The Moonshae
Isles

Sea of
Moonshae

Baldur's
Gate

River Chionthar

Sea of
Swords

N

0   300

miles

Memnon

Calimport

PART I

The approaching footsteps echoed off the many uneven surfaces of the small cave I lay in. I struggled to sit up, my shoulder sore where I had fallen on it, my wrists raw from the coarse rope tied around them. Flickering light appeared in the wide gap between the warped old wooden door and the stone floor. It was the first light I had seen in several hours.

The door creaked open.

A man stood in the portal, illuminated by the torch he held in his left hand. The light cast shifting shadows across his face, particularly under the brim of his broad black hat. Beneath the hat, a black bandana covered his right eye.

He entered, limping, favoring his left side. I quickly saw the reason: his right leg ended just below the knee, replaced with a weathered wooden peg.

After closing the door behind him, he pulled another torch from a loop on his belt, lit it, then placed the torches in sconces set on either side of the door. The light was still not much, and the shadows danced around the room. But at least I could see.

The old pirate turned toward me, lit ominously from behind, a silhouette, a shadow himself. His hand moved to the cutlass sheathed at his side, and I shuddered.

"Ye're a sailor, aintcha boy?" he said. "Yer skin's known the sea breeze, felt the sun. But it ain't yet leather like mine." He pulled at his many wrinkles, the sea-worn skin stretching in his hand. "But ye're on yer way. So be telling me, sailor-boy, how long ye been on the seas?"

I resisted the urge to answer him. It was the look in his eye. I knew he would kill me. I had been told often that pirates were merciless, bloodthirsty criminals—murderers and thieves—and that to be captured by one was death if there was no one to pay your ransom. I had seen it firsthand.

The pirate gave his cutlass a menacing shake and looked right into my eyes. "Ye thought I'd be coming in with me sword drawn and just cut ye down, didn't ye, boy?" he said. "But we could've done that when we took yer ship. Wouldn't have been much use for us to take ye all the way here and cut ye down, would it?"

I shook my head. "I didn't expect you to simply kill me. I expected—I still expect—you to question me first." I swallowed, attempting to still my trembling voice. "But you'll get nothing useful from me."

The pirate slowly drew his sword. "Well then, boy, shouldn't I just be killing ye now? I mean, if ye ain't gonna be giving me nothing *useful*." He burst into a laugh, the sort of laugh heard among friends sitting around a fire, sharing a drink. He slid the sword back into its scabbard. "Now, what be yer name, boy?"

"My name?" I had been prepared for an interrogation. But not for this. I pushed my back against the cave wall and sat up taller. I knew what I had to do.

"Yer name, boy. It ain't a hard question." The pirate smiled a crooked smile, showing as many teeth missing as remaining, several of them glinting with gold.

"My name does not stand alone," I said, the tremble gone from my voice. "It comes with a story. The tale of an artifact—tied to my soul through no fault or courage or heroism or hard work of my own. An artifact that has led me from one adventure to another, leaving a trail of destruction in its wake."

I stared at the dirty pirate a long while, forcing my mind down old roads I had tried to forget.

CHAPTER 1

I DO NOT KNOW WHAT NAME MY MOTHER GAVE ME.

I do not know, because every person who knew my name died—killed by a dark creature, a demon called Asbeel—mere days after I first entered the world.

Until I met Perrault, I was an orphan. And ten days after my twelfth birthday, I was alone once again.

Perrault lay unmoving on a bed in an inn. I had gone looking for help, but no help was to be found.

There was only Asbeel.

"Where are you, boy?"

". . . . boy . . . boy . . . boy . . . boy?" His voice echoed off every wall, shaking the timbers of houses all along the streets in that section of the city, shaking the ground beneath my feet. I looked around at the crowded marketplace, expecting to see panic, for how could the people of Baldur's Gate not react to that clamor?

But . . . nothing. Was the voice just for me? Was some demonic magic guiding it to my ears alone?

". . . boy . . . boy . . . boy . . . boy?"

I couldn't tell where the voice was coming from.

I darted frantically back and forth, looking for some clue, for some place to hide. A man leaning against a tavern door eyed me, thinking me out of my mind, no doubt. And perhaps I was.

The echoes grew louder. " . . . boy . . . boy . . . boy . . . boy!"

I raced down the alley beside the tavern and looked toward the sky. In that instant, all the sound came crashing together and nearly knocked me from my feet.

Asbeel stood a hundred strides away and thirty feet up, and I could see the fires in his eyes and the gleam of his teeth.

I knew—a sensation as heavy as drowning in cold water—that Asbeel had seen me.

I tried to run, but I could not, as if the cobblestones had reached up and grabbed my feet.

Asbeel jumped off the roof, landing in the alleyway with such strength that he hardly bent his legs to absorb the weight of the fall. The buildings shook and the ground trembled, and even the man at the tavern gave a shout, so I knew I was not imagining it.

But how could it be? Asbeel was no larger than an elf, a lithe and sinewy creature who seemed to weigh little more than I did. It made no sense, but nothing did.

The shock of the demon's jump seemed to break away the confining cobblestones, or free me from my own bindings. I knew not which and didn't care. I just turned and ran for all my life.

Not four steps out of the alleyway, I tripped and fell, skinning both my knees and jarring my wrists. But before I could begin to curse at my clumsiness, a huge crate soared over my head and smashed to pieces in the street in front of me.

I looked back just in time to see Asbeel kick another crate as if it weighed no more than a child's rag-ball. He laughed as it soared out for me, and I could only yelp and fall aside as it shattered precisely where I had been kneeling.

"Hey, now!" the man at the tavern cried, and another came out the door to see what was happening.

My mouth went dry, my heart sank. I wanted to call out to them to run away, to go back inside, but I could not. I hadn't the strength or the courage.

I just ran.

The ground trembled behind me as the beast gave chase. Then the shaking stopped, replaced by screams.

I covered my ears, but could not block out the cries. Not knowing where I was going, I turned every corner I came to, only wanting to be out of Asbeel's sight.

The ground trembled again and I knew he paced me. I ran into one of the main streets and the trembling grew more violent. I could hear his scaly feet slapping the cobblestones. He would grab me at any moment and tear me apart!

I should pull out Perrault's stiletto, I told myself, use its magic to make it a sword, and stab the beast through the heart.

I should . . . I should, I thought, but I could not.

Asbeel's face burned behind my eyes, evil and hideous and hungry, and the thought of it made my legs weak and my heart faint.

As I neared an intersection, a wagon driven by a team of four huge horses veered toward me. I couldn't stop. The driver screamed and tugged the reins with all his might.

The horses, neighing in complaint, barreled past me. I threw myself down and flattened myself between the wheels then managed to get out between the back two just as the driver stopped the cart.

"What, boy? Are ye dead, then?" the driver cried out.

I managed to scream, "No!" as I ran off.

Barely ten strides away, I heard the explosion as Asbeel slammed into the cart. I could picture the wagon shattering, its load of fruits flying wildly. I heard the driver yelp in surprise. I heard the horses whinny in terror and pain.

I peeled around the corner and looked back, just in time to see one of those horses kick Asbeel in the chest, sending him flying backward. He slammed against a wall and stumbled, but did not fall.

I yelled and ran. The demon refocused his anger—I heard more screams.

I turned down another cobbled street, and at last I knew where I was.

I had reached the heart of the temple district of Baldur's Gate. Massive structures all around dwarfed me, churches dedicated to each of the myriad gods of Faerûn, gargoyles and statues gazing down at me, leering or smiling with equal irony and equal uselessness.

The demon's voice rang out again, but it was farther away and full of even greater rage—an echo that would not die.

"You cannot hide, boy," the voice said. "Fall down and let yourself be taken."

But beneath his voice rang another, a woman's, perfect and clear as a clarion in the fog. It was but a whisper, but I could hear it distinctly.

Run now, and take heart.

Despite the clutch in my chest and the pain in my knees, the woman's voice compelled me.

I sprinted toward the sun that descended over the cityscape. The voices in my head grew fainter, and I felt less of the fear that had nearly crippled me. I felt myself coming under my own control again, aware of my surroundings. I slowed my pace.

As I tried to catch my breath, the leather bandolier I hid beneath my shirt dug into my shoulder, as if it were made of thick chains and not leather. In a pouch on that leather bandolier was a stone, dark as night and heavier than its small size suggested.

It had been in my possession for only ten days—a gift from Perrault—and already it had brought more grief than I had known possible. It had brought ruin to everyone I knew. And if I could not find a way to escape Asbeel, it would bring about my ruin too.

I glanced up and down the crooked street. The shadows grew longer; soon darkness would fall. I didn't want to be out alone, at night. And I didn't want to face Asbeel, alone, in the dark.

But where could I go? I thought of returning to the Empty Flagon, the inn where I had left Perrault only a few hours ago. By then the tavern would surely be full of patrons. The proprietor, a crazy old dwarf named Alviss, would be floating behind the bar and around the room on one of his flying blue discs. Flagons of mead would drift of their own accord out to thirsty customers then return, emptied, and with the coin paid.

And in the room at the back of the tavern, I would find Perrault, lying in bed. For a moment, I imagined I could race back to the inn, speak the password, enter the place, and have Perrault tell me what I should do. But Asbeel would surely come to look for me at the Empty Flagon. And I did not know the city well enough to find another place to hide. I had no other choice. I had to leave Baldur's Gate without him. The only question was how.

From the high hill of the temple district where I stood, I saw the whole sweeping descent of the bustling port and the long wharf at its end. The last of the day's vessels were just sailing up toward the city. I watched as one cut down the river, the small flag atop its mainmast fluttering in the wind. The weight lifted from my chest.

And a plan formed in my head.

CHAPTER 2

I SNUCK THROUGH THE INNER CITY AND MADE MY WAY TO THE RIVER WHERE I WAITED for morning to come. Nestled in a pile of crates at the end of the city's long wharf, I stayed awake all through the night. My heart raced at every sound, certain Asbeel had discovered me.

At last the sun rose and I felt safe enough to creep out of my hiding place. Many of the ships I had seen at anchor the previous evening were gone, having sailed out at first light. Those that remained had a steady stream of crew returning. I would have to play a waiting game.

The wind was strong and blew directly out to sea from the east, where the sun was rising. The air was warm despite the wind, and it felt good across my face.

I was sure no ships would be coming in against such a headwind, so to execute my plan, I had to pick one already docked. It would be a good day for departures, and I was sure most of the ships would be putting out before the breeze turned. All I needed to do was decide which one to hide aboard.

I moved along the wharf toward the city, and something caught my eye. Sure enough, a ship sailed upriver against the current and the blowing wind, tacking mightily and smoothly, cutting from side to side as if a ship were meant to sail like that, always like that, only like that.

I watched for some time, mesmerized, as the lone ship made its way toward the city. After a while, a small crowd began trotting along the docks. Several guards in uniform and a chubby man with a small stack of papers—the harbormaster, I guessed—prepared to record the new arrival. Then I realized they were gathering at the foot of the wharf I was sitting on.

I crouched behind one of the crates lining the wharf and prayed they hadn't seen me.

The ship stopped her tack and dropped sail, slowly gliding in along the dock. Her name, *Sea Sprite*, was painted in graceful though fading letters along her bow, and she was everything I was not looking for: small and sleek, in perfect condition, looking like the perfect craft for open water.

On her foredeck stood a human in very fine dress—the captain, I supposed. Next to him loomed a giant of a man, huge and imposing with long golden hair that shone in the morning sun. Beside him stood an unusual elf.

My gaze fixed on the elf. Something was not quite right about him, about the way he carried himself. He looked like a typical sun elf, with golden skin and light brown hair, but didn't seem comfortable in that skin. For a moment, it occurred to me that he was another of Asbeel's heritage, and I nearly ran away.

When he turned to look in my direction—to look at me, I realized, despite my hiding place—I recognized that discomfort again in his striking lavender eyes. That elf was different, I realized, and I felt the fool for thinking him connected to that beastly demon.

The ship was just putting in and would likely not put back out for a tenday. She was well cared for, and I figured that to mean an attentive captain and crew. She was small, with fewer places to hide than a great galleon. Every logical reason told me to pick a different ship.

But the elf intrigued me.

I decided right then and there that I would stow away aboard that ship. All her faults—which were really virtues—were outweighed by the look in the strange elf's eyes.

"What ho, *Sea Sprite?*" the harbormaster called to the captain. "Is Deudermont at your reins?"

The man in captain's garb called back. "He is! And glad to see Pellman, as well!"

Pellman, the harbormaster, had the look of a sailor, his skin leathered by the salt breeze, but his form spoke of a more sedentary lifestyle. Idling about the docks keeping his records, he probably took ample food from the various trading ships as they made berth, enough food certainly to keep his large belly full.

"Well met, Captain," the chubby man called. "And as fine a pull as I've ever seen! How long are you in port?"

"Two days, then off to the sea and the south," Deudermont replied.

Pellman called again. "I seek two adventurers—might you have seen them? Drizzt Do'Urden and Wulfgar by name, though they may be using others. One's small and mysterious—elflike—and the other's a giant and as strong as any man alive!"

Deudermont turned to his two companions, who were hidden from the harbormaster's view, and spoke briefly with them before calling down his answer. " 'Twas Wulfgar, strong as any man alive, who made the pull!" As he spoke, Wulfgar then the elf—Drizzt Do'Urden—stepped forward, showing themselves to Pellman.

That gave me a name for those violet eyes, and a name for the ship, and she was leaving in two days. Perfect.

The ship tied off quickly, smoothly, the crew executing its task to perfection. *Sea Sprite* had a shallow draw, and so was tied up close to the wharf. I saw my opportunity. Tied to the back of the ship was a launch, a two-person craft with oars, used to go ashore where there was no pier. The boat was tied to the back of the ship through a pair of small holes, too small for a man to crawl through.

Too small for a man, but not too small for me.

I watched as the crew disembarked and began loading supplies. I crouched in my hiding spot, hoping to catch a glimpse of Drizzt, but he was lost among the dockworkers. Wulfgar, the man I thought must have giant blood in him, helped from the deck, but never set foot off the ship. Midday passed, and before I knew it, the sun was moving into the western sky. With the day's work finished, many of the crew left the docks and headed for the taverns. A few guards took positions along the rails of the ship to keep watch.

I waited for the guard stationed on the aft deck to move to the far rail, then I quickly dashed forward. When he returned to the aft rail, I was almost directly below him. But he was expecting no trouble, and hardly even glanced in my direction. As he moved away, I began the more difficult part of the task.

The side of the ship was slick, even above the waterline, and the boards were fitted tightly together, but I managed to find small handholds to pull myself up. I climbed a few feet then sidled along the back of the ship until I was alongside the rowboat. My fingertips ached from the strain of holding myself, and I felt more than a few splinters dig in, but I would not let go. That ship was my freedom, and I saw only one way aboard.

The launch hung from ropes and dangled perhaps three feet behind the ship. I could climb no higher—the hull sloped outward, and I could see no more handholds. I would have to take a chance.

I pulled my legs up to my chest and braced them against the ship's hull. I took a deep, steadying breath, then let go with my hands and kicked out with my legs. I turned in midair, reaching for the launch. My hands made contact with the side of the ship . . .

And I slipped.

I lost my hold on the little boat, my only hope of getting aboard that ship. As I plummeted toward the water, I reached out in desperation, trying to grab the launch, the ship, anything.

My hand hit something solid, and I clutched at it.

It was neither the ship nor the boat, but one of the two ropes meant for securing the smaller boat. It had come untied—how, I do not know, for sailors' knots never come undone when they aren't supposed to—and the line had dropped right beside me.

The rope scoured my palm as I slid down it. But I held on with all my might, refusing to let go.

The launch swayed dangerously, and I thought it might tumble from its position—if one knot could come untied, the other could as well, as could the rope dangling from the aft deck. After a few moments I stopped swinging so wildly, and slowly pulled myself up the rope and onto the launch, my hands burning the whole time.

When I reached the launch, I realized my luck was even better than I had first thought. My plan had been to squeeze through one of the holes where the ropes tied the launch to the hull. Up close, I saw I could fit through the hole, but not with the rope threaded through the space. With a rope untied, one hole lay empty and I could pull myself through, bringing the rope with me. I tied it off, trying to duplicate the knot on the other rope. At last, the launch was secure enough, I was inside the hold of *Sea Sprite*, and no one was coming to investigate. I breathed a sigh of relief—breathed it into my aching hands, trying to soothe the pain—and moved some barrels to find a spot to settle in for the night.

CHAPTER 3

I SPENT THE NEXT TWO DAYS EXPLORING THE SPACE I HAD CLAIMED FOR MYSELF. WHEN there weren't sailors in the hold, I roamed around, finding barrels of dried fruit and jerky and filching enough to eat, but only a little from each barrel so it wouldn't be noticed.

I couldn't have picked a better place to stow away. I was far aft, away from the main hatch to the hold, and the containers were piled high. All the new cargo, mostly food, was stored near the bow of the ship. Back near the stern I found mostly trade goods, which wouldn't be unloaded until we reached a port, and with luck, not until I had safely made my getaway.

The goods were exotic and interesting—a barrel of a rare black spice, ground into fine powder; boxes of an ivory-like substance carved into various shapes; and crate upon crate of salt.

During those two days in port, I tried to turn my thoughts away from Perrault and what had become of him at the inn. But at night, he haunted my dreams. I tossed and turned in my makeshift bed, one nightmare after another startling me awake. I longed to go up on deck to count the stars like Perrault had taught me when I was six years old and couldn't sleep. It was the only way I knew to find peace, but I dared not leave the hold. And so I stayed, day and night, praying for time to pass quickly until the ship headed out to sea.

At first the solitude was nearly unbearable, but then I found a single barrel of ceramic marbles, each about the size of the knuckle of my thumb. Those marbles became my only amusement. I rolled them around, watching them move with the sway of the ship. I juggled them, tossing three or even four into the air, catching each as it fell then tossing it up again as the next came down. I even played with some of the rats on the ship, trying to roll a marble into a rat before it saw what was coming and darted away. I never actually hit one, but the game kept my mind occupied.

The third day, I awoke to much clamor from above, and to a great swaying of the ship. I darted to the rope holes, my only view to the outside world, and looked out to see Baldur's Gate receding into the distance.

Behind the city, the sun rose looking larger than I had ever seen it. The sun seemed to cover the entire city, that huge city I had been so impressed with when first I looked upon it. I stared into that beautiful sunrise, but I couldn't help but see darkness beneath it. The city faded behind me, and with it faded Perrault.

Down the Chionthar River we sailed, angling to port, to the south, almost as soon as we crossed the mouth of the river into the open ocean. The coast was in view, behind and to our left, for a good long way as we ran tight and parallel. As the sun moved to the west, we turned again, heading to the open ocean. I did nothing but watch the sea that day, not even thinking to play with the marbles and the rats.

I stayed hidden all day, waiting until the crew had gone to their crowded bunks on the deck above the hold. When night fell, I crept stealthily to the top deck.

I figured if anyone caught me out at sea, there was little they could do. Perhaps they would make me scrub pots in the galley, or swab the deck endlessly, or suffer at some other disgusting task. But they could not throw me off the ship—could they? Surely they wouldn't murder me. They were merchant sailors, not pirates.

Silent as a shadow, I stepped out under a sky filled with stars. The gentle ocean breeze welcomed me from my prison, and the air, which had smelled salty even below decks, burned in my nostrils with the brine of the sea.

Sailors were posted here and there, and though they weren't particularly attentive, I was careful to avoid them. I had decided that there was only one place to spend the night: the crow's nest.

As I made my way to the railing, I reached under my shirt and gripped the bandolier binding my chest. In only a moment, I would be rid of the cursed stone once and for all. I would throw it into the ocean and never think of it again. But as I opened the pouch that hid the stone, I hesitated. All I saw was Perrault, his face stern but his eyes smiling. I saw him in my head, and I felt him in my heart. But I also felt the weight of the stone, the weight of my guilt. And it was more than I could bear.

"Dangerous for a stowaway to be on deck, isn't it?" came a whispering voice.

I nearly yelped aloud. Such a scream would have alerted the other sailors, so I stifled it. I quickly closed the pouch, rearranged my shirt, and turned to face my discoverer.

He was hidden in shadow just beyond the mast, his form indistinct. All I could see were two points of burning lavender flame, the eyes of the elf, Drizzt Do'Urden.

"What are they going to do to me?" I whispered. I tried to seem confident, defiant even, but somehow the words only sounded scared.

"That depends," replied Drizzt, "on whether they catch you. But if they do, Captain Deudermont would be well within the law to throw you to the sharks."

I stammered, trying in vain to answer, but nothing intelligible came out.

The elf smiled. At least, his eyes brightened, so I assumed he was smiling, though I could not make out his facial features.

"But he seems an honorable man to me," the elf continued, "and would more likely put you to work. But that depends on whether or not they catch you."

"You aren't going to turn me in?" I asked.

He shook his head. "I'm a passenger, same as you. Well, perhaps not quite, since my passage is paid. But I have neither need nor desire to give you away. I would ask one question of you, though. Why do you risk so much to come out on deck?"

It was my turn to smile, in relief. "I can't see the stars from the hold." It wasn't a lie.

Drizzt looked at me for a long moment then gave a slight nod. "The stars are worth such a risk, indeed."

"Yes, sir, they are."

"Then I shall leave you to them." He turned and walked away before I could reply.

I made my way carefully, quietly, to the mainmast, looking over my shoulder, certain I would find the elf watching me. When I reached the simple ladder of metal pegs, I put my foot on the first rung and began to climb.

The view was as incredible as I'd hoped it would be, a clear sky stretching infinitely in all directions. The stars twinkled and blinked, and their reflections sparkled on the sea, and I could not tell where the sky stopped and the ocean began.

A cool breeze washed over my face and I took a deep breath, drinking in the salty smell of the sea. Perhaps it was something Drizzt had said, or perhaps it was just that spectacular view stretching before me, but the stone and Asbeel no longer weighed so heavily on my mind.

I shouldn't risk tossing the stone here, I decided. The time wasn't right. It could be too easily found again. Instead I would hide aboard the ship and sail to the ends of Toril—or as far as *Sea Sprite* could take me, and when I could sail no farther, then I would drop the thing into the ocean. And I would start my life again.

I wished I could spend the entire voyage in the crow's nest, but I knew that if I did, I would surely be discovered. And after what Drizzt had told me, I dared not take that chance.

I stayed in the crow's nest the whole of the night, though, only climbing down when the eastern horizon began to glow with predawn light. The crew was stirring as I slipped by, but no one took notice of me and I reached my hiding spot undetected. I was soon dreaming again, seeing Perrault, but the dreams were pleasant and warm.

I spent the next two days in a similar routine: sleeping during the day, and climbing to the crow's nest at night.

On our fourth day out from Baldur's Gate, something woke me.

It took me a long while to get my bearings, to realize what had stirred me from my sleep. I was still below, and no one had found me, but a great commotion took hold above as sailors rushed to and fro, shouting and yelling. Most of their words were lost to me, but one word, shouted over and over, told me everything.

"Pirates!"

CHAPTER 4

MY HEART DROPPED. PIRATES! IF THEY TOOK THE SHIP, THEY WOULD LOOT THE HOLD, and my hiding spot would be compromised. If pirates took me, they would not be so lenient as the elf had been a few nights earlier. They would throw me to the sharks, or keelhaul me, or worse.

I steadied myself. They would not take the ship, I thought, not with the elf and the giant aboard. And if they did, they would not take me easily. I would go down swinging.

I drew my dagger—Perrault's dagger—and rolled it in my hand, feeling its balance, its magic, its power. I had seen Perrault use its magic before: a simple flick of the wrist would extend it into a fine sword. I knew how to wield such a blade, and though I had never been in real combat, I was confident of my ability to defeat any drunken pirate.

If more than one pirate came, I would hold them off as long as I could. That corner of the hold was my kingdom, my little patch of the world, and it would not fall, no matter the foe. I would rather die than be taken by pirates.

But my determination died as *Sea Sprite* tried to evade her pursuers. A battle at sea is not like a battle on land, where armies line up and charge at each other, and the victor is usually the army that can bring the greatest numbers to the battle most quickly. On the sea, the battle is won or lost by positioning, by eliminating threats one at a time. *Sea Sprite* was a sleek and speedy vessel. I hoped the ships chasing her were not.

As *Sea Sprite* rolled, breaking through the swells, I thought about Captain Deudermont's tactics. The pirates would try to prevent his escape, while Captain Deudermont would try to get out of the pirates' range, so that he may face them individually. On the great expanse of the Sea of Swords, that probably meant hours of sailing before the first arrows were fired.

I peered out the holes in the stern, but saw nothing but open sea. With a heavy sigh, I settled myself down for an agonizing wait. I began tossing marbles, trying to bounce them off the crates and back to my hand without moving my wrist. I had become quite good at that game, and the repetition put me into something of a trance.

Without warning, I was thrown from my reverie.

I say "thrown," because I found myself suddenly in midair. The ship cut a turn, the sharpest turn I ever imagined any ship cutting. *Sea Sprite* cut so sharply that her bow lifted clear out of the water and she pivoted on her stern. The sudden move sent all the barrels and crates in the hold—as well as me—tossing and tumbling, head over heels and end over end, to bump and bang against each other. A cask of water burst, a barrel of salt spilled open, and a box of carved ivory slammed into the wall barely an inch from my head. With a crushing, grinding noise, the ship settled down as quickly as it had lifted.

Above decks, the hoots of victory and cries of rage turned to steel clashing against steel, shouts of pain, and the stomp of many, many boots across the deck. My blood raced, and I gripped my dagger, ready to stab any enemy who dared approach. But for the time being, no one entered the hold, and the waiting became unbearable.

I decided to peek at the action through the holes in the stern. I stuck my head out just enough to see that we were entangled with a larger ship.

In the distance, a ball of fire arced off the hull of another ship. As soon as the ball cut through the air, I realized what it was: burning tar, launched by a catapult and headed directly for *Sea Sprite*. Headed directly for the stern of the ship. Headed directly for . . . me!

I ducked.

I heard no crash of the missile against the hull, so I poked my head up to look. Directly below me, the water churned and I watched with great relief as the last lick of flames sank beneath the waves.

Another ball of fire soared over the other ship, but it didn't arc toward us—it didn't arc at all. My breath caught in my throat. What was it? Was it a dragon? Was it some powerful spell? If a wizard had thrown such a fireball, that wizard must be as a god, for it seemed as though one of the stars had dropped out of the sky.

Orange flames rent the cloudless blue. Sky and sea appeared as a painting, with a great fire roaring behind it, and someone tearing a jagged rip across that painting to reveal the flames.

I soon realized that the flames had a shape. It was no fireball or dragon—it was a chariot of fire, horses and carriage ablaze!

I lost my breath as the fiery thing cut sharply around *Sea Sprite* then soared toward the second pirate ship with purpose. The chariot plunged right through the pirates' mainsail, lighting the canvas on fire.

Then a silver streak blazed toward the ship from the chariot. A woman on the back of the flying craft fired a bow. Another bolt of silver leapt out. The catapult strained to respond, but its shot barely lifted into the air then it dropped back onto the deck of the ship.

I couldn't take my eyes off the spectacle. My heart raced as the chariot raced, and leaped as it cut graceful turns, and I nearly cried out when I spotted the driver—a red-bearded dwarf, hollering as if he were truly enjoying the wild ride. The chariot whipped around again, clipping the top of the pirate mainmast, lighting it like a candle. Then the flaming craft turned, moving toward us.

Something dropped off the back of the chariot—the woman archer, I guessed, had abandoned her ride. I leaned out, trying to see where she had splashed down, and to see where the chariot was headed.

I held my breath at the sight of a third pirate ship approaching. I prayed that the chariot would similarly cripple it.

But the chariot did better than that. I heard a cry for Moradin, a dwarf god, and that crazy driver steered the chariot right onto the deck of the third pirate vessel. If all the wizards of Baldur's Gate had lined up side by side and hit the ship with a fireball, it would not have been as grand an explosion! The sight of it stole my breath, then the brightness of it stole my sight.

I fell back and spent a moment blinking. As soon as I could see, I returned to my portal, not wanting to miss the incredible battle.

But then a scaly green hand, its long fingers ending in sharp, filthy claws, hooked over the hole right in front of my face.

CHAPTER 5

I FELL BACK AND LASHED OUT WITH MY DAGGER, MORE ON INSTINCT THAN THOUGHT. MY blade bit deep into the monster's hand, severing a finger. The hand withdrew, but didn't loosen its grip—it ripped a few planks out of the hull as it fell back.

I stared out the now-massive hole in the hull, hoping to watch the beast splash into the sea below.

But instead I saw it dangling from the launch by one hand. It would have been nine feet tall if it were standing, and its arms were long even for its body. It glared up at me, and its hideous pointed nose and crooked teeth would have been enough to unsettle the hardiest of soldiers—and I was no soldier! I looked into its murderous eyes and I felt as if my heart had stopped.

My mind cried out to stab it, to attack, to kill it while it hung from the rowboat. But my body would not answer that call. All I could do was retreat a few steps as the thing ripped at the hull, pulling planks off with ease. When the hole was large enough, it swung itself through.

A surge of fear snapped me from my stupor, and I took the only action I could think of. I turned and ran.

I hoped my small size would help me. I was able to navigate through the tight spaces of the hold easily, and the hulking thing surely could not. I realized my error as the first few boxes went soaring over my head.

"Come out, tasssty snack," the thing gurgled. Its voice was something between a roaring bear and a drowning cat, every bit as ugly as the monster itself.

I picked my way through the familiar cask maze, toward the hatch to the deck, to anywhere the beast was not. But the ship's sharp turn and the crash had tossed the contents of the hold, and I could barely keep my footing.

The troll tossed another barrel at my head, and it crashed among several casks of water, one of which burst open. Other crates and boxes tumbled about.

One of the crates, full of dried and salted meat, landed directly on me, knocking me down and blasting the breath from my lungs. The troll ripped through the last stack of barrels right behind me.

"Oh–ho! Cannot hide!" the brute shouted in delight. Then it stopped abruptly, and when I dared to glance back, it stood staring at me.

It stared at my chest, where my shirt had been torn open. Stared at the sash holding the black stone.

"Ohhh, the demon wantsss it, don't it be?" Its voice was a shrill whisper, like a nail pulled across glass. "'E'll pay me well, won't 'e, then?"

I snapped my wrist out, extending the magical blade, and swung as hard as I could. But the creature was quicker than I thought, and it stepped out of my reach.

"Eet hasss bite, eet does!" snarled the troll in a strange half-laugh. "But so does I!"

It lunged forward.

I dodged to my left and cut a quick backhand with my saber, aiming to hit the creature in the ear, or at least force it back.

But the beast caught my arm in its hand.

In desperation, I reached my other hand into the nearest barrel and grabbed a handful of powder. Without thinking, I hurled the white stuff into the beast's ugly face.

The sea-green thing howled but didn't loosen its grip on my forearm. "Sssalt!" it shrieked. "The tasssty snack attacks with salt! Oh ho! I leeve in the sea, foolish thing. Salt is my friend, is not yours."

At least it wasn't eating me as it spoke, I thought, reaching into the next barrel. Again, only powder, but I threw it in the troll's face, hoping to buy some time.

But this time the powder was black—it was pepper imported from the town of Nesmé, that rare spice I had found when I first came aboard. The creature yelped in pain.

It released my hand and grasped at its face with its filthy claws. I grabbed another handful and ran between its massive legs, heading toward the wall through the path the brute had just cleared, a plan forming in my head.

I pocketed the spice as I approached the gaping hole in the hull. Quickly I scanned the nearby barrels to be sure everything I needed was still there, popping open a barrel and a box. Then I went to the hole, using my sword to pull the dangling rope back onto the ship. Perrault's sword was a good one, and I quickly cut the other rope tying the launch to the hull, allowing the small craft to swing freely from the overhead rope.

Heavy footsteps thumped behind me like the beating of my own heart. I had no time!

I turned and grabbed three small objects from the open box—the ivory carvings.

Quickly I put them up into the air in a graceful juggle.

"Hey, you," I called to the monster. "If you don't eat me, I'll give you these!"

"Oh ho, the tasssty snack does not want to be snack, does it then? Eet bribes me! But no, I thinksss, I want the snack. Sailing is hungry work, so eet ees." The thing stopped, deep in thought—as deep as such a creature was capable of, I figured. It spoke again. "I can take the treenkets from eets corpse, can't I?" It moved forward again.

I tossed one of the pieces toward the beast, yelling, "Catch!"

Sure enough, the dim-witted troll glanced up at the flying object—not for long, but long enough. I pegged off the other two pieces, hitting the thing right between the eyes with both. But it hardly felt the blows.

It roared and charged.

I grabbed the open barrel and tipped its contents—hundreds of tiny ceramic marbles—directly into the wretch's path.

The monster slipped and fell, crashing heavily into the wall beside the gaping hole.

I did not wait. As soon as the barrel fell, I grabbed the loose rope and swung myself out toward the launch, climbing as fast as I could, hand over hand, up onto the small boat. The creature oriented itself quickly and appeared at the hole, snarling in rage.

"You die now." Its voice, that unearthly gurgle, was lower in pitch and more intense. Even several feet away, I could feel and smell its horrid breath.

The creature reached at me with its long arms and grabbed the side of the launch. Slowly, it began to pull the boat nearer.

I could have cut at those hands with my saber, but I knew I would not dislodge the thing. Instead, I grabbed the rope still attached to the launch and began to climb.

"You not escape," the troll promised, pulling harder, trying to bring the launch close enough to grab me before I got away. It leaned out of the ship, its foul breath billowing at me, its teeth gnashing hungrily. It leaned, and it pulled . . .

I gripped the rope more tightly with my left hand and swung my sword with my right, cutting the rope just about where my knees dangled.

Off balance, and suddenly burdened with the weight of the boat while leaning too far forward, the troll toppled and fell. It reached up to swat at me, but the strike had no strength and its claws did not dig in.

Down fell the launch and the wretched beast along with it. The boat landed with a splash, and the troll landed atop it, smashing right through, reducing the rowboat to flotsam. The ripples looked an awful lot like those created by the ball of pitch, in precisely the same spot.

The troll's strike had caused me to swing, and suddenly I was veering back toward the ship, toward the hole where the troll had ripped planks out of the vessel. I saw the sharp edges of broken wood rising up to meet me even as I fell, but I felt the pain of it gashing my chest for only a moment.

Then I felt no more.

CHAPTER 6

WHEN I AWOKE, I FELT AS IF I WERE GENTLY STEPPING OUT OF A DREAM. IN FACT, I thought I was still dreaming.

A most beautiful face hovered over me. Her eyes were the deepest, purest blue, and they smiled sadly at me, comforting me despite the burning pain in my chest. Her red-brown hair flowed over her shoulders, wet but still perfect.

Looking at her, I recalled the fiery chariot, its archer diving out right before it crashed into the pirate ship . . .

So that is why we won, I thought: The gods sent us an angel.

"Who . . . are . . . ?" My throat was so parched the words burned as spoke. I coughed, and pain seared my shoulder and my chest.

"Rest, child." The woman stroked my forehead until the coughing eased. "My name is Catti-brie. Everything is all right now."

I looked up to see the door opening. Three forms silhouetted against the incoming light—a dwarf, an elf, and a giant of a man.

My eyes fell on the middle figure, on Drizzt Do'Urden, his lavender eyes burning with intensity. His skin appeared black in the dim light, I realized, and it was no trick.

I had heard of dark elves before, of the drow who lived beneath the world. They were the subject of many nighttime stories, bogeymen who came out in the darkness to raid elven villages and kidnap babies.

But I was not afraid of that elf, that drow. He had not turned me in to the captain when he'd had the chance. He understood what a night spent staring at the stars might mean to someone like me. In the brief time we'd spoken, I sensed no malice, only sympathy. For whatever reason, he had chosen to protect me.

Drizzt stepped toward my bed, hesitation in his step. "How is he?" he asked in a low voice.

I remembered the first time I laid eyes upon the elf, when he had appeared as a surface elf but had looked so uncomfortable in his own skin. I suddenly understood why. He had been wearing some sort of magical disguise. And it was gone. Now that he could be himself, the discomfort I sensed was gone, too.

Catti-brie looked at the elf and his two companions. "I'm sure the boy appreciates your concern, but ye three are no help here." She waved them away and turned to me. "Ye all be going, now. I'll just be holdin' this one's hand a bit, while they take care of him." She nodded past me, and I followed her gaze to a pair of men entering the room. They carried a small bucket, steam rising off the top.

I tried to mumble something, to ask what was happening, what they were doing, but I could not produce anything intelligible.

I heard the door shut, and I felt her hand holding mine, strong and callused yet soft. The men set down the bucket—it was filled with black liquid, and I could feel the heat pouring off it. One of the men took up a large metal spoon.

Catti-brie whispered something under her breath—a prayer, I thought—and the man lifted the spoon up to my wounded shoulder.

Suddenly the pain worsened tenfold, a hundredfold. I tried to scream but there was no air in my lungs. I tried to focus on those blue eyes, but there was too much water, more tears than I knew I had. The pain was too intense and I passed out.

.:⌒:.

Some time later, I awoke. "The tar cauterizes the wound," said a voice—a man's voice.

"Cauterizes?" I mumbled, not even opening my eyes.

"It burns the flesh together, so the wound won't bleed."

"Sounds painful." I would have laughed if it didn't hurt so much.

"I've been told it is. But it's better than the alternative." The man's voice was firm, but not unkind.

"What is the alternative?" I was mumbling so badly, I could hardly believe the man could understand me.

"Bleeding to death. And that is no way for a lucky child like you to die."

At the words "lucky child" I opened my eyes, hopeful. But the man standing before me was unfamiliar—or, rather, I had never met him. He wore a regal, if threadbare, blue uniform, and he spoke clearly, with great dignity.

"I am Captain Deudermont of *Sea Sprite*, and you are unlawfully aboard my ship," he said.

Great, I thought. I save his ship from that troll and he's going to toss me overboard?

"I'm very sorry, sir," I said. "But I have an explanation. You see, what I am—"

"What you are, young sir, is a stowaway, and a thief," the captain spat.

In spite of my throbbing shoulder, I sat up. I tried to respond but the captain held out his hand.

"What you are not," Deudermont continued, "is a coward."

I perked up—that hardly sounded like a bad thing.

"Can you take orders?" he asked.

I blinked a few times before answering. "Yes, sir."

"Can you show dignity and bravery in the face of danger?"

"Yes, sir."

"Can you be loyal to those around you, peers as well as superiors?"

"Oh, yes, sir, I can, sir."

"Then, young man, I think I can find a place for you on my ship. If you so desire." For the first time, Captain Deudermont smiled—not a wide smile, but a dignified smile. And it was enough.

I started to respond, but he cut me off. "Do not answer right now. You have many days of healing before you could be useful, anyway. We shall care for you until you're fit, and then you can give your answer."

He turned to leave.

"Wait! Sir!" I called with as much force as I could.

He turned back. "Yes, young man?"

"My name is Maimun. You . . . you never asked my name."

PART II

"Took yerself long enough to get to the point!" the old pirate said with a chuckle.

"Exactly long enough," I answered.

"Gave yer name ter Deudermont pretty danged quick. Yer thinkin' he's better'n me, more deserving yer name? More deserving yer respect?"

"He didn't ask. You did. I do not reward greed."

The chuckle turned into a laugh. "Some'd say, greed be its own reward!"

"They'd be wrong."

"I'd expect you to say that, fool boy." In the blink of an eye his laugh was gone, his face a profound scowl. With surprising grace for a one-legged old man, he rose to his feet and snapped his cutlass from its sheath. "Ye learned from Deudermont, righteous old fart that he is."

"I learned much from Captain Deudermont," I answered indignantly. "He is a good man, one of many I've known, and all of them far better than you."

"Don't ye know better'n to insult a man holding a sword?" He brandished his blade but made no move to strike.

I waited, staring into that scowl, goading him with my eyes, challenging him to take the swing. But the cutlass did not fall.

"Well, perhaps yer captain'll pay yer ransom then. And my *greed*," he practically spat the word, as if it were distasteful to speak, "will be rewarded." He turned as if to leave, taking one of the torches from its sconce.

"Deudermont is not my captain," I said. "And he would not pay pirate ransom even if he were."

The old man stopped in his tracks and turned slowly toward me. "Yerself better start speaking again, and ye better start speaking fast, else I'll cut yer head from yer shoulders."

"Perhaps. But I have a question for you. What is *your* name?"

"Ye haven't earned enough of my respect to know it," he spat. "Now talk. Tell me of this artifact. Where did ye get it, and where is it? We ain't found it on ye when we pulled ye from the drink."

"You want the artifact?" I said. "Well, then, you should know its whole bloody story."

CHAPTER 7

I KNOW NOTHING OF MY BIRTH. I KNOW NOTHING OF MY PARENTS, SIBLINGS, NEIGHBORS. I do not know what day I was born, nor the name or location of my first home.

I do not know because when I was an infant, raiders attacked my hometown. They burned all the buildings, and killed all the people.

Somehow, I survived.

My parents' house had a secret room in the basement—a cellar where they kept their fine elven wines—and my mother hid me there. When the house was set on fire, the debris fell in front of the cellar door and blocked it. I lay down there, or so I was told, wrapped in one of my mother's traveling cloaks, crying.

The day following the raid, a stranger to the village rode into town alone and searched the rubble. He later told me that when he found me, a single, smoldering chunk of wood lay beside me—a piece of a ceiling beam that had fallen—and it had missed me by mere inches, but had kept me warm. I was alive, awake, staring at him. I even smiled at him, he told me. He smiled back then gently lifted me and carried me away from that ruined place.

We rode hard for a day and a night to the south, into the High Forest. His horse ran tirelessly, swift and surefooted even as night fell and the darkness of the old forest deepened.

The man delivered me into the safety of a small cave, into the arms of a skilled healer. Elbeth, she was called, and she was a caretaker of the forest—a druid. The man delivered me then rode away, and Elbeth never spoke a word of him again.

From that day on, Elbeth fed me—mostly the fruits and berries that grew wild throughout the area—and she kept me clothed and sheltered. She taught me to speak, and showed me the ways of the forest animals.

"Lucky child," Elbeth called me. I had no real name, and she had no inclination to give me one. A name did not define a person, she said. Instead, it merely marked things for recognition, like the beasts and the trees, and she needed no help to recognize me.

The anniversary of my arrival in the forest served as my birthday. The sixth of those days dawned dimly, the skies overcast with dense clouds. The rain began about noontime. The skies grew darker and darker as rumbles of summer thunder rolled through the trees.

Lightning pierced the sky as a figure strode to the mouth of our little cave, the brilliant bolts illuminating his silhouette, revealing his elf features. His skin was the golden red of an oak leaf in the early autumn, his hair the black of a raven's wing, long and silky and whipping in the rising wind. He moved with grace, and when he spoke his voice was soft and kind. But his eyes betrayed the lie behind that softness. They were dark, and hard, and empty of life.

"You cannot have him," Elbeth said before the strange elf could speak.

"That is not for you to decide, witch," he replied.

"I did not decide," she said. "He came to my door, and I sheltered him, and he needs my shelter still. So here he will stay. You cannot have him—you may not take him."

The elf's hand moved to his shoulder—toward the hilt of the sword sheathed against his back.

Elbeth laughed. "You wish to fight me, do you? Here, now, in my grove, in my home, you think you can defeat me?" She laughed again, and there was weight in her voice.

A flash and a tremendous burst of thunder shook the cave. I jumped, so startled that I tripped over my own feet and landed hard on my backside.

The elf scowled, again reaching for the hilt of his sword, and again stopping short. He started to speak then looked down at a spot on the ground less than five feet in front of him, blackened and charred where the lightning bolt had struck. In front of him—inside the cave.

"The next one does not miss," Elbeth said, her voice steady.

Still scowling, the strange elf turned on his heel and strode away from the cave.

As soon as he was gone, the wind whipped into a furious gale and the downpour began. Elbeth turned to me. "Let's have some supper, shall we? It is your birthday, after all."

"Who was that?" I asked.

I wanted to ask about the lightning as well. Elbeth had told me lightning prefers to hit the tallest object in an area, yet we were in a cave at the base of a hill surrounded by tall trees and the bolt had found its way through. But she seemed not to worry, so I took comfort in her confidence.

"He is none of your concern," she answered. "Just an old acquaintance." She waved her hand, spoke a few words, and suddenly the stone slab that served as a table was covered with a feast—sweet, sun-ripened fruits from the forest and a rare treat: heavy, sugared cream.

I dug right in. Elbeth stood at the mouth of the cave for a few moments, singing to the forest rain before she came to join me.

Despite the rain, the air was warm, and as always, the company was pleasant. Elbeth had a warm smile and hearty laugh, and our friends—small woodland creatures—joined us whenever we had a feast. I especially loved the chipmunks and squirrels, little rodents running up the sides of our cave as if gravity did not affect them. One particular chipmunk loved me too—or at least loved the berries and nuts I would save from my meals to share with him. He grabbed a berry off our stone table then ducked into a corner to nibble on it. I laughed at his boldness and tossed him a few more.

As darkness fell, with the rain continuing as hard as ever, the food ran out—though we were all long since full—and the animals cleared out to find their own shelters. I settled into my soft goose down bed to sleep.

When I awoke, I could not tell the hour. It was night and the rain continued, perhaps even more heavily, and the fire inside the cave had been doused. Elbeth crouched by the doorway, looking out into the forest. Something was amiss—I could tell instantly.

The forest was far too bright. Orange light seemed to pour in from every direction, despite the rain and the late hour. I pulled myself from my bed and crawled to the mouth of the cave.

The sight that greeted me was the most frightening thing I had ever seen. Sheets of flame rose up against the downpour. In all directions, the forest was ablaze; howls of the woodland creatures pierced the air. I took Elbeth's hand, but the cold sweat that covered it did little to comfort my fears. I looked at her face and saw, to my surprise, that her eyes were closed.

Not sure what to do, I closed my eyes, too. I focused on the sounds, and after only a moment I heard what Elbeth was listening to: a voice.

"Come out of your cave, witch," said the voice—the same voice I had heard earlier that day, the voice of that strange elf. "Come out of your cave, and let us see who is the stronger. Or sit and wait and let me burn the whole forest around you."

I opened my eyes and looked at Elbeth. A blue jay landed on her shoulder, chirped out a few notes, then swept back into the drenched forest. Elbeth turned to me, an unfamiliar expression on her face—fear.

"Come, Lucky Child, we must fly from this place." She cast her cloak over me and gripped my hand. Together we raced out into the downpour.

The storm intensified. The lump of fear that had formed in my chest from the moment the stranger had arrived filled my whole body. My arms felt numb with cold but the muscles in my legs burned as Elbeth pushed me to move faster than I had ever run before.

Once in a while, I tugged on her hand. "Please—can we stop for a moment and rest?"

"Not yet," Elbeth said, and she urged me to run faster, deeper into the forest.

After what seemed like hours, suddenly and without explanation, she slowed and veered off her course to a pine tree overgrown with vines.

She pointed toward the sheltered boughs. "There, Lucky Child. Now you rest."

I heaved a sigh and flopped down upon the pine needles. I bent over to rub my aching calves.

Above my head, Elbeth moved her hands in a circle, slowly chanting. As she finished, I felt my skin go prickly. It changed color, turning darker and rougher until it matched the hue and texture of the tree's trunk.

"Do not move," she said to me gently. "And do not cry out. Tomorrow, find the road and follow it. Someone will find you. The animals will help."

I swallowed hard and took a deep breath. "But you're coming back, aren't you?" I said, trying not to cry.

"If I can." She smiled. "But you are Lucky Child, remember? Everything will be all right. Everything always works out for the best."

Her smile faded and she turned back to the forest, toward the fires. I imagined the elf's voice echoing all around us.

As she moved away, I saw her crouch down on all fours. I saw her limbs thicken and lengthen, and her clothing melt into fur.

Soon, not a woman but a great brown bear was striding into the woods, roaring angrily, challenging the strange elf to face her.

As Elbeth raced away, I finally allowed my tears to fall. But only for a moment. Then I did as I had been told: I ducked under the boughs of the pine tree and soon drifted off to sleep.

CHAPTER 8

WAKE UP, CHILD." THE MAN'S VOICE WAS SOMEHOW COMFORTING, THOUGH I COULD not say why. "Wake up, young one. We must be off at once."

I opened my eyes. It was still raining, though it had turned from a downpour to a drizzle. The sky was pitch black except for the flicker of light coming from the sputtering torch in the man's hand.

The man gripped my arm and tried to pull me to my feet. "Come," he repeated, "we must hurry."

"But where is Elbeth?" In my heart, I already knew the answer. She was in the same place as my first family. I swallowed the lump that rose in my throat.

He winced, and tried to speak several times before he finally managed to utter one syllable, his voice cracking slightly. "Gone."

There was a strange finality to the way he said it. He reached out his hand again. "Come. We must be away before he returns."

For some reason, I was not afraid any longer. The look on the man's face when I had spoken Elbeth's name told me that I could trust him. And the thought of venturing out alone on the road seemed more frightening than following the man who promised to watch over me.

I took his hand. He pulled me to my feet then lifted me into his arms and carried me to his horse. After he helped me climb into the saddle, he slid in gracefully behind me, taking the reins and spurring the animal forward.

"Ever ridden a horse before, child?"

"No, sir." I ran my hand along the beast's mane. It felt surprisingly thick and coarse.

He gently patted her white coat. "This is Haze, as true a friend as you'll find in all Faerûn," he said.

She was beautiful, her coat glistening in the rain yet warm to the touch. I felt something different about her, different from all the animals I had known in the High Forest. She felt—magical, somehow.

"Where are we going, sir?" I asked hesitantly. Elbeth had told me the world was a large place, but had failed to give any details. The world I knew was a small cave in a sheltered grove in the middle of the High Forest. But that place was gone and I was riding into the unknown. I tightened my grip on this stranger's deep blue cloak.

"Wherever the road leads," he said gently. "And don't call me sir. Call me Perrault." He smiled.

"So, boy, what name do you go by? What did she call you?" he asked me, rubbing his neatly trimmed gray goatee. He peered at me thoughtfully, his blue eyes flashing. He was trying to ask the question lightly, but there was pain in his voice.

"I haven't a name, mister Perrault. She just called me 'Lucky Child,' 'cause I was lucky to live long enough to meet her."

"Yes. Yes, you were lucky, my boy, but that doesn't mean you shouldn't have a proper name. Twice lucky, now, to be alive to meet me again. Twice lucky . . ." He paused in thought. "There is a name I have heard of in my travels—a word in the language of the nomads of the Great Desert. *Maimun*, they sometimes title their children, and it means 'twice lucky.'" He smiled at me. "Maimun. What do you think, my boy? Does the name fit you?"

I shrugged.

"Well, try it out then!" he said.

"Maimun. Maimun." I spoke softly at first, letting the word roll out of my mouth naturally. As I gained confidence in it, my voice grew louder and a grin broke out on my face. "Yes, mister Perrault, it . . . fits me. Maimun, the twice lucky child." And then I remembered all that had happened, and a lump rose in my throat. "Only I don't feel lucky, mister Perrault. I want to see Elbeth again."

He wrapped his arm more tightly around me and began to hum a slow, sad tune, which soon turned into an even sadder song. He sang in a language I did not understand, but I knew he was singing to Elbeth, saying his farewell. The rain fell gently around us, but the drops never seemed to reach us.

As Haze carried us through the forest, my sadness began to lift. The sun peeked over the horizon, and orange and fuchsia painted the sky.

I looked at Perrault; he looked back at me, and managed a smile. The pain showed through his expression, but it did nothing to diminish the happiness in his bright eyes.

"Look there, to the east," he said. "Smile at the sunrise, for a new day has begun, and that is a beautiful thing."

"Why is it beautiful?" I asked. My tongue was thick from crying and the word fell awkwardly off my lips.

"Every day is a chance to start over. Any day can be bad, surely, but any day can be good, can be great, and that promise, that potential, is a beautiful thing indeed. And today will be a good day, little Maimun," he said. I heard a distinctly upbeat ring in his voice. "Today is the beginning of our new journey. Today we begin our ride to the south and to the east. The wind has come up, and I can feel it in my hair and on my skin. I can taste the salt on the breeze. Can you?"

I stopped and considered this odd question for a moment then shook my head. The air felt perfectly fresh, not at all salty.

He laughed. "You will, my boy, you will. Today we begin the adventure of your life. Tell me, little Maimun, have you ever seen the ocean? Did Elbeth ever take you there?"

Again I shook my head.

"Then you are in for quite a treat."

CHAPTER 9

"DID YOU KNOW THERE'S A DRAGON LIVING DIRECTLY BENEATH OUR FEET?" I ASKED.

"Well then, we'd best watch where we step," Perrault replied. His head never rose from the book on his lap.

Nearly six years had passed since Perrault had rescued me from beneath the boughs of the pine tree. He had kept his promise of showing me the ocean. From the High Forest we had headed directly to the Sword Coast, and we spent the following years wandering the lands along the sea. We slept outside or in a tent during the summer months. In the winter, we took shelter in the homes of farmers, who were always willing to share their hospitality for an evening of Perrault's stories.

Perrault loved to travel and after several days in one place, he would grow restless and insist it was time for us to move on. I longed for a real home, but Perrault said people like us weren't meant to be tied down to one place. So all I had to call my own was a bedroll.

That same night, after setting up camp and cooking our supper, Perrault stoked the fire and we both pulled out our books.

"The dragon's name is Adraedan," I explained, after consulting the heavy book on my lap, "and he was imprisoned beneath these hills by the Uthgardt barbarians. He was digging up the sacred burial places of the tribes, so they all got together and chose the best warriors from each tribe. They formed a new tribe, and they called themselves the Tribe of the Dragon." I turned the page and stared at our campfire's glowing embers. "Perrault, do you think my family might have belonged to such a tribe?"

"Read in silence, Maimun." Perrault didn't look up from the tome in front of him. "I have business to attend."

I was not surprised by his gruff answer. For the most part, Perrault was quick to answer most of my questions. He had taught me much about the world, from the names of the cities and small towns lining the Sword Coast to the great tales of the history of Faerûn. When the nightmares of Elbeth and the blazing forest woke me in a cold sweat, he would sit up late into the night, pointing out constellations and counting the stars with me until I fell asleep.

But when I asked him to tell me about the night of the fire or anything related to my past, he never gave me the answers I desired, save for the barest of details. I had learned that the night of the High Forest fire—the night of my sixth birthday—was not the first time Perrault had come to my aid. Perrault told me the tale of my rescue from my parents' home, and how he had delivered me into Elbeth's care. But any more than that, he did not know or would not say.

I sighed—loudly, but Perrault did not notice—and went back to reading the tale of the great battle between the Tribe of the Dragon and the mighty wyrm Adraedan, fought not a mile from the very ground I lay upon.

Like me, Perrault had a tome lying open before him. It was the only book among his extensive collection I was not permitted to read: a great, black, leather-bound thing with a heavy brass lock. I had never seen the key Perrault used to open the book—even though I'd hunted for it, had searched every place I could think of.

I only wanted to peek inside, to know what the book contained. It had no title, and I was desperate to know what secrets it might hold between its plain black covers. But the point was moot—I had never found the key.

Our campfire burned lower and my eyes grew heavy. I closed my book and carried it to the sack that contained Perrault's modest library. From the outside, the bag appeared to be a normal haversack, a satchel with a strap to sling over the shoulder. But the bag was enchanted to hold far more than should have been possible. I was pretty sure I could have fit inside that sack along with all the books.

I quickly scanned through the meticulously organized stacks of books, finding the appropriate place for the one I had been reading—in between *Demons and Devils* and *The Elven Folk*.

The bag held hundreds more books of all shapes and sizes. With those books, Perrault had taught me to read. And after six years on the road with Perrault, I had read each book in the collection at least once. Each book, that is, save one—that unmarked black tome.

With another sigh, I closed the sack and turned toward my bedroll. The night was warm, and the day's journey had been a long and hard ride across the rolling hills of the Crags, so I would surely sleep well.

I began to climb into bed, to wrap myself in a light blanket and in dreams of the mighty dragon I had been reading about. But Perrault's voice stopped me.

"Hold it. Back to the bag." I looked up to see him holding the black tome—closed and locked, I noted. I cursed myself silently. I had, for the thousandth time, missed the opportunity to catch a glimpse of the key.

I could not quite decipher the look Perrault leveled at me.

"It's all organized and neat, sir," I said hesitantly. "I put my book back right where it belongs."

"I do not doubt that. But I need you to fetch another book." The request was highly unusual—Perrault knew every book in the bag by heart, so the requested book could not be for him to read. But he rarely tried to guide my reading, instead allowing me to explore the books at my own pace.

"Which one?" I asked.

"*The Travels of Volo*. There should be a volume describing the central Sword Coast."

I reached into the bag, quickly pulling forth the appropriate book.

I was intrigued. In our six years of wandering, we had visited the northern Sword Coast and the southern Sword Coast, but we had always avoided everything between Waterdeep and Tyr. Perrault had never told me the reason, and I had never asked.

Perhaps that was about to change.

"Inside should be a description of the city of Baldur's Gate."

I nodded, and flipped open the book to that section and began reading. "'A thriving trade port and crossroads, Baldur's Gate lies halfway between Waterdeep and Calimport, and serves as a layover point for travel and trade in both directions, as well as . . .'"

Perrault's upraised hand stopped me. "Tomorrow, instead of dragons and barbarians and ancient battles, you will read that passage, until you know every word."

"Are we going there? Are we going to Baldur's Gate?" I asked, trying to keep the obvious hope out of my voice. I had never been inside a real city before—nothing larger than the town of Nesmé on the Evermoors. From afar, I had glimpsed mighty Waterdeep. The massive sprawl, the great mansions . . . the idea of tens of thousands of people living so close together was foreign to me. And in my mind, anything foreign, anything unknown, was worth investigating.

"As always, we are going where the road takes us," Perrault replied. "Where that will next be, I cannot say. But it is best to be prepared. Now, time for bed. Get some rest. We have a long day's ride ahead of us, and another after that."

Perrault turned away from me before I could respond, the surest sign he could offer that the conversation was finished. With a shrug, I put the book in the bag. I did not place the rich tome, penned by the incomparable traveler Volo, among the many other works in Perrault's collection. Instead, I placed it on top of the stack, in ready reach for the next day.

I went to my sleeping mat, lay down, and soon I was asleep. I dreamed of Baldur's Gate. I hadn't finished reading the passage about the city yet, but that did not stop my wandering mind from inventing all the necessary details.

I found little time to read the book the next day. We were up at dawn, as usual. It's difficult to remain asleep outdoors once the sun comes up. We rode for the entire day, stopping only for a brief lunch. We didn't ride too hard, but the landscape was uneven, and riding over such terrain is tiring. By the time we'd set our night's camp under a cloudless and moonlit sky, I had hardly the energy to lift the book, let alone read it.

The next day was the same, and the third and the fourth and the fifth. Each morning, when I awoke, Perrault would ask me how much I had read the day past. And each morning, I would answer that I had not read at all. Perrault would give me a slight nod, a sarcastic expression that told me he was trying to teach me something, though I hadn't the slightest idea what.

On the sixth day, the terrain changed. We quit the hills and turned southeast. We followed no road, but the land was flat and the run was easy. Farms dotted the landscape, their crops grown large in the summer heat. And what heat there was on that journey—not a cloud in the sky for the next twelve days, the sun bright and beautiful and scorching.

Despite the heat, our pace increased. I sensed a furor in Perrault, a desire to be at our destination as soon as possible. I shared the same desire, though I was sure our reasons were different. I wanted to see Baldur's Gate—I assumed that was our destination, though Perrault denied he had a location in mind. I thrilled at the thought of stepping inside a real city for the first time in my life. Perrault seemed only anxious, nervous, like he was on a dangerous mission and wanted the task completed.

The journey was not like any other we had taken. We had often traveled in uncivilized lands, where farms stood alone and held only nominal ties to a village. But even in the summer, even when we needed no shelter, we would stop at farmhouses along the way to exchange news and stories, and perhaps take a meal.

This time, we didn't pause at a single home or inn, didn't stop anywhere except to set camp. Our line was as straight as Perrault could manage, and we rode as fast as Haze could carry us without tiring.

My twelfth birthday passed without any mention from Perrault. He had never been one for grand celebrations, though he would normally give me some token to mark that one more year had passed since he discovered me in the ashes of my parents' home. But I didn't complain. I hoped my birthday gift lay at the end of our hard journey.

Around midday of the seventeenth day after Perrault charged me with reading Volo's description of Baldur's Gate, we crested a low, rocky ridge and saw spread out before us the mighty city. The sight took my breath away.

Perhaps four miles off, down a long green slope, it was more massive than I ever imagined. A great sprawl spread east and west, ending at a massive wall that I imagined was a hundred feet tall. Toward the center I could see another wall, surrounding a steep hill covered with massive structures, beautiful and graceful temples, great white towers ascending skyward like arrows aimed at the sun. The city rested on the banks of the mighty River Chionthar, which cut through the land to the sea like a great blue snake, wider than the city, twisting and turning its way through the green plain from the low hills to the east—toward the hills we stood upon.

"How many people live there?" I asked breathlessly.

"If you had read the passage, you would know the answer to that." Perrault motioned for me to dismount and I slipped off Haze's back as gracefully as I could.

I winced. "We rode too hard and I was too tired. I'm sorry, sir."

"So you did not learn the lesson I assigned you. But you learned a more important one in the process, did you not?"

"I don't know. Did I?"

"What do you expect you would have found, had you read the passage?" Perrault asked. I heard no anger in his voice.

"I don't know. Probably, the population and size and who runs it and who the important people are and things like that."

"Indeed." Perrault swung his leg over Haze's back and jumped to the ground. "And you would have found an accurate description of the docks, plus a list of fine inns worth staying at, monuments worth seeing, and the best market to buy your goods from. Here we are about to enter the city, and you know none of that because you did not read the passage."

"It wasn't fair! We were traveling all day and into the night. I didn't have time—"

"Life is not defined by how much time you have." Perrault was looking right at me, and I was surprised to see that there was no disappointment on his face. "It is about time you have *to spare*. You had seventeen days to read one simple passage—in the two days prior, you probably read more than that. And yet you chose not to spare the time. It is the smallest of choices that shape our destinies."

He turned away and gazed out down the hill toward Baldur's Gate. "Now, we must make our meal and rest a while. We enter the city at sunset."

CHAPTER 10

I COULD HARDLY WAIT FOR SUNSET. I SPENT MOST OF THE DYING HOURS OF DAYLIGHT moving about our small campsite, alternately staring at the looming specter of Baldur's Gate, or trying my best to put the city out of my mind. I groomed Haze, though she needed no grooming. I delved into Volo's account of Baldur's Gate, but it only heightened my anticipation. I tried closing my eyes and taking a nap. But none of it worked, and the harder I tried to put aside my excitement for the night's adventure, the more fully it occupied my thoughts.

After an eternity, the sun touched the western horizon, and we gathered our packs and headed for the city.

We carried no light—the risk of being seen was far too great. Though he never told me why, Perrault was determined to enter the city in secret. The walk across those four miles seemed unbearably long. With the city and its secrets just out of my reach, the anticipation as that distance became smaller and smaller was too much to take. But then, before I could blink, we were pressed up against the city's outer parapet.

I glanced up at the wall. I could see a torch directly above us, where at least one guard patrolled, but he was roaming toward the much larger flame anchoring the northeastern corner of the wall. A few other guards with torches moved along the wall, but none drifted near our position.

I looked to Perrault and saw him setting a coil of rope on the ground. As I watched, he began to hum a low tune, and he swayed gently back and forth. The rope rose up as a snake might, swaying in time with him. Slowly, so slowly, it ascended into the air, completely unsupported, until the end of the rope reached the top of the wall.

Perrault stopped humming and the rope stopped swaying. Perrault took hold and gave the rope a tug, smiling when it didn't fall down on us.

"Come on then, up we go," he said.

Without looking at me, he began to scale the wall. I followed a few moments later. As I reached the parapet, Perrault held out a hand through the crenellations and hauled me onto the wall. My hands felt raw and my arms burned, but Perrault had not even broken a sweat. For an older man, he was surprisingly strong.

After a quick glance to confirm that no one was around, Perrault reached out, grabbed the rope, and whispered a single word beneath his breath. The rope jumped up, twisting into a perfect coil in his hand. He slipped the rope into his pack, and pulled out two gold rings.

"Now comes the fun part," he whispered.

I could see the mischievous twinkle in his eye, despite the darkness. He slipped one of the rings onto a finger, and handed me the other. I followed suit and slipped the much-too-large ring onto the middle finger of my right hand. As soon as I let go of it, the band shrank to fit my finger perfectly.

"All right," Perrault whispered, "I'll count to three, and when I say three, we jump." He motioned to the inside of the wall, which was not crenellated. I stole a glance over the edge—it was more than twenty feet, and unlike the grassy field on the outside, the inside was a street of cobbled stones. I looked up at Perrault, and I could see him holding back a chuckle.

"Trust me," he said, and he took my hand.

He put his toes against the edge of the wall. With a deep, steadying gulp, I followed suit. I tried not to look down, but of course that was impossible, and the view turned my stomach and made me dizzy.

"One," he said, low and under his breath.

I thought I noted a trace of fear in his speech, but with the supreme voice control Perrault had developed from singing for so long, he could have hidden that undertone there just to unnerve me. He would get some amusement from that.

"Two," he said, a little louder.

The note of fear was clearer, but as I heard the clack-clacking of hooves approaching on the cobblestones, I realized his fear was no joke. I thought I should suggest we wait until whoever was approaching had passed, but before I could say anything I saw torch-light coming down the wall from the west. The darkness offered some concealment, but it seemed unlikely that the guard with the torch would miss us. We would have to jump, and hope the man approaching—

"Three!"

I felt a tug at my hand as Perrault leaped from the wall, and I jumped with him. A scream built inside me as my feet left solid ground, but I swallowed it.

As soon as we left the wall, I felt the ring on my finger grow slightly warm. I was not falling, but was drifting downward like a feather in a gentle breeze. I looked to Perrault, who had released my hand, to see him gently descending too. As he "fell," he reached into his pack and pulled out another object, too small for me to see.

The clack-clack of hooves grew louder, and before we landed I saw a man dressed in the uniform of the Baldur's Gate city guard trot around the corner. He was mounted atop a tall brown horse and held a torch in one hand, his spear resting casually across the front of the saddle.

"Oy, you there, speak and be recognized!" he said as we landed, his voice trembling slightly.

"Oh, sir, I would, but as it were, I prefer to remain anonymous," Perrault said. "So sorry."

He tossed the item he was holding in the direction of the guard. I saw it glint as it arced through the torchlight—it looked like a glass bead. Before I could get a clear view of it, it struck the ground at the foot of the guardsman's horse with a slight *pop*. As it broke, wisps of energy flowed up and around the guard, quickly weaving themselves into a solid, translucent bubble.

The guard recoiled and nearly fell off his horse. "Oy, what trickery is this?"

I could barely hear him. His voice was muffled by the magical bubble. He grabbed his spear and thrust it at the bubble, but it merely bounced off. He slid off his horse and tried to push through the sphere, but it proved unyielding.

I glanced up at the wall and saw the flicker of a guard's torch moving along the battlement.

The trapped guard saw his comrade on top of the wall. He stabbed wildly with his spear at the top of the bubble, to no effect, and screamed at the top of his lungs, though barely any sound passed through the magical barrier.

The man on the wall didn't hear him, and the torchlight moved on.

The guard's horse whinnied angrily at its master's yelling and put its head on the guard's shoulder, using its weight to push him to the ground.

The guard struggled, shoving the horse's head aside and trying—unsuccessfully—to stand, all the while yelling. That only annoyed the beast more. As the guard cursed and spat, the horse laid down, trapping the guardsman's legs beneath its belly. The watchman finally stopped yelling.

"Sorry, sir, but as I say, I prefer anonymity. This orb will guarantee that. Anyway, the bubble will fade. Eventually." Perrault's smile could easily have belonged to a troublemaking child, yet it somehow fit just as perfectly on his weathered face.

He turned to me and said, "Come, boy, we have appointments to keep."

CHAPTER 11

BALDUR'S GATE WAS UNLIKE ANYTHING I HAD EVER SEEN. TRAVELING THROUGH THE city that night, hardly a person was to be found—the only people on the streets were the vagabonds who had nowhere else to go, the guards on patrol, and those rogues who had managed to avoid the notice of the guards.

We fell into the rogue category, slipping through the cobblestone streets by moonlight. Occasionally I glanced up at the stars to determine the direction we traveled. But with all the buildings crowding around us, it was difficult to keep any significant portion of the sky in sight, and the city's roads were twisting and narrow.

We wound our way among old, run-down buildings and newer structures. At first, I tried to identify places from the map of the city in Volo's account, but we moved too fast and soon I gave up.

The sights were not impressive, but I found the smell of the place quite pleasant. The salt air of the ocean hung thickly over the city, where it combined with various spices and incenses brought for trade from all across Faerûn. The steady breeze mixed the aromas together into a soothing fragrance.

We roamed for a time, often ducking into alleys to avoid a passing guard.

At last Perrault stepped up to a closed doorway beneath a faded old sign displaying a drained mug and the establishment's name, The Empty Flagon. No light shone in the windows or door, and no sound pierced the night.

I figured the place was deserted. As Perrault opened the door, I saw I was correct. The tavern was empty. Stools were set on tables, and no one stood behind the bar.

"Well, what are you waiting for?" Perrault asked. "Head on in!" Again, that twinkle in his eye signaled mischief to me.

I hesitated for a moment, but Perrault just stood there. He would never do anything that would cause me real harm, I knew, so it was time to see what the game was.

I felt something strange as I stepped into the room, a sort of uneasiness, but I could not figure out what it was. I walked, slowly and cautiously, to the bar, looking around but seeing nothing. The tavern had no other exits save the way I had entered. I turned back to the door, seeing Perrault standing outside.

"There's nothing here," I called to him. "The place is empty."

"How would you know that?" he asked. His voice was quiet, yet I heard him quite clearly. "You haven't even entered the room."

"What do you mean?" I asked. "I'm inside . . ." I turned, sweeping my hand out wide. But as I turned to where the bar had been, I realized I was staring into the room—from the outside, as if I were still at the threshold.

"Behold the power of illusion," he said with a laugh. "Now, let's head in." He spoke a few words—"Good ale and fine stories,"—stepped across the threshold, and vanished.

I blinked a few times and looked around, but I could not see my mentor anywhere. I saw only one option.

"Good ale and fine stories," I mumbled, and in I stepped.

I crossed the threshold into sudden blinding light and a chorus of voices talking, shouting, singing, and cheering. As my eyes adjusted and I looked around, I saw an entirely different room. Every table was occupied, every chair filled—except a few whose occupants had fallen out in a drunken stupor—and many more people were standing or were seated on the floor around the hearth. Many of the patrons were not human, I noticed, and especially prominent were the dwarves and gnomes. Half a dozen women moved around the room, carrying trays that patrons simply plucked drinks from as they moved past.

Around the fire was gathered a group of dwarves, standing arm in arm and mug in hand, singing loud, raucous drinking songs—which, to dwarves, apparently meant songs about killing goblins. At each reference to a new and creative means of killing goblins, whether smashing goblin heads with rocks, bashing goblin skulls with hammers, or crushing goblin noggins with . . . another goblin, the dwarves let out a loud cheer.

They sang in detail exactly how to use a goblin as a weapon—hold him by the ankles, spin in place to build momentum, then slam him down in an overhead chop as if swinging a battle-axe. I knew from my reading that the goblin's head is the hardest part, and the best results are reached when the goblins hit head to head. The sound of the cracking can be quite loud and clear, and pleasing to the ear.

In all my years of traveling with Perrault, I had never seen anything like the place. And I couldn't help but listen, imagining the stocky, sturdy people swinging ugly goblins by the ankles, using the nasty creatures as weapons against themselves. Probably a sport in dwarven cities, I mused. I decided that someday I would have to travel to dwarf lands and see it firsthand.

"Perrault, my friend, it is good to see you again." A voice to my side, distinct among the crowd, broke the trance the dwarves' singing had induced.

I turned to see Perrault moving easily toward the bar through the crush of dwarves.

From the sound of the voice, I had expected a human or perhaps an elf, but I was surprised to see an old, gray-bearded dwarf balanced on a small pulsing blue disk of energy, drifting up and over the bar. Perrault and the dwarf talked, but their voices were low and I could not make out what they were saying.

I crept closer.

". . . waiting for you upstairs, but a man from her temple came calling and she left in a hurry. She said to leave it for—" The dwarf broke off his sentence abruptly and turned to look at me.

Under that piercing gaze, I suddenly felt naked, and I felt ashamed. I had sneaked into the conversation uninvited. I tried to sink into the crowd, but the dwarf's eyes softened and his thick lips turned up in a smile. His brilliant white teeth showed brightly through his dense beard.

"And this must be your ward, then," he said. Though the statement was obviously directed at Perrault, the dwarf's eyes never left me.

Perrault turned to look at me. There was surprise and, I thought, a bit of approval in that look. I knew immediately that Perrault had not noticed me, and was impressed that I had managed to get so close without alerting his attention.

"Yes, yes. This is my boy, my young apprentice," Perrault said, quickly composing himself. "Maimun, this is Alviss. He's a dear old friend. A bit surly—" he cast the dwarf a sidelong glance, to which Alviss only rolled his eyes and widened his grin—"but he's offered to watch you for me tonight."

"Watch me?" I asked. "I don't need anyone to watch me. Where are you going, and why can't I come?"

"I have business to attend, and it is not your concern. You stay here with Alviss. He'll give you a bed, and you can get some sleep." Perrault looked at Alviss as he spoke, and the dwarf was nodding before he finished.

"I'll give you a cot in the common room. It's mostly empty, anyway."

The dwarf put his hand on my shoulder and started to lead me away, but Perrault stopped him with an upraised hand. He leaned in close to Alviss and said under his breath, "Keep your eyes open. I'll be coming back fast and I'll need the boy ready to run."

Alviss nodded. Before I could say anything, he was leading me away to the common room and Perrault was exiting the tavern the same way we'd come in.

CHAPTER 12

I COULDN'T SLEEP THAT NIGHT EITHER.

I forced my eyes shut, tried to empty all thought from my mind, tried to embrace the weariness in my body, but despite my best efforts, my thoughts kept racing back to Perrault and his secret appointment.

After what seemed an eternity, I gave up, pulled myself from my cot, and dressed. I snuck to the door of the common room, quiet as a ghost so as not to disturb the two other people who had taken cots there, and put my ear against the portal. I heard nothing beyond.

Slowly, gently, I pushed the door open.

The tavern was empty of patrons, the chairs all placed atop the tables, the freshly mopped floor glistening. The only light in the room came from the bar—the pulsing blue glow of Alviss's magical floating disc. And there sat the old dwarf, mindlessly wiping down the bar with a rag and humming to himself.

Alviss seemed sufficiently preoccupied, and the room sufficiently shadowy, for me to cross the room without being seen. The exit was almost directly opposite the doorway in which I stood, so I would have to cross a lot of open space.

I moved quickly, keeping my weight on my toes—I had read a passage in one of Perrault's books detailing the proper way to move stealthily—and I used the tables for cover. The floor was slick, but not excessively, and soon I was reaching for the handle of the front door.

Alviss was still humming tunelessly and running the cloth over the bar. As soon as I touched the door, though, the old graybeard jumped.

He turned to look right at me.

He clapped his hands twice, the sharp noise shattering the silence, and the room was suddenly bright as it had been that evening when Perrault and I had arrived.

Alviss stared at me. I thought I saw his lips turn up in a bit of a smile, but it could have been the wrinkles on his weathered face. "Now, now, young'n, there's no way I'll be letting you wander out into the streets alone!" he said. "It isn't safe, you know."

"I won't get in any trouble. I don't get caught. You wouldn't have noticed me except for that . . . magic." I would have continued my protest except I saw Alviss, barely holding in a chuckle, patting his hands in the air to calm me down.

"I did not mean it wasn't safe for you," he said, a laugh escaping his lips. "I mean, it wouldn't be safe for *me* should Perrault return to find out I had let his nosey young ward out alone to follow him to a private appointment!" The dwarf's chuckle turned into a great belly laugh. On and on it went, sounding so out of place coming from that soft-spoken creature. After a moment I joined in.

He stopped laughing abruptly, leaving a note of my high-pitched giggle hanging awkwardly in the air. His face, however, did not lose its mirth—indeed, his smile seemed to widen, his lips curling in an almost sinister fashion.

"Come to think of it, though, all Perrault said to me was, 'keep the boy here.' He said nothing of keeping you from watching him."

"But how can I watch him if I can't leave?"

"Oh, there are ways." He turned and hopped off the magical floating disk—which instantly disappeared—and walked toward a small door hidden behind the bar. As he reached the door, he motioned for me to follow.

"Come, young'n, if you want to see." His voice was barely above a whisper.

I hesitated for only a moment, my curiosity outweighing my apprehension.

I followed Alviss through the tiny door into a pitch-black room beyond. No sooner had I stepped across the threshold than my foot caught on some heavy object on the floor. Down I went, directly into a bookshelf, and down it went in turn.

"Wha . . . what did you . . . watch where you . . . are you blind?" Alviss shouted. "Oh, right. Light." He clapped his hands twice, and the room was filled instantly with light as bright as the morning sun. "A dwarf needs no light to see. I still forget humans are not so blessed."

I sat up and looked around, rubbing the stubbed toe on my right foot, and could finally see that I had tripped over a huge tome bound in black leather and unlabelled, almost exactly like Perrault's mysterious book. It rested on a toppled bookshelf, which was precariously perched on top of what looked like a human skull—except it was several times as large, and instead of bone-white it was a fiery red. The contents of the shelf had spilled onto the floor, but many more books and scrolls lay about haphazardly than could have fit on the shelf.

"Well, get up already!" Alviss huffed impatiently. I stood up in one of the few open spaces on the floor and caught my balance.

Alviss, meanwhile, waved his hands and uttered some arcane words. The toppled furniture tilted upright again, spilling what little of its contents had not yet fallen out. The dwarf waved his hand a second time and many books and scrolls leaped from the floor onto the shelves, piling into whatever space they could fill.

Alviss cleared the room's only table. At its center rested a small object covered by a black cloth.

As soon as I stepped up to the table, Alviss stood straighter, pushing back his broad shoulders. With a flourish, he pulled off the cloth, revealing a clear ball of crystal set atop a pitch-black wrought iron stand.

The dwarf moved a finger to his lips, signaling that I should stay quiet, then began moving his hands slowly in circles above the ball. It took me several moments to realize he had also begun chanting—his voice was so low it was almost inaudible.

Suddenly, all light left the room except a brilliant pale blue hue emanating from the crystal ball. The dwarf's deep chanting changed, the words suddenly ringing with perfect clarity.

I leaned in toward the ball, closer, ever closer, the light growing brighter, the rumbling of Alviss's chant growing louder, louder, deafeningly loud, the blue light washing over me.

CHAPTER 13

THE ROOM WAS VAST, SO TALL IT SEEMED THAT CLOUDS SHOULD HAVE BEEN CIRCLING the tops of the enormous pillars. The floor, the walls, those dozens of great pillars made of pink marble, seamless and flat and shining. Great windows lined the walls, beautiful images appearing in the multicolored glass panes, allowing a dim, eerie light to shine through.

At one end of the massive hall lay an enormous dais, a raised platform three steps above the floor. On the dais knelt a figure, a human perhaps, though in the massive room, it was difficult to judge its size. A simple white robe completely covered the form.

My attention swung to the huge oak door at the other end of the hall. The door parted in the middle, one of its massive halves swinging open only a sliver. Then a man slipped through, seeming small indeed. I instantly recognized the midnight blue cloak slung around his shoulders.

Perrault.

The enormous door silently swung shut behind him as Perrault began the long walk across the room.

The figure on the dais rose and turned to face him. A hand reached up, gracefully pulling the hood back to reveal the most beautiful woman I had ever seen. Raven black hair was tucked behind a pointed ear that matched perfectly her angular face.

She descended the three short steps just as Perrault reached her. It appeared at first as though he would sweep her up in a great hug, but he slowed as he approached, instead grasping her shoulders and smiling gently. She returned the smile and spoke, her musical voice seeming to echo forever, yet somehow not disturbing the stillness that pervaded the great hall.

"My friend, it is so good to see you again. You should—you must!—come more often."

"You know why I do not," the man replied. His voice did not echo at all. It seemed out of place, as if it were not worthy to exist.

"Yes, of course, I know your excuses," she said. "Yet here you are, and there is no indication he has even realized."

"There will never be any indication, until I am accosted."

"You have been accosted before, and you have always escaped."

"But I am no longer concerned for myself. Elbeth's ward travels with me, and he is far more important." As he uttered Elbeth's name, the woman's smile disappeared.

She shook her head. "He is not Elbeth's ward any longer. He is yours, to keep and to keep safe. Even if it means poor Jaide cannot see you." She smiled. "Even if my only visitor is the dwarf!"

"At least the dwarf can keep his magical eyes on me," Perrault replied, "so you can hear of my exciting exploits. Perhaps those stories will convince you to reconsider your path, to return you to the road."

Again she shook her head. "My calling is here, for as long as it must be. Though I do believe the road will call to me again, perhaps even to your side. Perhaps I will again see the open air of the wide world, but until then I will stay here, in a world somewhat smaller, though no less beautiful.

"Anyway, to business." She waved a hand around her head, as if to brush off the distractions of the previous conversation. "I know why you have come."

Perrault stepped forward. "The boy turned twelve, and has shown remarkable maturity. He is ready to have it returned to him."

She nodded solemnly, her smile gone, and reached into a pocket in her robe. From inside she withdrew a small object, fist-sized, wrapped in white cloth. She looked at it, then looked at Perrault, then nodded again, holding out the object for him. "As I said, he is your ward now, so the decision is yours. But as you must care for him, you must care for this. It must not be lost, or he will be lost with it."

He reached out, taking the object reverently, and began to speak. Before any words left his mouth, Jaide rushed forward, wrapping him in a tight hug, her mouth pressed to his ear.

"It must not be lost again," she whispered, then pushed away from him. She turned and walked up the steps, taking her kneeling position. She pulled up her hood and bowed her head.

Perrault seemed as if he wanted to speak, but instead he nodded, turned, and began again the long walk across the enormous hall.

I opened my eyes—or perhaps they had never been shut—and staggered back from the table. I felt as though I had come running directly out of the crystal ball. My ankle caught on another giant book and I bumped into the bookshelf behind me and tumbled to the floor. The parchments on the shelf flew off and buried me in a great avalanche of paper.

From beneath the pile of stale-smelling parchment, I could faintly hear Alviss's chanting. I felt myself caught in the spell and pulled upward, but the tug was not enough to lift me.

I found my bearings and looked up to see Alviss staring at me. "Did that answer your questions, young one?"

"Yes sir. I mean, no sir, it . . . Who is she? Where was that? What . . . ?"

Alviss shook his head vigorously, first side to side then up and down. "Precisely. You sought answers to questions, but the answers were not for you. So you spied, you looked where your eyes did not belong. And what, young one, did you find?"

I pondered this for a while. "More questions. I found no answers and only more questions."

"Precisely. And on that note, it is past time you went to bed," Alviss said. "I hope you will remember this lesson, but I would appreciate it if you don't tell Perrault. He still may kill me if he finds out I helped you spy on him." He began to hum softly as he swept me out of the room, through the tavern, and to my cot.

I did not expect to sleep that night. I kept my eyes shut, but on the backs of my eyelids I saw the image of that woman, that elf, her black hair and her piercing eyes, and her voice, echoing softly, gently, perfectly . . .

"It must not be lost again."

CHAPTER 14

W AKE UP, CHILD." PERRAULT STOOD OVER MY COT, GENTLY NUDGING MY SHOULDER. He looked as if he'd just come from the road, covered in dirt and sweat. He held my clothes, ready for me to put on. I rose and pulled on my pants, then reached for my shirt.

"Hold on," Perrault said. "Put this on first." He handed me a leather belt studded with silver rivets the size of beans. In the middle of the strap, instead of a buckle, was a small pouch.

I moved to put the belt around my waist, but Perrault shook his head. "Wear it across your chest, right to left, like a sash. Put the pouch over your heart."

Isn't a sash worn over a shirt, and wouldn't it be a finer material than this coarse leather? I thought. But I did as I was asked, or tried to. The leather bit into my back and I couldn't find a comfortable position for it no matter what I tried. After a moment of fumbling, Perrault lent a hand, pulling the strap tight.

With the sash in a relatively comfortable position, I looked at Perrault and my heart nearly stopped. In his hand he held an object, fist-sized and wrapped in white cloth, the object Jaide had handed him earlier that night.

"Wha . . . what is that, sir?" I asked, all traces of weariness gone from my mind. I tried to keep my voice steady, but I was unable. I hoped the crack in my voice wouldn't alert Perrault that I had been spying. I was afraid, if he knew, he might not give the thing to me.

"This," he said with reverence in his voice, "is an heirloom—a gift for you. It has been yours since birth, but it has been hidden here within the city for safekeeping until you were old enough to have it—until today." He extended his hands toward me. He reminded me of a priest holding out a bowl of holy water to his disciple.

Slowly, I reached out and took the object. It was at once heavy and light. It didn't weigh much, but I felt as if I were holding something massive and important in my hand. I unwrapped the white cloth to reveal a black stone, perfectly smooth and perfectly round. As I turned the stone in my hands, it swirled with color—blues and reds, and a line of deep violet all wrapped around one another. It took me a long time to pull my eyes from it and look back at Perrault, who stared at me with a patient expression on his face, as though he'd expected that reaction from me.

"It fits perfectly in the pouch on the sash," he said to me. "Keep it there, and never let it be far from your sight."

"But why?" I stared at the stone in my hand. "What does it do?"

"There will be time later for your questions." He handed me my shirt. "Now, we must leave."

"Leave?" I asked. "Leave the inn?"

"Not just the inn. We must leave the city, tonight, and be far away by the time the sun sets."

In the predawn hours, very few people were on the street, and none took any notice of our passage. We walked quickly, for Perrault said running would have attracted the guards' interest. I believe we headed south, but the streets wound and meandered and I had trouble keeping my bearings. Perrault seemed to know exactly where he was going, so I just held on tightly to his blue traveling cloak and followed his lead.

All the while, I held one hand wrapped around the stone, which had settled in perfectly to the hollow in the center of my chest, directly over my heart. I felt a warmth from the stone, like it belonged there, had always belonged there, like I had not been a complete person until that night, when this part of myself had been rejoined to me.

I didn't notice that Perrault had stopped until I walked right into him.

I stepped around Perrault to see the reason for our delay. Standing before us, blocking the road, was a single figure. He looked like an elf, with a slight build and pointed ears. His head was clean shaven and his skin was almost the golden tan of a sun elf, with a hint of red to it.

"You should take more care in your travels," said the elf. He was dressed regally, in fine silks of violet and black, and he leaned heavily on an ornately carved staff of black wood, or perhaps obsidian. "You are far too conspicuous for one holding such sought-after goods." The elf's voice was lower than I expected, a solid baritone completely lacking the musical qualities common to the woodland folk.

"I was wondering when you would show one of your ugly faces, Asbeel," Perrault replied, venom dripping from every word.

"Now, now. Let's not insult one another," he chided. "Instead, let's discuss you turning over what is mine, and me not killing you for it." Asbeel displayed a disarming smile, but it was too wide, and appeared more than a little unsettling.

"It is not yours, and it never has been, wretch," Perrault said.

The smile disappeared from Asbeel's face. "What did I just say about insults, fool?" he asked.

Perrault ignored him, turning instead to me. "Maimun, are you tired?"

I hesitated. "No, I slept plenty."

"Good. Are your shoes tied?"

"Yes sir."

"Excellent. Run."

Immediately I was off and sprinting down the street.

Behind me, I heard a loud *pop,* followed by a sound like the hiss of an oil-soaked rag that had been set afire. I turned to look, but saw only Perrault filling my vision as he ran behind me. He caught me in mid stride and carried me, his strong legs far outpacing any speed I could have managed—far outpacing any speed a human should have been capable of. Behind me, I heard a laugh, deep and menacing, but it quickly faded into the distance.

Perrault ran, turning down every side street we passed. At first, I thought he was lost, but the expression on his face, stern and determined, led me to believe he had a destination in mind. He chanted under his breath as we moved, and once brought a tiny silver whistle to his lips. I had not seen the device before, but I was hardly surprised when the thing made no noise whatsoever as he blew into it. Another unexplained bit of magic, one of a hundred I had seen Perrault use.

We rounded a corner and reached the most open area of the city—the docks. A massive expanse along the banks of the Chionthar, the docks of Baldur's Gate contained no fewer than a hundred wharves, ready to take as many ships as the great ports both north and south could send their way. A road ran along the docks, as wide as four streets in the city, to accommodate the massive rushes of people and cargo getting on or off the ships in port. The far side of the road was lined with warehouses, tall and imposing and packed tightly together, giving the impression of a great wall separating the riverfront from the rest of the city.

At that hour, the docks were mostly empty. Only a dozen ships were moored, all at the long wharves on the northern end of the riverfront. Dawn was just about to break—the sky over the hills to the east were lightening to a pale blue to herald the sun's approach. The only bustle was around the ships, as crews rose from their sleep and went about their business. Not a soul wandered anywhere around us.

No one, save the pair of burning red eyes emerging from the shadows of the warehouse beside us.

CHAPTER 15

ASBEEL STEPPED OUT, GRINNING A HORRIBLE GRIN. HE LOOKED TALLER THAN BEFORE, his skin redder and not so perfectly smooth. He circled behind us, cutting off our route back to the alley we had just exited, but leaving open the wide street along the docks.

Perrault turned and ran down the street with all haste.

But Asbeel was in front of us, laughing.

The elf—or the creature that appeared as an elf—lunged forward. Perrault dropped me and leaped to meet him, producing from his boot a slender dagger. He sliced the stiletto through the air a few times to keep the creature at bay. I backed up, scrambling to put distance between myself and Asbeel, but not wanting to take my eyes off the spectacle.

Perrault advanced, advanced, advanced, swinging all the while. Asbeel gave ground, using his staff for defense, laughing all the while.

Then Asbeel was gone.

I felt a hand grip my shoulder—iron-strong claws digging into my flesh.

Perrault realized immediately what had happened. He turned and sprinted at me, but he was too late. I felt myself lifted off the ground.

I turned my head to see the creature holding me, no longer an elf but some demonic thing, half again the height of a man, covered in red scales, with great red wings extending from his shoulders. On his face was that same unsettling grin.

His wings beat once, then again, and up we rose a few feet, then a few more. I tried to grab his hand, to wrench it free of me, but his grip was too strong and I had no way to break it.

Then suddenly I was falling, dropping the ten feet back to the pavement. I landed hard, but not horribly—nothing was broken. Nothing, save the fabric of my shirt, which had torn away where Asbeel had held it, dropping me to the ground and leaving the airborne demon holding a shred of cloth.

The demon swooped in, but Perrault was there, fending it off with his stiletto. He grabbed me, picked me up, and turned to run. But again the demon was in his way, cutting off all retreat. With no other option, Perrault turned on his heel and sprinted down the nearest wharf.

He set me down and turned to face Asbeel, who landed behind us and was approaching, his obsidian staff pointed at us.

No, not at us, I realized. It was pointed at the dock in front of us.

The pier burst into unnatural, magical flame, leaping twenty feet in the air and spreading wide. The flames cut off the dock and billowed out, hovering over the water. The blaze was massive and intense and didn't subside, even as the wood beneath it was consumed.

Perrault pushed me behind him to guard me from the demon. He readied his stiletto and made a snapping motion with his wrist, as if to throw it, but he didn't let go. The movement seemed to roll along the blade, extending it, until the dagger turned into a sword, a thin and fine blade slightly curved at the end, sharp as glass and beautifully crafted. Perrault held it vertically in front of him and set his feet, one in front of the other, the rear foot turned sideways. With his left arm, he swept back his glorious blue cloak and he looked impressive, heroic, unbeatable.

The terrible demon stepped through the wall of fire, completely immune to the blaze, looking taller, fiercer, and more evil than ever. Before that monster, the man who was as my father looked puny indeed.

The demon no longer carried the obsidian staff. In its place he held a sword. As fine and beautiful as Perrault's bright saber appeared, the demon's blade was the perfect opposite. Black iron, the blade was longer than Perrault was tall, and the whole length of it curved. The convex edge, the sharp side, was wickedly serrated, with bright red barbs lining its length. Even the hilt looked capable of killing. Its crosspiece of twisted metal spikes, a dozen perhaps, jutted at odd angles, and several more spikes stuck out beneath the demon's red hand where a pommel should have been. More frightening still, the length of the blade blazed with red flame.

Asbeel glared at Perrault, his malicious grin gone. "Your blade is far too fine for such a weakling to wield," he growled. Perrault, still in his fencing pose, brought his blade up to his forehead and snapped it down again in a sarcastic salute.

Asbeel wasted no time setting himself, nor trading cautious jabs to take a measure of his foe. Instead, he charged at Perrault, beating his massive red wings once to create an impressive burst of momentum. The sword swung down with brutal force.

Perrault was ready for him, and knowing Asbeel's unearthly strength, he wisely didn't block the attack. Instead, he stepped toward the blade, ducking low and using his own weapon to divert the flaming sword over his head.

Asbeel overbalanced as his swing met no resistance, and Perrault, his feet solidly set and his balance perfectly centered, lunged forward. He couldn't bring his blade to bear, but punched out with the hilt of his sword instead, jamming his pommel into Asbeel's eye. The demon's head snapped back violently.

Asbeel staggered backward a step and beat his wings, thrusting himself away from Perrault. Perrault brought his blade to bear and lurched ahead. As he lunged, Perrault's own rapier burst into flame—a blue flame, not red like Asbeel's. Perrault's radiated chilling cold, not heat.

The demon's eyes widened. Realizing he could not back up far enough to avoid it, he took the only defense left—he fell to the ground, dropping hard onto the dock.

A light mist rose up around him, as if his presence so close to the water offended the river, and it was responding with fog.

Perrault was at full extension, his back leg straight out behind him and his forward arm locked in front. He was able to quickly regain his defensive position, but he was unable to press the attack before Asbeel scrambled away, rising to his feet and bringing his sword up.

The demon glared at Perrault, the hatred in his eyes mixed with newfound respect. He raised his blade, holding it horizontal to his body, and approached more cautiously.

The mist continued to rise and thicken, and I could see only the dim outline of Perrault as he fended off the demon. Their movements seemed slow, ethereal. I didn't feel as though I was watching a sword fight, but a slow dance, each participant moving in harmony, action and reaction and action again.

But the brilliant light of the flaming blades wasn't dimmed by the fog, and the speed of the swings wasn't slowed. As the swords cut and slashed, each time I felt as though a hit was inevitable, and each time I held my breath. And each time, the swords passed harmlessly or were parried successfully.

Then Asbeel changed his grip and reversed his direction, stepping forward and swinging his sword from low to high instead of high to low. Perrault was unable to step into the parries and under the sword. Instead, he had to leap out of the way, first to his left, then to his right. Blue flame crashed against red, and the clang of metal mixed with the angry hiss of fire on ice.

On the third swing, Perrault stepped straight back, leaning on his rear foot as the fiery blade swept just in front of him. For a moment, I thought the blade would hit him, and I nearly screamed—but the hellish red flame did not quite reach.

Perrault settled all his weight on his back foot, set firmly on the ground, his blade forward and ready. Asbeel, off balance, his sword out wide, had no defense. Perrault lunged, viciously, brutally, his sword tip reaching the five feet to Asbeel in the blink of an eye. The demon tried to fall back, to step aside, to get out of the way of that cold steel blade. But the motion was too fast, too fluid, too perfect, and the demon had nowhere to go.

The sword struck Asbeel in the chest and drove into a lung. Asbeel's howl of agony became a gurgle as blood surged from his mouth. The cold fire burned into his flesh, hissing wickedly.

In desperation, Asbeel brought his sword around hilt-first, but Perrault reversed his previous motion, retracting the blade and retreating a step, falling back into his fighting stance, at the ready.

"You are outmatched, demon," said Perrault. His voice showed not the least bit of fear. "Leave now and never return, or I shall destroy you."

Asbeel laughed.

"I think there may be a better way," the demon said. His baritone voice sounded slightly wet as blood choked his words.

He looked directly at me. I found myself staring into those fiery points of light where his eyes should have been. I tried, but I couldn't pull my gaze away, couldn't shut my eyes, couldn't move at all.

A voice sounded in my head—Asbeel's voice, but deeper, louder. *Come to me,* it said, and I found myself moving, crawling along the wharf toward Asbeel.

I tried to resist—oh, how I wanted to resist!—but I couldn't. My mind screamed, *Stop moving! Run away!* But my body refused to obey. It just kept crawling toward my doom. I felt disjointed, unattached to anything, as if I were simply an observer looking through eyes that had been mine. I saw tears well up in my eyes but I couldn't feel them as they ran down my cheeks. I saw my hands moving rhythmically, one in front of the other, pulling me along.

Perrault leaped in front of me, and he was saying something, but I could hear none of it. All I heard was that terrible voice, echoing in my skull: *Come to me.*

Then Perrault's cloak, that beautiful magical cloak, was flying around us. As it descended over me, the voice died.

I felt like myself again. I felt wet, and hot, and more than a little embarrassed, but I *felt*.

When Perrault rose, spinning to face the demon, I realized the cost of his action.

As soon as Perrault turned his back on Asbeel, the demon began moving. The horrible red sword descended.

It caught Perrault on the left shoulder and tore down, scratching across his chest, tearing a great gash, ripping at his skin and burning his flesh. Perrault staggered backward, one unsteady step after another, then he fell flat on his back.

"Now you die, foolish man, and I claim what is mine by right," cackled the demon.

"It is not yours, foul one. The stone chooses the wielder, and it has chosen the boy." There was strength in Perrault's voice, though he lay unmoving on the dock. The mist briefly swirled away from him, revealing his face—a bit pale, but smiling. "You can never use it, and you know it."

The demon laughed. "I was not talking about the *stone*, fool. I was talking about the *boy*. The boy I found, the boy I orphaned, the boy whose soul belongs to me." Asbeel coughed and spat out a mouthful of blood then he stepped toward Perrault, who lay still, barely keeping his grip on his sword.

"The boy's soul is his own," Perrault growled back, his anger matching Asbeel's. "You cannot use the stone through him unless he chooses to help you, which I find doubtful."

Asbeel laughed again. He beat his wings and threw himself at Perrault. Suddenly, the scene was crystal clear. The fog vanished, disappearing so quickly that I wondered if it had ever truly been there.

Time seemed to slow down. Asbeel hung in the air, his blade arcing toward Perrault, who had raised his sword above himself in a feeble defense. Over the hills just visible in the east, the top of the sun had risen over the clouds on the horizon, its light sparkling off the city and the river.

Above the demon, breaking through the wall of fire, came an object white and sleek: a magnificent horse, her eyes glowing with white light, her mane glistening in the suddenly-brilliant sunlight.

Haze burst through the flames in all her glory. Her head smashed into the demon's back and Asbeel was launched off the end of the dock.

He tried to beat his wings, but only one responded. The other, which had taken the brunt of Haze's charge, was twisted and broken.

Like an injured bird, the demon plummeted into the river, disappearing beneath the waves without a sound.

"He will be back," Perrault said, his voice low and full of pain. "But not soon."

With great effort, he pulled himself to a sitting position and reached into one of Haze's saddlebags. Out came a long white bandage and a vial of oil. He poured the oil onto the cloth then wrapped it tightly around his chest, trying to stem the flow of blood from his gory wound.

From behind us I heard a sharp crack, like lightning striking a tree, and a splash. A section of the burning dock collapsed into the river.

"Come. Let's get out of here," Perrault said. He managed to pull himself up into Haze's saddle. I followed, taking my seat behind him.

"Our way is blocked," I said.

"Only one way," came the response. "There are others." And with that, Haze wheeled around and took off at a gallop—directly off the end of the pier.

CHAPTER 16

A S WE HIT THE OCEAN, THE WAVES ROSE UP AROUND US, BUT THEY DID NOT SLOW
Haze's speed. She ran up and down over the cresting water. The jarring motion sent
my stomach reeling. I was afraid I might vomit, though thankfully I had not eaten anything since the night before.

I pressed my face tightly against Perrault's back, and after a while, I lifted my head to
look around. I should have done so much sooner. The sun was uncomfortably warm on
my head, but the salty ocean wind felt cool.

I noticed Perrault held Haze's reins with only his right hand, despite our swift pace.
The sight upset my stomach even more than the cresting waves.

I swallowed. "Are you sure your shoulder is all right, sir?"

"Maimun, do not pester me with your questions right now." Perrault said. But I could
hear the pain in his voice. "Close your eyes. We have a long journey ahead."

I did as I was told. The sounds, the smells, and the feeling of that glorious wind swept
over me, and soon all thoughts of my tossing stomach were lost—along with my sense of
time. I couldn't say how long we rode before Haze came to a stop.

I opened my eyes to a magnificent sight: a ship had grown from the ocean in front
of us!

I had seen ships before, but mostly in the distance—even the ones on the river at
Baldur's Gate—but I had never seen one up close. The sheer size of the mighty vessel
staggered me. It must have been a hundred feet long! It moved across the great flat plain
of the ocean with impressive speed, and Haze had to run to keep up with it. I studied
the deck and the massive square sails. I watched, my mouth hanging open, as the great
sheets of white furled upward, seeming to rise of their own free will, and the ship slowed.

A dozen sailors stood at the rail. Their expressions mirrored my own, mouths hanging
open, eyes wide, and it took me a moment to realize what they were staring at. Then it
hit me: The ship they stood upon, for all its size, was *supposed* to be there. The horse on
which Perrault and I rode was not.

Another man joined the crew at the rail. I knew he must be the captain, for he was
well dressed—or would have been, if his clothing hadn't been so old. The blue jacket he
wore must have once been covered with ornaments, but all that remained was one brass
button and loose golden threads. Upon his head sat a dusty hat much decorated in brass.
It had a strange shape, almost flat, with corners sticking out far to the sides of his head. A
tassel of the same golden thread as his bandolier hung down on each side of the hat. He

would have looked like a gentleman, even a noble, except his brown hair was wild and untrimmed, and the look in his eye was just as wild.

"Give me one reason not to have you killed where you ride," the captain called down. He had the voice of a street thug, coarse and harsh, but with the inflection and pronunciation of an educated man.

"We've given you no reason to attack, good sir," Perrault replied.

"That devil horse is reason aplenty, I'm thinking! It ain't natural, a horse ridin' on the waves!" As he spoke, he grew visibly and audibly agitated, and the other sailors at the rail bristled and nodded their agreement.

"Devil?" Perrault replied. "Hardly. Angelic, more like! I come as an emissary from the Temple of Tymora at Baldur's Gate. If you attack us, you shan't be allowed back in that city, which"—he looked deliberately at the front of the ship—"is your port of call, judging by your flag."

Perrault was lying. Even if I hadn't known we were not such emissaries, I could hear the lie in his voice. I hoped the sailors could not.

The men seemed suddenly less comfortable, and the captain stuttered several times before he managed to respond.

"Prove it, then! I ain't heared o' no emissary o' no temple comin' out 'cross the water on a damned horse afore, an' I ain't been told o' nobody lookin' for my ship. So prove it, or we'll kill ye as ye ride!" Any semblance of dignity had left his voice—he sounded every bit the salty seafarer.

Perrault reached into one of the pouches on Haze's saddle and pulled out a rolled piece of parchment. "A message from the temple, for your eyes only, Captain," he called.

"Oy, toss it up then."

Perrault obliged—almost. He threw the parchment at the captain, but it didn't quite reach his hands. Its momentum seemed to die about three feet from the rail. The captain reached out for the parchment, leaning out a bit too far. A sudden gust of wind caught him full in the back and he tumbled right over the rail, dropping with a splash into the water beside us.

He came up, gasping and choking. His hat floated beside him, but even as he reached for it, the heavy brass weighed it down and the object disappeared from sight.

The captain struggled just to stay afloat. Haze wheeled around, and Perrault grabbed the man's arm and held him. Perrault couldn't lift the man, but kept his head above the water, and as Haze trotted along beside the moving ship, the captain was pulled with us.

"Oy, what're ye waitin' fer!" he screamed at the crewmen on the rail, who were staring at us in shock. "Drop us a damned launch, ye fools!" The men ran from the rail and soon returned with a rowboat on ropes and pulleys, which they began to lower into the water.

Before the boat was halfway down the side of the ship, the captain ripped his hand away from Perrault and *jumped*. Somehow, he pushed the entire upper half of his body from the water, despite having nothing to brace against, no footing, and a heavy, soaked coat weighing him down.

He sputtered and stuttered and shouted, but his words were unintelligible. He began swimming furiously, trying to find a handhold on the side of the ship, but there were none, so he screamed at the men above.

"The launch! Lower the damned launch! It just brushed my foot—it just . . . damned shark! There's a damned shark in the water and it . . . There it is again! Get that boat in the water!"

The men hastened to obey their captain at the word *shark*. In a matter of seconds, the launch reached the water—mostly because two of the crewmen lost their grips on the ropes in their haste. The boat plummeted the last ten feet, narrowly missing the captain, and landed upside-down.

The captain seemed unconcerned with the graceless landing, and hardly seemed to notice the boat wasn't right. He quickly climbed up onto the keel of the small craft and yelled up for a rope.

Again, the crew responded with speed but not grace—a coil of rope was thrown down. The crewman who threw it had fine aim, it seemed—the rope caught the captain square on the forehead, knocking him off his feet. Somehow, he stayed on the boat, despite the lack of handholds and the rounded surface. He seemed afraid that even touching the water would mean a painful death, and his fear lent him acrobatic talents he could not normally command.

The captain didn't even berate the sailor for his errant throw. He simply grabbed the rope and hauled himself up, hand over hand, with remarkable speed. Once he reached the top, he turned and called down to us, "Are you coming, or shall I haul the rope up?"

"Neither, and both," Perrault replied. Haze trotted beside the overturned launch and Perrault grabbed one side of it, flipping it over easily. Then Haze stepped into the launch, and Perrault hopped off the horse. I followed suit. He took the rope and tied it to the boat. "Toss us three more ropes, then haul them all up when we're set."

The captain offered a nod, then walked from the rail. The crewmen threw three more ropes and we tied them to the boat. The light craft groaned in protest at the weight of the horse, but it held strong, as did the pulleys—and the men working them—on deck.

Barely a moment later, Perrault and I were in the captain's cabin, the door shutting behind us with a soft click.

CHAPTER 17

T HE CAPTAIN'S CABIN WAS RICHLY FURNISHED WITH A THICK RED CARPET, MANY CABI-
nets, and small tables of fine dark wood—all bolted to the walls or the floor. Dozens of
knick-knacks lay scattered around the room: here an ancient oil lamp of tarnished brass,
there a finely crafted tea kettle and four cups inside a locked cabinet with a glass door, and
over there—hanging above the other door to the cabin—a strange object with a wooden
handle and a long metal tube. It looked very much like a drawing of a thing called an
arquebus I had once seen in a book titled *Unusual Armaments*.

The captain sat comfortably on a worn chair behind an enormous table, on which lay
heaps of papers—notes, charts of the stars, maps of varying scale detailing the sea from Waterdeep in the north to Calimport in the south. Apparently he had a spare hat, identical to the
one he'd lost, for it was atop his head as if nothing had happened. And a spare coat, it seemed,
since the one covering him was dry. The only indication that he had been in the water was the
puddle slowly spreading beneath his chair. I tried not to look at it, out of politeness.

The captain motioned to the two chairs opposite him.

"Please sit," he said, the saltiness of his voice hidden beneath his trained accent.
"What can I do for an emissary of the Temple of Tymora?" I heard a note of sarcasm, and
surely Perrault did as well, but he ignored it.

"That depends largely on the course you've set," replied Perrault.

"We make for Luskan with all haste, to sell our cargo and refill our holds, that we
might leave for the south before the ice of winter traps us in port."

Perrault sat silently for a moment, hand on chin, deep in thought. "Then what you
can do for us, good Captain . . ."

"Smythe," said the man. Perrault nodded.

"What you can do, Captain Smythe, is divert your course to Waterdeep. I have business there of the utmost urgency."

Captain Smythe scowled, but only for a moment before he caught himself. "If we
make for Waterdeep, we shan't make Luskan in time to load and head south, so we'd have
to sell and buy in Waterdeep instead. The prices will not be as high, and the goods we take
on there shall be of lesser quality. So tell me, will the temple compensate me for this loss?"

Perrault only smiled. "The temple's compensation comes in the form of the flag you
now fly."

Captain Smythe didn't even try to hide his scowl. "The loss is too great. I cannot agree."

"You would deny an emissary of the—"

"I never saw proof that you are from the temple!"

"Only because you dropped the parchment." Perrault's tone was mocking, insulting.

Smythe stood up, his voice rising with him. "I dropped it because you threw it so poorly!"

Perrault stood, matching the captain's intensity. "You asked that it be thrown, instead of inviting us aboard! You threatened to kill us without proof, then when proof was offered—*you* demanded it be thrown. And you dropped it. Deliberately, I say! You dropped it so you wouldn't have to recognize my authority!"

Captain Smythe's hand moved to his sword, but Perrault was faster. In the blink of an eye, his fine stiletto was in hand, pointed at the captain.

Smythe stopped and took his hand off his sword. "Regardless, I will not divert my course without some proof of your claim or a promise of compensation." He sat down, and after a moment, Perrault did as well. "But I will allow you to sail with us. I will even offer you the comfort of my own cabin for the journey, and free run of the ship until we reach Luskan. It is not far from there to Waterdeep. It will take only five days' sailing or maybe a tenday's ride. That's the best I can offer you."

Perrault nodded. "Very well. Though the temple will not be pleased to hear of my treatment."

"A risk I must take," replied Captain Smythe. "Now, if you will excuse me, I must see to the crew. Please, make yourselves comfortable."

CHAPTER 18

A S SOON AS I WAS SURE SMYTHE HAD GONE, I TURNED TO PERRAULT. "YOU AREN'T AN emissary from any temple," I whispered. "You lied to him."

"Repeatedly and continuously, and for his own good," Perrault answered. He leaned back in his chair and gazed up at the ceiling of the captain's small cabin. His shirt had come untucked and I caught a glimpse of the stark white bandage wrapped around his chest.

"But lying is bad," I said.

"So I was bad." Perrault stood up and circled the captain's desk. He picked up one of the maps and studied it intently. "And I didn't even get what I wanted, did I? We're still sailing for Luskan, but we need to be off this boat a good deal sooner."

I shook my head, not understanding. "What was on the parchment you threw to him, anyway?"

"Absolutely nothing," he replied without looking up from the map. "It was blank."

"So if he had caught it, what would have happened?"

"Many bad things." He set the map down on the desk and looked at me with that familiar twinkle in his eye. "The captain probably would have ordered us killed, and then I would have had to take the ship myself, one against dozens. It might have taken an hour to accomplish!" He began to laugh then stopped abruptly. He held his arm against the wound on his chest, flexing against the pain. "Perhaps two hours, with this gash slowing me down. And then we would have had to sail this ship to Waterdeep all by ourselves. Trust me, that is no easy feat!"

I would have been laughing, surely, but the pain on his face when he clutched at the wound sobered me.

"You threw the parchment so he couldn't catch it, didn't you?" I asked, the picture coming clear. "Then you said *he* dropped it deliberately, so he wouldn't be able to accuse you of the same thing!"

Perrault bowed slightly. "Precisely."

"And the wind," I said. "Did you conjure that wind to knock him off the ship?"

"You overestimate me. That was fortuitous coincidence."

"Fortui . . . what?"

"Fortuitous, like fortune. Luck. That was lucky chance."

"So why did the captain give us his cabin?" I had seen Perrault get whatever he wanted with merely a well-worded question, but the cabin had been offered up, not asked for—and that immediately following a near sword fight!

"Etiquette." I opened my mouth, but Perrault held up his hand to stop me. "Etiquette . . . manners. When a distinguished guest is aboard the ship, the captain is supposed to offer his cabin. He probably has a spare cabin below made up and ready for him for just such occasions."

"But he didn't believe you. He doesn't think you're a distinguished guest."

"He's hedging his bets. He refuses to obey my request, because he doesn't think I work for the people I claim to represent. But to not offer me his cabin, if I were telling the truth, would be a tremendous insult. This way, if he's wrong, I can tell my superiors that he didn't obey, but he wasn't rude. And if he's right, all he's lost is a small amount of comfort for the journey."

I was nodding before he even finished, seeing the logic. "But why do we need to trouble him, anyway?"

"I have business in Waterdeep. You heard me tell as much to the captain."

"What kind of business?" I laid my hand over my heart, feeling the lump that was the stone against my chest. "Business with this stone? Why is it so important? What does it do?"

"Enough." The finality of the word and the weight of his tone stopped my next question in my throat. He crossed the small cabin to the door in a few strides. "I must see to Haze. You must sleep. I can see in your eyes that you are tired."

"I'm not tired!" I shouted back at him.

But he was already gone.

I moved to the other door, which predictably opened into the captain's sleeping quarters. The room was much more sparsely furnished, with only a cot and a dresser. I moved to the cot and flopped down atop the neatly tucked blankets.

I lay there for a while staring at the cabin's ceiling, my hands clenched at my sides. Perrault still treated me like the day he had found me under the pine boughs, the day I was six years old. He must think I was too foolish, too weak to know the truth. Even after the fight with the demon and our race across the sea—all of that, and still Perrault wouldn't see fit to trust me with the answers I most wanted to know.

CHAPTER 19

I AWOKE TO THE SOUNDS OF MOVEMENT AND A CLAMOR FROM ABOVE. LIGHT STREAMED in through the small round window. The sun had still been up when I fell onto the cot, and it was up again now. I must have slept as the dead! My stomach ached—it had been so long since I'd last eaten. Or perhaps it ached due to the constant toss and roll of the ship. Either way, I figured food would do me well.

Perrault was not in the room, but since I was under the covers and my traveling gear was neatly piled beside the bed, I assumed he must have come to tuck me in. I rose, dressed, and walked into the outer chamber of the captain's suite.

As out of place as Haze had appeared the previous day, running along the ocean swells, she seemed even more out of place kneeling in the captain's private room. She leaned gently against a bookcase. Her head lolled as the ship rocked, and she whinnied softly. I could not tell if she was enjoying the ride, or if she was about to vomit. Fearing the latter, I skipped by, pausing just long enough to run my hand through her fine mane, and walked out onto the deck.

About half the sun peeked above the eastern horizon. There used to be land there, I thought. The sun appeared huge, more massive than I had ever seen. Its brilliant rays caught the spray off the cresting waves and lit the drops like crystals. The air felt alive with light, and the deep blue sea danced beneath it. I stood staring for a long while, until the bottom edge of the sun passed the horizon and the magic in the air faded.

I thought of what lay ahead. At least, for once, I knew where Perrault was taking us: Waterdeep, the Jewel of the North, the greatest city of the Sword Coast. Baldur's Gate had been impressive—Waterdeep would be amazing. And demon-free.

It was early, but every crewmember was on deck. Some were moving about, securing this rope or moving that line, some were on hands and knees pushing a heavy horse-hair brush across the deck to clean it.

I climbed the narrow ladder to the aft deck. A few sailors stood there at the wheel, plotting a course. I crept past them to find Perrault leaning heavily against the rail, facing west.

"Sir," I said as I approached him. "I'm sorry for shouting at you last night."

He didn't reply. Standing beside him, I could hear that he was singing under his breath. I knew better than to interrupt him. I would have to find him again later, I thought. I slipped away and climbed back down to the main deck.

There Captain Smythe called out orders. "Raise the mainsail!" he shouted. Above him, climbing amid the rigging, were the lightest and most agile of the crew, shinnying along crossbeams to unfurl the sails.

The wind blew from almost directly behind us, and as soon as the men dropped the lines, mighty white sheets billowed out. The sails caught so much of the wind that I could actually feel the ship lurch forward, moving at a great clip.

High above all that activity, a girl about the same age as me stood perched in a large wooden bucket fixed to the mainmast. She had long hair the color of wheat whipping about her head.

White and gray seagulls circled her, and whenever she held out an arm, one would swoop in to land on it. She would hand the bird a small piece of bread and the gull would take off. Occasionally, she would turn to the aft deck—to the captain—and yell something. She spoke the common tongue, but with the wind and the sails, I couldn't understand a word she said.

I watched her for some time, fascinated by the gulls. I tried to keep track of them, and before long I was convinced of it: The same gull never landed on her arm twice in a row.

Watching the gulls feed made my stomach growl, so I headed back to the narrow ladder to find Perrault.

But before I even made it to the deck, a sailor approached me. He tipped his head, motioning to the aft deck where Perrault stood. "Your friend there said to give you this when you woke." The sailor handed me a cloth wrapped around a hunk of bread and a small piece of cheese.

I found a place against the railing, in a patch of shade. The bread was a bit stale and the cheese was too sharp—but after a full day without food, it was enough to satisfy my rumbling belly. I devoured my meal then lay back on the deck and closed my eyes.

I listened to the captain as he barked orders, and to the cawing of the gulls, and to the splash of the ocean waves against the hull of the ship. The sounds mixed so well they seemed to become one, a perfect harmonious rhythm, the song of the sea, I thought.

The previous day had been horrible; today could only be an improvement. Perrault's wound would be on the mend. Asbeel would be farther away.

But in the back of my mind, questions nagged at me. What if Perrault got worse? What if Asbeel found us on the ship? Dark thoughts crowded my head, but I didn't even try to shake them.

"Oy, you awake, kid?" It was the girl from the crow's nest, poking me.

"No," I said without opening my eyes.

She smirked. "Then how are you talking, eh?"

"I talk in my sleep all the time. Just ask Perrault."

"Who's that, then?" she asked.

I knew I was being rude, but I couldn't help myself. The last thing I wanted to do was make small talk with a girl. I sat up and stared at her. "Perrault's the guy I came here with." I filled my voice with as much venom as I was capable of. "You think a kid like me could make it here all alone?"

"I didn't think a kid could make it here at all," she said. "You weren't here when we set off from the Gate. And I ain't recallin' us stoppin' to pick you up! How did you get here, eh?"

"Perrault and I rode. How else could we have come?" I said it as if it was so obvious, as if there were no other choice, but of course that made no sense. How could someone *ride* to a ship, particularly across the open sea?

She just rolled her eyes at me and smirked. "So he's your father, then?"

I was shaking my head before she finished. "No. He's just . . . He's . . ." What was he, I wondered. Surely Perrault was the closest thing I had to a father, and he cared for me and protected me as a parent should, yet when she asked that question . . .

"Say no more. You're an orphan, ain't ya?" She smiled again, but this time there was only gentleness there, so I abandoned my planned response—spittle—and just nodded. "An orphan, just like me. Name's Joen. What're you called, then?"

"Maimun." I could barely get the word out—a orphan, just like me, she'd said. Something about the sound of that word, leveled at me by someone other than Asbeel, shook me up. I'd never thought of myself as an orphan, though of course I was. I had always had someone, and even if Elbeth and Perrault weren't my parents by birth, they surely were by deed.

"Well then, Maimun. Wanna come with me? I'll show you 'round the ship, eh?"

I shrugged. "I guess so." I had nothing better to do while I waited for Perrault.

Joen led me around the ship, and pointed out each detail. The foredeck had a carving of a mermaid out front she called a "figurehead." Joen said we could have climbed out there, if the boat wasn't moving so fast. She showed me the crew's quarters, with the galley behind, where we swiped a loaf of bread. Then the hold, full of wool, dried fruit, and pottery from the Heartlands for trade in the North.

When we made it back to the deck, the captain was looking for Joen, wearing an angry scowl that seemed so at home on his grizzled face. But as soon as he saw me, his expression tightened.

"Joen, quit your playing, your break's over. Get up in the crow's nest before I have you whipped."

Joen lowered her eyes and nodded, moving toward the mainmast. I followed close behind. She tucked the loaf of bread into her belt and began scaling the mast—it was set with pegs specifically for that purpose, I could see—but she stopped a few rungs up. "Oy, ya wanna join me in the crow's nest?" she asked.

I hesitated. I had been rude to this girl, this fellow orphan, had all but told her to leave. But she had not, and was even asking me to join her. Asking me as a friend? I had never had a friend—save Perrault—and I realized I wouldn't know what to look for in one. Or maybe she was just planning to drop some of her work on me?

"Hurry up!" she called over her shoulder.

Worth finding out her intentions, I decided.

"Shouldn't this place be called the gull's nest?" I asked as I set my foot on the first rung. "Those birds aren't crows, they're gulls!"

Joen smiled widely. "All right, come join me in the gull's nest, then."

We spent the rest of the day up among the birds. I had never been so high in the air, and the view was dazzling.

I leaned over the side of the tiny bucket, and saw the sailors milling around on the deck. "They look as small as halflings." I laughed.

I stared down at the little people on the big ship and imagined they were oversized rodents, scurrying about from hole to hole, as they appeared and disappeared among the massive sails, the holds, and the many nooks not visible to a person from above. I made up a story on the spot about a rat who wished to become a sailor and the captain who made that dream come true. I told my tale to Joen in my best imitation of Perrault's storytelling voice.

When I finished, she clapped. "You should come up here every day," she said. "This ship's a whole lot more interesting with you aboard. Where did you hear that tale?"

"I made it up, just now. I guess one day I . . . well, . . . maybe I might like to learn to be a sailor, too."

"Here's your first lesson, then," Joen caught my hand and pointed it to the east. "Do you see the land there?"

I shook my head. To every side, the horizon appeared perfectly flat.

"Look harder! If you wanna work the crow's—I mean, gull's nest, you gotta keep a sharp eye out for anything." Joen jabbed my hand, tracing a line. "See? The color of the horizon is different out there, darker."

I squinted, and a line of gray came into focus atop the shining blue sea. "I can see it!"

"And there, moving parallel to us in the west—" She whipped me around and pointed my arm at the other side. "Sails! See them?"

The sun was bright and the horizon hazy, but I could just make out a speck of white riding the edge of the sea. I nodded.

Joen laughed. "You're a natural, then! I gotta lot a stuff I could show you. Tell your father—or whatever you call him—that you wanna stay aboard. Maybe the captain'd give him a job or something, eh?"

I shrugged. "We have to leave at Luskan." My stomach twisted and I remembered the argument Perrault and I had had the night before.

Joen picked up the loaf of bread from the floor of the crow's nest and ripped off a piece. "Well, maybe you can come back some day." She held out the piece of bread and a gull swooped out of nowhere to land on her arm. The bird gobbled it up in one bite, then dropped off her arm, wings outstretched. I followed his flight until I lost sight of him on the horizon. How would it feel to be so free?

When we ran out of bread, the gulls circled a bit longer before swooping off. They dropped into the ship's wake, skimming off the waves. Joen explained that the cook would be preparing the night's meal, and his scraps would be tossed out a porthole. The gulls would scavenge it all. Their appetites were infinite, it seemed.

After what seemed like hours, the thin clouds lit up, flaring brilliant red, as did the sea. The sun descended into its own shimmering reflection, orange meeting orange, and it seemed rather than setting, the sun was collapsing on itself.

"Wait till you see this." Joen smiled at me. "You ain't seen a sunset until you've seen a sunset at sea."

I had always loved to watch colors explode across the sky, orange, pink, red, and sometimes even a regal violet, but somehow this was different and not just because I was at sea. As the sun dipped lower, a shadow spread across the ocean to the east, coming from the land toward the ship like some great dark wave. As it reached the ship, I watched as the shadow climbed up the side, then onto the deck, then slowly up the mainmast.

When the shadow touched us in the gull's nest, the sun disappeared from sight. On the eastern horizon, the stars were already twinkling, growing brighter and more numerous by the second.

"I gotta get down to the galley and help Cook." Joen put her foot down on the mainmast's top peg and began to descend. "But maybe I'll see you around the gull's nest again."

I watched as she headed below then followed her down. At the bottom, I rushed to the eastern rail of the ship. I had seen sunrise then sunset at sea; now I intended to see the stars' bright lights. The night sky always seemed darker when few lights were about, like the open countryside. On the sea, there was no light save the tiny beacon at the bow of the ship. I stood transfixed for a good while, counting the stars as they appeared, trying to identify constellations and individual heavenly bodies.

I tried to remember the lessons I'd learned about navigating by the night sky, to figure out where we were and where we were heading.

After a time, Perrault joined me. "You missed the meal," he said. "So I brought you some." He handed me a plate of hard biscuits and salted meat.

I took the food gratefully, but could only nibble. Instead, I gulped deeply at the sights and sounds of the ship, and the salty smell of the sea.

Perrault stayed by my side for a moment, gently cradling his left arm and gazing out at the sea. He slipped away after only a moment, saying something as he went. It might have been, "Don't stay out too late," but I couldn't tell.

I couldn't say how long I stared out across the sea, first at the east rail, then at the west. All my favorite constellations were either west or south of the ship that time of year.

But some time later, a tiny speck on the horizon caught my eye. It was so small that it could have been the reflection of the stars off the water, except it didn't waver with the waves. At first I wasn't sure if I was imagining it. Perhaps I had spent too long staring at the stars. I closed my eyes and listened to the waves against the boat, the creaking of the wood, the low howl of the wind. I breathed deeply then I opened my eyes and scanned our ship.

Only two lanterns were lit, one at the prow and one at the stern, and a single lookout stood near each lantern, gazing out inattentively. My eyes swept back out to sea, along the horizon, and there it was again.

The tiny fleck didn't move at all—except, I noticed after a short time, it appeared to be growing. More to the point, it was *closing*. I realized with a shock that it was a ship. And it was coming right at us.

CHAPTER 20

I LET OUT A GASP AS I BACKED OFF THE RAIL, UNSURE WHAT TO DO. PERRAULT WAS ASLEEP, surely, and he had told me not to be out too late—what time was it? If I woke him, and it was nothing, he would know I had disobeyed, and I would be punished. But if I did nothing, and the ship was heading to attack, the consequences would be worse. So I settled for the middle path. I had to alert somebody, just not Perrault. I rushed to find the forward lookout.

"Wake up! Wake up, sir," I said. He didn't answer, so I repeated my request more forcefully, accentuating it with a push. He responded with a loud snore, and an empty bottle tumbled out from its cradle in the crook of his arm. He would be no help.

Frustrated, I ran to the stern and climbed up on the aft deck near the ship's wheel. The guard was awake, but when I rushed over, he spoke in a language I didn't understand.

" 'Ey boy, 'ows enyt trit'n or ees?" he said through a mouth devoid of teeth. My blank stare prompted a repetition, but the words came no more clearly.

I decided to speak to him and hope he could understand me. "Sir, there's something out there," I said, pointing to the western horizon.

"O ah, der sum'n ery ware, ya know, boy," he replied with a kind-hearted smile. Again, I couldn't make any sense of the words.

"A ship is out there, coming directly at us. It's closing fast. I don't know what to do!" I pronounced every word very clearly, and this time it seemed to sink in. The kindly smile disappeared from his face, replaced by a look of fear.

"A chip?"

"A ship. Yes. Right there." I moved to the rail and pointed straight at it. The man followed me, and stared into the darkness.

He fell back from the rail and sounded the alarm.

"A chip! A chip! Cap'n, wek de Cap'n, ders a chip an its lik'n be'n pirates! Pirates, Cap'n!" he screamed loudly as he rushed to the ladder and down, toward the cabin Perrault and I had taken. Realizing his error, he galloped below decks. I could hear his screams echoing up from below. The only word he could pronounce clearly was "pirates," and I heard it over and over, each time sending a chill up my spine.

Soon the deck was a flurry of activity, men scrambling all around. Many went up the mainmast to unfurl the sails, sure-handed even in the darkness. The helmsman, the captain, and Perrault all made their way to the aft deck, where I stood. Anyone without a task gathered at the west rail, watching the ship as it closed.

As soon as the sails were unfurled, they were turned to catch the wind, but the wind blew in from the west, from starboard, and though we could catch a fair breeze, our pursuer had it full on her back. Soon we were turning, running in a straight line with the pursuer. But still the ship closed.

"We cannot outpace her, Captain, she runs too swiftly," I heard Perrault say quietly, so none of the crew would overhear. "We should consider surrendering."

The captain's face turned red. "You have no authority to make such a decision. I say we run, and we hope at dawn to see friendly sails to deter the pirates! And if not, we'll deter them ourselves, at sword point!" The captain's voice was loud, and several nearby crew turned to look. A few let out a halfhearted cheer at the captain's proclamation.

"If you run," Perrault replied, lifting his voice to match the captain's, "and are caught, they will be far less merciful. If you fight, they will slaughter you, every one." No cheers at that, but a few of the sailors nodded in agreement. The captain's face was turning toward purple.

"Are you telling me," Smythe said, straining to keep his tone level, "to surrender my ship, to entrust the fate of myself and my crew to the mercy of pirates?"

"My own fate, and that of my ward, are tied to yours."

"Not so long as you have that damned horse!" He was screaming and the crew stared, but Smythe didn't notice. "I'll kill the thing, and then we'll see if you want to surrender!"

He took a step toward the captain's cabin, where Haze was resting. But only one step, because suddenly Perrault was armed, his sword pointed at the captain's throat. "You have but one more step to take, sir. Choose it wisely."

Smythe turned slowly to face Perrault. "Get off my deck," he said.

Perrault nodded and turned to me. He took my hand, gently, and led me to the captain's quarters. All the way, I could hear a stream of curses pouring from Captain Smythe. I tried to ignore him, but it was impossible. By the time the cabin door closed behind us, I was shaking.

Perrault checked on Haze—she was still exhausted from the taxing run so far out to sea. I wanted to suggest we ride away before the pirates arrived, but seeing her, I knew there was no chance. She could run forever across the ground, but running over water cost her great energy. Looking at her now, I was amazed we ever even reached the ship. I wondered if Perrault had known where the ship would be before we set off, and the thought chilled me—running blind across the great open ocean, hoping to find a ship, a mere speck on the great blue emptiness. . . .

Perrault led Haze into the captain's bedroom and I followed. He slid the heavy dresser in front of the door and stood near the porthole. I realized I was exhausted, so I dropped onto the cot. Despite my tiredness, no sleep would come. A question pressed at my mind until I could hold it no longer, so I had to ask Perrault, "What will happen when the pirates catch us?"

Perrault's expression was grim. "If the crew fight, they will die. If they surrender, who knows?"

CHAPTER 21

IT WAS PAST DAWN BEFORE THE PIRATES CAUGHT US. THE CAPTAIN'S HOPE OF FRIENDLY sails had not come true.

Nor had his plan to fight.

Wisely, the crewmen ignored their captain's call to arms. Badly outnumbered, they laid down their weapons and hoped for mercy. The pirates were happy to oblige—the only thing better than looting a ship, after all, was looting a ship without anyone in the way.

The captain's quarters were by no means protected from the looting, and it was not long before we heard several men enter the outer room. I heard furniture skidding across the floor and small crashes as the pirates tossed items about.

I peered out the tiny crack between the door and the jamb to see a pair of pirates ransacking the place. They were dirty, filthy, covered in the grime of tendays at sea without a bath. The room lay in ruins, each piece of furniture meticulously tipped over. Parchment and shattered wood lay everywhere.

One of the men held a small horn with a leather strap. The other held the arquebus I had seen earlier. They poured smokepowder down the barrel of the oddly-shaped thing—copious amounts of it—far, far too much.

After a moment, the one holding the weapon stepped back, said something, and pointed it directly at the other man, laughing all the while. The other threw his hands up to cover his face and dived backward.

The first pirate lifted his thumb to the hammer at the base of the barrel, pulled back, and let go.

The flash blinded me, the blast deafened me, and the ringing in my ears took a good while to fade. As I reoriented myself, I heard cursing, laughing, and shouting from the next room. The pirates had survived the blast. A shame, I thought.

Then I heard a different kind of blast—the banging of a heavy fist on the door to our barricaded little room.

"The ship's been surrendered, ye need to be lettin' us in!" came the call from outside.

"This room is off limits, good sir," Perrault replied.

"Ain't nowhere off limits! Open the door!" The banging fist was replaced by a much heavier thud as the man threw his shoulder into the door.

The door had no lock, and the barricade wasn't especially sturdy—every slam slid the dresser a few inches. It wouldn't be long before the pirate pushed through. Perrault knew this. He held his sword out—but in his left hand. His right was pressed tightly against his chest, which appeared to be bleeding again, staining his shirt.

"You err badly, sailor. Fetch your captain, and he will confirm: this room is off limits to you." How Perrault could keep his voice so calm despite his pain and such obvious danger amazed me. I wanted to hide under the bed, or scramble out the porthole, but I took courage from Perrault and did neither. Instead I hid behind Haze, stroking her mane to keep her quiet.

The banging at the door stopped and was replaced by heavy, sharp footsteps. A deeper voice spoke from behind the door.

"I seek the man called Perrault. Open this door."

Perrault hardly seemed surprised. "Captain Baram, I presume?"

"Indeed."

Perrault moved the barricade and opened the door, with great effort. Standing patiently was Captain Baram, looking every bit the pirate and every bit the captain all at once. His clothing was similar to Captain Smythe's outfit, but black instead of blue. His hat was three-pointed, also black, of old and well-worn leather. His face bore the scars of countless battles, and his beard was thicker than Smythe's, yet it looked regal, neatly trimmed, and well kept. The creases on his face spoke to years of salty ocean winds, his skin as leathery as his hat.

"Come, then, let us speak in private," said the captain. Perrault nodded, and led Haze and me out of the cabin.

On deck, the pirates had lowered two gangplanks—merely thick slabs of wood—across the gap between the ships. Baram led us across the nearer gangplank onto his ship.

We were not the only ones moving in that direction. A pair of armed pirates stood at the other plank, and a line of prisoners marched across. The crew of Captain Smythe's vessel were bound at the wrists and ankles then tied together, each to the person in front and behind. They walked with their heads down, hopeless, helpless.

At the back of one of the lines came Joen.

Her head was down, but her eyes were not. They peeked out from beneath the tangle of her hair. No fear filled those eyes, not even the resignation so visible in the older crewmen.

Her roaming gaze settled upon me. She, a captive, tied to the captive in front of him, looked at me, walking free, walking behind the pirate captain himself. Joen slowed and lifted her head. The pirate guard prodded her hard with the hilt of his cutlass, but Joen didn't flinch or lower her gaze. She looked directly at me, and whispered something. And though she only whispered, and a great distance stood between us, I heard her clearly.

"I forgive you."

Forgive me for what? I wanted to shout. But Joen had already walked across the plank and out of sight, into the hold below.

Perrault tugged on my arm and I continued walking, following him and Baram to the pirate captain's quarters.

Once there, Captain Baram opened a glass cabinet—not glass, I realized, but a magical glass known as glassteel, infinitely more solid and expensive than normal glass—and withdrew a dusty bottle. He poured a thick brown liquid into two glasses then looked at me and smiled. He reached for a third glass and moved as if to pour, but a look from Perrault stopped him. Captain Baram laughed and put the bottle away.

"To good health and good fortune," Baram said, raising his glass.

"Both come to those who seek it," replied Perrault, tapping his glass to the captain's.

"And to those who are shown it!" Baram replied, roaring with laughter.

"Your fortune and mine are the same. That I sought it and you found it is no coincidence."

"Ah, but only if I deliver you where you wish. I am a pirate, after all, and Waterdeep is out of my way. Why should I take you there, when it would be more profitable to return home with my new goods, and a valuable prisoner to boot?"

"Your reputation speaks otherwise, good sir."

"Indeed, indeed, and the other pirates will not cease to tease me about it!" Again came that great belly laugh, and Perrault joined in. "Very well, very well. Waterdeep it is. We should be there inside four days."

CHAPTER 22

PERRAULT SEEMED TO KNOW HIS WAY AROUND THE SHIP, AND AFTER FINDING SHELTER for Haze, he led us to an unoccupied cabin near the bow. I waited until we were alone before I allowed myself to say what I'd been thinking.

"You know the pirate captain." It was not a question—it was an accusation.

"Never met the man," Perrault replied.

"But you knew he was coming." I paced the small cabin.

"Yes." Perrault sat down on the edge of the bed, his back turned to me.

"How did you know?"

"I called him. It was a simple spell, really, to send my voice out across the miles and tell our good Captain Baram about a ripe and cooperative take."

I stopped pacing. It took me a moment to regain enough composure to say anything. "You . . . called him?"

"I did. For good reason." Perrault loosened his traveling cloak and laid it on the bed beside him. I could see dark patches of sweat staining the back of his finely woven shirt.

"What reason?" I clenched my fists and tried not to shout.

"The captain would not divert his ship's course," Perrault said with no emotion in his voice. "We needed to be off the sea a good deal sooner than Luskan."

I covered my face with my hands. "But what about Captain Smythe's ship, and his sailors, and all their stuff? They're all captured. Joen's captured. And it's all because of us . . . because of you . . ."

Suddenly I knew exactly why Joen had forgiven me. She knew the terrible thing that Perrault had done. My eyes began to fill with tears I didn't want Perrault to see. "If the sailors hadn't surrendered, they would have been killed. You nearly got the whole crew killed! Is getting to land sooner than Luskan worth the lives of every person on that ship?"

"Yes." Perrault said without turning around to face me.

I let my hands fall to my sides. "But why?" My voice was choked with unshed tears and I could barely push out the words.

"Because Asbeel has eyes everywhere. The demon was wounded, surely, but not badly. He will not stop looking for you, so we must step quickly to keep you out of sight. We cannot remain still, the way we were on the ship."

I shook my head. "But a ship is not still. It's always moving. That makes no sense."

Perrault stomped his foot hard, his boot cracking sharply against the floor. "I tell you where we're going, and there we will go, and that is the end of it. I know how to keep you safe. You do not."

My tears had dried, and I was just angry. "Why is that so important? Is my life more important than the sailors'? More important than Joen's?"

"It is to me!" Perrault swung around from his seat on the bed and glared at me. I could see what he'd been hiding. His silk shirt was soaked with blood, from the top of his wounded shoulder all the way to his waist.

The sight caught me off guard, and left me breathless. A million questions spun in my head then disappeared. I wanted to respond, to say something, anything, but no words came out. Perrault continued.

"A lesson for you, *child*,"—he spat the word angrily, as if it were an insult—"the most important one you shall ever hear from me. You protect first those you love then yourself, and last everyone else. You are my ward, so I will protect you first among all the souls in this world. And if doing so means harming others, even those who deserve no such harm, then so be it."

He grimaced then turned his back to me, pulling off the shirt and the bandage beneath. I saw the wound only for an instant, but it was long enough to horrify me.

The gash was an angry red, dripping watery, pale fluid. The flesh around it was blackened and burned where the demon's fire had touched it. It looked as if it had not healed at all—it looked as if it had grown worse.

Perrault got up and opened the cupboards. Finding what he sought, he pulled out a fresh linen sheet. He murmured a few words, poured some liquid on the fabric from a vial in his pocket, and tore the sheet into strips. Quickly, sure-handedly, he wrapped the linen tightly around his torso then pulled a fresh shirt from the cupboard and put it on.

"It's not about me—is it?" My words came out in a rush. "None of this is about me. It's about this stone. If you really cared about me, you wouldn't have cursed me with it." I ripped my shirt open and tugged the bandolier off my chest. "Why don't you just take it back?"

I marched over to Perrault, shaking the leather strap with every step I took. "Because of this stone, I'm an orphan. Because of this stone, I don't even know my real name. So tell me, why is it worth so much to everyone? To everyone but me?"

Perrault turned to face me and I could see the pain in his sunken eyes. His beard seemed more white than gray; his pale skin sagged.

"That stone is your heirloom and it will be forever intertwined with your destiny. I cannot answer any more than that, Maimun. There are some things you must learn for yourself." He looked as if he'd aged a decade in the past hour. His breath was labored. "Now please, child, help me to the bed."

I took his hand and was shocked by how cold it felt. He shuffled to the bed and helped him slide beneath the woolen blanket.

"We will make port in three days," Perrault said. "From Waterdeep, we make for Silverymoon with all haste. I've a friend there who will hide you."

"But what of you?" I asked. "You're hurt. You need help."

"I'll be fine. And besides, the finest healers in all Faerûn are in Silverymoon. Now, get some rest."

I supposed the plan was as good as any, though I knew the journey to Silverymoon would be long. Perrault had just placed a salve and fresh bandages on his wound, and he was a skilled healer. The oil he poured on the linen was surely magical, so I hoped the wound would heal soon.

I pulled some blankets from the cupboard, wrapped myself in them, and lay on the floor, affording Perrault the comfort of the cabin's only bed.

Perrault spent the next day in the cabin, barely moving, and sent me to fetch our meals. I had planned to seek out the captured crew, to learn Joen's fate, but Perrault's condition seemed far more urgent and I had to push my plan aside.

The second morning, he couldn't even rise from bed. The ship's healer came to see him, but was unable to do more than simply change the bandage. Captain Baram personally delivered our meals, to check on Perrault, and he informed us—informed me, as Perrault was asleep—that we were making fine time and were near the coast, but a powerful storm was battering Waterdeep and we couldn't sail into the harbor.

The third morning, Perrault did not wake.

CHAPTER 23

YOU SHOULD WAIT TILL WE HIT PORT." CAPTAIN BARAM'S VOICE WAS GENTLER THAN I'D ever heard it, full of something like pity. Somehow, that made me angry.

"Can't wait. Can't stay here with pirates," I spat.

We stood on the deck of the pirate ship mere moments after I had tried—and failed—to wake Perrault. I knew right away that we couldn't stay aboard and wait out the storm. Perrault didn't have that kind of time.

"Plenty of good healers in Waterdeep," Baram continued. "They'll fix him up right. You won't make it to Silverymoon."

I hefted Haze's saddle onto her back. "Best healers in Faerûn are in Silverymoon. Perrault said so."

Baram gave Haze a long look. "You sure she'll make it to shore?"

"She wouldn't let Perrault down. No chance, not ever." I finished with the saddle buckles and moved to Perrault, who lay on a cot the crew had dragged onto the deck. "Help me, would you?" I said, and a pair of crewmen obliged, helping me hoist him onto the saddle. His skin was hot and feverish, and his eyes flickered but never fully opened. He seemed halfway between sleep and waking, halfway between life and death.

I began to tie Perrault into the saddle.

"You'll be riding straight into a thunderstorm," the captain said. "Storm this far north, this time of year, gonna be a rough one, I'll tell you that much."

"We'll make it." I took Perrault's cloak from his back and fastened it around my neck. It was too long and dragged on the ground, but I didn't care. I reached into his boot sheath and withdrew his magical stiletto, sliding it into one of my belt loops. I slipped the straps of our haversack over my shoulders. Though it contained hundreds of books, it felt light as a feather.

"I have no doubt you'll make it," Baram said. "But you must make haste, or he will not."

I nodded, and swung up into the saddle. "I thank you for your hospitality, Captain Baram," I said, holding out my hand.

He took it in his strong grasp, and gave a firm shake. "If ever you find yourself in Luskan, do come find me," he said.

I gave him one last nod, took up Haze's reins, and headed overboard.

I had no plan to travel to Silverymoon, nor to trust Perrault's fate to the healers in Waterdeep, but I wasn't about to confide my real destination to a pirate.

I knew the one who could save Perrault, and she lived in Baldur's Gate.

Baldur's Gate, where I had been only a few days ago.

Baldur's Gate, the city where Perrault had been wounded trying to protect me.

We ran southeast, covering a great distance in a short time. After a few hours, the coast was in sight—and not a moment too soon, as I could feel Haze growing weary beneath me. At first, it had felt as if she were running on a cloud, but her hooves soon began to splash the water with every stride. We would be ashore soon, but along the coastline loomed a massive black cloud. Lightning rent the air, and waves of thunder rolled out to greet us like some ominous warning.

Turn back, said the thunderstorm. *It is futile. You are doomed. Turn back.*

Soon we were riding through a downpour, bolts of lightning crackling overhead, thunder following close behind. The storm increased in fury as bolt after bolt blazed out, the thunder chasing it like an evil laugh, the world laughing in my face, taunting me.

But we made the shore.

Haze stumbled and nearly fell as her hooves finally touched solid ground. Tired and soaked, I tumbled head-over-heels off her back, landing hard. Perrault remained firmly tied in place. His breathing was exceedingly shallow, and the bandage over his wound was saturated.

I climbed to my feet and walked to Haze, laying my face against hers. Those intelligent gray eyes looked at me, exhausted.

"I know you're tired," I said to her, "but if we stop now, he dies."

I could see in the way she reacted that she understood me. She pulled herself up, forced her back straight, and stood with pride, power, and grace.

"That's my good girl," I whispered, pulling myself back into the saddle. Haze was off and running before I even settled into my seat.

A normal horse moving at a normal pace can cover about fifty miles in a day if the weather is good and her rider lets her run. The journey from Waterdeep to Baldur's Gate is about five hundred miles, so the journey should have taken about ten days.

We made it in two.

We thundered through the city gates at a full gallop, Haze still managing a run despite having not slept, not even stopped her run, in forty hours and five hundred miles. The city guards shouted in protest and tried to stop us, but they couldn't keep up. Soon we were pounding through the city streets. Haze knew our destination without my guidance, and finally we skidded to a halt in front of the Empty Flagon.

Alviss, who had seen us coming, met us at the door.

I swung off the horse and handed her reins to the dwarf. "Take care of them," I said, turning to leave.

"Where are you going?" he asked.

"I must find Jaide. Where is she?"

"She's . . . she's in her temple," he stammered. "But you shouldn't be here. The demon is still looking for you!"

"I don't care. I need to find Jaide, to save Perrault," I said. "Which temple is hers?"

"The Lady's Hall," he said. "But wait! Don't go just yet." Alviss ran through the Empty Flagon's door and returned a few seconds later, sweat beading on his brow. He motioned for me to hold out my hand, and into my palm he pressed a slip of parchment. "You'll need this. Read the word aloud and she'll know it's you. It's the only way to enter her temple."

I was running toward the temple district before he could say another word. I heard him yelling after me, a stream of words lost to the wind, but his last two broke through clearly enough: "Be careful!"

CHAPTER 24

THE LADY'S HALL—THE TEMPLE TO TYMORA, GODDESS OF GOOD FORTUNE AND A matron deity to Baldur's Gate—was like nothing I had ever seen. It was huge and magnificent. High walls of white stone had statues placed every few feet depicting the goddess Tymora, her sister Beshaba, or one of her heroes fighting some dragon or devil. Mighty towers rose all around the building. Carvings covered them, layer upon layer of reliefs winding up the walls. Each tower was a giant work of art. At their tops were bells, perfect in both shape and sound.

I didn't stop to stare at the massive building. I had a purpose, and I moved deliberately, circling the temple to the east. I came to a narrow alley between the temple and another large building—it looked like a wealthy person's home—and moved along, looking for the door. But I found no entrance on either of the structures.

Behind the large house I found a ramshackle, run-down hut. The hovel's weather-beaten door had a carving of a sun with a face on it, eyes closed and mouth slightly upturned.

I reached into my pocket for the parchment and when I pulled it out there was another object in my hand. I unfolded the parchment, intent upon reading the word and entering the place.

"Took you long enough."

I started, because I recognized that voice.

Asbeel.

"At last you have come to fulfill your destiny. And you brought me the key to the priestess's home. Well done!" He laughed a terrible laugh.

I crumpled up the paper with my left hand and slipped it into a pocket, reaching with my right for the stiletto on my belt. I tried to keep my hand steady, but the unfamiliar weight of the stiletto and the cold feeling in my gut made that impossible.

"Begone, snake," I hissed at him.

When I drew the weapon, Asbeel laughed even louder than before.

"The bard's cloak, and his dagger too! The rumors must be true—mighty Perrault is dead!"

He was defenseless; he had no weapon, not even his obsidian staff. His eyes were half-closed as he laughed. I snapped my wrist—the stiletto lengthened into a fine saber—and leaped at him, lunging for his throat.

But my sword passed harmlessly though him.

I knew my mistake as soon as I heard the beat of wings behind me. The illusion in front of me faded as I spun to face the real Asbeel, swooping down from the rooftops, his obsidian staff swinging for my head. I barely managed to get my sword up to block, but the strength of the blow was incredible. I went flying backward, the sword falling from my hand, and landed hard.

"No more games, little one. You were mine from your birth, and with the bard gone, I claim you for my own. As it should be. Do not resist, or I will have to hurt you." He stalked forward, staff at the ready.

I had seen Asbeel fight Perrault and I knew I couldn't hope to defeat the demon. I got to my feet and retrieved my sword, quickly thinking through my options. What could I do? What could I use against him?

Then there was a blinding flash that set the world alight; and there was a voice, a woman's voice, cool and velvety and powerful all at once.

"Let him be, demon, he is beyond you," said the voice. "Come and play with me a while." Somewhere I heard a door click shut. The light was suddenly gone, and standing in the alley was the beautiful Jaide.

She was unarmed and unarmored, but still she looked formidable. Asbeel sensed it too. He turned from me, dropping his staff and drawing his sword. The blade burst into flame as he rushed her. A staff appeared in her hand, not a physical object but a concentrated beam of light, and she parried his blow and struck back hard.

Asbeel barely managed to dodge, and he fell back a step. Jaide pressed the attack, her every movement graceful, the staff an extension of her will. The fight was dazzling, but it could not hold my focus, for suddenly a voice spoke in my head.

Run away, Maimun, Jaide said without speaking. *Run and hide.*

Perrault is sick! I mentally screamed back, somehow knowing she would hear me. *You need to help him!*

I have always helped him. But there is nothing more either of us can do for him now except to keep you and the stone safe. There was a finality to her words, but also serenity. I felt my heart clutch in my chest at the confirmation that Perrault was truly gone.

I don't want the stone, I replied.

That's not your choice to make. Keep it, and keep it safe.

Where should I go? I thought, defeated.

Anywhere but here. It is best if I do not know. Don't let the city guards see you, if you can, for many of them are allied with your foes. Run now, and take heart, for you will be blessed with luck in whatever travels you take.

I nodded at her, though she could not see—the battle raged on, sword and staff clashing together, bursts of fire and light illuminating the shadowy alley. I turned and ran.

I stopped at the end of the alley, one final thought coming to mind, and I hoped she could still hear me. *Will you kill Asbeel?*

Her response was faint, so faint at first I couldn't understand it. But she repeated it over and over, or perhaps it was merely an echo: *That is for you to do.*

PART III

A sharp bang on the door startled me from my tale. "Grub's up, Cap'n," came the muffled call from outside.

"Good, good. Bring mine in here," the pirate sitting before me replied. He paused a moment. "Make that a double ration."

No response came from outside save heavy booted footsteps walking away.

"So you're the captain then?" I asked. "That's new."

"What, ye think we'd let any old salt interrogate ye?"

"Is that what you've been doing?"

"Something like that. Found out who ye sailed with, didn't I?"

"You found out who I sailed with long ago," I said.

Again the knock, and the door swung open, revealing a sandy passage leading to . . . was that the night sky? The rhythmic pounding of the waves against a cliff drifted up the corridor, along with the smell of salt water. A flicker of light at the end of the hall told me there was probably a campfire, and there was a low hum, like a song being sung in the distance. The other pirates were nearby.

I pondered the possibility of escape—bowl over the captain, maybe take his sword, and fight my way past this other pirate whose hands were full. But that would put me outside, among the whole crew. Their mooring would surely be someplace hidden, a cove or an island. There would be nowhere for me to run.

No, I decided it wasn't the time for an escape. Perhaps when the captain left.

Once the captain had his food, the door swung shut again.

"Thinking it, weren't ye?" he asked.

"I don't know what you mean."

"Ye were gonna make a run fer it."

I shrugged. "It wasn't my moment."

"No, it weren't. Ye think yer moment'll come soon, do ye?"

"I've been through worse than this."

The captain set down his food—a lump of some shapeless slop and two small cuts of blackened, salted meat—and began picking at it.

"Hungry, are you?" I asked.

"You bet yer ugly arse I'm hungry. Captainin' be hard work."

"Hence the double rations."

"What, did ye think some of it was fer ye? Ye don't get food till I says ye get food."

I shrugged. "Then you get no more of my story."

The captain stopped. "Ye finished yer story, didn't ye? Ye already told me what happens next. Ye ran off from the demon, found Deudermont's ship, and stowed away. Ye met the drow, fought the sea troll, and made good with yer captain who offered ye a job aboard his ship. Got back to where ye started from."

"I did, but there's still more to tell."

"Yar, I know. Let me tell it. Ye sailed with Deudermont fer the next six years and then ye got yerself caught by me crew. Good tale. Not worth me giving ye any o' me food." Some of the colorless slop spilled from his mouth with each word.

"If you believed that, you wouldn't have taken your meal here."

The pirate stared at me for a long while. "Clever boy, ain't ye?" He reached down, took one of the slices of meat, and tossed it to me. "Speak, then."

I took a bite. It wasn't half bad, despite its appearance, and I was famished.

"Very well," I began. "Let's pick up back on *Sea Sprite.*"

CHAPTER 25

S *EA SPRITE* HAD NO EMPTY CABIN TO HOUSE THE SEVERAL SAILORS WOUNDED IN THE skirmish with the pirates. Instead, Captain Deudermont had a spare sail hung wall-to-wall in the crew cabin, separating the dozen bunks nearest the stern of the ship.

Deudermont said that would prevent dirt and diseases from the other sailors from creeping into the same area as the wounded and causing infection. I figured it was to keep the garish injuries, some much worse than my own gash, out of sight of the rest of the crew.

I was given the bunk closest to the port side of the ship, directly beneath a small porthole. As the ship sailed south, my porthole faced directly into the sunrise, and I took advantage of it on the second morning after the battle. The porthole was too high to see out of without standing on my cot, and I still felt lightheaded, but I hauled myself up and stared out at the brightening sky.

From my low vantage point, the horizon was an unbroken stretch of water. The rising sun appeared, slowly at first, then growing, until it filled my view, the brilliant light blinding me.

I thought of Perrault, of the first sunrise I had watched with him those many years ago. A new beginning, he had called it. A new day. Was this the same? Could I begin anew, right now, right here?

No, I decided, I could not. A weight still hung around my neck, and I couldn't start over as long as I carried it.

I was so wrapped up in my thoughts that I didn't notice the laughter behind me. It was more wheeze than laugh, filled with phlegm and more than likely some blood. Only when the laugh turned into a hacking cough did I take note.

I turned to face a wounded sailor. He wasn't too old, but his face was worn, wrinkled, and leathery. I didn't see his wound at first—he was covered foot to neck by a blanket, and heaving with that awful cough—but when I saw it, my stomach turned. His left leg was missing from the knee down, and from the bloodstains on the sheets, it had been freshly amputated.

Gradually his cough subsided and the man was peaceful, but lathered in sweat. I knew that if I were to touch him, his flesh would be burning but that sweat would be cold. His cheeks were pale, his muscles slack. But his eyes were bright, staring at me.

"Are you all right?" I asked him. Only when he started laughing again did I realize how foolish the question was—he had lost his leg, and from the sound of that cough, he was seriously ill.

This time, the laugh didn't turn into a cough. Instead, it turned into words. "All right? I suppose I am, then. I didn't expect to see another sunrise at all, but there she is! 'Course, there's a boy blocking my view, but that don't bother me so much. He isn't hogging all the light." His voice, like his laugh, was choked with phlegm. He had the sound of a dying man, and my stomach dropped at the thought.

I flushed red and sat down on my cot. "Sorry, sir," I said. "I didn't realize you were awake."

"That's all right, kid," he replied. "But my name ain't sir—it's Tasso—and I'd much prefer if ye called me by it."

I nodded slowly. "I'm Maimun," I told him.

"You ever watch a man die, Maimun?" he asked. I heard no fear in his voice, only curiosity. "And I don't mean, have y'ever seen a man cut down by a sword. That's one thing, and it's horrible, but it ain't the same as watching a man die. I want to know—have you ever been near a man who could talk to you one moment, and the next he's gone?"

I started to shake my head, to say no, I hadn't ever seen that, but I stopped myself, thinking of Perrault. One day he was talking, trying to lead me to safety. The next day, he was asleep and I'd never hear his voice again.

"Is that a yes or a no?" Tasso asked.

I quickly shook my head. I knew where his questions were leading—Tasso was telling me that he was dying. And as much as I wanted to keep the truth about Perrault from myself, somehow I couldn't bring myself to hold back the truth from a man who was not long for the world. It didn't seem right that the last conversation he would ever have should be soiled with a lie, or even a half-lie.

"I've seen a man dying." A lump rose in my throat. "But I've never seen a man die."

"If ye don't think ye can handle it, you probably should get out of here soon," he said. Already his voice was lower, quieter than it had been, as if the energy of the conversation was draining him. "I was supposed to go east," he continued. "Supposed to follow my family out there, past the Sea of Falling Stars. Promised 'em I'd come find 'em."

"Why didn't you?"

"Never had the time."

I blinked a few times, remembering what Perrault had once told me about time.

"How old are ye, Maimun?" Tasso asked.

"Twelve, sir. Er, twelve, Tasso."

He wheezed out a laugh. "Same age I was when I first took to the seas. Been on the ocean twenty years, been in the world thirty-two. I had plenty of time, didn't I? But I ne'er made it to the east."

"It isn't about how much time you have, it's about how much time you have to spare," I said quietly.

He looked at me for a long while. "Now ain't them just the wisest words I've ever heard?" He reached out and grasped my arm, pulling me toward his face. I felt his hot breath on my cheeks, but I was not revolted, I didn't try to pull away. "Time ain't spare, kid," he said, his voice low and choked. "Ye don't get given yer time, ye make it for yerself. Ye've got twenty years to catch me. Don't let it slip, waiting for something. Go east."

He let go and fell back onto his cot, his breathing shallow and labored. He sounded as if he was in pain, as if the air burned his lungs and throat as he gulped down his breaths. But a look of peace stole over his face, a serenity in his expression that I had not seen before.

I took his hand and held it. His breaths grew less frequent, and quieter, until I had to put my face close to his to hear it at all.

Less than an hour after he introduced himself to me, I held the hand of the sailor Tasso and watched his very last breath leave his body.

I sat on the edge of my cot, holding Tasso's hand even as it grew cool, for a very long time. The sun had risen beyond my porthole view, the diffuse light in the dusty cabin giving it an eerie feel. I sat there, holding the dead sailor's hand, imagining it was Perrault.

Only a few days earlier, I had raced to Baldur's Gate with Perrault, determined to find a way to save him. When I had the chance to say one last good-bye, right before I headed to the wharf to stow away on this very ship, I had passed it by. I had told myself that he would be better off without me, that the danger from Asbeel was too great. But I knew that wasn't true.

Perrault had raised me for six years, had dedicated his life to my protection. He had taught me, had shown me the world. He was wounded in my defense, had died to protect me. He was the only family I'd ever known. And I hadn't had the courage to be there, holding his hand as he slipped into the next world.

What had he felt, I wondered, when he died. Had his face worn the same look of peace that Tasso's had? Had he perhaps awakened, seeking to speak to me, if only for a moment, to admit he was done and would soon be gone?

Who had held Perrault's hand when he died?

The ship's healer arrived to find me holding the dead man's hand and weeping softly. He gently separated my hand from Tasso's and helped me back to my cot.

I barely heard him as he talked to me, and to the two crewmen he'd brought with him. Tasso had died because his wounds were infected, and to leave him would risk infection for the other wounded. He would be removed, and would be buried at sea that very day—that is, he would be wrapped in cloth, tied to a plank, weighted with stones, and released overboard.

Would I be buried at sea if my wound became infected and I died? I had no ties to these sailors. Would they care if I disappeared? If I died? Would anyone?

I fell back onto my hard cot and wept, crying alternately for Perrault, for Tasso, and for myself, the orphan boy, wounded and wandering, with no roots or home to call my own.

"Self-pity does not become you." The voice caught me off guard. It was quiet and gentle, but full of strength. I looked up to see a black hand pulling back the corner of the canvas separating the makeshift infirmary, and a pair of violet eyes staring at me from beneath the raised corner.

"It wasn't self-pity," I lied, indignant. "I was crying for Tasso." I motioned to the empty cot.

"You barely knew Tasso. You were crying for yourself."

"You barely know me."

The dark elf Drizzt nodded his assent. It was true, of course, that we barely knew each other. But looking into his eyes, I felt again the bond I had sensed when I first saw him.

I felt again that I had known him all my life. And I was sure he knew it, and I hoped he felt the same connection.

"You're right. I wasn't crying for Tasso. I was crying for someone else, but it wasn't for me."

"Why do you cry for this other person?"

"Because he's dead!" I practically screamed.

Drizzt nodded. "Of course," he said. "But why do you cry for the dead?"

I stuttered a few times before I could answer. "Because he's gone and he won't come back."

"But where has he gone?"

"I don't know. Tymora's realm in Brightwater, I suppose. He's gone to be with his goddess."

"If you believe that, then why cry for him? If he is in a good place, shouldn't you be happy for him?"

"I . . . I don't know."

"Look inside. You were crying because you lost him, not because he is lost. You were crying because this world is suddenly less full than it was before. And that is a fine reason to grieve. But be aware of that fact. You were crying for yourself."

I stared at him for a long time, at that dark elf so full of wisdom. He knew things, many things, I realized. He knew the truth about me before even I knew it.

"When a sailor dies, why do they bury him at sea?" I asked, trying to hold back tears.

"People are always buried near their families," Drizzt said. "So when a sailor dies, his family at sea will always be nearby."

"What do you mean, his family at sea? Do sailors take their parents or their children out on the water with them?"

"Sometimes. But I meant the others on his crew." Drizzt stepped into the room and sat beside me on my cot. "There are all kinds of family, as you shall learn. Every sailor on this ship is brother or sister to every other. Now, enough of this discussion. How is your arm?"

I hesitated for a moment before I realized what he was talking about. Unconsciously, I started moving my left arm in circles. "The pain is gone," I said, "but it feels . . . tight."

Drizzt nodded. "Can you stand? Can you walk?"

I shrugged. "I can stand. Haven't tried walking."

"Do." He offered me his arm, which I accepted and used to pull myself up off the cot. I stood unsteadily for a moment. "I feel a bit woozy," I said. "But I think I'm all right."

"Good. The captain wants to see you." He handed me a small sack, which I opened to find a fresh outfit, complete with a clean shirt, a leather belt with a sheath for my stiletto, and a worn pair of boots. And the leather sash holding the magical stone.

I looked up to see the flap of the canvas fall behind the departing drow. "Drizzt!" I called after him. My chest hurt from the effort of the shout, but the flap lifted and the dark elf reappeared.

"Forget something?" he asked.

"If I die, where will they bury me? I have no family."

He looked at me for a moment. "You have a family. You just don't know it yet."

CHAPTER 26

WHAT DO YOU KNOW OF THE SEA?" CAPTAIN DEUDERMONT ASKED ME.
"The ocean is vast and unknown, stretching away from the western coast of Faerûn forever, to unknown tracts of water and perhaps land," I recited. "It serves as a means of conveyance between the points along the coast, much faster than travel by land, though often more dangerous. The first . . ."

Captain Deudermont stopped me with an upraised hand. "You have read Volo," he said.

"Yes sir."

"That is good. But what do you know of the sea that is practical?"

I paused for a moment. "I don't know what is practical at sea," I answered truthfully.

"Have you ever been aboard a ship before?"

"Just once." I winced at the memory, and Deudermont noticed.

"You didn't enjoy the experience?"

Again I hesitated. How could I explain the events of my previous sea voyage? Of course, one word would fully and accurately describe my troubles. "Pirates, sir."

Deudermont nodded. "So twice you have been to sea, and twice your ship has been attacked. You have some terrible luck, Maimun."

"Apparently so, sir."

"Back when you were at sea before, what did you do?"

"I spent most of my time in the gull's . . . I mean, the crow's nest, sir." Deudermont perked up at that.

"Did you have the eyes for it?" he asked. "Could you make out objects on the horizon?"

I nodded. I had seen the ship Joen had pointed out. I had even seen a ship at night, that horrible night, and I told him so.

"That is impressive. It usually takes a sailor months, even years, to attune his eyes to the tricks of the light on the open ocean."

"I was only at sea for short time, sir."

Deudermont smiled. "Your manner and honesty have confirmed my choice for you. Your position on the ship will be as my cabin boy. Your tasks will be mostly menial. While at sea, you will run orders to the crew, and you will bring meals to me. You will maintain the cabinets where the captain's log and the charts are kept." He motioned to a large piece of furniture I had assumed was a cupboard. "When we're in port, you'll watch the ship if I go ashore. In exchange for all these tasks, you'll be paid a modest wage in silver, and you'll also be paid in knowledge. You'll learn, from the crew me, all forms of seamanship—tying knots, navigating by the stars—"

"Oh! I know how to . . ." I blurted out the words before I realized how rude my interruption was. Captain Deudermont's gaze was stern, and I flushed bright red.

"Where did you learn to navigate?"

"I read it in a book."

"There's a big difference between a book and the real thing."

I shook my head. "When I was traveling with . . . my father, he wouldn't tell me where we were, so I'd use the stars to figure it out," I answered. "There isn't any difference between starfinding on land and on sea, is there?"

Deudermont's expression softened a bit. He looked almost curious. "It is easier, in fact, at sea, since the horizon is flatter. My young man, I think you have a remarkable mind. Here is your first task. Run these orders to the guards at the brig, where the pirates are being held."

I was beaming at the compliment as I bounced out of the room, across the deck, down into the hold, and toward the brig.

Like any seafaring vessel, the ship was fitted with a simple prison, a single cell made of iron bars. The cell had no window and only one door, which was securely locked from the outside. The brig was large, but full. Two dozen pirates sat on the floor, packed as tightly as they could fit. Two of *Sea Sprite*'s sailors stood guard, leaning against the wall beside the cage. One of them absently twirled a ring of keys around his finger. The other appeared to be dozing, his chin resting on his chest and his shoulders slumped. Neither took any notice of my approach.

"Orders from Captain Deudermont," I said meekly. The guard with the keys jumped and nearly dropped them. The other didn't even stir.

"Oh, so the Cap'n's got you runnin' orders to pay your debt, does he?" he said, his voice loud and rough. It awoke his companion, who had been asleep on his feet. Startled awake, he jumped forward, his body moving too quickly for his legs. His feet tangled and down he went, landing with a heavy crash.

In the blink of an eye, the guard was back on his feet, brushing himself off and waving his fist at the caged pirates, who were laughing at him.

One man, standing against the bulkhead at the back of the cell, wasn't laughing, though, or even smiling. He was short and thin, with a wide nose and too-small eyes. His skin appeared a pale blue, and his hair was the bluish white of a breaking wave. He was just staring—at me. Suddenly I felt very uncomfortable.

"Well then, hand them over," said the guard with the keys. I obliged, passing him the note, which he unfurled and scanned quickly.

"Oy, Tin, you're relieved," he said, looking at the other man. The clumsy sailor nodded and left without saying a word.

"His name is Tin?" I asked.

"Oh, no, his name's Tonnid. But we call him Tin-head, 'cause he's got as much brains in that skull as an empty tin cup. And I'm called Lucky, 'cause, well, I'm the luckiest salt you'll ever meet. What's your name?"

"My name is Maimun. It means 'twice lucky'."

Lucky broke out laughing. "Twice lucky, eh? But you're half my size!"

I joined in the laugh for a moment then looked around. "So, if he's relieved, who's relieving him? Or does it say you have to guard alone?"

"Naw, naw, I ain't guarding this lot alone. You're supposed to fetch his replacement. Guy named Drizzitz." He cackled, and I knew he was directing it at me, though I didn't know why. "You're the stowaway ain't ya? Paying back the Cap'n for stealing his food by running these orders?"

"Yes, and no," I answered. "I stowed away, but the captain offered me a place on the crew."

In the blink of an eye, Lucky's mirth was gone. "Offered you a job? For stowing away and hiding through the fight? That don't seem half right. No it don't."

"I didn't hide. I fought. Got wounded, too!" I reached to the neckline of my shirt, intending to show him my scar. But that pirate who had been staring at me seemed to perk up as I reached, and I realized that to show him the wound would also reveal my leather sash. I hesitated.

"Well, then, let's have it, eh? Show me your wound, else I'll know you for a liar."

Thinking quickly, I reached out and grabbed his hand, pulling it toward my chest. "Feel that?" I asked, putting his hand on my shoulder where the scar began. "You feel the wound?"

By the look on his face—a mix of horror and sympathy—I knew he felt it, the raised welt where the gash had been. "Ye got tarred," he said, low. "That's one of the things I been lucky about. Been sailing some thirty years and I ain't never got a wound so deep it needed the tar. You have me apologies, boy. But I didn't see you in the fight. Ya mind telling me what happened?"

Again I hesitated. How could I tell him about the fight, about the troll that had come looking for me? How could I tell him without revealing the artifact strapped to my chest—which the pirate in the brig seemed interested in. Worse, how would Lucky react if he deduced, as I had, that the pirates had attacked *Sea Sprite* because they were looking for me?

I couldn't tell him. I would have to lie.

"A pirate got into the hold where I was hiding," I began. Lucky immediately looked suspicious. I figured he'd been on the deck, and he knew no pirate had entered the hold that way. Time to improvise. "He climbed up the stern. Had a big axe. You know that big hole in the aft hull? That's his doing—cut his way in."

"Must've been one big pirate to cut through the hull of a ship!" Lucky exclaimed.

"The biggest man I've ever seen," I replied. "I figure he had some orc—or something—in him. Anyway, so he chops into the hold right where I'm hiding. And he wants to go through the hold and up the hatch and attack the crew from behind. But I couldn't let him do that. So I sneaked up and tied a rope to his ankle then tied it to the rowboat and dropped the boat into the water."

"Oy, good thought! But how'd that get yourself a wound?"

"He crashed into me on his way out of the hold," I said. "Knocked me right into the splintered wood he'd cut through."

Lucky winced. "Guess you ain't as lucky as your name says, then."

"He's a liar." The voice caught me off guard. It was deep and powerful, but not harsh. It reminded me of the distant thunder of a storm on its way out, damage done but mercifully leaving. It belonged to the pirate in the back of the cage—only he was no longer at the back of the cage. He stood right against the bars, staring at me, unblinking.

"Oy, shut your mouth and don't talk no more, you wretched wretch!" Lucky drew his cutlass from its sheath and waved it threateningly at the man.

"The child is lying to you. He is concealing something."

Lucky spat at the pirate and stepped between us. "If ye think I'll trust you over the boy, you're dumber than a sea sponge."

"I don't ask for trust. But I have a question. Little Maimun, what is that lump in your shirt beside your heart?"

Lucky turned to look at me, staring intently. I was sure he'd see the lump and ask about it, and I couldn't answer him. I slowly moved my feet, one behind the other.

"I need to find Drizzt to relieve Tin," I said, and before Lucky could say anything, I turned on my heel and sprinted away.

I found Drizzt on the deck at the prow of the ship. The disguise that made him appear as a sun elf was off, his black skin exposed to the summer sun. He held his head high, eyes closed against the breeze, feeling the sun on his face and the wind sweeping back his thick white hair. I crept up silently, not wanting to disturb his meditation, but he heard my approach.

"Greetings, Maimun," he said, not opening his eyes or turning his head. "Captain Deudermont told me of your new position. Congratulations."

"Thank you, sir," I said. "I have orders from the captain for you."

"To take my shift at the brig, I'm suppose," he said.

"Yes sir."

"Thank you, then." He opened his eyes and turned to face me.

"Can I ask you a question?" I said.

"You just did."

"I mean . . . you know what I meant." I stammered, suddenly nervous. "Where . . . where is your home? Where is your family?"

He looked at me for a moment, studying me intently. I don't know what he was looking for, but apparently he found it. He nodded, and answered. "My home is wherever my family is, and my family are my friends and traveling companions. It is not a large family, so far, as few trust me. Few trust any of my dark heritage."

"But the others who fought the pirates here," I said. "Wulfgar, and the dwarf, and the woman. They trust you, right?"

"They do. And those three are my family. Well, those three and a fourth who is not here. You're an orphan, aren't you?"

"I am." I sighed. Thrice an orphan, I wanted to say. "How did you know?"

"You understand what I mean by family. Most do not. Most think of a family as parents and siblings, aunts and uncles, but really, a family are those people you know here," he pointed to his head, "and trust here." He laid his hand over his heart.

I nodded my agreement. "So who is the last of your close family?"

"A halfling named Regis. He was taken from us and is being held prisoner in Calimport by a very powerful and evil man. For his sake, we sail south."

"Sounds dangerous. Are you sure he wishes you to save him?" I asked. I immediately thought I should have picked my words more carefully, but Drizzt didn't seem upset.

"How do you mean?" he asked. I think he knew exactly what I meant, but he was leading me on. Perrault did the same thing. He'd lead me on, knowing the answer, to force me to articulate it. Because, he'd say, only after I had spoken it would I truly understand what I meant.

"I mean," I began, "are you sure he isn't in a cell somewhere, scared to death that you and your family—his family—might try to rescue him but fail? That one of you might be killed for his sake?"

Drizzt nodded again, his expression somewhere between grim and hopeful. "I am quite certain he's thinking exactly that."

"Then why go?"

"Because he cares more for us than for himself. We'd be terrible friends if we didn't return the favor." With that, he bowed his head slightly then stepped to the ladder to the hold.

"Drizzt!" I called after him. "If you die, where should they bury you?"

"It doesn't matter. My friends will know where to look for me."

Instinctively, my hand went to my heart—because, of course, he meant his friends would only need to look within. But in reaching for my heart, my hand bumped against something else. Something the size of a child's fist, held in a leather pouch. The stone.

CHAPTER 27

THE NEXT SEVERAL DAYS WERE A BLUR. I SPENT MY WAKING HOURS RUNNING AROUND the ship delivering small scrolls of parchment, or verbally passing orders to the sailors who couldn't read. I ran Deudermont's meals from the galley to his cabin, and was rewarded with the privilege of dining with him. During those hours, Deudermont, true to his word, began to teach me the craft of seamanship, telling me of the tactics of running a ship—when and how to set sail or make port, weather signs, and all the things a captain should know.

When I was idle, I learned the practical art of sailing. I spent hours sitting on the deck watching the crew as they went about their affairs. I memorized the knots they tied. I watched them furl and unfurl the sails, and turn those sails to catch the wind. I listened to the calls from the helm, usually just numbers, to change our bearing. Soon I was confident I could have undertaken any job on the ship. For the first time in my life, I felt at home.

I learned most of the crewmen's names, and some snippets of their stories, but I kept to myself and they did the same. I was worried that I would have to tell my story again, to lie again. I was worried that Lucky, in particular, had pieced some of it together, and that I would be blamed for the pirate attack. But even Lucky was friendly toward me, and he never once asked about the lump on my chest.

The days flew by, and before I knew it, we were sailing into Memnon.

I thought Baldur's Gate to be a great city, but it would have fit a dozen times into the sprawl that was Memnon. As the northernmost port in Calimshan, the city was built where the Calim Desert met the ocean, where the sea breeze could break up the stifling heat of the parched sandscape. The sprawl reminded me of the poorest parts of the lower city of Baldur's Gate mixed with the richest parts of the upper city, thrown into a mixing pot and stirred well. Ramshackle huts built of driftwood stood against mighty palaces of white marble. Low warehouses lined the docks, like in Baldur's Gate, but the windows were empty of glass, and by the sheer volume of people moving in and out, I figured most of the structures served as homes for those who could find nowhere else to be, rather than as storage for trade goods.

The sprawl made its way into the harbor as well. The docks were completely full, and a hundred more ships were anchored beyond them. Great trade galleons mingled with tiny fishing vessels, and the flags of a hundred ports of a dozen kingdoms flew from the masts.

Moving around the ships were longboats, each crewed by a dozen men chained to their seats and pulling at oars. Each boat bore a beacon lantern at the bow, and a flag flew from the stern, marking them as official vessels of the city of Memnon. Captain Deudermont informed me that they were the Memnon Harbor Guard, and they were searching incoming vessels for contraband. Or, more accurately, they were forcing those ships holding contraband to pay bribes. Otherwise, they would be refused access to the port.

They would also be the ones taking the captured pirates off our hands. A reward was offered for bringing captured pirates to Memnon. But Deudermont said the Harbor Guard would surely make up some reason the reward could not be paid. They were experts at extorting money, he said, but very bad at paying it. And they wouldn't be checking our ship for at least a day.

On the first day in port, Drizzt and his companions prepared to depart.

Drizzt talked to Captain Deudermont in his cabin, and I wasn't invited to sit in. I tried to listen at the door, but their voices were low and I couldn't make out what was said.

On the way out, Drizzt gave me a look. "I'll see you again," the look said—and he put his hand over his heart in salute. His skin was as light as a sun elf's again, just as it had been the first time I'd laid eyes upon him. Though I knew it was an illusion, it was still strange to see him again in his magical disguise. At least he didn't look as uncomfortable as he had that first time. I felt a strange kinship as I watched him walk away. Something had changed for him aboard *Sea Sprite*, just as it had for me.

Drizzt and his friends boarded a hired launch, and he was gone, drifting through the harbor toward the docks. All I had left of him was that look.

I awoke the next morning to shouts coming from the deck. I quickly dressed and scurried above to discover three uniformed members of the Memnon Harbor Guard climbing aboard. Captain Deudermont rushed from his cabin to meet them. He looked somewhat disheveled, obviously surprised by the quick arrival of the inspectors. He'd told me to expect them late that day or early the next.

I quickly moved to his side. As soon as I reached him, he said, "Maimun, go rouse the crew. Tell them we're unloading the pirates."

I opened my mouth to say something, but Deudermont waved his hand at me and turned back to his conversation with the guards.

I did as I was told, and soon the pirates were marching up from the hold, each man tied at the wrists and ankles, and each tied to the man in front of and behind him. On the captured pirate vessel, a similar scene occurred, but I noticed many more pirates crossing the deck than the two dozen crossing ours. It seemed the pirate ship had a larger brig than *Sea Sprite*.

But the pirates on our ship were more intimidating. The strange pirate who had confronted me was on deck, and he stared right at me again. I turned to the nearest crewman—it happened to be Tin.

"What's that one's problem, Tonnid?" I asked him, motioning toward the staring pirate.

"I dunno, bud. He's just rude, I think."

"Aren't all pirates rude?"

Tin paused, thinking over his answer. "Yep, I figure they is," he replied. "That one's just even ruder."

Tin smiled at his almost-joke, and I laughed a little. It wasn't funny, but Tin liked people laughing at his jokes.

In the blink of an eye, Tin's smile was gone, replaced by a look of shock and horror.

Behind me I heard a soft thud, followed by loud shouting. I turned to see the strange pirate free of his bonds, the ropes uncut but lying on the deck. The man charged right at me.

"Hey, you's gonna get it for that, mister ruder!" Tin shouted, jumping in front of me, fists up in front of his face, ready to throw a punch.

The blue-faced pirate didn't hesitate, and didn't flinch when Tin threw a heavy punch at his jaw. The blow landed with a crunch, the sound of bone breaking, I thought. But the pirate didn't even slow. Instead, Tin fell back a step, clutching his wounded hand. The pirate bowled right over him, shoving him roughly to the deck, and reached out for me.

My stiletto was out, thrusting for his hand. Like Tin's, my blow struck squarely, but had no effect, bouncing harmlessly aside. The hand grabbed the front of my shirt and I was airborne.

The pirate, with me in his grasp, took two running strides and leaped over the side of the ship. With a splash, we hit the water and plummeted to the bottom, as if we were tied to one of the ship's anchors.

I struggled against that iron grip, but he was strong and I couldn't break free. I swung my stiletto at him, but the water slowed my movements, and I felt as though I was striking stone. The pirate ignored me and ignored the water, walking along the floor of the harbor as if he were strolling down a sunny street.

I held my breath as long as I could, until I felt as though my lungs would explode. I hadn't had a chance to take a deep breath before we entered the water, and the exertion of swinging my dagger used up my air. The pirate took no notice of my struggling. He walked along, uncaring that I was about to drown.

I could take it no more. My breath came out in a bubble, and I inhaled deeply.

But somehow, air, not water, entered my lungs.

The pirate finally acknowledged my existence. He pulled me in front of him, face to face. He looked at me as I took my first few unsettling breaths then he began to laugh.

"Fool," he said. His voice sounded even more sinister distorted by the water. "Did you think I would let you die? You are worth twice as much alive! Though truly, the sum for your corpse would still be worth my time." Again, that terrible laugh.

An old horror jolted through me. Only one person—one creature—would put a bounty on my head. The foul blue pirate meant to sell me to Asbeel.

That notion sent me into a frenzy. I tried with all my might to pull away. I stabbed at him, at his chest and his face, again and again. I kicked and screamed, though my words were so distorted as to be unintelligible. I fought desperately, but I only ripped my shirt, and as soon as that happened, the pirate adjusted his grip, holding firm to my wounded left shoulder.

And all the while, Memnon's docks approached.

The water in front of the pirate turned white. Not noticing, he continued walking—right into a thick sheet of ice.

At the instant of impact, I felt his grip loosen. I jerked sharply, bracing my feet against his thigh and pushing off with all my might, and I was free.

But in my next breath, I caught water, not air. I was choking, sputtering, with no air in my lungs and none to bring in. Instantly my chest ached, a horrible, acute pain, and I tried to resist the urge to breathe. The pirate reached for me, and I was tempted to grab his hand just so I could take a breath. But I knew if that hand caught me, I wouldn't be free again. I wanted to swim for the surface, but the surface was a long way off, and I was weighed down by my sodden clothes. I would surely die before I made it.

Then I was rising, streaming through the water, and before I knew it I broke the surface—not just my head, but my entire body. I coughed and sputtered, and gulped down air and expelled water.

Glancing around to orient myself, I found I was much closer to the docks than to *Sea Sprite*. Somehow I was lying atop the water, floating perhaps an inch off the surface. A slight depression, like a bowl on the waves, formed beneath me, as if I repelled the water. Curious, I reached down to touch the surface, and some invisible force pushed back against my hand. I pushed harder, but it pushed harder back, the depression in the water growing deeper, my hand barely moving.

I looked up, wondering at the source of that miracle, and found it standing above me.

The man wore a deep blue robe and had a bearded face, which in turn wore an expression of pure amusement.

"Done coughing, boy?" he asked, his voice dripping sarcasm.

I nodded, taking a few more deep breaths to steady myself then stood bobbing in my invisible bowl. "Who are you, sir?" I asked.

He seemed pleased to be addressed as "sir," as if that was an uncommon occurrence. "My name is Robillard, and I work with the Memnon Harbor Guard. I was overseeing the transfer of Captain Pinochet and his pirates from *Sea Sprite* to our control, when that fool"—he motioned toward the water—"grabbed you. You're lucky to be alive, boy."

I shook my head. "He wasn't going to kill me, sir."

"Then what did he want with you?"

I hesitated. "It's personal," I finally said.

"You knew that pirate?" There was no sarcasm in his voice—he was accusing me.

"No, sir. He's working for someone who wants to capture me."

"So you're a runaway?" Robillard arched an eyebrow. "What is your name, child?"

I glared at him. "My name is none of your—"

Suddenly, the force that had kept me above the water gave way, and down I went with a splash. As soon as I was completely under, I was rising again. It happened so quickly that I landed perfectly on my feet, stunned but unhurt.

"Beware whom you speak to so rudely," Robillard said. "And more importantly, beware *when* you speak so rudely. Fool."

Another voice carried across the waves—a familiar voice. Lucky. "Oy, Maimun, you look all wet!" Then a friendly burst of laughter. "Not hurt, are ye?"

I turned to face the voice, and saw that *Sea Sprite* had already replaced her ruined launch. Lucky and two other crewmen glided toward me—Lucky standing at the prow, the other two rowing. They were still a good distance away, but would come alongside me quickly.

"No, I'm not hurt," I called. "How's Tin?"

"Broke his hand, he did. I always told him, never swing with a closed fist, you'll break it for sure, but did he listen? No sir, 'course not, he ain't smart enough to listen to me."

My mind spun in a dozen different directions as I watched the launch approach. Mostly my thoughts focused on Asbeel and his cohorts, on the troll I had thrown from the ship, and the strange pirate who had taken me captive. I had thought that out at sea, I would be safe from Asbeel. But I was wrong.

I had already caused the deaths of several men in the battle with the pirates—Tasso, and more whose names I didn't even know. I couldn't stand the thought of Deudermont, or Lucky, or Tin dying on my behalf. I couldn't allow it to happen again.

I turned to Robillard and asked, quietly so Lucky wouldn't hear, "How long will this enchantment last?" I motioned toward my feet.

"Hours, if I let it," he answered with a wink that was not unfriendly. "Why?"

"Hey, Lucky," I called, without breaking eye contact with Robillard. "Do me a favor." "Whatsat?"

"Tell Captain Deudermont—thank you for your hospitality, and for your offer, but I am resigning my position aboard his ship."

I heard the oars stop rowing, and Lucky stuttered out something like, "What?"

Robillard looked at me hard then nodded and smiled. "So you *are* a runaway."

"A runaway." I almost laughed. "I guess you could say I've been running my entire life, sir."

And with that, I turned and sprinted across the water toward Memnon.

CHAPTER 28

MEMNON'S SPRAWL PROVED EVEN MORE CONFUSING ON THE GROUND THAN IT HAD appeared from the ship. The streets weren't paved, and didn't seem to have been laid out according to any kind of plan. Instead, a street was simply any space not occupied by a building. The vast majority of the structures were shoddily built and atrocious to look at, but the people were amazing. As I pushed through the crowded streets, I saw that almost everyone was brightly dressed, their heads wrapped in turbans of red and blue and black. Most of their faces were covered by veils, some dark and obscuring, others sheer and showing a hint of the features beneath.

I moved with as much haste as I dared. I had no idea whether the city guard could be influenced by the demon. But I had learned that Asbeel's agents could be anywhere, and I couldn't risk attracting anyone's attention. I no longer had anyone to protect me—I no longer had anyone to fall on my behalf.

And how could I, in good conscience, associate with anyone ever again knowing a demon followed me? My heart sank as I pictured my future: a life of solitude, always moving, until one day I slipped and Asbeel caught up to me.

I considered leaving Memnon. I could head south, into the harsh Calim Desert. I had read books about survival in harsh climates, including the parched sandscape of the desert. I would be able to journey a few days into the desert, at least. Out there, out in the wasteland alone, I could bury the stone, and bury it deep. No one would follow me, and no one would find it. I would be free. And no one else would be hurt on my behalf.

But what would become of me then? Somehow the stone was linked to my family. Somehow it was part of my destiny. Perrault had told me so. How would he feel to know that I planned to toss it away? My face flushed at the thought and I knew the answer.

After all those days aboard *Sea Sprite*, I had learned one thing for certain: no matter how far I traveled, across the sea to the ends of Toril, through the sands of the Calim Desert, Asbeel would never be far behind. And I was so tired of running.

The streets of Memnon wound randomly and sometimes ended suddenly, but just as often met at the intersection of half a dozen streets, each looking exactly like the next. The sprawl was an enormous maze, and before long I was completely lost.

Just before sunset, I found myself somewhere in the middle of the city, with neither the outer walls nor the docks in sight, and no real idea where either might be. I couldn't wander around the city all night. Even if I wanted to leave Memnon, I had no idea how.

Lost in thought, I turned down a darkened alley. My feet throbbed and my stomach ached with hunger. Soon I would have to find a place to rest.

A movement farther up the alley caught my eye, a shadow moving among the shadows.

In an instant, my pain flew away and my heart set to racing. Asbeel, or one of his dark agents, had come calling.

I turned back the way I came, and looked directly into a pair of glowing yellow eyes.

CHAPTER 29

S TARTLED, I BARELY MANAGED TO STIFLE A SCREAM AS I BACKED UP, REACHING AWK-
wardly for the stiletto sheathed in my belt. Just as my hand found the thin dagger's
hilt, my heel found a crate, and already off my balance, I tumbled hard to my backside.

The yellow-eyed creature leaped in surprise at the sound, hissing and baring its feline
claws at me, then darted into the shadows. I found myself laughing despite my situation.
Defeated by a mere tabby cat!

I was left staring up at the sky, feeling ashamed that a tiny cat had so frightened me. I
thought I heard footsteps clattering along the rooftop at the end of the dark alley.

Had Asbeel found me, even here? Or was I being paranoid?

I stared up at a pile of old crates, reaching nearly to the roof of the building. As I
pulled myself to my feet, I thought of a phrase I had heard before—luck favors the bold.

It was time for me to be bold.

The crates proved easy to scale. The sturdy wood easily supported my weight and the
pyramid shape of the stack formed almost a stairway. The topmost crate was barely three
feet below the edge of the roof, and soon I was climbing out of the gloomy alley and into
the glowing sunset.

Here the light was even brighter than it had been in the streets. The rooftops all
around were made of some kind of white tile, and at that moment were perfectly angled
to catch the rays of the descending sun. The glare stung my eyes. I shaded my eyes and
glanced back and forth across the glimmering rooftops.

I could see almost the entirety of Memnon laid out before me. At least I wouldn't be
lost in the jumble of streets. I turned to the west and thought I saw a lanky, elf-like figure
in a black and violet cloak slipping around the chimney of the rundown building.

I gripped my dagger tighter and took in a breath. If Asbeel wanted the stone, he
would have to fight me for it. I would not let him chase me anymore.

I broke into a full run after the shadowy figure. Not three streets away, the figure
seemed to slip down the side of the building and disappear. Even from a distance, I could
see the stands of the marketplace below. They bustled with more people, I imagined,
than lived in the entirety of Baldur's Gate. I had to hurry or I would lose him among the
many people.

I leaped the last five-foot-wide alley onto the roof of a brick building. Directly below
me, vendors' carts hustled down the street that led into the market square. The only
question was how to make my way down from the rooftops back onto the street without

anyone spotting me. It was perhaps twenty feet, a fair fall indeed. But I had read in one of Perrault's books that when falling beside a wall, martial warriors and monks of Shou Lung would use their hands and feet to slow their descent. Upon landing, they tuck and roll to absorb much of the momentum. It was a move I had longed to try since I'd first read about it and it seemed as good a time as any.

I tucked my dagger into my boot and dropped.

As I plummeted toward the ground, I realized that reading about a move and performing it were two very different things. With nothing to grasp at, I couldn't possibly slow myself. The surprised shouts of the people below barely registered. All I saw was the inevitable end of my journey, the unpaved dirt road, rushing up to meet me.

But then a pale form cut in front of me, a great white sheet of fabric, billowing in the breeze as it dangled from a clothesline. The sheet caught an unexpected gust of wind and fluttered toward me, a helping hand reaching out to catch me. I wasn't about to argue—I grabbed for the fabric.

The clothesline bowed and the sheet stretched, until finally the pins keeping the line and the fabric together surrendered to the force and popped loose, dropping me the last fifteen feet.

Instead of the hard-packed dirt road, I landed directly onto a cart of fresh melons. As I thumped down into the cart, melons exploded all around me, covering me, the laundry, and the street in red and purple juice and pulp.

"Oy, oaf! What've ye done?" A man rushed toward me, brandishing a gourd like a club. "I'll smack yer little head in, I will!"

I rolled out of the fruit cart and reached into my pocket. I pulled out what few coins I had and tossed them at the man. It was not nearly enough to pay for all the fruit, I knew, but it was something.

As the coins arced through the air, they caught the sun, distracting the man and the other onlookers long enough for me to turn and sprint down the road.

The man continued to yell, though I couldn't make out the words, and a woman's shrill screech joined in. "He ruined my best bed sheet!"

I raced into the market and pushed through the crowd of people as best I could. Ahead of me I heard gasps, curses, and the crash of an overturned vendor's kiosk. It was Asbeel. It had to be. I couldn't let him hurt any more people on my behalf. I cut turn after turn, weaving around people's legs. At last I saw the figure dart into an alley, and I picked up my pace to follow him.

But as soon as I crossed into the shade of the narrow lane, I felt a little shiver roll through my body.

My heart pounded in my ears, but I was unable to move.

CHAPTER 30

ON'T FRET, YOUNG MAIMUN," A VOICE SAID. A WOMAN'S VOICE, IT WAS MELODIC AND beautiful, and not at all threatening. "I have placed upon you a spell of holding. You will be unable to move for a short time. I am sorry for it, but it had to be done."

She stepped from the shadows, though it took me a moment to see her. She was completely covered in a dark robe, her hood pulled up, a black mask covering her face. The mask was a solid piece of obsidian, I figured, carved to look like a human face, completely blank of expression. It covered her whole face, even her eyes.

I tried to scream at her, to tell her to let me go, but I couldn't speak through her spell.

"Do you know what the stone you carry is, Maimun?" she asked. "It is an artifact blessed by the goddess Tymora, the bearer of good fortune. To the soul it has chosen, it will bring good luck, as long as it is close at hand."

And so I learned the answer I had wished so long for Perrault to give me, the power the stone held over me. The events of the past few moments fell into sharp focus. It was good fortune that I had found a billowing sheet to break my fall. And the melon wagon, coming at just the right moment—the stone had brought that good fortune upon me too. The pieces began to tumble into place, and they threw my whole journey, my whole life, into question. I had thought it was my choices that had led me to *Sea Sprite*. But had the stone itself given me the luck I needed to stow away unseen? Had it given me the strength to fight the troll, to save the ship? Without it, would I have ever found my place at sea?

"Unfortunately," the woman said as she crept closer, "luck in this world is finite. One person's good luck means another's misfortune."

The woman's objective became crystal clear, and I struggled mightily against her spell. My own purpose became clear.

For better or for worse, the stone had shaped my past and was meant to shape my future. I could not let it go. I could never let it go. The stone had been bestowed upon me for a reason. Perrault had trusted me to discover that reason and to protect the stone at all costs. After all that he had done for me, I couldn't betray his trust.

The woman calmly began opening my shirt. "This stone throws luck out of balance. While it favors you, it will hurt others. And that is not acceptable."

My shirt was open, and she reached around me to gently unfasten the buckle and remove the whole sash. I felt it pull away, as if my skin were stuck to the leather, as if my body stretched out, trying to hold onto it. But then it was gone. My chest stung where the stone had rested, and my heart felt empty.

She tucked the stone under her robe and stepped back. "The stone will be kept safe from those who seek to use it for ill gains, and you shall be free of your burden."

I had once dreamed of being free of the stone's burden. But now that it was gone, I realized how wrong I had been. This *hurt*.

"Now, Maimun, I'm going to cast another spell on you. This one will put you into a deep sleep. You'll wake up tomorrow morning, refreshed, and I urge you to look upon it as a new life."

I don't want a new life, I thought. I want the stone. I willed myself to reach for Perrault's dagger and for a moment, I thought I had broken her spell.

My voice broke through the silence. "Give . . . it . . . *back!*" I shouted.

But the woman began an arcane chant, and soon I found myself following along mentally. I drifted along the river of soothing sound she created and soon I was fast asleep.

The strange woman was wrong. I would not sleep until morning light. I woke up sometime long past darkness, to someone prodding at my shoulder.

I found myself staring at a pair of shiny leather boots. Rising from the boots was a pair of legs, clothed in fine black silk pants, and above that, a pristine white shirt.

And above that, a snarling, red-skinned elf face.

"Where is it, boy?" Asbeel spat at me. "Where is the stone?"

PART IV

Light poured into the tiny, dirty chamber, waking me from my sleep. I looked up and shaded my eyes. Sunlight shone directly in through the short passage that led to the beach outside. But I couldn't tell if it was morning or evening, if we faced west or east.

At that moment, it hardly seemed to matter. A tall man stood in the doorway, leaning slightly to his right, awkward on his wooden peg leg. With a shuffle and a clomp, he stepped into the room. The door swung shut behind him, snuffing out all the light save what little came in through the crack at the bottom of the portal.

"Ye got more story to be telling me, or is this the day I be killing ye?" he asked gruffly. He placed something between his knees—a torch, I guessed. I heard the scrape of flint across tinder as he tried to light the thing.

"You're planning to kill me when I finish the story?" I asked.

"Yar, probably so. The boys don't like holding prisoners fer too long, seeing as it means we can't be out sailing."

"Out plundering and murdering, you mean."

"Call it what ye will," he said with a chuckle.

"If you're going to kill me anyway, why should I continue the story at all?"

The pirate laughed. "Ye've seen men die before, whelp. Ye know what tha's like. Ask any o' them what they'd've done fer one more day! I be sure telling an old salt like me a bit o' story wouldn't be too much trouble."

Steel clicked against flint once more, and a few sparks flew out, revealing the old pirate's face and the horrible gold-toothed grin splayed across it. But the sparks didn't take on the torch, and again he was in shadow.

"This coming from a man who wouldn't know," I said. "You've never cared about death, not your own nor anyone else's."

"Strong words, whelp," he snarled. "But ye're off yer mark. I had me day o' dying once, and I were bargaining much as I could, with any who'd listen. And only by the grace o' the gods did I live."

Again sparks flew as steel struck flint. The pirate's smile was gone, his face flat in the eerie light. But again the torch did not light.

"And I see you've paid the debt you promised them," I said sarcastically.

"That I have, that I have!" the pirate replied. "I swore I'd live each and ev'ry day as if it were my last. And I ain't missed one yet. Now, I'm offering ye a chance, boy. Either this day is yer last, or ye tell me the next part o' yer story."

A third time flint and steel struck and sparks flew. Finally the oil-soaked rag of the torch caught a spark and lit.

CHAPTER 31

WHERE IS THE STONE?" THE RASPY VOICE WHISPERED FROM ABOVE ME.

I scrambled back on all fours. Asbeel's boot paced me. I felt the dull impact in my midsection, but I hardly noticed the pain through the mental fog that clouded my memory. Where had the stone gone?

"Where is it?" Asbeel's boot lashed out again.

A black mask of carved obsidian, a shadow beneath the hood of a flowing black robe, leered at me from my mind's eye. She spoke, her voice so soft, so gentle. Her voice . . . I had heard it only once, yet it felt so familiar.

The boot leaped at me again, aiming for my head. I brought my arms up, absorbing the brunt of the blow, but the force was still enough to send me into a roll. The wall of the narrow alley met me halfway through the tumble, and the impact knocked the breath from my body.

I turned my gaze upward, following the arc of the muscled leg hidden beneath black breeches; to a leather vest, and the red-tinted arms crossed in front of the chest; to the leering face, angular and bald, its red eyes glowing with angry fire. And beside the creature's head, the hilt of a sword, a horrible creation of jagged metal—an evil blade to match the demon's evil soul.

The demon. Asbeel. He had pursued me across the length of the Sword Coast. His sword. That same blade had felled my mentor Perrault.

Time moved more slowly, all sensations becoming more distinct: the loose sand of the alley; the rough stone of the wall behind me, unfinished and easy to climb; the sky above, lightening with the sunrise, taking away the demon's advantage of darkness. Without realizing I had moved at all, I found my hand resting on the hilt of my own weapon, the stiletto Perrault had once wielded. The fog lifted from my mind; my vision was suddenly remarkably clear.

Asbeel spoke again. "Where is the—"

"I do not have it." My voice did not crack, did not waver at all. "And neither shall you."

I jumped to my feet, and my hand snapped forward, bringing the narrow dagger to bear in front of me. The momentum of my sudden motion rolled down the blade, lengthening the weapon into a fine saber. I fell into a lunge as the sword tip leaped for Asbeel's black heart.

But Asbeel simply stepped backward.

I teetered at full extension, my trailing foot against the wall, the tip of my sword a foot from Asbeel. My moment of vengeance turned to defeat; my elation turned to fear. My mind raced as I tried to recall the swordfights I'd read about or seen. My feet scrambled to form an L shape, and I struggled to hold the sword vertically in front of me.

Asbeel reached up to his shoulder. Somehow he found a handle to grip among the sharp, twisting spikes on his sword. The wickedly serrated, curved blade slowly rose from behind him. As soon as its tip cleared its sheath, the whole blade burst into red flame. Still moving slowly, deliberately, Asbeel gripped the hilt in both hands and tapped the dull edge of the blade to his forehead in a mock salute.

The blade's fire danced wildly, mesmerizing, tantalizing, beautiful and horrible all at once. My heartbeat drummed in my ears.

With a snarl, the demon leaped forward. He swung his sword in a wide arc. The fire seemed to hang in the air behind the curved blade.

But I was ready. I brought my sword to bear against his in a textbook-perfect parry.

Or so I thought.

The sheer force of the demon's blow nearly ripped my saber from my hand. I tried to roll with the momentum of the strike, to absorb some of its power. I could not hold my footing, and my skull cracked hard against the ground.

I felt warmth on the back of my head, a trickle of blood. A wave of dizziness washed over me. I could not catch my breath. The demon would be upon me before I could right myself.

But the killing blow did not fall.

After what seemed an eternity, the world stopped spinning. I rose unsteadily and turned to face Asbeel. The demon had not moved. He matched my stare, but in his eyes I saw not rage, only amusement. Again he tapped his sword to his forehead, saluting me, mocking me.

"You wear his clothes, boy," said the demon. "But you do not honor him with your fighting."

"You know nothing of honor," I growled.

"I know your mentor would be ashamed to see you fight so wretchedly."

"The only thing he wouldn't like," I said calmly, "is that I bothered to talk to you." I lunged forward suddenly. Steel clashed against black iron, but my blade cut nothing but air.

I retracted my arm quickly and struck again. I did not fully commit myself, but shortened my lunge. When the demon brought his blade across to parry, I rolled my wrist, twisted my saber around the demon's sword, and pushed my leading leg forward, extending my arm to its full length. My sword's tip reached out for Asbeel's chest, stretching, reaching. . . .

Asbeel's empty hand shot across his chest and grabbed my sword by the blade. My sword slipped a bit. Its perfect edge drew a line of blood across the demon's hand, but he did not seem to notice.

"You do not deserve that sword, boy," he said with a wicked laugh. "So I shall take it from you."

I gritted my teeth and yanked at the sword. I felt its edge dig in to the demon's flesh, but he only tightened his grip in response. The sword would move no further.

I wanted to release the sword, to leap at Asbeel's smug face, to punch him, kick him, whatever I could do to fight back. But the idea of my sword—Perrault's sword—in that beast's possession, even for a moment, made me ill. How many times had I seen Perrault use that sword—for show more often than for combat—twirling it about expertly, mixing the straight lines of lunges with dazzling curving strikes, the blade's magical blue flame trailing behind it.

Blue flame . . .

A brilliant line of cerulean fire pierced the dark air, engulfing my sword from crosspiece to tip—and Asbeel's clawed hand with it.

Asbeel's unearthly scream cut the stillness of the dawn. The alley became a clutter of motion as rats and bats fled its shadows. I wanted nothing more than to turn and follow them. But I stood my ground.

Asbeel's face twisted in pain. After a long moment, he released the sword, and I stumbled back.

For the first time, I had the upper hand against the beast. I took a step toward him, then another. I would kill Asbeel with the sword of my fallen mentor. I was worthy of the weapon.

I lunged ahead one final time, lunged right past the demon's outstretched arms, lunged right at his black heart.

But as my sword reached the demon, he disappeared.

Asbeel's fist clubbed the back of my head. I tumbled forward, away from him, yet somehow I landed right at his feet. He kicked at me several times. At last I managed to scramble away.

I pulled myself up to all fours and took an awkward half-running, half-leaping step, propelling me over the short stack of crates separating the alley from the market square.

But he was already there as I landed. He stood over me, his sword upraised.

"Stop."

The word was whispered, but its effect was immediate. The demon and I turned in unison to face a hooded figure emerging from the shadows across the square.

She wore a black robe, her cowl pulled low, her face hidden in shadow. No, not shadow, but a shadowmask, black as night and carved into an expressionless human face. A cold chill ran down my spine. It was the same woman, the same creature, who had assaulted me the previous night, the same being who had stolen from me that which was most precious.

"Child, come to me," the woman said, beckoning. I took the first steps to oblige, relieved to step away from the demon and be rescued from the impossible fight. But I stopped after a few short paces.

The demon cackled behind me. "You call to him now, do you? Twice you abandon him, yet now you call to him?"

"Ignore him," she said sweetly. "Come to me."

Every instinct I possessed cried out that I should go to her. But somewhere in my rational mind I remembered her words from the previous night, and how I had fallen asleep against my will. Was there magic in the words she uttered?

How else could she have stopped Asbeel so completely, just as he was readying a killing blow? Or was she in league with the demon, tricking me into letting my guard down so he could kill me with ease? What more could she want from me, given that she had the stone?

I flexed the fingers of my left hand instinctively, and a slight tingle traced its way from my fingertips to my heart, to the hollow of my chest where the stone had once rested in its leather pouch.

I yearned to be reunited with that stone, wanting it back with every fiber of my being. It had been my curse. Before I returned to Memnon, I had intended to be rid of it. It was powerful, to be sure, and the luck it provided had saved my skin more than once. But its power was not the reason I craved its return. It was my destiny, my legacy, the only thing that remained of my family. And yet the masked woman had the stone. She had stolen it from me, and it belonged to me, not to her.

I raised the sword, still burning a fiery blue. "Where is it?" I asked her. "Where is the stone?"

Again Asbeel cackled. "Yes, do tell," he said sarcastically.

"Begone, wretch!" Gone was the woman's whisper, replaced by a roar as loud as a riled bear's. A group of ravens lifted off from the rooftop above me, their wings shining in the light of the new dawn.

I heard a faint popping sound. When I turned, Asbeel had disappeared.

I dropped to a crouch and brought my sword above me. I looked up, scanning the rooftops for the demon. I was certain he would be swooping in to attack me at any moment. But the first rays of sun broke over the horizon, illuminating the sky, and no dark shadows floated there.

Asbeel was simply gone.

I glanced back at the cloaked woman just in time to see her fade into the shadows of the market's eastern edge.

"Wait!"

CHAPTER 32

I FLEW THROUGH THE WINDING, NARROW STREETS OF MEMNON, FOLLOWING THE slightest flicker of darkness. The masked woman's black cloak seemed always but a few yards in front of me, just on the edge of my vision. Every turn I took, every new street I entered, there she was, just rounding the next bend.

I had not come to Memnon looking for the woman. I had entered the city to save *Sea Sprite* and her crew—the crew I had put in danger. I had planned to pass through Memnon on my way to some place where I could safely be rid of the stone without fear that it would fall into the wrong hands—Asbeel's hands. But she had found me and changed everything. As soon as she had wrenched the stone from my possession, I wanted nothing more than to hold it again.

People filtered out of the low stone buildings that crammed both sides of the narrow lane. The bustle hardly slowed me, as I moved nimbly around the pressing crowd. Each building looked like the last, each beggar the same, as I dashed past them. The only constant in my vision was that fleeting speck of black, the flowing robe of the masked woman.

A man cut in front of me, but I darted between his legs, and he seemed not to notice my presence. I flew as if nothing could stop me, desperate not to lose my target in the swarm of brightly colored robes and exotic headwraps. If I lost track of the masked woman I would be adrift in the winding, confusing streets of Memnon. And somewhere out there, Asbeel hunted me.

I turned onto the next street, and there again was the flutter of the woman's cloak, just rounding a corner. There the road widened and brightened. A thin bit of smoke wafted into the street, and the noise and bustle increased tenfold. I hastened my step, knowing, fearing, what lay around that corner.

I reached the bend in a rush, and saw precisely what I had feared: an open market square, huge and packed with shoppers. Ahead, through the crowd, I saw her moving. The people hardly slowed her measured pace. I tried to push through the crowd, but it was no use.

She was escaping.

I could not follow.

I was lost.

I heard a flutter of wings behind me, and the crowd parted. Several voices cried out in a language I did not understand.

I turned, moving purely on instinct, my stiletto out, ready to face Asbeel again. As would surely be my lot in life, until one of us was dead.

But the wings did not belong to Asbeel.

Nine ravens, black as midnight, stared up at me. Eight had formed a circle on the ground, their wings stretched, touching tip to tip; but each had turned its head to me. The ninth stood in the middle, its chest puffed out proudly, and opened its beak.

But caw it did not. It spoke.

"Flee," said the bird. "Do not pursue."

I blinked a few times and looked around the street. No one around me seemed concerned by the strange events. They continued about their business, though they did give the birds a wide berth.

I stared at the bird, and it stared back at me. Feeling quite foolish, I asked the most obvious of questions. "Do not pursue whom?"

"Us." The bird's head twitched to one side.

"Why would I pursue you? Who are you?"

"Birds."

I could hardly find words. The situation seemed so ridiculous. "I'm not pursuing birds," I said. "I'm pursuing a thief."

"No thief," the bird said.

"A woman took something from me without permission. That makes her a thief." My eyes darted through the crowd's sea of colorful robes, desperate to catch a glimpse of the dark cloak.

The bird skittered toward me. "Savior. Do not pursue."

I stared directly into the raven's beady eyes. "How do you know about . . . any of this?" I asked.

"We see."

"You've been following me, haven't you?"

The raven nodded. The strange gesture sent a shiver up my arm.

"Then you're a spy, and no better than the thief." I advanced a step and brandished my sword menacingly.

The birds lifted off from the ground in a flurry of feathers, their wings beating at the air, throwing up a cloud of dust in their wake. Their caws—the cries of ordinary ravens, not words—faded rapidly into the distance.

With the birds gone, the crowd of shoppers pressed closer to me. I sheathed my sword and let myself fall into the flow.

I shook my head. Of all the bizarre creatures I had met on my journey, that had to be one of the strangest sights of all. A talking bird? At least it had not tried to hurt me. The bird—as odd as it was—seemed to want to help me, in its own strange way.

But I would not heed its warning. I would not give up on the stone. True, I had little to go on. I knew nothing of the thief who had stolen it. I had no magic to aid me. And I knew no one who did.

I let out a heavy sigh. Elbeth, Perrault. Everyone who had tried to help me was hurt, missing—or dead. I briefly considered returning to the docks. But the thought of facing *Sea Sprite*'s crew again filled my heart with shame.

Pirates hunting me had attacked the ship, and though we had won the battle, several crew had been killed, and the ship was damaged. Our victory came thanks only to Drizzt

Do'Urden and his friends, who had disembarked the ship more than a day before. If I returned to *Sea Sprite* and brought on another attack, the crew would be overwhelmed. And I would never forgive myself.

The crowd pressed me on to the edge of the market. In my darkest days on board the ship, Drizzt had spoken to me about family—not the family you are born to, but the one you find. I knew he was talking about the crew of *Sea Sprite*, telling me that they were my family. I hung my head. Maybe I should return to the only family I had left and give up my foolish journey. The stone had caused me nothing but pain.

A feeling like a thousand tiny pinpricks shot up my arm. I shook my hand reflexively, and accidentally slapped the wide backside of a shopper passing beside me.

"Aii!" the woman shouted. "Keep your filthy hands to yourself!" She shoved my shoulder—hard.

I lost my balance and crashed into the side of a small tent at the edge of the market. The tent wall crumpled, and the pole it was attached to dropped directly on my head, dazing and blinding me. I stumbled forward and fell to the dusty ground.

A large hand, heavy and strong, grasped my shoulder. A deep, throaty laugh filled my ears.

Asbeel!

CHAPTER 33

I THRASHED ABOUT, ONLY SERVING TO FURTHER ENTRAP MYSELF. THE TENT CLOTH wrapped about my arm and entangled my legs. I felt like a fly in a spider's web, each movement only ensuring my demise. I tried in vain to grip the dagger in my belt to cut my way out of the trap. But I could not reach it.

A second hand joined the first, gripping me tightly, holding me still.

"Relax," said a deep voice, a voice not Asbeel's. "You try to move large, but you are trapped, so you move not at all. Move small, and you will move far."

"What in the world does that mean?" I asked, my voice muffled by the drapery.

"Be still," the voice said quietly—as quietly as a thunderstorm could be. "And I will help you."

The hands released me, tentatively. When I did not resume my struggle, they began slowly to unwrap the tangled mess I had become.

A few moments later I lay on the dusty floor inside the tent. Its remaining cotton walls rippled gently in the breeze. The fourth strip of fabric lay in a pile on the ground where I had tumbled into it. The air was hazy with smoke leaking from the pots of incense placed around the room.

"Greetings, maimed one," said an old man. He spoke with the cadence of a bear shambling through the forest: not in a rush to get anywhere, not wasting any energy where it wasn't needed; but with the confidence of a creature secure in its own great strength.

"How do you know my name?" I asked, climbing to my feet unsteadily.

"What?"

"My name. You called me Maimun." I took a step back. "How did you know my name?"

The man towered over me, his head nearly touching the top of the small tent. Everything about him seemed out of place in those tight quarters. "I called you 'maimed one.' Scarred one."

I felt him staring at my chest. My shirt had fallen open, revealing the long black patch across my chest. "Tar," I said. "To cauterize the wound."

"Yes, and it must have hurt greatly," said the man. "But I wasn't speaking of that wound. There is magic about you, and that is scarred as well, more than your flesh." He stepped closer, leaning heavily on a single bone, as tall as his shoulder, which in turn was as tall as most men. The great thing was blackened along one side, and from its top dangled feathers, claws, and teeth.

The hair on the back of my neck pricked up. "Who are you?" I asked.

"I have no name," he said.

I took another step back and glared at him. "How can you have no name?"

"I had a name once, but it was taken from me. I shall not get a new one until I rejoin my tribe in the next land." He raised his bone staff and pointed to a corner of the tent filled with pillows. "Now, come, Maimed One, sit with me a while, that I may look at you."

I glanced over my shoulder. Behind me, I could see the open street, filled with bustling shoppers, a clear path to escape should he attempt an attack. If I sat in the corner of his small tent, I would be in a much more dangerous position.

"You have questions, yes?" He said, smiling. "I can look at you and maybe see the answers." From behind his long hair, pale blue eyes, like the midwinter horizon a moment before dawn, stared at me, unblinking. I felt weak, naked, beneath his piercing gaze.

I shook my head. Had I truly fallen so far? Had Asbeel really chased me to such a frightened state? There was no doubt I needed help. I had no one else to turn to. Perhaps the man could tell me how to find the masked woman and retrieve the stone. I took a deep breath and decided to trust him.

As I sat down on the pile of pillows, a cloud of dust rose up, stinging my eyes and nose. The pillows were not as soft as they looked. I rubbed the new bruise on my thigh and shifted to a more comfortable position, as the old seer settled cross-legged on the bare floor in front of me.

I had witnessed divination magic in practice only once before: when Perrault's dwarf friend Alviss had used his crystal ball to allow me to spy on Perrault and his friend Jaide. I knew from various tomes that scrying often used such tools—a crystal ball, a mirror— to peer through to a distant place, so I scanned the room for any such object. But the space was sparse, almost bare. A chest sat against the wall opposite the tent's door (the proper entrance, not the fallen wall), with a stack of books atop it. I thought back to Perrault's collection of books, which I had taken such care to organize. The seer's books were stacked haphazardly; only three of the seven were spine-out, and those were in no particular order, with one of Volo's accounts sandwiched between what I could only assume was a spellbook and one written in a language I could not read.

Smoke wafted about the large man, drifting up from a lit candle set at his feet—where did it come from? Ever so slowly, the man began to rock back and forth; his lips moved, but I heard no sound. The smoky haze moved with him. His features wavered within it, and though I knew I could reach out and touch him, somehow I felt as if he was not fully there.

After a moment I found myself swaying in rhythm with him. A wave of calm washed over me.

I leaped to my feet, my eyes darting around the room. I felt as though I'd been startled awake from a long nap, though I was sure I hadn't been asleep. The old man's eyes flew open, and he took in a quick breath.

"What just happened?" I asked, trying to keep my voice steady.

"I looked at you, and someone looked back." He leaned heavily on his staff and rose up beside me.

"What do you mean, 'looked back'?" I asked.

He paused, as if searching for the words to explain. "I told you before, there is magic about you. I looked at you to find that magic and to follow it."

I nodded and gestured for him to speak more quickly. Suddenly, I felt as though there was no time to lose. "And what did you see? Did you find the magic?"

"No." The old man replied, not seeming to notice my panic. He spoke in the same measured pace. "Someone else was following the same line. He seeks what you seek."

"Who? What was his name?" I asked, then shook my head. Divination magic surely didn't work like that. The old man must be thinking me a fool. "I mean can you describe him?"

He nodded, and suddenly I felt less absurd. "A stranger to these lands, of skin and manner. Magical by nature, not by practice."

"That is all?" I said. "You see nothing more?"

The old seer picked up the candle and blew it out. "If you can find him, his journey will aid your own." He stared at the candlewick. "That is all I know."

I paced the tiny tent and flexed and unflexed my left hand, which tingled as if I'd sat on it too long. My mind was spinning, rolling over all the possibilities. Who could the magical person be?

The woman in the mask? I had no idea what her nature was, nor her skin, nor anything about her. But no, the seer had said "*he* seeks what you seek." The masked stranger already had what I sought. And she was female, that much I was sure of.

Did he mean Asbeel? The thought made my heart race. I scanned the crowds outside, but the demon was nowhere to be seen. Asbeel did seek the stone. But he also knew who had it. I thought back to when the woman in the mask had appeared in the alley. He had seemed to know her somehow, but I certainly couldn't ask Asbeel who she is. If I were to find him again, he would surely try to kill me. That thought sent cold chills up my spine.

I glanced again at the stack of books, at the Volo in particular. I recalled a passage in one of Volo's books describing one of the rarest sentient races seen on Toril's surface. "Creatures of magic themselves, they are in tune with the unique magical nature of the deepest parts of the world." The book described the various sub-races of the elves; the passage described the drow.

The drow. Magical by nature. Pitch black skin. Strangers to our world. I had only ever seen one drow in my life. He had entered the city only a day earlier to complete a journey of his own.

"Drizzt?" I raced toward the seer. "Was it Drizzt Do'Urden you saw?"

The seer gazed at me for what seemed like an eternity, and he slowly nodded. "It matters not what I see. It matters only what you feel."

With that I was certain. Drizzt was the answer. He was searching for the stone. And to find it, all I had to do was find him.

CHAPTER 34

I PUSHED MY WAY TO THE EDGE OF THE MARKET CROWD, AND FOUND MYSELF STARING down a lane to the city gate—or rather a hole in the wall that served as a gate—to a road out into a sandy wasteland. Four guards flanked the portal, leaning lazily against the cool stone of the wall, staying in the shade.

I ran to the gate, passing a group of beggars along the side of the road. As I passed, they pleaded for scraps and coins, but I did not slow my pace. "Hey," I called. "Hey, guard!"

If Drizzt and his friends had left the city here, the guards would know it; if not, I would attempt to navigate the maze of the city to another gate, and so on.

None of the guards stirred as I approached. I wondered for a moment if they were asleep.

I cleared my throat. "Excuse me? Guard!"

At last the biggest man spoke. He scarcely moved a muscle, as if he had perfected the art of pure laziness. "Go away, beggar rat," he said.

I stepped closer. "I am no beggar. And I need some help."

He opened one eye. "You look like a beggar, and it ain't my job to help."

"It's your job to protect the people of the city. And I don't look like a beggar. Have you ever seen a beggar with a cloak like this?" I waved Perrault's magical royal-blue cloak, exposing the finely-crafted hilt of Perrault's dagger, belted at my hip.

The guard stood and faced me. "You're right, I suppose. You don't look like a beggar. You look like a thief." He took a step forward, trying to appear menacing. He stopped to rub the sleep from his eyes, and I nearly laughed aloud, but thought better of it.

The guard would be of no use to me, I knew. And I needed some answers—now.

"Any of you, then," I said, turning back to the row of beggars on the street. "Any of you see a dr—" I nearly said drow, but caught myself, remembering that Drizzt would surely be wearing his magical mask. "Any of you see an elf come through here, probably with a dwarf and two humans?"

After a moment, no one answered, so I moved farther down the lane and repeated my question.

Someone answered, a boy who looked to be about half my age. I winced when he stepped forward. Dirt coated his face and bare chest. His ribs showed through his hollow chest. "Yeah, I seen 'em." His voice was weak, almost flimsy. "Elf, woman, dwarf, giant."

My heart leaped. "That's them!" I fished around in my pocket for coins, and found three, all silver. I brought one out and presented it to the boy. All the other beggars perked up at the sight and began moving toward me. I ignored them. "A silver for you if you can tell me where they went and how to find them."

"They left the city through them gates," he said. "I dunno where they's heading." He smiled, for no reason I could see.

"Where does that gate lead then?" I asked.

"I dunno. The Calim Desert, I suppose. Get a camel and follow 'em." He held out his hand.

I placed the coin in it, but did not let go. "Who sells camels?" I asked.

"Lotsa folks sell camels."

"Who near here?"

The boy thought for a second, then pointed down a side street. "Sali Dalib, he sells camels. His tent is at the next market down that road," he said. I released the coin, and the boy scampered off into the shadows.

Sali Dalib's tent stood almost directly in front of the street, just as it opened into a relatively small market square. The large pavilion had recently been damaged, I saw, as two men worked on a makeshift scaffold raising one side of it. Outside there was an empty enclosure, for camels I assumed.

A goblin sat beside the door. He held a small bag to his head. His face was discolored around the bag—a bruise, I realized. In his other hand was a small wand. He pointed it at me, briefly and subtly. I pretended not to notice as I approached.

"We are not open, no, no," said a voice from within. A man in a brightly-colored flowing robe and a shining yellow turban came outside. He carried a large traveler's pack as if he were heading out on a long journey. "No food for de beggars today, no, no. Go away." He shooed me away, but the goblin grabbed his robe and whispered. The man stopped.

"But perhaps we can make an exception. Yes, yes, we can," he said. "You wish to buy, yes, yes? Or maybe to trade?" His voice rose an octave as he spoke, his tone switching from the gruff dismissal of a beggar to a honeyed sales pitch now that he considered me a potential customer. Perrault had always told me to judge a person by their actions when they have nothing to gain from you; by that standard, I did not much like Sali Dalib.

I opened my mouth to speak, but the man cut me off. "Inside. We should talk inside, yes, yes," he said, closing the few feet to me in the blink of an eye and putting his arm around my shoulders. He herded me to the tent. The goblin followed behind, quietly.

"I be Sali Dalib, purveyor of de finest wares, yes, yes! I have everything you need, at de bestest prices in de whole city!"

The interior of the tent looked much like the exterior: fine silk in many mismatched colors pieced together somewhat haphazardly. It would have been a fine shop, were it not partially destroyed. On one side of the tent lay a mess of broken trinkets, shelves, and ropes. On the other side a case of magical instruments caught my eye.

Sali Dalib hopped over to the shelf, following my gaze. "You wish to buy a Doss lute? I have one on sale cheap!"

I opened my mouth to answer, but Sali Dalib had already moved to the next shelf. "Or perhaps a nice traveling cloak? You already have one, yes, yes, but dis one is so much finer!" He held up a coarse yellow cloak, patched in several places. "We can trade, yes, yes!"

"How about some broken shelves?" I asked sarcastically, looking past him at the shelves and ropes scattered around the floor. "You seem to have a lot of those."

"Yes, yes, we have many," he said, apparently not catching the joke. "A minor accident, we had, yes, yes. How many would you like?" He beamed at me, bouncing up and down slightly in obvious anticipation, until his turban slipped and fell over his eyes.

"None. I just want information," I said. I could almost feel Sali Dalib's expression drop.

He pulled his turban up, eyes narrowed. "Information about what?" he asked. His voice, so round and robust before, was utterly flat.

"About an elf. He would have been traveling with two humans—a small woman and a huge man—and a dwarf." I meant to continue, but a groan from behind me—from the goblin—cut me off.

Sali Dalib stared at me. "You be friend of de drow?" he snarled.

"Friend? Not really, I'm just looking for—" I choked on my own words. He had identified Drizzt as a drow. "So you did meet them?" I asked, trying not to show the trepidation I was feeling.

"Friend of de drow is not welcome here," Sali Dalib said, standing up as straight and as tall as he could manage and pointing at the door.

"Wait, wait, I'm not his friend," I said. "I'm looking for him. He owes me gold." It was an outright lie, of course, but I figured perhaps I could connect with Sali Dalib in terms he could relate to. "I just need to know where he went."

"Calimport," the goblin gurgled behind me.

I rolled my eyes—of course they were headed to Calimport. "I mean, how? By what path?"

"By camel, yes, yes. By de caravan—" Sali Dalib's voice seemed to lighten mid-sentence. "No, no, not de caravan road, by de bestest road." The goblin groaned again, but Sali Dalib shot him a glare, and he stifled his complaint.

"The bestest road?" I parroted.

"Yes, yes, de bestest road. It be marked by signs. Yes, yes, just outside the city, and it be de fastest and safest road to Calimport! De bestest, it be! That be why they call it de bestest road, yes, yes!" Sali Dalib was positively beaming at that point. "You need a camel, yes, yes. Sali Dalib will sell you a camel and cheap, yes, yes."

"I have no money." I would have felt worse about the lie if I were not so sure Sali Dalib was trying to swindle me.

Sali Dalib did not miss a beat. "A trade then, yes, yes? A camel for . . . " he looked at the goblin. "For your cape? It be a cape from de North, yes, yes, to keep you warm. But in de south it be warm anyway!"

"In the south, a good cloak keeps the sun off so you don't die of heat," I replied. "I'd not make it far in the desert without a cloak."

"We throw in a Calishite cloak then, yes, yes, And de deal is done!" Sali Dalib clapped his hands loudly, excitedly, and bounced over to the shelf with the ugly old cloak. He turned back to me, holding the ragged thing aloft, to see me shaking my head.

"I can't trade this cloak," I said. "It belonged to my father, and I can't part with it."

Again, and instantly, Sali Dalib's eyes narrowed, and his voice flattened. It amazed me how quickly he seemed to swing between incredible excitement and a seething anger. "Den we are at an impasse," he said.

"Maybe you can loan me a camel?" I said. "I told you, the drow owes me gold. I'll pay you for your help once I collect."

Sali Dalib started to answer, then stopped, then started again, then stopped again, until finally his goblin cohort answered for him. "Camel can die. Not a good loan."

"How is it going to die?" I asked. "Are you trying to sell me a sick camel?" I tried to sound angry.

"Maybe drow kills it."

Sali Dalib was nodding again. "Yes, yes, camel can die and drow maybe kills it or steals it. Yes, yes. But maybe we loan something else?" He bustled over to the shelf with the lute, but ducked behind it. I heard the click of a trunk lid opening, then some shuffling as the merchant rummaged through a container.

"Here, dese bestest boots in de city! Make you run faster! You run on de bestest road, catch drow, and make him pay, yes, yes. Give Sali Dalib his fair cut, yes, yes!" He held up a pair of boots, a skin of water, and an open sack holding enough dried bread to last a few days. It was not much, I saw, perhaps enough for a day or two. It would certainly not get me anywhere near Calimport, no matter how fast the boots would make me run.

But I nodded and accepted the objects as he presented them. "I'll bring them back soon," I said.

"You will, yes, yes! With money to pay me for a camel, too! You look trusty, yes, yes!" he said.

"Trustworthy," the goblin muttered quietly, doubtfully.

I was suspicious. But I had no other choice, surely no better choice, so I accepted his boots and his far-too-vigorous handshake, and I bid Sali Dalib farewell.

I returned to the same gate where the guards had brushed me off but an hour earlier, and found them standing in exactly the same positions as when I had left. None of them batted an eye as I strode forward to the gate. None of them said a word as I left the city. But I could feel their eyes on me, and I knew what they were thinking, because the thought crossed my mind as well.

A single traveler, without a mount, with few rations, heading into the desert alone. I had no chance.

But I also had no choice. Drizzt had only a slight head start, but I would have to hurry if I wanted to catch him. I could waste no more time gathering supplies.

I said a quick prayer to Tymora—though I doubted that any of the gods would watch over me, she seemed the best bet—and walked out onto the hot sands of the Calim Desert.

CHAPTER 35

I HAD READ OF DESERTS, HAD OCCASIONALLY BEEN IN CITIES ON THE EDGE OF THEM, HAD endured the heat of crowded Memnon for the past two days. But the truth of the desert—the scorching heat, the shifting sands, and the utter dryness of the land—had never reached me through my books.

I traveled all afternoon, stopping only to take a sip of water or a small bite of stale bread every so often. But I hadn't covered much ground. Each time I came to the crest of a dune and turned around, I could still see Memnon there in the distance. Yet my feet and legs ached as if I had marched a hundred miles. The sands of the desert provided no solid surface to step on. Each stride felt like walking across a soft mattress. My boots sank into the sand, and I pulled them back out, again and again and again.

Not far outside Memnon's gate, I passed a sign, written sloppily, reading "De Bestest Road" with an arrow pointing east, not south.

Instantly I knew Sali Dalib had no intention that I would ever reach Calimport. I had read about such deceptions in my books. Had I followed his directions and taken "De Bestest Road," I would have been intercepted by some of his minions. All Sali Dalib had to do was alert them to the presence of the boots, and his "loan" would be recovered, along with everything of mine he coveted: Perrault's cloak, my dagger—and quite possibly my life. And so I passed the sign and kept walking south.

The sun, thankfully, proved less of an obstacle than I had feared. Despite Sali Dalib's warnings, my cloak proved ample protection from the brutal rays. I kept the hood up and the cowl low to keep the glare out of my eyes. I had always known Perrault's cloak carried some protective magic—he had used it to sever the mental connection Asbeel had placed upon me during a fight on Baldur's Gate's docks—but on that trudge through the desert I came to believe its protective magic extended much further. But even with the cloak beating back the worst of the sun, I was sweating profusely and going through my water far more rapidly than I wished.

Dehydration, not heat, was the greatest danger of the desert. I had walked only a few miles, only half a day, with at least seven more days to go, and had spent nearly half my water.

And the boots Sali Dalib had loaned me were obviously fakes. Then again, I was a fake in the manner I had borrowed—or, rather, had stolen—them. I had no intention of ever giving them back.

But I was justified, I told myself. Sali Dalib had meant to have me killed, to take back what he had lent me and more. He had lied to me, and I had lied to him; he had tried to steal from me, and I had stolen from him.

I wondered what Perrault would think of me now.

Would he approve of my theft? Probably, I thought. I recognized Sali Dalib for what he was and cheated the cheater. But Perrault probably would have lamented that such a decision had been necessary. He wished to protect me, in everything he did—not just from demons, but from the necessity of compromising my principles.

I remembered the lesson he had tried to teach me after we fled Asbeel in Baldur's Gate. Perrault had lied to the captain of a ship to get us onboard and had attempted to change the captain's course in order to facilitate his goals.

His goals. My safety. "You protect first those you love, then yourself, then everyone else," he had said.

Perrault's lie to the captain had disgusted me then; yet perhaps I finally understood his lesson. I myself had lied, and I had been rewarded.

That memory led to another: Joen, her hair flowing in the sea breeze from her perch high atop the mainmast, in the crow's nest of the ship; of her smiling as she tossed a hunk of bread up to the circling gulls, that they might share her mirth; of her eyes, staring in silence at the sunset.

Of her wrists, bound in chains, as she was led belowdecks on the pirate ship.

On the ship Perrault had called.

To protect me.

Abruptly I stopped and shook my head, as if I could shake loose the painful memories. The sun had gone down, and the night air was much cooler, cold even. My legs ached, but I decided to press on.

Travel in the desert at night was much cooler than during the day, but no less difficult. The sand still shifted beneath my feet, and the desert creatures, which stayed hidden beneath it through the hot hours under the baking sun, came out in force as night fell.

I drew my stiletto and enacted its magic, lighting the blade with a blue flame. I was pleased to see the fire worked even when the weapon was not in its sword form. My blazing blade provided sufficient light to move by, and occasionally revealed a strange beast: a whip-tailed scorpion; a small, quick lizard with teeth too large for its mouth; a snake that skittered sideways. Each time I saw an animal, it moved quickly away from my light. But I was reminded that there could be another right behind me, following in my shadow.

I tried to keep such thoughts from my mind—and thoughts of the rarer, larger monsters of the desert, which I had read of in my books—but as my weariness grew I found I could not push the dark beasts from my mind.

And even darker thoughts crept in. Why was Drizzt searching for the stone? How could I really be certain that he would help me if I found him? What if he wanted the stone for himself and killed me to keep me from stopping him?

Drizzt had been in my presence along with the stone for some time on *Sea Sprite*. In fact, he had sat beside me when I was lying helpless in bed, seriously wounded. If he had wanted the stone, he could have taken it then. Had I hidden it that well? Perhaps he had known I had it all along and concealed his intentions, fooling me into trusting him until the time was right to steal the stone—or to trick me into giving it to him. I gulped. Was

Drizzt in league with Asbeel? I glanced up at the sky, half expecting to see the demon here, following me. . . .

I broke into a light jog. I tried my best to maintain a southerly heading, using the stars to guide me. Perrault had taught me how to navigate by the night sky, but I had never tried it on my own. All through the night I worried I had lost my way. By the time my strength failed me and the horizon grew light, I had no way of knowing whether I was on course or far, far off.

When the sun rose, directly to my left, I breathed a sigh of relief. I had stayed true, and had made good ground to the south. Safe in that knowledge, and too tired to do anything about it anyway, I took a few sips of water and a bite of bread and lay down, wrapping Perrault's magical cloak around me to stave off the sun as I slept.

And so I continued toward Calimport and the only hope I had left. By night, I trudged through the shifting sand, dark thoughts crowding my mind. By day, I slept under the protection of Perrault's cloak.

On the third night, my waterskin ran dry. Sometime that same night, I dropped the sack with my old boots and my food ration in it. The weight only slowed me down, and dry food was no good without water.

But I walked on.

I felt the sweat bead on my neck as the sun rose on the fourth day. I did not stop to sleep. I was not halfway to Calimport, but was too far from Memnon to turn around. And I knew if I lay down, I would never rise again. The hot wind whipped the sand into a frenzy, obscuring my vision. It diffused the light but amplified the heat of the blazing orb above me.

But I walked on.

The wind stopped suddenly. The sand fell to rest, and the dry air sucked the moisture from my breath before it left my lungs. I pulled the cowl of my cloak over my head, and I could not see the sun, but I could feel it still, reflecting off the hot sands to bypass my magical cloak's protection. My legs burned, my knees felt weak. I stopped sweating. My body had run out of water.

But I walked on. And I was not alone.

Perrault walked beside me, humming a tune, matching my pace. I tried to remember the words that went with the melody, but they were in Elvish, and I could not recall them.

Jaide, the most beautiful woman I had seen in my life, walked beside me, her hand resting gently on my shoulder. She tried to assure me that I would be all right. But her words did little to comfort me.

Ahead of me, Drizzt Do'Urden strode with purpose—white hair, jet black skin, and two swords belted at his hip. Drizzt had lied to me, had hidden his intentions from me. I sought him to confront him. Strength flowed out from him, yet it was not enough to keep my spirit alive.

No, it was the most unexpected companion who saved me. Her hair flowed in a wind that did not exist, long strands of wheat whipping about, without a care, free. A bird sat on her arm, picking at a loaf of bread in her other hand. After what seemed like days, Joen turned to me and beckoned, motioning to her eyes, then to the horizon.

I followed her gaze, over the dunes to the east, away from the descending sun. Through the hot haze it took me a while to see what she had seen, but there it was, clear as could be.

Trees.

Trees meant water.

Water meant life.

I looked back to Joen, but she was not there. Nor was Drizzt. I turned to Perrault, but he was gone, and Jaide's hand no longer rested on my shoulder. The sun beat down on me.

But the trees remained.

CHAPTER 36

AS I MOVED CLOSER TO THE TREES, MY VISION CLEARED, AND MY HEART BEAT FASTER. I was not dreaming them, could not be dreaming them. The oasis was real—a small spring of water, barely a pond, surrounded by a few tall trees. They were not like the trees to the north, but were thinner and without branches until the top, where several great fronds extended into a natural umbrella. My heart lifted at the sight. The oasis had water, and shelter, and possibly food if those trees bore any fruit.

Along the northern side of the pond, I saw a group of men had set camp right at the shore. I suddenly felt nauseous. There were at least two dozen men, all wearing brightly colored clothing, their heads wrapped in cloth, presumably to beat back the sun. A dozen unsaddled horses milled about, chewing the thin mossy grass growing by the pond's shore, or sipping at the water.

Each man carried a sword or spear. Each had rough, gnarled facial hair and was covered in dust, as if he had not seen a town in months. There were no women with them, unless they were hiding in the tents.

Bandits. There was a good chance they held the water hole, and would share only if I paid the toll. I considered my own meager funds. I had two silver coins left—certainly not enough. I wished I could wait until nightfall, when it would be so much easier to sneak past, but my thirst would not wait. I had to go immediately, or I would never make it.

I stayed low to the ground as I crested the last dune before the oasis, feeling fully exposed. The pond was no more than ten yards across in any direction, more a glorified puddle than a true lake. The sight of the water made my throat ache. But how would I reach its shore without being spotted? I crawled down the dune with the sun directly at my back.

The trees had thin trunks, but on the southwestern corner of the pond they formed a dense grove. I slipped in between the trees, moving as quickly as I dared.

I placed my hand upon one of the tall trees, feeling the roughness of its bark, delighting in the sensation, in any sensation besides sand. Suddenly, commotion broke out from the bandit camp.

I scrambled behind the tree. I heard mugs clanging loudly. I glanced around the trunk and breathed a sigh of relief. The bandits were toasting. Water sloshed over the sides of their cups. What could have so excited bandits such as those, I tried not to imagine. I hoped they were merely happy about the discovery of a water source, not about the death and robbery of their victims. But that was not my immediate concern. My immediate concern was the utter dryness of my throat, the pounding behind my temples, the weakness of my legs, the aching in my joints. I needed water, and I needed it right away. So whatever they were toasting, I was glad for their distraction.

I dropped flat to my belly. The sand was covered by a springy sort of short grass. I pulled myself along, arm over arm, making hardly a whisper and staying as low to the ground as possible. I inched along until finally I pulled myself right to the edge of the water.

I drank deeply, gulping down water like I had never seen it before, like I had been parched my whole life. I dipped my hands in the water, and then my face. I let out a sigh, then stifled it until I realized the loud celebration continued, and no one could possibly have heard me. I silently toasted the bandits, feeling like I deserved to join their celebration. Then I filled my belly until it sloshed.

"Hey," said a voice behind me. "That water ain't yours."

I froze. "It's water. It's everyone's," I replied quietly. I subtly drew my dagger as I turned, tucking it tight against my wrist and keeping my hand beneath my cloak.

"Not in the desert it ain't," said the man. He was dressed like the others at the camp, in a bright red tunic and simple, functional breeches and boots. His head was wrapped in a slightly darker red turban, which had come partially unwound, but he seemed hardly to notice. His face would have been rough even without the days of stubble growing on it.

"I'm sorry, I didn't realize," I said. "I'll just move along, then."

"No, you won't," he said, his voice emotionless. "Not 'til you pay me what I'm owed."

"Are you the toll-man, then? The leader of these ban—?" I interrupted myself, before I could say "bandits," hoping he would not catch my slip.

He scoffed. " 'Course not. I'm the lookout. But right now I'm the guy you're gonna pay not to kill you." His eyes were dark and menacing and, I thought, merciless.

"Looks like they're having a party over there." I said, motioning to the ongoing celebration. "Why weren't you invited?"

"I see what you're trying to do, kid, and you might as well stop now. It don't work like you think it works, got it? I like being the lookout. It lets me collect from the wretches like you who stumble over here while the others are busy, and don't no one else take a cut."

I considered pushing further, trying to drive a wedge between him and his cohorts, or perhaps threatening to reveal his scam to the rest of his crew. But something in the man's eyes made me stop. He knew I was powerless. There was nothing I could say that would turn him away.

I leaped to my feet, then immediately doubled over in pain. My belly ached, my head ached, my very skin ached. I wondered what dark magic the man was using on me. Then I realized. The water I had just consumed was working its way into my system, trying to rehydrate me far too fast.

The bandit laughed and held forward his long spear, its barbed tip glinting in the last rays of daylight. "Now, you gonna pay me, or am I gonna take the coin from your corpse?"

I swallowed the bile bubbling up in my throat. "If you want my silver," I said, "you'll have to come claim it." I snapped my hand forward, lengthening the stiletto into a fine saber.

"Well all right then, kid, if you insist." The bandit came at me, his spear tip leading.

I whipped my sword up and out, pushing aside the thrusting spear, and moved to lunge forward. But with a simple twist of his wrists the man reset the spear, its tip directly in my path. I stopped and pulled back, shuffling a step to the left to stay ahead of the prodding spear.

The bandit circled with me, his feet crossing over in perfect harmony. He jabbed again. I blocked easily, tapping my sword against the shaft of the spear and redirecting its head aside. Still I held no illusions about my fighting prowess. I knew the bandit was testing me.

Steel crashed against wood. With each motion, a wave of nausea washed over me, and with each impact, the fingers of my left hand tingled. After each thrust and parry, I took a step to my left, and the bandit did the same, and soon we had reversed positions, with his back to the water and mine to the desert.

I hoped that the sound of our battle would not carry above the loud celebration. I could still hear the loud laughter and mugs clanging. I considered running. But I doubted I could outrun the man in my current state, let alone the horses he could send after me. No, I needed to win the fight, and I needed to do so quietly, without alerting the other bandits.

But the task was not a simple one. The bandit had apparently taken enough of my measure. He jabbed again, but even before I had finished my parry he retracted his spear, moved his trailing right hand over his left, and stepped forward. I found my sword out of position as he stepped and lunged, his spear tip covering the three feet to me in the blink of an eye.

I fell back, and threw up my hand in desperation. And somehow, I clipped the shaft of the spear to raise it harmlessly over my head.

I stumbled backward. The bandit brought his hands up and thrust the spear brutally toward me.

I fell flat on my back to avoid the wicked tip. Its barbs glinted in the setting sun. Suddenly I knew what to do.

I somersaulted backward. The bandit came at me again. I came to my feet just as he lunged forward for the third time, and I brought my sword to bear.

I did not try to parry. Instead, I brought my sword up under the thrusting spear and hooked my blade right at the hilt against the spear's barbs. In the same motion, I dropped my trailing shoulder. I rolled my sword over myself, pulling with all my strength and weight.

The man was perfectly balanced to thrust his spear. But his feet were not set to resist my tug. I rolled all the way around, pulling him forward, pulling us together, pulling his spear past my body. When our momentum played itself out, we found ourselves barely four inches apart. I was far inside his spear's reach, but my sword was out wide.

I expected him to try to retreat, to reset his spear, and to continue the fight. So I moved forward. I brought my sword in tight, hoping to get at least one good strike, to win the fight right there. But he did not retreat. He dropped his spear and stepped forward, wrapping his arms tight around me.

I struggled a moment, but could not even begin to break his clinch. He was strong. Not abnormally strong, not as strong as Asbeel or the strange pirate who had pulled me off *Sea Sprite* into Memnon's harbor. But the bandit was a man, and I a boy, and he had the better position: his arms were wrapped all the way around me, pressing my own arms tight against my body.

I felt as though he would crush the life out of me. Each time I exhaled, he squeezed tighter. Each breath was more difficult than the last.

I had only one option left. I held up my sword and put it flat on his back. He barely seemed to notice. I had neither the angle nor the strength to try to stab him with it.

But I did not need to stab him. I thought of blue fire, and suddenly my sword was ablaze.

The bandit screamed. I fell to the ground, gulping down air.

I looked at my fallen foe and gripped my sword, preparing to continue the fight. But he lay curled in a ball, weeping.

I jumped to my feet and spat, the taste of sour bile still lingering in my mouth,. "I guess you won't be taking coins from my corpse then, will you?" I said. And that's when I saw the bandit's back, where the fire had burned him. His tunic had been torn open, and his skin was bright red and blistering, as if badly sunburned. The torn clothes were wet. The bandit rolled over, and he howled again.

The camp across the pond was silent. But only for a second.

Then all sorts of commotion broke out. I glanced across the oasis to see the rest of the bandits running to their horses, saddles and bridles in hand. Others ran at me along both banks of the pond.

The nausea came back up again, and I did not fight it. I vomited, and though the bile burned at my throat, it felt somehow good.

Then I turned and ran full speed into the desert.

CHAPTER 37

THE SOUNDS OF THE OASIS RECEDED BEHIND ME AS FAST AS THE TOP EDGE OF THE SUN disappeared beneath the western horizon. My strides were long—impossibly long— like a deer bounding through the forest. My boots did not sink into the loose sand; they barely left a footprint even. "They make you run faster," Sali Dalib had said. I had thought them a hoax. But I had never even tried running.

I sprinted until my lungs burned before stopping to catch my breath. I stared down at my waterskin, hanging from my belt, empty.

I had been right at the watering hole and had not filled the skin, and I felt truly the fool for it. Calimport was no less than five days away from me, and I would not survive that long without water. I would have to wait a day and try to sneak back, hoping the bandits had moved on.

But as it turned out, I would not have the chance. I caught the faint sound of approaching hoofbeats, muffled by the sand. I turned to look only seconds before six men on horses, three brandishing spears and three carrying torches, crested the sand dune not thirty yards behind me.

I forced my tired legs to move, one then the other, as fast as they could carry me. I skipped across the surface of the sand, while my pursuers dug in with every galloping stride, throwing up a great cloud of dust behind them.

But horses were still faster than I. After mere moments they were around me, beside me.

A rider prodded at me with a spear. "Thief! Stop!"

He narrowly missed my arm. I could hardly breathe, and I feared I might vomit again. I glanced ahead through the shifting sands, but I saw nowhere I could hide. Panic rose in my chest.

I remembered seeing a fox chase a rabbit once, when I lived with Elbeth in the forest. The fox was faster than the rabbit, and whenever the chase moved in a straight line, the fox would gain ground. But the rabbit was more agile, and changed direction often, never allowing the fox a good straight line to run.

I would have to be as the rabbit.

I planted both my feet and leaped out to my side as forcefully as I could. My magical boots pushed hard against the loose sand, propelling me out and away. I hardly lost momentum despite my sharp turn.

The horses could not shift so quickly. They skidded and stomped right past the spot where I had pivoted.

I changed direction again, turning sharply to my right. The horses tried in vain to keep up with my darting movements. Just like the rabbit and the fox.

Of course, I couldn't help but think of the end result of that chase. The fox had caught the rabbit, and I had been given a lesson on the laws of the natural world: win, or die.

I turned to my left, and four of the six horses changed to follow. The other two, one with a spear and one with a torch, continued in a straight line. Soon they were far out to my side.

I cut hard right, and two of the four turned with me, and suddenly I knew my folly. The horses running in straight lines stayed even with me, flanked me.

"Nowhere to go now, thief. No way to get past us," a bandit said. He wasn't wrong, but his high-pitched squeaky voice made him seem less frightening.

Two behind, two right, two left. I could not turn, or I would run into the flankers; I could not reverse, or I would meet the pursuit. And I could not outrun the horses if I stayed to my course.

My path led straight up the side of a great, tall dune, and I saw the flanking pairs moving farther out from me, to stay low around the mound. Horses would not travel so well up the dune. I could use the terrain to my advantage.

My legs ached, but I pushed them on, running as fast as I could in a straight line, directly for the top of the dune. The flankers were at least a hundred yards to my sides, whooping and hollering and staying dead even with me. The riders behind me stayed close, but on the uphill I gained some distance. On the downhill, I knew, I would be caught.

So I would not reach the downhill. As soon as I crested the top of the dune, I dug both my feet into the sand and drove myself to a halt. I felt my left leg go numb, felt my knee shift, but I ignored the pain. I turned fully around, facing directly at the oncoming riders.

And I leaped.

I leaped as no human is meant to leap. High and far and fast I soared through the desert air. I cleared the riders and horses by several yards, and landed so lightly I could hardly believe it, so lightly I did not even break stride. I heard the riders yelling and the horses whinnying. I heard a thud. I glanced over my shoulder and saw a torch, and the man holding it, lying on the ground, and one of the horses milling about.

I smiled. I am the rabbit, I thought again. But I beat the fox.

I crested the next rise to a beautiful view of the moon rising over the desert, appearing huge and bright and beautiful. I slowed my pace to a jog and listened carefully for hoofbeats, but I heard none.

My throat burned, and my tongue felt thick. My thirst nearly overwhelmed me. I had no choice but to stop and catch my breath. Perhaps they would not try to follow me, I thought. Perhaps I was in the clear. But the thought did nothing to comfort me. Bandits or no bandits, I would never make it to Calimport without water. To make matters worse, the wind picked up, howling and cold.

I wrapped my cloak tight around my shoulders. If I died here in the desert, at least I could say I had fought with honor at the oasis. I smiled at the memory of my final maneuver. The bandit had not even noticed me drawing my blade, let alone the blue fire, burning his back and leaving his tunic torn and wet.

I drew my blade, still in its saber form, and stared at it for a long moment. I took in a short breath. Could it be? I wondered. I ripped my cloak from my back and whipped it around the blade. With a thought, I lit the sword. The blue fire did not burn through the cloak. But when I unwrapped the blade, I saw something spectacular.

A layer of frost had formed on the blue fabric and it was quickly melting. Melting into precious water. I folded the cloak to make a trough, put my mouth against one end, and tilted it. Water trickled down, sweet and pure.

Again and again I lit my blade and nearly danced as the frost melted to a puddle on my cloak. But as thirsty as I was, I forced myself to drink slowly, letting the water settle in my stomach before sipping again. Once I had drunk my fill, I wrapped the cloak around my body and set off again at a jog, headed south.

CHAPTER 38

OVER THE PAST SEVERAL TENDAYS MY IDEA OF A CITY HAD CONTINUALLY EXPANDED. Despite my young life spent traveling with Perrault, I had never been in a city until a month before, when we had entered Baldur's Gate. Until then I had never seen so many people living so close together. Then I had sailed into Memnon harbor and seen a true sprawl. Miles of city, of buildings and makeshift shacks, rich and poor, were thrown together in a huge crowd. Baldur's Gate could have fit inside Memnon several times over. But even Memnon had not prepared me for my first view of Calimport.

Beneath the rising sun, the largest city on the face of Toril spread out before me, as endless as the sea beyond it. A million people must live there, I thought.

I walked down the last dune before the city gates. The wrought-iron bars were capped with golden spikes, each likely worth more than the average citizen's lifetime earnings.

I was weary and starving. I hadn't eaten in six days, since the night before the oasis. But I felt so elated by the end of my long road through the desert, I practically jogged into town. The guards, like those in Memnon nearly a tenday earlier, barely spared a glance.

The children, on the other hand, stared.

They reminded me of the boy in Memnon who had pointed me to Sali Dalib. They were thin, waifish, wearing whatever clothes they had stolen or salvaged, if any at all. Their skin was burnt, their bellies swollen with hunger. They stared at me as I walked past, not expectantly but hopefully.

I fished about in my pocket for my last two silver coins and moved to one of the several carts of food and supplies that lined the street. The fat vendor grinned as I handed him the coins, and without a word I took the two largest loaves of bread from his cart and moved away. I had certainly overpaid, but I was in no mood to haggle. I needed food, and I needed information, and the bread would get me both, I hoped.

The children, predictably, followed me, their hands out. A round-faced boy hung back in the shadows, watching. He looked about eight years old, larger than the others and healthier. Their leader, I guessed.

"Listen up," I said after I had led them all down a lonely road off the main entrance to the city, far from the guards' prying eyes. "You can all have some food if you help me. I'm looking for an elf by the name of Drizzt Do'Urden. He'll be with two humans, a man and a woman, and a dwarf with a red beard. Do you know where I might find him?"

A hush fell over the kids. I had expected to get a flood of responses, and to have to sift through a dozen false leads to hopefully find the one truthful one. But they were obviously frightened. I broke a piece of bread off, and they all stared at it, practically drooling. They were also obviously hungry.

One boy stepped up to me. I gripped my dagger, half worried that he might try to challenge me for the bread.

"No food's worth that fight," he said. He motioned to the rest of the children, and they all turned and shambled back to the gate, leaving me alone on the side of the road holding my bread.

I sat down on the dusty cobblestones, feeling much like a beggar myself. Had I been thinking clearly, I would have found some more people to question and continued my search for Drizzt. But I was holding two loaves of fresh bread. My stomach grumbled. By the time I fully realized I had taken a bite, I was brushing the last crumbs of the second loaf from my lap.

I breathed a satisfied sigh and looked up to find a boy right in front of me. It was the child who had hung back, watching from the shadows.

"You're looking for the drow," he whispered.

I started to nod, then stopped. "Elf. I never said drow."

"You don't have to say it. And you shouldn't be asking about him." He leaned his hand on the wall above me, and tilted his head toward the end of the road. He looked like all the other urchins on the street: dark hair, tanned skin bearing witness to years without shelter, oversized clothes probably stolen from a drunk passed out in an alley. But there was something different, something odd, about his eyes. "Entreri claimed him."

"What's an Entreri?"

He nearly choked and staggered back a step as if he'd been slapped in the face. He started to speak and stopped several times before finally managing a sentence. "You can't be walking around Calimport and not know the rules," he said.

"What rules?" I asked, scrambling to stand beside him. I wasn't exactly tall for my age, but still I towered nearly a foot above him.

"The rules of the streets, kid. The rules the pashas make. And the first rule is, don't cross Entreri."

"So Entreri is a person, then?"

"Yeah." The boy kicked a loose stone down the narrow road before turning back to look up at me. "Used to be, at least."

"Used to be? Is he undead?"

"I meant it figuratively. But he's as cold as the undead, that's for sure." The boy let out a short laugh. I couldn't help but stare as deep wrinkles creased the corners of his eyes.

"Who are you?" we both asked at the same time.

I waited a second, but he didn't answer. "My name is Maimun," I said.

"Twice lucky." He stared at me, studying my face. "That's a desert name, but you don't look like a desert person."

I nodded. "I suppose I am now, since I crossed the Calim on foot alone."

"You crossed the desert alone, looking for the drow? Gutsy, kid, but not too smart."

"Why do you keep calling me 'kid'? I'm probably older than you."

He chuckled. "Not a chance, kid." Again his skin crinkled around his eyes, and that time I was sure he wanted me to see it.

I took a step toward him and jabbed my finger at his chest. "You're not a kid," I said. "You're a halfling."

"And you're perceptive," he said, pushing my hand aside. "Been a street kid for about twenty years. Name's Dondon."

"You pretend to be a kid so you can rob travelers. So why tell me your secret?"

"So you'll believe me when I tell you to drop your search. Besides, you don't have anything worth stealing. I already checked."

I instinctively patted myself down—cloak, weapon, all there. Somehow I felt offended that he didn't consider those things worth stealing.

"Too hard to fence," the halfling said with a wink. He started walking down the road.

"Wait!" I ran after him. "Why do you care? Why are you telling me this?"

He chuckled again, but kept walking. "I don't care if you get yourself killed, kid."

I put my hands on my hips. "I can handle myself, you know."

Dondon kept walking until he reached the street corner. Then he stopped and looked at me over his shoulder. "I got no reason not to warn you," he said. "No gain either way. Besides, I like you. You were gonna give the urchins some food, even if they were smart enough not to accept. Under the circumstances."

"All I need is information," I called to him. "Can you at least point me to someone who knows where I can find Drizzt?"

"Hells, kid, I know where you can find him. It's the telling you part that isn't going to happen."

"Then point me to someone who will tell me!" I said, throwing up my hands.

"Why do you want to find him so bad?" asked the halfling.

"He has something of mine," I lied.

"So that's it then." He sauntered back to me. "Drow stole from you, did he? What'd he take?"

"None of your business, is what," I snapped.

"Hey, you don't share with me, I don't share with you, got it?"

I frowned. I had no reason to trust him, but I had no better options. "I have to talk to him," I mumbled at last. "He has some information I need."

"Oh ho! So you want information about the whereabouts of the guy who's got your information. That's something, ain't it!" Dondon laughed. "Well, sorry, I can't help you then. There's no way you would get close enough to him to talk, that's for sure. If it were, you know, a sack of gold or a magic ring, that'd be one thing. Entreri's a killer, not a mugger. He's not after the loot. I could've maybe helped you get it back, you know what I mean? But information?" He sliced his hands through the air. "No way." With that, he disappeared around the corner.

I waited a few moments. Then I slipped around the corner after him. I had often shadowed Perrault before, and was quite competent at it. The trick, I knew, was not staying hidden, but blending. Of course, there were plenty of tricks to counter shadowing—choke points, sudden direction changes, backtracking, all designed to make obvious the person trying to blend in—but using these methods relied on the knowledge, or at least suspicion, that one was being followed. Which, I hoped, Dondon did not possess.

Dondon walked quickly, moving deftly through the crowded street, very possibly picking a few pockets along the way.

All the squalor that plagued Memnon was abundant in Calimport as well. We passed by makeshift hovels made of shoddy driftwood, leaning against the sides of great mansions. Towering spires looked over broad slums. A horde of beggars flanked the doors of a great temple. And Calimport had a distinctive smell to it: the stench of unwashed bodies covered with far too much rich perfume. It was as if the city's wealthy had tried to hide the odor of the poor.

The longer I followed Dondon, the more certain I was that he had a destination in mind. And given our previous conversation, I figured he was probably heading to Entreri, or someone who knew Entreri, to let him know I had been snooping around.

But would that really be so bad? Dondon and the urchins on the street surely feared Entreri. Drizzt, on the other hand, had never even mentioned him. Though that wasn't the only thing the drow hadn't mentioned to me. He had never told me what he wanted with the stone, either. I had no idea which of Drizzt's words were true and which were false, and no way to determine between the two.

But I needed to find Drizzt. I needed to know why he was after the stone. And I needed to know if he could help me, if we could search for it together.

A great bell in the temple ahead of me began to ring. My eyes darted through the sea of worshippers streaming out of the temple doors, and I cursed. I had lost track of Dondon. I raced up the street, passing row after row of driftwood shacks. As I passed a dark alley, an arm reached out and pulled me in. I couldn't help but let out a yelp.

"I knew you'd follow me, foolish kid," Dondon said, but his voice was not as harsh as his words. He sounded almost impressed.

I leaned against the high stone wall, willing my racing heart to slow back to normal. "I need to know what I'm up against."

"Of course. Allow me to show you." He pointed down the alley. "The road out there is Rogue's Circle. At the end of the road you'll see a three-story brown storehouse. Outside are four men who look like vagrants."

"Look like, but aren't," I said, beginning to piece the puzzle together.

"Precisely. They're guards. The house belongs to Pasha Pook."

I peered down the alley to try to catch a glimpse of the house or the so-called guards. But all I could see at the end of the alley was a sliver of cobblestoned road lined with iron grates and what looked like a tavern door across the way. I turned back to Dondon. "Who's Pasha Pook?" I asked.

"He's the most powerful man in Calimport, kid," Dondon replied, crossing his arms over his chest. "Even more so since his assassin came home."

"His assassin?"

"Entreri. Most dangerous man in the city."

I let out a frustrated sigh. "You just said Pasha Pook was the most dangerous man in the city."

"Pook's the most powerful. He can have anyone killed, anytime, for any reason. Don't cross Pook. But Entreri's the most dangerous. He's the one doing the killing."

"Okay. So what's this got to do with Drizzt?"

"The drow crossed Entreri, and the assassin led him here to die. He and his buddies went to Pook's house yesterday, which means they're either dead or captured. If the drow's your friend, hope he's dead. And either way, forget about him." Dondon punched my leg, nearly knocking me down, despite his small size. "This is the last time I tell you to drop it. If you don't, I won't shed a tear when you disappear."

I looked at him long and hard, trying to discern if the concern on his face was real. "You're heading to Entreri right now to tell him everything."

He laughed in my face. "What would I say?" he said when he'd caught his breath. He raised his voice to a mocking high pitch. "Hey, Mister Entreri, sir, there's some little kid from out of town asking about the dark elf. Want that I should kill him for you?" His voice dropped back to normal. "He'd probably kill me for wasting his time!"

Dondon kept laughing as he walked away. I briefly considered running after him, knocking him out, maybe taking him prisoner. Perhaps I could arrange an exchange for Drizzt?

Or perhaps I would simply end up dead. I had enough powerful enemies as it was.

My shoulders sagged, and I sat back against the alley wall. What was I supposed to do? Luck had always been on my side. I had been named for luck; the stone I sought was an artifact of Tymora, the goddess of good fortune herself. And yet Tymora smiled on me no more. I shook my left hand, which had grown completely numb ever since I fought the bandit in the oasis. Pinpricks were creeping up my left foot as well.

I'm just tired, I told myself. I hadn't slept since the previous day, and had run many miles across the desert since that last rest. I needed to find somewhere to sleep. And I knew just the place.

In a sprawling city like Calimport, it would take years for me to learn my way around. But there was one exception, one landmark I could find easily in any city.

Locating the docks was a matter of using my nose, following the breezes carrying the salt of the sea. In Calimport, the docks stretched for miles along the coast, and extended as far as the eye could see onto the water. Some piers had as many as eight ships docked alongside—and not small boats, but huge oceangoing trade ships, four-masted, six-decked monstrosities that put *Sea Sprite* to shame. At the foot of each dock, a lamp-post stood over a bubbling fountain. The fountain offered clean water to disembarking sailors—and to the many vagabonds roaming the wharves—and the lamp offered light when night fell.

I walked along the expansive docks for nearly an hour before I found my hiding place: a collection of blackened crates, waiting to be loaded into a warehouse farther down the pier. I was careful to choose a stack that had no activity around it and found a nook in the seaward face of the pile.

One of the crates had cracked open on one side, and through the split wood, I spied slivers of dried, salted meat. My rumbling belly would not listen to any objections about stealing. I ate my fill with no second thoughts.

The sea breeze felt good on my face; the salt smelled like perfume to my nose. The sounds around me all felt so familiar: the gentle lapping of the sea against the base of the docks, and the creaking of the ships as they rose and fell on the tidal swells. Sailors and deckhands and dockmasters shouted commands as they rushed by. They raised sails and lowered them, loaded and unloaded cargo, called out permission to dock, permission to come aboard, "yes Cap'n, no Cap'n."

I wished I could find another ship at the docks and sail away, but I knew that I could no longer run from my troubles.

I steeled my resolve, determined to follow my path to its end. When night fell, I would go to Rogue's Circle. Drizzt and his friends were in danger at the hands of a crazed assassin, and there was a good chance I was the only one who knew it. How I would get past Pook's guards or fight Entreri, for that I had no plan. I would have to improvise. Once I had saved Drizzt, I could question him; perhaps then he'd have no choice but to tell me everything he knew about the stone. I dared to hope that he would be so grateful, he would agree to help me, and we could track down the woman in the mask together.

It was a dangerous plan for sure, but I had come too far to let any setback stop me. Even if it led to my death.

For a long time, I stared at the boats, enjoying the smell of the sea breeze for what I was sure would be the last time. Eventually I drifted off to dreams of sailing on Captain Deudermont's ship, scanning the open sea from the crow's nest with a wheat-haired girl by my side.

CHAPTER 39

WHAT HO, *SEA SPRITE*?" THE CALL ECHOED DOWN THE DOCKS.
I rubbed the sleep from my eyes. The sun was low in the western sky, but not yet set. The tide was coming in. I had slept well and long, but still I was weary, and still my hand and foot were numb. I could hardly believe the call I'd heard was anything but a dream, but I couldn't help myself. I had to scan the docks.

And sure enough, there she was, tying off alongside a pier not two hundred yards from my hiding place. It had been less than a tenday since I'd seen her last, but it felt a lifetime ago.

I pulled myself to my feet and walked toward *Sea Sprite*, trying not to put too much weight on my weaker left foot. I could hardly fathom her presence—how, and why, had she come to Calimport?

I had trekked across the desert, had nearly died of thirst, had nearly been killed by bandits. I could have simply stayed with *Sea Sprite* and reached the same place at the same time!

I thought of the reasons I had left the ship: the pirate attack, the troll, the danger my presence brought. My intentions had been honorable when I abandoned *Sea Sprite*. Could I really bring her crew back into all of that? How selfish was I?

No, not selfish. It was not just my fate that hung in the balance. Many more lives than mine were at stake.

I reached the pier where *Sea Sprite* sat docked, to find two familiar faces at the end of the deck.

"Oi, it's Lucky-Twice!" said Lucky. "How'd you get 'ere? Stow away on another boat, then? We'd've given you a ride if we knew you was heading here to Calimport, you know."

Tonnid laughed along with Lucky, but he seemed less sure about the joke.

"I walked," I said. My throat choked up a bit: Lucky and Tonnid had been the closest thing I'd had to friends on the ship. I had thought I would never see them again.

"You walked. From Memnon?"

"Well, ran, really." I shrugged. "Most of the way. Walked some of it."

"Sure, kid, and I'm a Lord of Waterdeep." Lucky scoffed and rolled his eyes. "Ain't that right, Tin?"

Tonnid's laugh turned into a great, uproarious cackle. Quickly every head on the pier—and for several piers in each direction—stared at us.

I shielded my face from their stares and stepped closer to the ship. "Listen, Lucky. Can I come aboard? I need to speak with Captain Deudermont."

"You don't need to come aboard to speak with me," said the captain, as he marched across the deck. "I had planned to look in on you once we returned to Memnon, a few tendays from now. I did not expect you to beat me to Calimport."

"Nor did I expect to come, sir," I said. "But here I am."

"Indeed. What can I do for you, then?" Deudermont asked as he ambled down the gangplank.

"I'm not looking for a job, or for passage, or anything," I said.

"Based on the circumstances of your departure, I didn't expect you were," he replied curtly.

"Yes, sir. But you see—" I cleared my throat. "I need a favor."

How best to say it, I wondered. If I blurted out that Drizzt had been captured by the most dangerous man in Calimport and I needed to get him back, so he could tell me where the stone he never expressed any interest in is, so I could get back that same stone, which I left *Sea Sprite* intending to be rid of as soon as possible, Deudermont would probably give me a funny look, and bid me farewell. At the least.

"Drizzt is in trouble," I began. "He's been captured by dangerous people."

"I knew he sought dangerous people," said Deudermont. "But he is himself dangerous, when he needs to be. Are you sure he is captured?"

"I have it from a good source," I said. But then I reconsidered my only source: Dondon, a halfling posing as a child. A professional liar.

My doubt must have been written across my face. "You are not so sure," the captain said. "But I will trust your judgment. Who holds him?"

"Pasha Pook."

Deudermont winced at the name. "I have no desire to fight a man as powerful as Pook," he said.

I nodded. "I didn't really expect you to. But thank you anyway." The words tasted bitter in my mouth. I had in fact expected Deudermont would help. He was after all, a noble man. But I couldn't blame him for not wanting to get mixed up in my troubles. I began to walk away.

"Hold up there, Maimun," he said. "I said I have no desire to fight him. But there are other ways to get things done in a city such as this."

I turned back. "What do you mean?" I asked.

"I am fairly prominent among the merchant sailors, and I am connected to Waterdeep. I have some political power at my disposal. Political pressure can be a great tool."

Suddenly things didn't look so bleak. "Can we go right now?" I walked backward to the city, eager to get moving immediately.

I was sure Deudermont would feel the same way. He wouldn't want to see Drizzt and his friends held, and likely tortured, any longer than necessary.

But Deudermont only took one step onto the dock, then stopped.

I motioned him forward. "Come on! You never know how long it could take for you to apply pressure, or whatever. If we want to rescue Drizzt from Pasha Pook, we have to go right now!"

Deudermont just smiled, even laughed a bit, as he looked right past me.

I turned to see what he was looking at and walked directly into the lamppost behind me.

I bounced back and rubbed my head. Only then did I realize it was no lamppost, but a leg. A leg attached to a tall flaxen-haired barbarian.

"Wulfgar!" I shouted.

"Sounds like you've got a solid plan there, Maimun," said Wulfgar. On one of his shoulders rested a massive warhammer. The bicep of his other arm was wrapped in a clean white linen bandage. "So whom are we pressuring? I am a fair hand at applying pressure myself, you know." He swung the hammer down from his shoulder, slapping it into his palm. He winced slightly at the impact.

"Yeah, like ye pressured that hydra into not eating ye," said a rough and gruff voice behind the barbarian. The red-bearded dwarf, Bruenor, shambled into view. Had he been hiding behind Wulfgar deliberately? His axe was belted at his hip, his shield was slung over his back, and his one-horned helm sat crooked on his head. "Ye only let him take the one bite!"

He reached up to slap Wulfgar's wounded arm, but the barbarian simply raised his elbow a bit, and the dwarf could not reach his target. Bruenor settled for a sharp punch to the barbarian's side instead. Wulfgar hardly seemed to notice.

Beside him stood Catti-brie, the woman who had held my hand on *Sea Sprite* many tendays before. My hand moved to my chest instinctively, to the black mark where my wound had been tarred over. Seeing Catti-brie made the scar ache once more, but the sight of her auburn hair blowing in the sea breeze was worth the pain.

"Ye're not one for subtlety," said Catti-brie to Bruenor. Her voice carried the same accent as the dwarf, but sounded far sweeter. "Ye'd rather kick down the front door."

"Hey! The door I kicked down was in the sewers, remember?" Bruenor said.

"It was a thieves' guild," said a voice from nearby. It took me a moment to locate its source: the rooftop of the warehouse beside the pier. "The sewer door is the front door."

I took in a sharp breath.

He was wearing his magical mask again, I realized, which made him look like a surface elf. But his violet eyes could not be hidden. I scanned his face, my stomach roiling, terrified he would greet me as a foe, not a friend. But he seemed happy to see me. "Come on," Drizzt called out. "Are we going to go to Pasha Pook's house to rescue me, or not?"

"You mean Pasha Regis's house," Wulfgar said. They all burst into laughter. Even though I didn't understand the joke, I laughed too, grateful for a reason to smile again.

"All right, enough of this," said Captain Deudermont from behind me. "There is some storytelling to do, and I think this story will be enjoyed best in the privacy of my cabin." He turned and walked back up the gangplank. The four adventurers followed, still laughing.

A new energy lightened my step. It would not be long before I had the information I needed.

But when I reached the gangplank, Captain Deudermont held up his hand. "You are welcome aboard my ship," he said to me. "But I will speak with these four in private first. I expect that you will not eavesdrop."

I started to object, but Deudermont's look was so harsh and unbending that I thought the better of it. "Of course not, sir," I mumbled.

"Good. I will speak to you when I have finished with them," Deudermont said. Without another word he led Drizzt, Wulfgar, Catti-brie, and Bruenor onto and across the deck and into his cabin. I slunk up the gangplank a few moments later and onto the deck.

We were in port, and night was falling. I looked up at the mainmast. There was no lookout posted in the crow's nest.

Soon I would confront Drizzt and demand answers. I would very likely have to leave the ship, and my friends, once more. But before that, I would sleep in the crow's nest underneath the stars. I would be exactly where I wished to be.

CHAPTER 40

THE SOUND OF SOMEONE CLIMBING THE LADDER BROKE MY TRANCE PERHAPS AN HOUR later, just as the last rays of light disappeared beneath the horizon. I pulled out my dagger, ready to strike.

"The captain said you were looking for me," Drizzt said, pulling himself gracefully into the broad bucket beside me.

"I was." I put my dagger back in my belt, but kept my hand on the hilt.

"For what purpose?"

"I . . . I need to know something." I hung my head. All the time I had been searching for the drow, I had never really imagined what I would say once I finally found him. I knew Drizzt was a formidable fighter. What if my questions made him angry? I gulped. Fear weighed down my voice. My question came out at barely a whisper. "What do you want with my stone?"

"What stone?" He looked genuinely puzzled.

"The magical stone. The stone I carried in a pouch here," I said, tapping the hollow of my chest. How could he pretend to not know what I was talking about? My voice grew stronger. "I had it last time we were on this ship. I nearly tossed it away the night we met, when you found me on deck. I'm sure you knew about it then, didn't you?" I said, though in fact I was not at all sure.

But Drizzt did not deny it. "And you have lost it now," he said.

"Not lost—it was stolen!" I practically spat out the words. "It was stolen by a woman. She wears a shadowmask and a robe, and the ravens said she was trying to save me and—"

"Ravens?" Drizzt interrupted.

"Talking ravens," I said. "Nine of them. Or, one of them talked, I don't know about the rest."

"Where is your stone now?" Drizzt asked.

"That's what I'm asking you." I was growing desperate. "Where is it? I have to get it back, and I thought since you were after it too, you would know!"

"I am not after your stone, Maimun." Drizzt looked down at me, with no menace in his eyes. "Why would you think I was?"

"I met a seer in Memnon." The words sounded foolish to my own ears, and a blush crept over my cheeks. "He told me you seek what I seek." Had the old seer lied to me? A feeling like hot needles shot through my left leg.

Drizzt shook his head slowly. "All I seek right now is passage back to the north, to help my friend recover his home. I know nothing of any such stone."

My heart sank. I clenched my fist, trying in vain to relieve the pinpricks shooting up and down my arm as well.

"What is the matter? Are you in pain?" Drizzt said, pointing at my hand.

"No," I said. I tried to blink back the tears in my eyes and look normal.

He ignored my obvious lie. "You are wounded."

"It's nothing." I stared at my hand and wiggled my fingers. "My hand just feels a little numb."

"Just your hand?"

My gaze dropped to the bucket's worn floor. "My left foot too," I admitted.

"Since when?" There was genuine concern in his voice and on his face, and I felt ashamed for ever having doubted his motives.

"Since . . . Since I left *Sea Sprite*, I suppose," I tried to think back to exactly when the feeling had started, to what had caused it. "No, since I lost the stone. It's powerful magic, brings luck and stuff. And it's been mine since birth even though I only got it this summer, and it's tied to me somehow and . . ." My voice rose in speed and intensity as I rambled on frantically.

Drizzt patted the air and motioned for me to be calm. "I know little of any of this," he said. "But it sounds to me like the numbness and the stone are connected." He squatted down and reached out to touch my leg. I jerked it back reflexively.

Drizzt looked back at me, deep concern in his eyes. "You must find your stone, or I cannot say how much worse this pain and numbness might grow."

I took a few deep breaths until the pinpricks began to subside. "Can you help me?"

"I will do what I can, but I fear that is not much."

I dropped my head.

"But," the drow continued, "I do know of someone who may be able to help."

I looked up again. "Who?" I asked.

"A man, a wizard, named Malchor Harpell. He lives to the north, in a hidden tower. I can take you there, if you will trust me."

My head swirled with hope. I had a destination, a place to begin again. I nodded.

"Good," Drizzt rose to his feet and headed for the ladder. "Now, the captain is waiting for you in his cabin."

PART V

So ye went down to the cabin and ye spilled yer beans to Captain Deudermont," the pirate said. He sat on a boulder in front of me, his elbows perched on his knees, his head resting in one hand.

"That's right," I said. I cast my gaze behind the pirate. I could see that the light coming through the door had changed significantly. It no longer came through the door so directly. But a faint glow still seeped through the cracks. It was indirect sunlight pouring into the tunnel that led to the beach. I would not have even noticed it, except that I had been watching for it, waiting for the answers it would bring.

The sun was rising, not setting.

The cave faced east.

"So then ye sailed north," the pirate chanted. "And ye found this Harpell person, and—"

"If you want to tell the story, be my guest," I snapped.

"A story that boring? Why'd I want to tell it?"

"Why would you want to hear it, is the better question."

The pirate laughed and pulled himself to his feet. "Good question, that be," he said, hand going for the hilt of his sword.

He brought the sword up and advanced menacingly.

"You don't want to kill me," I said.

"Not if ye got more to say," he said. "And if it ain't boring."

I made no response, just locked my gaze with his. After a moment, he sat back down. "So, ye talked Deudermont into taking yerself north, then."

"He volunteered, actually," I replied. "For the second time, he offered me his help unconditionally."

"So long as ye give in to his will."

"That's right."

The pirate leaned forward. "Pretty strong condition, that be."

"Are you going to stop interrupting me?"

He laughed again, a great belly laugh that rolled for what seemed like several minutes.

"I'll take that as a no," I said when he'd finished.

"I be a pirate, boy! We ain't known fer politeness."

"Nor for bathing either," I said, unable to resist.

"Nor that," he agreed. "Now, do continue with the tale. There be a long way between Calimport and Waterdeep."

A big part of me wanted to simply stop talking, to let him kill me, to deny him the pleasure of knowing the end of my tale. But I could not do that, not after what I had learned.

The cave faced east.

It faced open water.

That meant we were on an island, somewhere off the Sword Coast.

That meant the pirates would have ships, boats, some means of reaching the mainland, near at hand.

The beginnings of a plan formed in my mind. A desperate plan, true, but a plan nonetheless.

I could not let this pirate kill me. After everything I'd been through, I would not be killed like an aging animal too old to serve its purpose. But for the moment, I had no choice but to give the pirate what he wanted, until the time was right to make my escape.

CHAPTER 41

"Sails on the horizon! South by southwest!" I called down from my perch in the crow's nest. We had been at sea for seventeen days, harnessing a strong autumnal wind blowing from the south to push us up the Sword Coast at a good clip. Autumn was dragging on toward winter, and the ice floes and icebergs of the northern seas would soon begin creeping down toward Waterdeep. We had passed Memnon more than a tenday ago. We were but a few days from Baldur's Gate, where we planned to make port and take in more supplies. I almost wished we'd never get there.

I had been there twice before, both times ending worse than my worst nightmares. I had battled Asbeel there, had watched Perrault take a grievous wound defending me, and had abandoned him to die there. I would surely have died there myself, had I not found *Sea Sprite*. And back aboard her again, I felt like I had come home.

After we departed Calimport, Deudermont assigned me the job of carrying his orders, the same job I had held before taking my sudden leave in Memnon. As the numbness in my left foot grew worse, it became more and more difficult to walk. In spite of the pain, I was willing to continue my duties without complaint, but Captain Deudermont would hear nothing of it. He said I had eyes as sharp as any on the ship, and could make better account of myself as lookout.

"Sails on the horizon!" I called out again. The season was late, so we saw relatively few ships, and nearly all of those sailed from the north to Calimshan. "She's tracing the horizon," I called down. "Looks like she's heading for land."

Odd, I thought. The coastline nearest us was Tyr, its purple hills meeting the sea at rocky and often sheer cliffs. There were few, if any, good berths due east of that ship's position.

We were faster than her, but her angle would bring her closer to us as she passed directly south of our due-north track. Her choice of path was curious, surely, but something else was amiss. I couldn't quite place it. I watched her move ever so slowly across my field of vision, away from the darkening western horizon . . .

The darkening western horizon. Darkening, in the early afternoon. Suddenly the ship was the least of my concerns.

"Captain!" I yelled down to the deck below. "I need the captain!" A boy named Waillan, who had taken over my duties as deckhand, darted below deck and emerged a moment later with Captain Deudermont in tow.

"What is it?" Deudermont called up. Even yelling, his voice sounded regal.

"Ship south-southwest, moving due east," I called down. "I think she's damaged, looks to be listing."

Deudermont nodded. "Heading for Tyr, for repairs," he said.

"No sir, I don't think she's on course for any city. She's just aiming for the nearest land."

"Any thoughts on why?"

"I think she's running from a storm," I yelled, more loudly than I had planned.

A hush fell over all the crew on deck. A storm so late in the season likely meant a tempest. A tempest could make a ship like ours disappear.

"You think?" Deudermont said. "Look again and tell me if there is a storm or if there is not."

All work on deck halted. All eyes turned to look at me.

I turned back to the horizon and peered out, squinting my eyes to cut through the glare of the high sun. And again I saw it: the western horizon growing dark, dimmed by the approaching thunderhead. The clouds would be visible in a matter of hours, I knew. And a few hours after that, we would be in the thick of it.

"Storm," I called down. "Huge, too. Covers the whole western horizon."

Deudermont nodded and looked me straight in the eye. Then he moved to the port stern to scan the horizon himself. I felt a twinge of bitterness that the captain hadn't trusted my eyes.

"Sails to full!" he called after only a moment. "Get all hands on deck! Tie down the cargo, close the portholes, and make the ship ready! We'll run 'til we're caught, then ride it out!" The crew leaped into action immediately. "Helm, set us bearing zero-four-zero. Head toward land until the coast is in sight. We'll need the reference to reach the Gate in a storm."

"Aye," called the helmsman, turning the wheel to the right. Though it was only a slight movement, up in the crow's nest, I felt the boat tilt distinctly.

I glanced out at the listing ship. "Wait! No!" I called down.

But with all the hustle and bustle on deck, Deudermont could not hear me. Men climbed the rigging to open the sails. Others scrambled about with ropes to tie down and brace all the various moving parts on deck. A constant stream of activity entered and left the hold.

"Relief!" I called down below. There should have been someone ready to take my place whenever I conceded the watch. But Deudermont's new orders had trumped that plan. My appointed reliever was busily battening down a hatch somewhere.

I scanned the deck. "Relief! If you please!"

Still no one heard me. At the front of the deck, I saw Wulfgar pulling up the anchor chain—the entire anchor—over the side of the ship, along with a few other crewmen. If the anchor were allowed to hang, as it usually did, and the storm damaged that part of the ship, the anchor could drop into the sea and be lost. Or worse, it could drop into the sea but not be lost, instead catching something on the seabed below and holding us in position. Not being able to rise and fall and move with the swells of the storm could cause catastrophic damage.

Bruenor leaned over the rail, bidding a fond farewell to his lunch for the seventeenth straight day.

Drizzt was walking in the rigging, moving with ease and grace beyond anything I'd seen. He walked along the narrow beams and ropes as if they were solid ground. He was busy helping unfurl the last of the sails, bringing us from half to full. The sight made me a bit nervous. If our sails were out fully when the storm caught us, they'd be ripped to shreds. Deudermont was betting the extra distance we'd cover in the run before the storm would be worth the risk. He would order all sails furled and secured before the front of the tempest hit us.

"I've got ye," came a call from below, a female voice. I knew without looking it was Catti-brie, the only woman on the ship.

I slid down the mast. I had become quite good at dropping from the crow's nest to the deck. She climbed up, offering me a wink as she passed.

As soon as I reached the deck, I set off in a limping sprint, straight to the captain.

"Sir, you missed something," I tried to keep the trepidation out of my voice.

"What's that, Maimun?" Deudermont replied curtly. He did not take his eyes off the horizon, which visibly darkened even from our low perch.

"The other ship."

"What about her?"

"She's listing, sir, and I think she's damaged. We have to help her." Visions of the last ship I hadn't helped flashed in my mind, visions of Joen in chains . . . "We can get to her before the storm does if we turn and set full," I said.

Deudermont turned to face me. "We'd be sailing straight into the wind."

"No, sir, you're wrong," I pointed toward the thundercloud. "See, the storm is coming from the west; it should push the wind in front of it. The storm is probably cycloning, spinning, so the wind will come in from the southwest. If we set to intercept the ship, we'll be headed southeast. The wind won't be perfect, but we can still ride it."

He stared down at me. "Then we'd both be caught in the storm."

"We're going to be caught in the storm anyway," I said, stepping up on the bottom edge of the rail to meet his gaze. "She's already listing, Captain."

"And unlikely to survive the storm. Our presence near her won't change that," Deudermont said. He turned back to the rail, indicating the end of the conversation.

I tugged on his sleeve, willing him to turn back around. "We can take her crew on board, shelter them," I said, fully aware of my own rudeness.

Deudermont continued to stare at the horizon. "I will not risk my own ship and the lives of my crew. Thank you for your opinion, but my decision is made."

I stomped my foot. "Your decision is wrong, sir," I said.

Deudermont whirled back to face me, a fire in his eyes I had never seen. "I am captain of this ship, not you. I am charged with making these decisions, not you. And do not think you are the only one who can see clearly here. I know what is likely to happen, I have weighed all my options, and I have made my choice. When you have an opinion to voice, I will hear it, but once my decision is made, you will not question it so long as you remain on my ship. Am I clear?"

"Yes, sir," I mumbled.

"Good. You are relieved from duty." Without another word, Deudermont stomped away from me toward the stern.

I could barely breathe, let alone speak, as I watched him walk away. I limped to the hold. Belowdecks, I found the hammock that served as my bunk, and fell into it. But I was too humiliated to sleep. Deudermont had just relieved me during an all-hands situation. Never before had he done such a thing to any of his sailors. I could hardly fathom an insult of that magnitude. I flexed my numb hand, and felt the pinpricks traveling up my forearm. Had the other crew heard the discussion—the fight? Would Captain Deudermont tell them how insolent I'd been? I turned my head to my pillow. I'd never be able to show my face abovedecks again.

"The storm's turned," said a voice—Tonnid's voice, low and slow and steady. "Cap'n said you should know."

"Turned south?" I asked, rubbing sleep from my eyes.

"Nopers. Turned north."

I sat up. "Running alongside us?"

"Yepper, just a few miles to our'n west. She's giving us a good wind too, right in our backs! Like a big guy blowing on us!" He puffed up his cheeks and blew a puff of air—and a mouthful of spit—right at me.

I wiped my cheek. He blushed bright red, and offered a small apologetic giggle.

But I was hardly concerned with a little spittle. "What of the other ship? Did the storm catch her?"

"Nope, turned before it got to her. We all had a good cheer on deck."

I smiled. "Thanks, Tonnid. That makes me feel a lot better."

"Good, 'cause the Cap'n said if you feel better you should come back up on deck." He laughed a little. "Never knew you to get seasick, Lucky Lucky." He turned and walked away.

Seasick? Captain Deudermont had told Tonnid I was seasick? I felt my anger at the captain disappear. I vowed never to cross him again. I tugged on my boots—my ordinary leather boots. Waillan had outgrown them, so he'd passed them on to me. I still had Sali Dalib's boots of course, but I kept them tucked away with the rest of my things in a canvas pack. They were hardly suitable for life aboard a ship.

I raced back abovedecks. The storm was just off our port side, due west of us. That is to say, sheets of rain were just a few miles off our side, clearly visible. Where we were, the sky was overcast, and the wind was howling, sweeping up directly from the south. The sails had been reduced to half—the wind was so strong it would've ripped our rigging apart if the sails were up. But still we moved at an incredible clip.

Up in the rigging, a few of the more agile crew, including Drizzt, held position, waiting for the call to stow the remaining sails. The decision would have to be made fast if the storm turned. Even a slight change would have it atop us in a matter of minutes. Catti-brie was still up in the crow's nest, and when she saw me emerge from below she waved and beckoned me to join her.

"Won't be long now 'til we reach the Gate," Cattie-brie said. "Perhaps the captain will give ye leave for a few hours and ye can visit with some o' yer old friends?"

My friends. Though Catti-brie had meant to comfort me, my stomach flipped at the thought.

There were two people in Baldur's Gate whom I could call friends. Alviss, Perrault's dwarf wizard friend, had used his magic to help me spy on Perrault before. Like the seer in Memnon, he could probably try to peer through that crystal ball of his, to locate the stone, to help me if I asked.

And then there was Jaide: the beautiful elf, the priestess of Tymora. She surely could help me, and just as surely would offer her assistance should I ask.

But I did not dare to ask. To find Jaide, I would need to speak to Alviss. And to find Alviss, I would have to visit his inn, the Empty Flagon. The Empty Flagon where I had delivered Perrault, just before he died. I shuddered. I never wanted to see that place again.

Malchor Harpell, I told myself, was all the help I would need. We'd be in Waterdeep in a tenday, and at his Tower of Twilight before winter made the land impassable. Until then, I would not leave *Sea Sprite*, where I could pretend to be an ordinary sailor, relieved for just a little while of the burden of the stone.

I spent the last few hours of that day watching the curious behavior of the storm from my high vantage point, praying it would push us off course and delay our arrival. But when I rose in the morning, the storm's steady wind stayed behind us, driving us even faster toward Baldur's Gate.

CHAPTER 42

THE STORM DID EVENTUALLY TURN EAST AND OVERTAKE US A DAY AND A HALF LATER, JUST as we sailed up the Chionthar and made port at Baldur's Gate. Our initial plan had us stopping in the Gate for merely one day to resupply. But the storm had other ideas. It sat over Baldur's Gate, hardly moving, keeping us locked in. The first day was agony for me. I waited belowdecks, avoiding the sight of the docks. I was afraid of the memories they would bring back, mostly. But I was also certain Asbeel would be there, watching, waiting for me.

On the second day, with the ship supplied but the storm not breaking, Captain Deudermont gave shore leave to any of the crew who desired it. Lucky and Tin tried to get me to go to a tavern with them, but I pretended the captain had given me work to do. I fell asleep that night, praying for the storm to end. I tossed and turned, my sleep torn apart with nightmares about Asbeel.

The next morning, I crawled abovedecks, certain I would see blue sky. But still the rain poured down in sheets. Through the low clouds, I thought I saw a dark plume lazily rising from the city. I climbed up to the crow's nest to see where it was coming from. The outer district? My stomach clenched.

Without thinking, ignoring all my previous reasoning, I rushed down the gangplank and into Baldur's Gate, limping along as quickly as I could. I had only been in the city twice, but somehow I had memorized the route. After only a few minutes I rounded a corner to see the familiar sign, the single mug, drained of liquid: The Empty Flagon.

The building was ablaze, and a small crowd had gathered to watch as the flames leaped high into the air in defiance of the torrential rain, sometimes accentuated by a pop or a hiss or a small explosion. The buildings beside the inn were pressed tight against it, as were most structures in the city, but the flame didn't seem interested in them, barely licked against their wet wooden walls.

I moved to the crowd of bystanders, asking quietly if anyone knew what was going on.

"Dunno, really," one man said. "Place just lit up like a candle. No warning, didn't see no one there."

"What about the owner?" I asked.

"The dwarf? He ain't been around in o'er a tenday. Just up and disappeared one day, and the people stopped coming."

"Actually been nice, not having them ruffians coming through all the time," a woman nearby said. "Got nothing against dwarves, you know? But they like to drink, and drunk people always want to fight, you know?"

"Anyone know where Alviss went? The owner?" I asked.

"He didn't tell no one, didn't pack up and move or anything," said the first man. "Just up and vanished, like I said."

I started back to the docks, then thought better of it. Something odd was going on, and I had a feeling a certain demon was behind it. And if he'd gone after Alviss, he may have gone after another one of our friends . . .

I could hardly manage a run, with my left leg numb from the knee down, but I went as quickly as I could to the temple district and the great Temple of Tymora.

The massive structure was imposing indeed, even more so in the downpour. Its gargoyles leered out menacingly through the rain, and its smooth walls glistened as if possessed by some inner light. I considered going around the back of the building, to where I knew there would be a door. But I did not have the password, so instead I ventured through the main entrance.

The nave of the main temple was huge, lined with tapestries depicting Tymora and her legendary heroes, sometimes in battle but more often simply in some heroic pose. Huge marble columns lined the nave, with yet more tapestries strung between them, dividing the structure into three paths.

Down the center aisle, before the altar, a young man in white robes holding an armful of candles approached one of the tapestries.

I moved swiftly toward him, taking note of his jet-black hair, his slightly pointed ears, his angular face. He was half elf, I was sure.

"Excuse me," I said. "I was wondering if you could help me."

"I am quite busy, but I'm sure one of the disciples will aid you," the half-elf priest replied. He arranged his candles—seven of them, long of neck and longer of wick—side by side under the center of the tapestry. The tapestry depicted Tymora in a white robe holding a lit candle, standing side by side with her twin sister, Beshaba, goddess of misfortune, wearing black and holding an unlit candle. The priest lit the wick of the candle closest to Tymora's side of the tapestry, and knelt before them.

"What are you doing?" I asked. I knew I was being rude, but I couldn't help myself.

"I am praying for one of our lost sisters," he said in a nasal voice. "That Tymora will guide her home. Now leave me to my prayers, child." He began whispering under his breath. As I watched, the wick of the lit candle fell sidelong onto the next, and after a moment the second candle was alight.

"It will only take a moment. I just need to speak with Jaide."

"I said—" The priest's words caught in his throat, and he rose suddenly, spinning to face me, and nearly lighting his white robe on fire with the candles. "How do you know that name?" he whispered harshly.

"She is a friend. And I need to find her."

He studied me up and down and looked at my face, at my tunic—at my cloak. His eyes widened with surprise and what I thought might be horror. "You are Perrault's ward," he said, still whispering.

Behind him, the second candle fell into the third, and that one caught fire as well.

"Yes," I said, "I was Perrault's ward. And now I need help. So tell me where Jaide is."

"She left a tenday ago. It is for her that I pray." He sounded somewhat angry. "But there is someone who needs to see you. Please, wait here." He motioned to a disciple, then disappeared through a well-concealed door behind the altar. The disciple came over to the tapestry, bowed to me, and knelt before the tapestry, apparently to continue the priest's prayer. The third candle, in the meantime, dipped into the fourth.

I motioned to the line of candles. "What is that?" I asked.

"A prayer to Tymora," said the disciple. "The candles can fall either toward or away from the next in line. Tymora guides them, to tell us whether luck will be good or ill for that which we pray about."

"So the more candles are lit, the better the luck?"

"Not quite. Misfortune is often just good fortune taken too far, so teaches Tymora. The best position for the candles is the fourth, where the fire is now. But any farther"—as he said it, the fourth candle dipped into the fifth, which then fell onto the sixth, and that into the seventh, in rapid succession—"and the luck is ill. Oh, this is not good. I must pray for our sister, please. Wait at the altar for Priest Aridren to return." The disciple pushed through the door behind the altar. Through the dark crack, I thought I saw a flash of red skin.

I leaped off the altar, sprinting as far and as fast as my lame leg would carry me, all the way back to *Sea Sprite*.

I knew whom Priest Aridren had gone to fetch. I did not wish to be there when Asbeel emerged from that door.

The storm did not break for another thirteen days, during which neither hide nor hair of me could be seen anywhere but belowdecks on *Sea Sprite*. I spent much of my time those days playing a card game called *Three Dragon Ante* with Lucky and Tonnid. Tonnid, despite his generally slow mind, turned out to be quite good at odds. We did not bet money, but rather duties and chores, and by the time the storm finally broke and the sun came out, I owned most of Tonnid's turns cleaning the bilges, or clearing the galley after meals, or aiding the galley cook, or any other unpleasant task he had wanted to be rid of, all the way to Waterdeep.

It would be a long journey. But at least I would not have much idle time. Any time not spent doing something would find my mind wandering to Asbeel and Priest Aridren, whom I was convinced was his servant; to the stone, and the uncertainty I had surrounding it; or back in time, to Perrault, Alviss, Jaide, and Elbeth, all of whom had tried to protect me and suffered instead.

A cooperative wind could've gotten us to Waterdeep inside ten days. But on the fourth day out of Baldur's Gate, the biting north wind blew in, trying to drive us back to fairer waters.

The northern breeze more than doubled the time of our journey. During the day, we would have to tack into the wind, slowing us greatly. At night, we could not sail, for fear of colliding with the icebergs from the Sea of Moving Ice far to the north.

I hoped the wind would break, but the more experienced sailors all knew that was impossible. Once the wind had turned, it would not shift again until the spring. We would have to cut through it if we meant to reach Waterdeep.

The farther north we sailed, the slower the going became. On the eleventh day, the fears of an iceberg proved true, and though it appeared by daylight, we had to tack off course to avoid the massive, deadly chunk of ice.

From that evening on, all sails were firmly stored each night, the anchor dropped, and the launch's beacon was lit. The small craft rowed a few hundred yards out ahead of the ship each night with two men assigned to it, tasked with staying awake and watching for dangerous ice.

I drew that duty once, and it was among the worst nights of my life. The temperature dipped far lower than I thought possible—it was late autumn, not winter!—and the breeze bit through even Perrault's magical cloak. By the time dawn broke and we rowed back to *Sea Sprite*, my teeth were chattering so badly I feared my jaw would rattle right off my face.

But something else happened that night, something that gave me hope. For in spite of that terrible cold, my left hand held fast to the oars. There on that freezing little boat, I realized that the colder it got, and the closer we got to Waterdeep, the less numbness and pain I felt. From that day on, my condition, though not cured, did not grow any worse. I knew not what it meant, but after that night, my nightmares ceased, and I no longer hoped to stay aboard *Sea Sprite* forever. I couldn't wait to reach the Tower of Twilight, where Malchor Harpell could give me answers and I could begin my journey anew.

CHAPTER 43

T HE CAPTAIN HAD TAKEN THE HELM HIMSELF THE LAST FEW DAYS, AND AS WE SAILED around the last bend into Waterdeep Harbor, I saw why. The entirety of the harbor was choked by ice floes large and small, with hardly space between them for a ship. The captain masterfully guided *Sea Sprite*, with Wulfgar pulling the guide ropes as mightily as any man could. The captain's great skill and the barbarian's great strength worked so well in concert I felt as though I were watching a dance. *Sea Sprite's* movements through the choked harbor, missing ice on each side by mere feet, were as graceful as any waltz.

When at last we pulled up to the pier, the stunned expressions of the harbormen, busy breaking down the last of the dock equipment for storage for the winter, were a sight worth seeing.

Soon, they had the pier cleared and ropes ready as we pulled alongside to a chorus of cheers.

Captain Deudermont moved to the rail. "Permission to come ashore, Harbormaster?" he called down.

"Granted, with pleasure, Captain Deudermont!" a man called back, and a second round of cheers went up. "We had hoped you would reach the city before winter locked you out."

"You had hoped?" Deudermont repeated.

"Oh, yes. You are summoned to a council of the Lords, good captain. I believe they've an offer to make you. This very evening, in fact."

Deudermont gave a quick set of orders, and his well-trained crew sprang into action. A group began hauling the trade cargo from the hold, while another began taking on foodstuffs and essential supplies. The sails were furled, all but the main were taken down and stowed; everything loose on the deck found its place for storage. I had not witnessed that particular dance before, but I could surmise its meaning: *Sea Sprite* was making ready for a winter in port.

As if to accentuate my thoughts, a light snow began to fall. Big, wet flakes whirled and spun through the air on the sea breeze, before finally melting into spots of water on the ground. I doubted the snow would stick at all, doubted it would even leave a coat of fresh powder anywhere on the city. But it did signal things to come.

Winter had arrived.

Which meant Drizzt and his companions would wish to be out of the city and on their way. And I with them.

R.A. & GENO SALVATORE

I had next to nothing to pack—just the small sack I kept near my hammock—so instead I leaned on the forward rail and watched the snow fall on Waterdeep, watched the dockworkers at their tasks, watched the girl with the short yellow hair walk past.

My eyes stopped roving and fixed upon her. Despite the cut of her hair, I knew her instantly. I had seen her in my dreams, and until then, I had not imagined that she was still alive, had not imagined anything of her past her disappearance into the hold of that pirate ship.

I could hardly breathe as I limped across the deck, down the gangplank, toward Tonnid standing guard at the end of the pier.

"Hey, Maimun, you ain't got shore leave," Tonnid said, stepping in my way.

"Yeah I do, Tin," I said. "Captain just gave me leave."

"But he ain't even on the ship."

"He left me a note."

Tonnid blinked a few times, stared up as if seeking answers from on high, then finally nodded and stepped aside.

I felt bad for tricking him, until I remembered how many times I'd had to take his shift cleaning out the bilges on the trip from Baldur's Gate to Waterdeep. It served him right, I decided.

But I had more pressing business. Joen was nearly out of sight, her short stature making her difficult to see in a crowd. But I was determined not to lose her. I sprinted off, as fast as I'd managed to run since the desert.

Waterdeep was a northern city, and I was thankful for it. In the south, in Memnon and Calimport, any patch of land without a structure was fair game for erecting a hovel. As such, the roads were unpredictable, winding, often coming to dead ends suddenly and forcing long backtracks. In the north, in both Baldur's Gate and Waterdeep, the streets were clearly marked (in the better districts, cobbled stone and not dirt), and they followed a somewhat logical order.

Many times over the next hour, I lost sight of Joen as she rounded a corner. But each time, when I rounded the same corner, I could either see her, or see exactly which roads she had taken. Had we been in the South, I surely would have lost her, and been lost and confused myself. But in Waterdeep, I managed to track her all the way through town, until I saw her enter a run-down inn near the middle of the city.

The inn was in such a state of disrepair, I was surprised it was even open. A sign hung above the door, but one of the ropes holding it in place had snapped, leaving the shingle dangling awkwardly. The picture on the sign was that of a simple wooden dagger; the faded letters below it spelled out one word: "Shank." A fitting name for such a place, I decided; anyone entering was surely at risk of being stabbed.

I crept up to the inn's door. It stood slightly ajar, and flickering light and plenty of raucous noise came out of it. I glanced behind me. The street looked abandoned, so I peered through the door's crack without fear that someone outside would see me.

Three dozen men and women, one dwarf, and one female halfling stood or sat within. They each held a mug of frothy ale—several people held two. They sat in a semi-circle, all talking with each other, but staring at a figure in the middle. He sat there, his head down and obscured by a great wide-brimmed violet hat, his frame clothed in fine silk of royal purple. Nowhere in the inn did I see Joen. Had I just imagined her after all? The concern fled from me as soon as the figure in the center raised his head.

His face was the blue of the southern seas, his hair the white of ocean spray. I had seen his face before, seen his cold eyes staring at me, felt his mighty grip as he pulled me beneath the water. My hand dropped to my dagger. I gripped the edge of the door tighter, but still I did not dare enter.

"Greetings," the blue pirate said, his voice sweet yet flat. "I am Captain Chrysaor, and you all are now my crew." A murmur went up through the crowd. I blinked. That was highly unusual. It was the crew's choice to sign on with the captain, not the other way around.

Chrysaor held up his hands, signaling for the murmur to die down, then continued. "That you have shown up here tells me you seek gainful employ. And I promise you, in my employ you shall find only the greatest gain."

"What sort of gain?" someone from the crowd called out. By the rough voice, I thought it must've been the dwarf, but then again all those people were pirates, so I couldn't be sure.

"Gold and silver, gems and jewels. A veritable dragon's hoard." Chrysaor replied. "A fortune to be split evenly among all of you. I won't even be taking a share; I want only one artifact from the entire take."

Each person inside apparently decided that was his cue to strike up conversation. The noise level went from a patient silence to a deafening roar instantly.

But I still heard the whisper in my ear with perfect clarity. I felt the sharp edge of the dagger resting against the side of my neck.

"You should not have come here," Joen whispered. She placed her strong hand on my shoulder and pulled me around to face her. I smiled at her, my heart racing. But she did not take the dagger from my neck.

I wanted to tell her everything, everything I'd been through up until the moment that I saw her on the docks. But I couldn't push the words past the lump in my throat. So I settled for a simple question: "Why are you here?"

"You heard him. Gainful employ."

"But you're a sailor, not a pirate." I felt foolish even as the words left my mouth.

She scoffed. "I was a sailor, before my ship was taken by pirates," she said. Her voice was full of venom, full of accusation. "And what makes you think this is a pirate crew?"

"Because the captain is a pirate. One who tried to kidnap me even."

She hesitated. "That isn't true."

"Yes, it is," said a voice from behind me—a deep voice, a strong voice, the voice of Chrysaor.

Joen took her dagger from my neck. She stared over my shoulder with fear in her eyes. I turned to face my onetime assailant.

The blue-skinned pirate smiled, the expression at once comfortable and out of place. "Though really, I wasn't after you, child. You are of no consequence." Chrysaor said.

"Then you wanted the stone," I said.

"What stone—" Joen began.

I cut her off. "And you're still after the stone, aren't you?" I said. "That's the artifact you want this crew to help you recover. You know where to find it, don't you?"

"You are very perceptive," the blue man said. "But you shouldn't tip your hand so easily. Your one advantage is knowledge your opponent does not possess."

My mind was swirling. "Where is the stone?" I cried.

Chrysaor laughed, a bubbly laugh that reminded me, for some reason, of my childhood in the High Forest. "You don't even know what you had, child, and so you do not deserve it. And so you have lost it, and so you will never recover it." He jabbed my left shoulder and looked down at my leg. "And so you will die."

My hand again dropped to the hilt of my stiletto, but Chrysaor ignored me. He swung the inn's door open wide and stepped inside.

"So what do you think, friends?" he cried, raising his voice for the first time. Shall we set sail come springtime?" A great cheer went up within, followed by another.

"Joen, I have to tell you something," I whispered.

She looked at me—glared at me. "You should not have come," she said. She pushed past me into the inn, slamming the door behind her.

CHAPTER 44

B Y THE TIME I RETURNED TO *SEA SPRITE*, THE SNOW HAD TURNED TO RAIN, AND MY whole body—along with the whole city—was soaked through and chilled to the bone.

Almost the entire crew was still hauling boxes and crates of cargo out of the hold. But no one was hauling anything belowdecks. I was somewhat surprised. We had been in port long enough that most of the stuff should have been offloaded. Most of the food and supplies should have been securely stowed within.

I reached the wharf just as Drizzt and his friends trudged down the docks.

"Ready to go?" he asked me.

"Uh, I . . . I'm not sure."

He cocked his head. "I wasn't aware you had much to pack," he said. "Catti-brie and the others are gathering our supplies, and we plan to be off before nightfall today. Best you make ready quickly."

I paced up the dock, my heartbeat thudding in my ears, my head tumbling through all I had just seen. Joen. Chrysaor. Chrysaor was hunting the stone. I thought of the seer in Memnon and his prophecy. "He seeks what you seek . . . A stranger to these lands, of skin and manner." I swallowed. Could it be?

I turned back to face Drizzt. "I'm not coming with you," I blurted out.

Drizzt stared at me. "Give us a moment," he said, addressing his companions.

"Of course," said Wulfgar. "We'll see to securing some horses." He walked past me, patting me on the head with his giant hand. Bruenor followed, muttering something about "durned fool kids." Then Catti-brie wrapped me in a hug before skipping off after them.

"So you've found a better course than Malchor Harpell?" Drizzt asked when the others had left.

"I think I've found someone who knows where the stone is. And that's why you were taking me to Malchor, isn't it?"

Drizzt's brow furrowed. "Are you sure of your source?" he asked.

"No," I said, hanging my head. And then I spoke aloud the fear I had kept hidden for the past several tendays. "You have no way of knowing that Malchor has any insight into the stone and my troubles, do you?"

Drizzt shook his head. "But I do know that my friends and I are willing to protect you on the journey, if you join us. Are you certain you wish to stay here and take this risk?"

I shrugged. I could hardly admit my true motives even to myself right then. "It's a risk either way," I said.

"It is indeed," Drizzt said as he rested his hand on my shoulder. "My friend, I am saddened that you will not be joining us on the road. But I admire your bravery."

"So you think I should stay here?"

"I think you have wisdom enough to decide for yourself," Drizzt said. "And you did not approach me to ask my advice, did you? You approached me to say goodbye."

I nodded.

"Then goodbye, and safe travels, Maimun. I hope you find everything you are looking for." Drizzt offered me one last nod of assurance, then walked away.

With a heavy heart, I turned back to face *Sea Sprite*. The captain stood at the bottom of the gangplank, shaking hands with a man in blue wizard robes. I reached them just as their conversation apparently ended.

I recognized the wizard: it was Robillard, the same wizard who had pulled me from the harbor in Memnon.

"What are you doing here?" I blurted out before I realized I had spoken.

"I have been hired by the Lords of Waterdeep," he said. "To accompany a newly commissioned vessel to hunt pirates."

"But I thought you worked for the Memnon city guard."

"Waterdeep pays better," Robillard said.

"But . . . What vessel?" I asked.

"Well, Captain Deudermont's, obviously." He shook his head in what I hoped was mock annoyance.

"Enough," Captain Deudermont cut in. "What are you doing here, Maimun? Drizzt and his friends have just left." He gestured to the end of the dock. "You'll have to hurry to catch him."

"I'm . . . I'm sorry, sir," I stammered. "I'm not going with Drizzt." I took a deep breath, then relayed what I saw at the Shank. As I reached the end of my tale, my stomach filled with butterflies. "You once said that you and your crew would help me on my journey, sir. Can you help me go after Chrysaor?"

"Things have changed, Maimun. We are no longer a simple merchant crew," Deudermont said, his voice taking an air of formality. "We are now commissioned to hunt pirates. Dangerous work in the best of circumstances."

"Chrysaor is a pirate, sir," I said.

Robillard looked down at me. "I know of this Chrysaor. He's an underling pirate, not a captain. Serves—"

"Asbeel, I know," I cut in.

"Pinochet, actually, last I'd heard," Robillard said. "Who's Asbeel?"

"Oh, um, another pirate. I got confused." I wasn't quite sure why I was lying to Robillard, and based on his disapproving stare, Deudermont wasn't so sure either. But the captain did not say anything.

"Well, Chrysaor's a water genasi, not exactly common in the city," Robillard said.

"A what?" I asked. I had heard the term before, but could not place it.

"Genasi, descended of creatures of the elemental planes. He's got the blood of a water elemental in him."

"But . . . Aren't water elementals just, you know, water? How can they have kids?"

"Elemental creatures, not elementals specifically," Robillard said, rolling his eyes at my ignorance. "Maybe his great-great-great grandmother was a water nymph, and his great-great-great-grandfather was damned lucky," Robillard said, laughing at his own joke. When he saw we weren't joining in, he shrugged. "In any case, I can keep eyes on him easily enough."

I looked from Robillard to Deudermont, my eyes pleading. "If you help me, I'll do anything. I can fight. I can clean the bilge or the galley. Whatever you wish."

Deudermont sized me up. "You made good account of yourself on the last voyage. You have sharp eyes, and I could use a good lookout."

"So does that mean you will help me?" I asked.

Deudermont nodded. "Now grab some crates and follow the crew. We've a new ship to prepare."

I was off and running before the captain had finished giving his order. My goal seemed so much closer than it had even a day before. And, I dared to think, so was Joen.

CHAPTER 45

THE NEW SHIP, WHICH CAPTAIN DEUDERMONT NAMED *SEA SPRITE*—PROMPTING AMONG the crew a long series of jokes about his creativity—was beautiful, for sure. She was smaller than the old *Sea Sprite*, sleeker, with a different cut to the sails that would supposedly let her run faster and turn more sharply than any other ship on the seas. She was built to overtake a pirate ship in a chase, but not to overpower her.

But she was not built for the comfort of her crew. On the old ship, our quarters had been cramped. On the new vessel we were packed in so tightly it was a wonder no one was crushed to death while sleeping. The galley was about half the size of our old one. Every time Tonnid or Lucky asked me to play cards, I turned them down. I didn't want to get stuck with any of their lousy shifts on the new ship.

In truth, we didn't have much time to spare for games. And none of us were given shore leave for more than a day at a time. Instead we spent our hours on deck, with a pair of swordmasters hired by the Lords of Waterdeep to train the crew.

For three months we sat in port, and for all three we drilled.

At first, Deudermont told me he wanted to keep me from fighting pirates once the ship set sail. He said I would be of more use in the crow's nest. But I finally wore him down with my constant begging, and he agreed it couldn't hurt for me to have some formal training in combat tactics and swordplay.

I was part of the crew, fully and completely. It should have made me happy. But the drills were more difficult than anything I'd tried to do before. My condition, while no longer worsening, left me terribly clumsy at best. The instructors were merciless, not accepting any excuses. The crew never passed an opportunity to laugh at my stumbles.

Each night I would find a note from Robillard on my cot. He magically watched Chrysaor, who made no attempt to hide his actions. Like us, Chrysaor couldn't set sail until the winter storms had passed Waterdeep. But he did everything he could to prepare his crew to leave come spring. Shortly after the meeting in the tavern, Robillard left me a note that told me Chrysaor had purchased a ship, a two-master called *Lady Luck*. Later notes detailed the supplies Chrysaor bought each day. It was clear he and his crew were stocking the ship for a long, long journey. Each note ended the same way: "So when are you going to pay me for this service?" followed by Robillard's overly grandiose signature.

Then one day, six tendays yet before the vernal equinox, a burst of warm air flowed up from the south, and Waterdeep found herself thawing.

I came above deck, wrapped in my winter clothes, along with the whole crew. We had the day off, but the quarters below were so cramped that no one desired to stay put. We were to begin the next day with tactical training—which I guess meant moving as a unit—and we were all pleased, as we expected it to be less physically taxing than the sword fighting we had been learning.

But the air was warm, and the sun was bright, and we found ourselves distracted by a strange sight at that time of year: sails.

A single ship made her way through the still-icy waters of Waterdeep Harbor, headed for open seas. She was far from our berth, and the glare of the brilliant sun on the ice made her hard to distinguish. But somehow I knew exactly which ship she was.

I rushed to the captain's cabin and banged my fist against the door. "She's leaving! She's leaving! Captain!"

The door swung open, and I nearly tumbled in. Captain Deudermont stood before me, fully decked out in his regal captain's attire; behind him, Robillard appeared to be laughing. At me, I knew.

"Who is leaving?"

"Jo—uh, Chrysaor's ship. *Lady Luck.* She's leaving, right now, and we gotta go catch her."

Deudermont ushered me inside, motioning to a comfortable seat at the round oak table, between the wizard and Lucky, who had been appointed the boarding crew's tactical leader, a position of high honor. I gave my friend a brief smile as I took my seat, but if he noticed he paid me no heed.

"Robillard, what has your scrying revealed?" Deudermont asked, taking a seat across from me.

"Memory going in your old age, captain? I just told you."

"Yes, and now you will tell our newest arrival," Deudermont said, gesturing at me. "The short version will do fine."

Robillard rolled his eyes. "Captain Chrysaor and his ship have left port and are making slow speed to the south," he said.

"And beyond that?" Deudermont leaned comfortably back into his chair, seeming almost disinterested.

"There's a great storm brewing to the north," The wizard replied. "If it turns south, it'll put Waterdeep under several feet of snow in three days' time."

"Now Maimun," said Deudermont. "What do you suppose would happen to a ship caught in such a storm?"

"She'd be covered in snow," I said. "I don't care."

"You should care," Deudermont snarled. I had never seen him angry like that. "The crew care for you; you should care about them."

"I do, but—" I started, but the captain cut me off.

"But, you care more about yourself and your own goals."

"You promised, sir. You promised you would help me however you can."

"I did. But this I cannot do."

"Why not? They have the guts to sail out, why don't you?"

"It's not about guts. They risk utter disaster, for small gain. I will not take that risk."

"Small gain? My life is small gain?" I realized my mistake as soon as the words left my mouth.

"Your life is at greater risk if we sail out than if we stay here. And your life is not more important than the lives of all the rest of the crew."

I had heard that speech before, but from the other side. My life was more important than the whole crew of a ship, Perrault had said. But he had also said, protect first the ones you love.

"Captain, we're supposed to be pirate hunters, right?" I asked, putting on my most naïve expression. "Well, there's a pirate ship. And she's sailing away. Why aren't we hunting her?"

Lucky turned to look at me then at Deudermont, his eyes wide.

Deudermont rose up. "This conversation is over. You are all dismissed."

I started to say something, but Deudermont had already turned his back on me. Lucky punched my shoulder lightly, then headed for the door. Robillard, still sitting next to me, barely contained a laugh; and not for my sake, I knew. If Captain Deudermont hadn't been there, Robillard would have been taunting me mercilessly.

With my shoulders slumped, I wandered back out onto the deck. The rest of the crew was enjoying the warm weather, but I felt cold inside, and no amount of sun would change that. I slunk below, fell into my bunk, and drifted off to a fitful sleep, and dreamed I had followed Drizzt and his friends out of Waterdeep.

CHAPTER 46

I AWOKE TO A GRATING, GRINDING SOUND AND A VIBRATION IN THE SHIP. THE WAVES swelled up beneath us, moving us far more than any ship should when tied safely to a dock. Either the storm had arrived early and the seas were tossing beneath us, or . . .

I leaped from my cot and raced to the ladder, barefoot and bare-chested, wearing only the breeches I'd slept in. Up I went, into the afternoon sun, just in time to catch the spray as *Sea Sprite* cut through a wave.

I glanced around, hardly believing what I was seeing. Captain Deudermont had the helm, and the sails were set and full of the wind blowing down from the north. The crew moved about in a slow waltz, securing a line here, untying one there, following the captain's orders almost before he called them.

"Mister Maimun, to the helm," the captain called. "After you dress yourself, that is." Without a word—I couldn't have found one if I'd tried—I dropped down the ladder and raced to my cot, quickly gathered my things, and sprinted back to the deck. The sway of the ship on open water beneath my feet felt wonderful.

"Yes, sir," I said as I skidded to a halt before the captain, trying to sound formal and calm.

"Relieve Mister McCanty in the crow's nest, if you please," Deudermont said.

"Yes, sir. And thank you, sir."

"Don't thank me," he said tersely. "Thank your friend Lucky. He polled the crew, and they agreed, to a man, to take the incredible risk and pursue our blue friend."

I could barely draw breath as I walked to the crow's nest.

My head was still spinning when I reached the top of the mainmast. The mast was shorter than on the old *Sea Sprite*, so the view was not as good and the bucket was smaller—or I had grown. But the ship moved with a speed unlike anything the previous one could have managed, and the chill wind in my face was refreshing indeed.

I took it all in: the smell of the air and the feel of the wind; the view of the crew moving about, a perfectly choreographed dance; the shining sun reflected off the sea, and off the—

"Iceberg! Ahead, off the port bow!" I yelled.

We cut sharply, avoiding the massive chunk of floating ice. And the next, and the next, and on and on, huge bergs drifting down from the Sea of Moving Ice. The thaw had dislodged them from their winter rest, but it was not warm enough to melt them. It would be a dangerous journey indeed. I hoped it would be worth it.

My mind wandered back to the previous summer. I had seen only snippets of actual combat on that journey, had watched much of it from a porthole in the hold of the ship, until a particularly nasty troll pirate had climbed aboard. I had defended the ship from the troll and had eventually knocked the foul thing from the boat.

After the fight, Captain Deudermont had offered me a place on his crew, citing my courage. But it had not been courage, it had been self-preservation that drove me. The troll had found me, and would have killed me had I not fought back. I looked down at my scar. That was the end result of my so-called courage.

And I was leading the crew into trouble yet again. We were following a pirate ship—all because of me, because the crew had agreed to help me. I remembered Tasso, a sailor aboard *Sea Sprite* during the other fight. He had been wounded, and had died in the bed next to mine. More could die because of me and my selfishness, I knew. Would Lucky fall, or Tonnid, or even Captain Deudermont?

I shook the thought from my head. This time would be different, I vowed. We would capture Chrysaor and force him to tell us where the stone was. And if anyone died in the trying, it would be me.

"Look alive, Maimun!" I caught sight of Lucky down below hefting a coil of rope over his shoulder. He looked up at me, his eyes shaded from the sun. "Why the long face? Ye're going to get yer pirate after all!"

"Seems so!" I called out. "I can't thank you enough!"

"How's about you join me and Tonnid in a game of cards later on then, eh? We got a few chores we wouldn't mind putting on the table for a lucky fellar like yerself." Lucky's face broke out into a wide grin.

I nodded and laughed along with him. And that was all the confirmation I needed that we were on the right path after all.

For seven long days we followed *Lady Luck*, each colder than the last. The ship had turned due west, then northwest, and was heading out into open water far, far from shore. We never caught sight of her, but Robillard kept his magical eyes upon her.

He also kept his eyes on the northern storm, which hit Waterdeep right on schedule, bringing nearly three feet of snow. Even if we had wanted to turn back, we couldn't. The harbor was sealed shut.

I remembered the voyage from Baldur's Gate to Waterdeep: the constant tacking, the long nights in fear of a berg, the cold so deep it felt as if I'd never feel warmth again.

Each day, I took my post in the crow's nest. The biting wind was brutal. I wrapped Perrault's cloak around me, but it wasn't the magic that kept me warm. I leaned into that frigid wind. I thought of what might lie at the end of the journey, and the cold never touched me.

On the seventh day out from Waterdeep, I sighted a dark line of clouds, due west and moving toward us.

"Storm! Dark clouds ahead, due west!" I called down.

Everyone abovedecks halted whatever they were doing. Then a moment later, they began again, working more furiously than ever.

"Hold course," Deudermont called out.

Right into the storm, I thought. The man who had initially refused to sail out of port for fear of a winter storm, was ordering us to hold course directly into one.

"What do you see, Maimun?" Deudermont yelled.

"No bergs ahead, just the storm, sir," I called. How had Robillard not scryed it? Or perhaps he had, but he and the captain had kept it secret from the crew? The captain would have no reason to conceal something like that, would he?

"Just the storm? Are you sure?" I got the distinct feeling he knew something I did not.

I peered out into the distance scanning the horizon in all directions. Nothing north, nothing south, nothing east, a storm west . . .

A storm, with a white spot on it. A growing white spot. Sails.

"Sail ho! Due west, and it looks like she's closing!"

"Very good," the captain called. "Can you make her heading?"

"Looks like she's sailing right at us, sir."

"Very good. Mister Lucky?"

"Oh, right," Lucky, who was standing beside the captain, said. "All hands make ready for battle!"

CHAPTER 47

WHOOSH!

The catapult on *Sea Sprite's* foredeck released, throwing a ceramic bucket of burning pitch high into the air, spinning end over end, to splash into the water three hundred yards short of *Lady Luck*.

A ranging shot. And a close one.

I looked across the water to the fast-approaching ship, to the bustle of activity on deck, and the single spot of yellow in the crow's nest. Somehow I knew Joen sat there with her hair cropped short, her piercing green eyes, and her figure so tall for her age. And I knew she looked back at me. She would have turned thirteen, I knew; her birthday was in the winter.

As *Lady Luck* drew closer, our catapult sent another bucket of burning pitch into the sky. I watched its arc, a trail of red on the black clouds of the approaching storm. It seemed to drift on the air, in defiance of gravity, moving oh so slowly toward its target.

Oh so slowly, toward *Lady Luck's* mainmast.

Toward *Lady Luck's* crow's nest.

My eyes widened in terror. Joen ducked down into the crow's nest.

The flaming bucket skipped off the mast barely four feet above her, sending the thing swaying. But the ceramic did not break, and the whole bucket plummeted through the furled rigging into the water below. Joen poked her head up again, her head bobbing up and down. Sobbing?

No, laughing. Thirteen and fearless. That was Joen.

I scanned *Lady Luck's* deck. She had no catapult, and it seemed to me that we would get many more shots before the ships closed the last few hundred yards. But a pirate stood on the forward deck, waving his arms in tiny circles, chanting. An odd time to be singing and dancing, I thought.

Crack! I whipped back to look at our foredeck. A massive fireball burst directly over our own catapult. The whole catapult crew dropped to the deck. Small fires sprang up all around them, and fingers of flame reached out for the stacked buckets of pitch.

The crew rose up and immediately began to scramble, pails of water in hand. I tried not to imagine what would happen if the fire reached the pile of pitch before they could extinguish it. The blaze of fire, the screams of pain, the smell of burning flesh . . .

"They've got a wizard!" I called down. "Forward deck, wearing pirate clothes." A bolt of lightning arced out from the hands of the wizard. "He's casting a sp—"

The lighting struck the side of the crow's nest, splintered right through the wood, and crashed into me. Energy jolted through my chest, and I flew up into the air.

I squeezed my eyes shut and held my breath, waiting to plummet onto the deck below.

But a second later, I realized, I was not falling.

I opened my eyes.

I was drifting, as light as a feather. I looked at my hand and caught a glimpse of the gold band circling my finger. I remembered gliding down from the wall in Baldur's Gate, Perrault's hand in my own. He had given me the magical ring then, but I had completely forgotten I still wore it.

The deck drifted up to meet me, slowly, dreamlike.

From below, I heard several crewmen gasp. At first I thought they were merely astonished by my gentle fall. Then I looked down.

The ship was sailing out from under me. I would not land on the deck, but in the frigid ocean beyond!

I snatched my stiletto from my belt. I thrust it into the sail, or what little of the canvas was exposed. My fine dagger cut through the sail as if it were paper. I heard a few lines snap. But my momentum slowed.

At last I came to a stop, dangling ten feet above the deck.

The wind picked up. The crew scrambled around the deck below me.

"Help!" I called out weakly. But my words were lost in the growing storm.

A fine white powder of snow churned all around me. I peered through the tear in the sail at *Lady Luck*'s forward deck, my heart in my throat. The wizard who had attacked me had disappeared. But her captain, Chrysaor, still held fast to the wheel. Snow settled on the crossbeams of her rigging, on her rails, on Chrysaor's violet hat. Then, without warning or any apparent reason, Chrysaor flung his hands from the wheel and stepped back. I took in a sharp breath. He mounted the forward deck railing. For a moment he stood there, riding the storm, his blue-skinned face lifted into the wind, his ocean white hair whipping out behind him. He turned to flash me a wicked grin. And then, he plunged into the sea.

"No!" I called out. "Captain! Chrysaor is abandoning his ship!" I looked down at our own deck just as Captain Deudermont's hat blew off, lost to the storm.

The sky grew dark. The sail I clung to whipped around, as if it were trying to buffet me loose. My arm ached. I could not hold on much longer. No one was coming to help me.

I pulled my dagger free, kicking off from the sail.

I landed hard, sending numbing pain coursing up my left leg.

As soon as I hit the deck, the storm unleashed its full fury. The air was thick with snow, and sleet blew sidelong across the deck. The wind swirled. Those few sails that were open threatened to tear from their rigging. But they could not catch and harness the wind, and we did not move. The other ship was completely obscured. The crew slipped and slid, and I slid with them, finding my balance impossible to keep on the slick deck in the tossing seas.

Only Captain Deudermont held his ground, his grip firm on the wheel.

At last I pulled myself up to the railing and glanced down at the rolling ocean. But I could see nothing but white-capped waves. Chrysaor was gone, racing to safety beneath the sea.

Suddenly the deck beneath my feet heaved. The whole ship rose into the air, caught on a huge swell. The water carried us with it, carried us faster than the wind ever had.

A voice cried out over the wind—Lucky's voice. "Captain! She's—" The rest of his warning was garbled in the wind.

But his meaning became clear a second later, as *Lady Luck* came racing up alongside *Sea Sprite*, her deck barely ten feet from ours.

With a colossal bang, her mainmast and ours collided.

Both ships stopped in their tracks.

I, however, did not. Nor did the rest of the crew.

We flew across the deck. I crashed into a rolling barrel and bumped into Lucky before I finally came to rest at the forward deck.

The snow cleared just long enough to reveal Captain Deudermont, standing firm and tall at the helm, holding his sword high. The wind died just enough to hear his voice calling out to us.

"To arms," he cried, "and to the rail! To the fight!"

"To arms!" echoed Lucky, scrambling to his feet.

CHAPTER 48

I WATCHED AS THE MEN OF *SEA SPRITE* ROSE UP UNSTEADILY AROUND ME. THEY SHOOK OFF their bumps and bruises. They drew their weapons.

Then they raced to the pirate ship's rail.

We had trained hard the last few months, in swordplay and in tactics. But in the span of that last second before the throng of pirates crashed into the crew, all that training disappeared.

The fight descended into chaos.

I huddled behind an overturned barrel. I had promised the captain that I would stay out of the fighting. And I meant to hold fast to that vow. After all, with my leg aching and my still clumsy swordwork, what good could I possibly do?

Sounds of steel on steel echoed across the water, with battle cries turning fast to howls of pain.

The first time a cry of pain ripped through the air, I found my breath hard to come by. I watched as the battle lines formed and broke, as the throng surged toward the rail, then halted and pushed back the other way. I watched as the snow piled up on the deck, listened as the wood of the tangled ships creaked and groaned against the strain, against the wind.

I watched in horror as the snow piles turned red.

I peered around the barrel to see a man go tumbling over the rail, screaming all the way into the icy water. I could not tell if it was one of ours or one of theirs.

I wedged myself farther behind the barrel and hugged my knees. I had brought all of it about, I reminded myself. I had started the voyage. But here I was, hiding, while men died for me. I could hold back no longer.

Gathering all my courage, I pushed back the barrel and stood up. I took a step, then another, then broke into a run across the slick deck. I would leap the rail, join the fray. I flicked my dagger into a long blade.

And then I saw her.

Around the side of the melee, a tiny figure moved: a girl with hair the color of wheat and the purest green eyes. She held a dagger in each hand, and walked like a warrior, stepping lightly and in perfect balance.

And then she saw me.

Twenty yards separated us, but I felt as if we were standing face to face. Her expression was as cold as the storm, her teeth gritted, and her jaw set.

Joen crossed the deck at a run, leaping the rail in a single, graceful leap, landing but a few yards in front of me. The wind picked up again, drowning out the sounds of combat. The snow came down faster, obscuring the battle still raging around us.

I held up my arms, sword out wide, trying to indicate that I meant no harm. Joen rushed toward me, her arms tight to her body. For a moment I thought she was going to embrace me.

Instead, she punched out with the pommel of the dagger. It slammed me in the forehead and sent me reeling. I fell and skidded halfway across the deck.

I lifted my sword and looked up, expecting her to be right atop me. I rose unsteadily to my feet, my weapon at the ready.

"Never drop your guard in a fight, eh?" she said, stalking toward me. "That's a free lesson for you. The next one's gonna cost you, got it?"

I brought my sword up, touching the blade to my forehead right where her blow had landed, then snapping it back down in mock salute. "So you have more lessons for me, then?" I quipped, settling into the stance the Waterdeep swordmasters had taught me.

"Many more, kid," she promised, spitting the last word like an insult.

I knew she was angry at me so I decided to allow her the first attacks until her rage played itself out.

Left, right, left, she slashed with her daggers, aiming not for me but for my blade. She meant to knock my sword out of line—her eight-inch daggers would not reach me if she could not move her body past my sword.

With a simple twist of my wrist, I kept my sword in line with her through each contact. The numbness in my left side was almost a memory. The quality of my swordplay surprised even me.

"Feeling better yet?" I asked sarcastically.

"You're still standing."

"So that's a yes?"

She snarled and repeated her attack. If she meant to kill me, she surely could have in that initial strike. But neither was she dropping her weapons or her guard. My pulse quickened. Perhaps she did mean to kill me after all.

Left, right, left; but that time, as the second left hit my blade, she took a quick step to her left and brought her right-hand dagger close to her chest. As I twisted the blade in, trying to keep her at bay, she stepped toward me. I had not reacted quickly enough to her step, and the angle was wrong. When I tried to compensate, to angle my sword farther in toward her, I merely hit her right-hand dagger.

She shuffled toward me, quickstepping in and disengaging her left dagger at the same time. I tried to pull my sword in, to cut off her line of attack, but she pushed with her right dagger, and I could not maneuver my much longer sword into a good position.

She thrust out with her left hand, blade tip leading, and all I could do was fall back to my left and skip away. I felt the rush of air as the dagger swept past my head, felt the tiny prick of pain, felt the little drop of warm liquid dripping from the nick on my ear.

I hopped back a few steps, settling again into my defensive pose; again, she did not press.

"I suppose I'm feeling a bit better now," she said. Her eyes were still icy cold as she crept forward, her daggers at the ready.

"You're about to feel a lot worse," I said.

I would not let her lead again. As she approached, I thrust out, once, twice, and again, short jabs that did not come close to hitting the mark. But neither did she get close enough to attack me.

But I could keep her at bay for only so long like that. My sword was light, but still heavier than her daggers. I was expending more energy than she, and I would surely tire faster.

She knew it too, and she allowed me my simple attack routines.

I jabbed again, a short stab from my elbow, my body staying still and in balance. Joen shifted her weight, staying out of my reach, her daggers at the ready but a parry not necessary. I started to repeat the motion, but planned to push off with my back leg, drop my trailing arm, and fully extend my sword arm. I would reach out fully three feet farther than the short jab, and the whole move would take only a fraction of a second longer. I would catch her completely off guard.

But I hesitated. Could I really hurt her? Could I really kill Joen?

My body reacted when my mind could not, and I did indeed attack, but there was little strength behind my lunge. And Joen was not surprised by the move at all, anyway. She dropped into a crouch, bringing both daggers up in a cross, catching the bottom of my blade and driving it up.

Before I could retract, she pushed off with her legs from her deep crouch directly at me. She kept her right hand up, her dagger holding my sword at bay; her left she thrust forward, tip leading, right for my chest.

I brought my trailing left arm around in desperation, and only through some luck did I manage to contact her thrusting arm and drive it aside.

But she still had a vastly superior position to mine. She brought her right hand in, and though I found my sword free, once again she was far too close for me to use it effectively.

Instead, I bulled ahead before she could line up her strikes. I shoved my left forearm into her chest and pushed off with all my might.

She brought both her daggers in from the sides. I felt them hit me, but she was falling backwards and there was no strength in the swings. They did not even cut through my tunic.

She let herself fall, rolling backwards with perfect grace, then coming to her feet and skipping back another step, out of my reach once more.

I took a breath. "You fight well," I said.

"That makes one of us."

"For a girl," I finished.

"Still just one of us."

I growled and took a step forward, ready to strike, but stopped short. "Why are you doing this?" I asked. "Are you really trying to kill me?"

She opened her mouth as if to speak, then closed it, shaking her head.

"Answer—" Before I could finish, she rushed forward again. She swung her arms as one, both blades moving at the same time, in the same direction, barely an inch apart. As she swung her swords, she moved her body the opposite direction. If she hit my blade, she would drive it away from herself, and she would be upon me in an instant.

I stepped back furiously, trying to keep her weaving dance in front of me, trying to keep my sword between us.

I managed five steps, then my rear foot hit something solid.

The rail. I had run out of room. I had no retreat; and I did not know how to defend her attack.

So I didn't try. I swept my sword out, horizontal at eye level, the fine saber edge leading. Joen ducked, bringing her blades up to deflect and ensnare my sword.

But the slash was only a feint. The real attack was my body. I pushed off from the rail with all my might, colliding with her and driving her backward. I kept my legs pumping, kept pushing, preventing her from bringing her daggers to bear.

I pressed her straight back, across the deck, into the base of the mainmast. We crashed into the solid wood hard. I felt her breath leave her body. The daggers fell from her limp hands.

I stumbled back a step, dazed. Joen stayed with me, wrapping her arms around me for balance.

She buried her head in my shoulder, coughing and crying. I could not tell if the tears were from physical pain or some emotion.

I did not ask.

All I could do was let my own sword fall from my hand, and wrap my arms around her, holding her tight.

"I'm sorry," she whispered. "I was going to . . . I wanted to . . . I'm sorry."

"It's all right," I said. "I forgive you."

CHAPTER 49

THE BLIZZARD GREW WORSE. THE WIND SWIRLED AND CAUGHT THE SAILS OF THE TWO ships, twisting them one way or the other. Their fouled riggings groaned in protest.

Waves pulled the ships apart then slammed them back together again and again, deck to deck, with a great jarring impact and a crash that resounded like thunder.

Most of the crew of both ships were aboard *Lady Luck.* The pirate crew—outnumbered, captainless, facing a better armed and better trained crew—had surrendered, but the crew of *Sea Sprite* did not dare cross back to their own ship in that weather. Nor did anyone dare climb the masts to untangle the lines. Aboard *Lady Luck,* all of the men of both crews vanished belowdecks, evidently intending to ride out the storm in warmer quarters. Aboard *Sea Sprite,* two remained above.

Joen had settled in next to me. The pair of us rested against the mainmast, Perrault's magical cloak wrapped around us. While I wore it, the cloak never seemed especially large; it did not billow nor drag on the ground. But covering myself and Joen it seemed more a blanket than a cloak, and it wrapped around us both completely, a warm cocoon against the wind and the blowing snow.

Our ship looked terrible. The rail was broken in many places. Scorch marks scarred the deck near the catapult and on the mainmast. And our rigging was hopelessly tangled with that of the ship across the narrow stretch of water. But *Lady Luck* looked even worse. She listed steeply toward our portside as wave after wave rolled beneath her.

Joen's breathing had steadied, then slowed. At first it had frightened me, but when she nestled her head into my shoulder and snored loudly, I realized she had simply drifted off to sleep. I would have gladly followed her, but I told myself that if we both slept, I would lose my grip on the hem of the cloak, and the cloak would fall wide open to the furious elements. So I stayed awake, one hand holding the cloak closed, the other gripping, through the cloak's fabric, a rope tied around the mast. Joen could have her rest, I decided. I would protect her while she slept.

Besides, I had no idea where I would put my hands if I did not have something useful to do with them. I flushed red and shifted uncomfortably.

Joen stirred and looked up at me. Even in the fading light her eyes shone, emeralds boring into me. She could see what I was thinking, I knew it. She was about to toss off the cloak and storm off the deck.

But she did not. She merely gave me a curious smile, and wrapped her arms around my waist. Her arms were thin but strong, and her grip was tight as she pulled herself closer. She felt warm beside me, and I was grateful for it. I let go of the rope on the mast and put my arm around her shoulders, my hand resting awkwardly against her side. She did not seem to mind. She put her head down again on my shoulder, and a few moments later she was fast asleep.

I know not how long I stayed awake. Even as I dozed my dreams were filled with images of the here and now. The storm blew snow across the deck, falling in piles only to be shaken off again. The wind howled, and wood crashed against wood. And screams—real or imagined—echoed across the waves. Joen slept on my shoulder, her arms wrapped around me.

.:⌒:.

When I woke in the morning, it took me a good while to realize that I was indeed awake, and that the pair of polished black boots on the deck in front of me were indeed real.

"Look alive, sailors," Captain Deudermont said.

Joen and I both started. She jumped to her feet. But my cloak caught my ankles as I rose, and I tumbled back to the deck.

At that precise moment, the ship gave a mighty lurch. I skidded toward the broken rail on our starboard side, nearest *Lady Luck*. I could see a great hole in her hull just at the water line. I thought I saw a flicker of movement beyond the hole, but could not discern what it was before another wave rolled up against her, covering the hole. *Sea Sprite* gave another lurch beneath me. I grasped at the planks of the deck to prevent myself from sliding yet farther.

One man stood on *Lady Luck*'s rail—quite literally. Robillard rode the rail itself, seeming unfazed by the ship's sharp motion. He simply went about his business, waving his hands in some arcane gesture, mumbling some chant, and tossing what looked like blue ropes toward *Sea Sprite*.

The ropes stretched above the water and grabbed *Sea Sprite*'s rail. Some tied themselves there. Some grabbed the already-set lines and tied across. A net of sorts formed before my eyes.

Behind me, Captain Deudermont tapped his foot. I allowed myself to skid all the way to the rail. There I leaned against it to stand, and walked unsteadily across the deck.

I took my place beside Joen, who stood at attention in front of the man who was not her captain.

"You'll need better balance than that, Maimun, if you want to be a sailor," Captain Deudermont said.

"Yes, sir. Sorry, sir," I mumbled.

"As soon as Robillard has finished his work, you're going up the mast. We need to get untangled."

I swallowed. "Yes, sir. But why now?" Though the storm had given up much of its rage in the night, the winds still swirled around us. The last thing I wanted to do was to climb back up the mast. I pointed to the dark clouds above us. "Why not wait for the storm to blow out?"

Joen gave me a startled look, but only for a second; clearly, she did not think it wise to question the captain's orders.

I thought I caught a little smile flash over Deudermont's face. But when he spoke, he looked directly at Joen.

"*Lady Luck* is sinking," he said. Joen did not flinch. "We need to untangle, or she'll take us down with her."

"Yes, sir," I said for the third time.

"And you," he said, addressing Joen. "Did I not see you in the crow's nest aboard the other ship?"

"The gull's nest, aye, sir. That's my post, eh?"

I felt a strange elation climbing in my chest. Deudermont was sending Joen up the mast with me! My fear vanished. I knew there would be a lot of tough work. I knew there would be the ever-present danger of a fall, a danger made more keen by the blowing wind and the swaying of the ships. But working near Joen was worth any danger.

"Well then," the captain said to me, "you have another job before you climb the mast."

I hesitated a second, sorting out Deudermont's words. "I do, sir?" I asked.

"Yes. First you'll escort this young woman to our brig."

"But, sir, she's not a pirate," I said.

"And you'll not question your orders. Now get to it." With that, the captain turned and walked away.

Beside me, Joen chuckled. "Don't look so stunned, eh? Soon as he recognized me, I knew I'd be going below. Be a fool to think anything else."

"Well, I'm a fool then," I muttered.

She just laughed. "Oi, course you're a fool. Probably thought he'd be sending me up into the rigging with you, didn't you? Don't be a disobedient fool, though, he won't much like that, will he?" She started to walk to the hatch that led down to the hold, still chuckling.

I followed a few paces behind her.

"Oi, ain't you supposed to be escorting me to the brig?" she asked, looking over her shoulder at me.

"Ain't that what I'm doing, eh?" I replied, doing my best to imitate her accent. I was so happy to have her here, safe aboard *Sea Sprite*, that I couldn't help but joke a little.

"Then why am I walking in front?"

"Prisoners always walk in front," I quipped.

"Oh, yeah, right, so they can't stab the guard in the back, eh? You figure I'm gonna try and stab you?" She laughed, but her laugh turned into a painful cough. She stopped walking and doubled over, clutching at her chest.

"I think you already tried to stab me," I said. "And you got that cough instead."

Joen glared up at me, her eyes burning behind the veil of her hair. "That ain't funny," she said, her voice stern.

"It wasn't so funny when you cut my ear, either." I said, matching her tone.

Slowly she straightened, standing tall and proud, not looking away. The intensity of her stare was intimidating, and it was all I could do to maintain eye contact. But I would not look away.

"Prisoners walk in front," I growled, motioning toward the hatch.

She did not say another word all the way to the brig.

CHAPTER 50

ALF A DOZEN OF US TOOK TO THE MASTS A SHORT WHILE LATER. THREE *SEA SPRITE* sailors accustomed to working in the rigging climbed up from each deck. There was almost no activity beneath us. Only Robillard stood on deck, or rather sat, looking quite comfortable on the sterncastle of *Lady Luck*, his feet dangling over the rail. His magical net stretched between the two ships. It looked solid despite the fact that it was formed of what appeared to be tendrils of blue light. As the ships pulled apart, the net stretched, but the gaps did not seem to grow. As the ships crashed together once again, the net swelled upward, as if a breeze from below had caught a bit of fabric and made it billow. There was no way for someone to fall through, I hoped.

Soon after we had reached the fouled riggings, it seemed the gods decided we should not be allowed to escape our fates.

The wind blew steadily and with such force that it was all I could do to maintain a grip on the ropes. Up here, so high above the deck, the air was much colder, and with the wind whipping about there was no way I could keep Perrault's cloak wrapped around me. I felt the stinging burn of the cold and the numbness of frostbite creeping into my fingertips. It was a welcome relief from the other numbness, which had nearly disappeared.

I did not complain. Instead I let my anger warm me. At first it was simply a vague sense of anger, a hatred of the way things had been for as long as I could remember. But then my anger found focus. First at Asbeel, who had stolen so much from me; then at Chrysaor, the blue-skinned pirate captain, who had led me so far astray only to disappear. Then at Deudermont, my captain, who had locked up Joen when he should have been sending her up here to work with me.

And there my anger found a home: Joen.

She had attacked me, had cut my ear. It still stung quite a bit, especially in the cold. Then she had called me a fool, and refused my orders. And that was just since sunrise!

I lay my torso down on a thin crossbeam. My feet braced against the mast, and my arms reached out for a tangle of rigging. As *Lady Luck* was sinking anyway, our orders were not so much to untangle the ships, as to free *Sea Sprite* from the burden of the crippled vessel. At each point of entanglement, I would seek the lines that belonged to the pirate vessel and cut them loose, then move on to the next point I could reach.

The whole journey had been for Joen, I realized. I had told myself I was seeking the stone, but it was a lie. I had never really believed we'd get any information from Chrysaor.

I should have gone with Drizzt to see Malchor Harpell. He would have pointed me in the right direction.

My hand snaked down a line of rigging from *Lady Luck*.

But instead I had followed Joen out to sea, to save her from the pirate crew she had willingly joined. And after I had saved her, all she could do was laugh at me and call me a fool.

I sliced through the rigging with such force, I nearly sent my dagger down with the falling rope. Again, I located a line, and again I tore through it. At each line I found a new reason to vent my rage.

I was still lying on the thin wooden crossbeams, when I felt something graze the back of my head. It felt like someone wearing a heavy cloak had walked past me, and the cloak had brushed against me. My heart beat a little faster.

I tried to turn, but I couldn't twist around from my already-precarious position without risking a fall. So instead I had to pull myself back to the mast, then straighten up. In the time it took me to reestablish myself, whatever had hit me had disappeared.

It must have been a loose line, I forced myself to think. Again I moved out along the beam, making sure my position was more secure, and I could turn around if needed. Sure enough, after a minute I felt something. It was not so much contact as something rushing past my head.

I turned quickly, but saw nothing.

I squinted. A tiny black shape spiraled in the distance. But it remained indistinct, blurred by the blowing snow, its dark shape uncertain against the equally dark midday sky. It was too small to be Asbeel. I let out a breath I didn't know I had been holding.

I watched the shape move, graceful and smooth. It seemed equally at home riding a gust of wind or cutting right through one. The air suddenly cleared, the storm giving us a reprieve, and the speck flew back to the mast.

I gasped and very nearly lost my perch. A raven!

I knew it could be no ordinary raven, for no ordinary bird would brave the weather, and a raven would never be so far out at sea.

The bird alighted on the crossbeam in front of me and stared into my eyes. It was the same bird I had seen in Memnon. What on Toril was it doing here?

Its chest puffed out proudly, the bird opened its beak.

And it cawed. It raised its head and gave a slight nod—a truly odd thing to see a bird do. Then it took off, its wings beating hard, cutting through the snow to the southeast.

The raven disappeared from sight for a minute, then circled back in, landing again in the same spot. It let out a caw and took off again, repeating the circle.

I peered off after it, trying to track its flight, trying to see what the bird so obviously wanted to show me. But I saw nothing but swirling sleet and darkness.

Darkness . . .

"Land ahead!" I screamed as loudly as I could. But my words were lost in the storm. I waved my arms, trying to signal the captain, or Robillard, or anyone below, but I was invisible in the blizzard.

I scurried to the mast, shimmying along the rigging. I had to climb down and warn Deudermont.

But I was not fast enough.

With a tremendous crash, *Sea Sprite* slammed into the beach.

I grasped with frozen hands for a rope, a beam, anything. The grinding noise of wood splintering on rock echoed even above the wind. My hands tangled in a pair of lines, and I regained my balance. I withdrew my hand to find blood on my forearm. The rope had cut me, but thankfully it was not deep.

Then *Lady Luck* hit us. The jarring impact sent me spinning over the rigging and down toward the choppy sea.

But as before, I drifted downward—like a feather on a light breeze. I wafted clear of the wreckage, until I landed with a roll on the beach.

The sand was soaked, but no snow had accumulated. Numerous jagged rocks lined the shore. *Sea Sprite* had run aground against several of the rocks, I saw, but she had mostly hit sand and plowed forward. Half her hull was beyond the water line.

Lady Luck had not been so fortunate. As far as I could tell, she had crashed against *Sea Sprite,* then bounced off some rocks. The waves were pulling her back out to sea, dragging *Sea Sprite* along with her, where they would both surely sink.

I stumbled to my feet, dizzy but unhurt, just as the exodus began. Men on *Sea Sprite* threw down lines and climbed onto the beach. Those on *Lady Luck* simply jumped into the icy water and swam.

Lady Luck's hull breach had grown, and apparently had torn open the brig, for the pirate crew were among those swimming most desperately—battling waves and narrowly avoiding the rocks.

I saw Lucky and Captain Deudermont walking down the beach. I breathed a sigh of relief. Tonnid was climbing down a line from *Sea Sprite*.

But there was one person missing. Apparently *Sea Sprite*'s jail had not broken, and no one had thought to open it.

I ran to the ship. *Sea Sprite* listed badly to port as she slid backward into the open sea. Tonnid was just dropping off the line as I started to climb up. He mumbled something at me as I approached. But I did not reply. I simply clambered right past him and pulled myself up onto the deck.

The mainmast was leaning dangerously, ripping up planks from the deck. It looked as if it could fall into the water at any moment. The deck was slick with sleet. I ran as fast as I could manage, slipping often but always bouncing right back up to my feet.

I reached the hatch that led below and threw it open. I raced down the ladder, through the hold, fighting against the ship's list, feeling the slide, knowing I was nearly out of time.

Joen sat patiently, calmly, on the brig floor. Her legs were crossed, her head rested on her hand, her elbow on her knee. She was the only person in the brig.

"You came back for me," she said quietly when I skidded to a halt at the iron-barred door of the cell. She made no attempt to rise though.

"Of course I did."

She offered the slightest smile and rose slowly to her feet. "Took you long enough, eh?"

"Well, you know, it's kind of a long walk from the beach," I said, scanning the wall where the cell keys would normally hang. The pegs were all empty. "We ran aground, didn't you notice?"

"Not much of a view from here," she said. "So you got off the ship, then got back on? Not very efficient, are you?"

"I got thrown off the ship, actually," I said. I dropped to my knees and scrabbled around on the ground, looking for where the keys might have rolled.

"What, your captain kicked you off? Oi, what did you do to him, then?" she said laughing, and she leaned against the bars. I could feel her watching my increasingly desperate movements.

"No, I mean, literally thrown off the ship. When we ran aground." There was no sign of the keys. A few crates were piled against the port wall; by their haphazard arrangement I could see that they had fallen there in the crash.

"So how're you alive, then? Seems that'd be a long way to fall."

"There's a lot about me you don't know," I said. "I have powers you can't even fathom."

She laughed. "More likely you landed in the mud, eh? I bet you sank in good and deep, and they had to pull you out by the hair!"

"Then I'd be covered in mud, wouldn't I?" I snapped, and she fell silent. I reached behind the crates, hoping the keys had tumbled there—and I found open air and cold, blowing wind. I pulled back, startled.

"Something wrong?" Joen asked. For the first time there was a note of trepidation in her voice.

I couldn't answer. I just pushed against the crates, shoving them roughly out of the way and revealing a small but not insignificant hole in the wall, leading directly out into the storm.

I turned back to Joen. Her face was ashen, her eyes wide. Without a word, she sat back down, put one elbow on one knee and dropped her head onto her hand.

The ship continued to list, but I hardly felt it. I lost my balance and slipped to the floor, but I made no effort to right myself. My mind whirled, searching for an answer, for a way to open the cell without the key. But the brig was built solidly, and there was no way we could pry open the door. I didn't know how to pick a lock, and I did not have the necessary tools anyway.

The keys had fallen through the hole in the wall, I was sure of it. But there was no similar hole on the other side, within the prison, through which Joen could escape.

I looked back at Joen. I wanted to say something, but the words sounded hollow in my head before they ever reached my mouth.

With a jerk, *Sea Sprite* slid further backward, and I could feel the deck beneath my feet heaving in the high surf. Soon we would be out on the open sea. *Lady Luck* would not stay afloat much longer, and we would go down with her.

Joen didn't say anything, she just stared, her emerald eyes piercing the dim light. I thought she would be angry with me, thought she deserved to be angry with me. We had parted in anger, and I had done nothing to apologize.

But there was no anger in her eyes. "Leave me," she said, "before it's too late."

I rose unsteadily. Could I abandon her to a watery fate? Could I leave her to die?

I looked at her again, long and hard, and sat back down.

Behind me, the door crashed open. I leaped to my feet and turned to see the most beautiful sight imaginable.

"What're ye doin', Maimun?" said Tonnid. "Ship's gotta be abandoned, ye know?"

My mouth hung open, as dry as the Calim desert. So instead I pointed at Joen who had once again lifted her head from her hand and was slowly rising to her feet.

"Oh, uh," Tonnid stammered. "Well, that ain't good, is it?"

I started to answer, but Joen spoke first. "That'd depend on your perspective, eh?" There was a sharpness, a bitterness, in her voice.

"Who'd think it good ye're stuck in the cage?" Tonnid asked, patting himself all over with his hands. I thought he looked like he was trying to pat out some invisible flames, like Joen's words had somehow burned him.

"Oh, I don't know, maybe the one who put me here, eh?" Joen said.

"How can you say that!" I yelled. "I was following orders! I didn't want to lock you up!"

Joen turned to look at me, as if for the first time. "Oi, I wasn't talking about you, then. I meant your bloody captain, eh? I done nothing wrong, and he throws me in here like, like a . . ."

"Like a pirate," all three of us said at the same time.

"Look, maybe—" I began.

Tonnid gave a sudden shout. He was striding to the door, his hand held aloft, holding something small. Holding a key.

"Where did you get that, Tin?" I asked, my voice barely a whisper.

"Always have a backup plan, ye know? Captain said I'd be the one he could trust with the spare, ye get it? In case something happens to the key."

Joen said what we both were thinking. "In case what happened, exactly?"

"Oh, I dunno, in case th' ship gets damaged, and the key falls out a hole in the wall, or something like that," he answered sarcastically. The cleverness of his joke astounded me; the one we called Tin-head had always been thought of as a decent man, and a good sailor, but never a particularly sharp thinker.

Of course, I could hardly make comparisons between me, the kid who had tried to free someone from the brig without a plan at all, and Tonnid, the man who had thought to bring a key.

The key clicked in the lock. The door fell open into the cage with a loud bang. The ship gave a mighty lurch.

And we three sailors ran for the deck.

CHAPTER 51

J OEN, TONNID, AND I CLEARED THE HATCH NOT A MOMENT TOO SOON.
Sea Sprite's teetering mast gave a final creak and ripped from the deck. Lines snapped as the towering pillar toppled sidelong into the water. The deck gave a mighty buck, the force that had held it at such a deep list being relieved. Like a pendulum it rocked back and forth, back and forth, all the while drifting out on the waves with the outgoing tide. And bringing us with it.

I ran across the deck, trying hard to keep my balance on the slick wood. Joen and Tonnid shambled along behind me. After many stumbles I reached the rail.

Lady Luck had sunk almost fully beneath the waves beside us. Only her sterncastle and her masts poked above the water, the fouled rigging still pulling *Sea Sprite* out to sea. Our own ship had not completely cleared the beach, but it would not be long. The lines which had been dropped to the beach dangled in the water.

I grasped one and swung a leg over the rail, but stopped halfway, stunned by the scene below.

On the beach, the crews of the two ships had divided and were facing each other, their weapons drawn. On one side, the crew of *Sea Sprite* stood in a fighting formation, their swords raised. On the other side, the crew of *Lady Luck*, sodden from their swim, held rocks, broken planks of wood, and whatever other makeshift weapons they had picked up on the beach. They stood clumped together, shivering, with no sort of battle formation and no captain to guide their battle. What appeared to be an attempt to create a campfire sat in front of them. But it remained unlit.

The crew of *Sea Sprite* advanced slowly, deliberately. I heard Captain Deudermont's voice. I could not hear the words, but I knew it would be a call to battle. It was with some surprise that I noted *Lady Luck's* sailors bristling, moving forward, their primitive clubs at the ready.

"Why do they not throw down arms?" I asked Joen as she joined me at the rail.

She paused to take in the scene, then snarled an unintelligible answer and went over the side, landing with a splash.

"Wait!" I cried, leaping over the rail after her. I slipped off the rope but landed smoothly in the water, thanks to Perrault's ring.

Tonnid splashed down beside me. I rose, soaked, sympathizing with the crew of *Lady Luck*. But only for a moment.

Then I saw Joen sprinting off to join the pirates, scooping up a couple of rocks as she went.

I had nearly left her for dead in *Sea Sprite*'s brig just minutes before. I had nearly failed to save her. That would not happen again.

"Wait!" I called, running to the battle lines. "Captain, wait!"

I rushed forward, yelling all the way. Slowly, the sailors on each side saw me, and to a one they stopped in their tracks.

By the time I reached the center of the field, directly in front of Captain Deudermont, over a hundred people—every one of them older than I was, every one of them a more experienced sailor—were staring at me.

But would they listen?

Captain Deudermont's eyes were slit like daggers. "What is it?" he asked, his voice low.

"You have to stop this, Captain," I said.

Captain Deudermont looked very un-captainly in that moment. His clothes were torn and soaked. His face was drawn into a tight scowl, accentuated by a bloody cut on his left cheek. I had seen him angry before, but not such a rage, pure and simple.

"Once again, you dare question my orders," he spat.

I swallowed hard. "I'm sorry, sir, but you cannot do this," I said quietly. "This battle, it's wrong."

His eyes widened. "Wrong?" he said, his voice rising. "This crew destroyed my ship, killed my men, and we are the ones who are wrong? They deserve death, to a one."

The crew around him bristled, but only for a moment. Across the beach, *Lady Luck*'s crew advanced a few menacing steps, brandishing their weapons.

I waved frantically at them to stop. The last thing I wanted was a battle, and I knew one was coming if I did not quickly make my case. I grasped around in my thoughts, searching for a reason Deudermont should not kill all these people.

For a reason Joen should not die.

Joen should not have been among those pirates at all, I knew. She was not like them. And I could not allow her to be killed because of them. But there was no way I could bargain for her life and not the others, not after she had run to them though the battle lines were so clearly drawn.

"We fought them before, and you ordered them captured, not killed." I said at last, trying to keep my voice calm and reasonable. "What's changed?"

"They sank my ship!" Deudermont roared, and the crew of *Sea Sprite* cheered. A great crunch echoed in off the water as if to accentuate his point, as *Sea Sprite* collided with *Lady Luck* once more.

"We sank theirs first," I said, and the pirate crew roared in approval. I shot them a glare to silence them, but they paid me no heed.

"They sail out, pirates looking for plunder, and they attack us and they sink my ship. And we're in the wrong? You're a foolish child, foolish indeed, and I should never have let you on my crew! You're no better than they are, no better than a pirate yourself!"

"*Lady Luck* wasn't a pirate ship. She was a treasure hunter," I said. I felt bolstered by my own words, sure the captain would see my logic. "She was hunting a treasure that belongs to me. And I say we forgive her."

"Not a pirate ship?" Deudermont snarled. "You yourself named their captain as a pirate."

I pointed to the clump of pirates. "But the captain is not among them now."

Deudermont stepped toward me. "I don't care where their captain is. When he ordered the attack on us, his crew became our enemy. Every one of them."

Including Joen. I felt myself deflate, felt my argument falling apart.

Captain Deudermont glared at me. "I will not tolerate any more of this insubordination from you, Mister Maimun." He motioned to the crew assembled beside him, and the one across the beach. "Choose your side."

I stared down at the sand. If only Joen hadn't run from me. We could have stayed out of the fight. No one would have faulted us. Surely Captain Deudermont would have spared Joen's life then.

But she had chosen to side with the pirates to the death. And I was powerless to stop it.

I felt a hand on my shoulder, and at first I thought I was imagining it. I turned to face Joen, standing beside me before the captain.

"Our captain did not order an attack on your ship, sir," she said. Her voice was quiet. "You fired first."

"She's right!" I stared up at him. "The first shot was from our catapult!"

"A warning shot," he replied. "Which your captain did not heed. Your wizard attacked us from your deck. Or did he not count because he isn't here either?" Deudermont was taunting me. I felt my face flush red with hot anger.

"Look, sir," said Joen quite calmly. "I know you're angry. You want revenge. But what good is revenge now? This storm's sunk both our ships."

As she said that, a great form darkened the seaward sky. The hull of our ship, with its mast ripped up and laying on deck, slid ashore with surprisingly little noise.

"Well, it sunk one ship then, eh? The other it just broke and beached." Joen chuckled. She always managed to find the humor in the darkest of situations.

"There's no way your crew could repair your ship after fighting the rest of us," Joen went on. "You've not enough men. And your crew's already injured as it is."

The storm seemed to feel the mood changing. The wind howled a little less loudly; the sleet slowed to an icy drizzle. The dark sky on the edge of the horizon revealed a lighter patch where the sun was trying to poke its light through.

"What are you proposing?" Deudermont asked. The rage had not entirely left his voice, but it had surely lessened. Slowly, his sword arm fell to his side.

"We help you repair your ship, you give us a ride back to Waterdeep, eh?" Joen stepped closer to Deudermont. "No charges, no trial, nothing. We want to go home."

Deudermont was shaking his head. The idea of letting the pirates go surely did not settle well with him. But he could not argue with Joen's logic. He needed every man on the beach. If he did not accept their help, we were all doomed.

The clouds blew off the western horizon just enough to reveal a sliver of golden light. Black forms danced about in the setting sun, birds flying up in the light, near the top of the short hill that formed the center of the island.

With a start, I realized they were ravens. They turned and flew closer, until they landed all as one, on the sand.

My blood ran cold as they formed a circle, their wings touching. All nine stared up at me, directly at me, only at me.

And then they were not ravens.

Where the birds had stood were nine people, each wearing billowing black robes, their faces obscured by shadowmasks.

CHAPTER 52

WE ARE NOT HERE TO HARM YOU," SAID THE MAN CLOSEST TO ME. "WE COME WITH A message. Which is the captain?"

Deudermont did not hesitate, but strode up right before the speaker, unblinking. "I am the captain," he said. "And I am not in the habit of talking to men in masks."

"Talking will not be necessary," the man replied. "Only listening. We have brought you here for a reason."

"Brought us here?" Deudermont said. "We crashed here in a storm!"

"You said you did not want to talk," said the masked man.

"And we agreed with you," said the one to his right.

"The storm brought you here, yes," said the next in line, that one a woman.

"But we controlled the storm," said another man. I was paying more attention to their voices than to their words, listening for a specific voice, the one I had heard in Memnon. The voice of the woman who had stolen the stone from me.

"We have brought you here for a reason," repeated the man who had first spoken, apparently the leader. "You have among you a treasure we must protect."

"What treasure?" Deudermont sounded unconvinced.

"A child."

"No children on my ship."

In unison, the nine robed figures all cocked their heads to the side, a curious expression made all the more odd by the expressionless masks they wore.

"A young man, then," said the leader. He motioned to me. "He led you out here, or for his sake you came. We know you would not dare brave these waters in such weather, Captain."

"We came following another ship," Deudermont said defensively.

"Yes, and now you are both wrecked and trapped here. So let us be done with the fencing. You have the boy. We want the boy. We will not let you leave with him. You may stay as long as you like. But be warned there is not enough food for the lot of you. Or you may leave without him. But he may not leave the island."

Deudermont puffed up his chest. "I am Captain Deudermont of the good ship *Sea Sprite*, commissioned by the Lords of Waterdeep. I do not need your permission to do anything." With that, he spun on his heel and turned his back on the strangers.

"Captain Deudermont, however good your ship may be, she still needs a fair wind. As we have said, we can give or deny that wind." As he finished, the wind gusted once, mightily, the robes of the nine whipping around in fury.

Then, suddenly and completely, it stopped.

The whole of the island seemed to have fallen into silence. The only sound was the waves, lapping gently against the shore. They were peaceful and serene, so unlike the wind-whipped breakers of but moments earlier.

Deudermont slowly turned back to face the robed figures. But he did not look at them. He stared into the distance, as if looking right past them. "Who are you?" he whispered. "And what do you want?"

"We are simply called the Circle," replied the leader. "And we exist, like many of our brother and sister Circles, to maintain the balance of a region. And these past dozen years, the balance of your Sword Coast has been failing. We will keep the boy here, so that balance can be maintained."

Captain Deudermont did not appear to be listening at all; he just continued to stare into the sunset behind the robed man, the leader of the Circle. I knew the captain was angry with me, but I was sure he wouldn't be so cruel as to abandon me to those thieves. Not after everything I'd been through—after everything we'd been through together.

After a long pause, Deudermont turned to his crew, his face calm. "Let's get some fires burning. Dry off, warm up." He put his hand on Joen's shoulder. "Tomorrow we work, pirates and sailors alike. We fix Sea Sprite, and we sail back to Waterdeep." Then he fixed his gaze on me. "Without you."

I stood, my mouth agape, unable to believe what I was hearing. But Captain Deudermont ignored me, and he walked away up the beach.

The pirates cheered as they followed Deudermont. The crew of Sea Sprite slumped after them.

Only one remained.

I stepped toward Joen, my hand reaching out for her.

Her hair fell around her eyes, concealing her expression. After a moment, she turned away from me and followed the rest of the crowd to the shore.

The last sliver of the sun disappeared behind the island, and the mysterious Circle vanished with it, as suddenly and as completely as if they were flames on a candle that had just been blown out.

PART VI

A few moments passed before the pirate noticed I was no longer talking. I stared at him, and he stared back at me.

"Well?" he finally asked.

"I told you not to interrupt me," I said lightly.

"I didn't interrupt ye! Ye just stopped!" he snapped.

I laughed a little; he seemed none too pleased. "I was just testing something," I told him.

"Testing? Whaddya mean?"

"I wanted to see how long you'd wait before interrupting the story."

He snarled and rose to his feet. "I didn't interrupt, ye fool boy. Now quit yer mocking and get on with the tale!"

"Not just yet," I said. "First we have to settle something."

His hand dropped to his sword, and he started to speak, but I cut him off.

"I know you aren't going to kill me. Don't bother with the sword, it's getting old."

"It's getting old, like ye ne'er will," he said. He advanced a step and pulled out his cutlass. "And what makes ye think I ain't gonna gut ye right here?"

"You want to know where the story goes," I said, keeping my eyes fixed on his simmering ones.

"I know where it goes," he said with a half-snarl, half-laugh. "It goes right here, to this li'l cave on this li'l isle."

"You know where it ends," I corrected him. "But you want to know where it goes. You want to know what happens between that island and this one. And if you kill me, you'll never find out."

He stood there, glowering at me, for a long while. I kept my gaze locked with his the whole time, watched as the rage in his eyes died just a little, his stare softened just a bit.

"What did ye wan' to settle, then?" he asked.

I smiled at him; he did not return the gesture. "I need a few things from you if we are to continue. First, I need food."

"Ye've been fed," he snarled.

"Barely, and at your leisure. I want full meals. Second, I want a light. A lantern or a torch, and the means to keep it burning."

He pointed to the torch in the sconce on the wall. "Alright, so I be leaving the torch when I go, an' I get ye something ter eat, an' ye'll finish yer tale?" He did well to mask it, but I heard the slightest hint of relief, of contentment, in his voice. He really did want to hear the rest, and my demands apparently seemed reasonable to him.

But I had one more demand. "Third," I said, "and last, I need your word."

He blinked a few times, apparently not comprehending what I was asking. "Me word on what?"

"That when I finish my story, you will not kill me."

He laughed uproariously, a rolling belly laugh that stretched on for what seemed like minutes. Each time he paused to catch his breath, and opened his mouth to speak, another bout of laughter came pouring out. I half expected some of the other pirates to hear him and come to investigate, but after a few minutes none had arrived, and he finally managed to speak.

"Me word ye can have," he said. "But ye know the score: a word's only as good as the man giving it. An' I ain't a good man!"

"No, you aren't," I said, prompting another burst of laughter. "But Captain Deudermont, he is a good man. And I've seen him break his own word. So I put little value in anyone's word, good or bad."

"Then what do ye want me word fer?" he asked.

"I asked you before not to interrupt me, and you didn't. So you can keep your promises. I'll choose to believe you when you say you won't kill me."

"A bold choice."

"Perhaps," I said, smiling mysteriously. "But I think you'll see how it will pay off—for both of us—in the end."

CHAPTER 53

L IGHTNING FLASHED IN THE SKY OVERHEAD, ACCOMPANIED BY THE THUNDEROUS snores of the crewmen sleeping around the campsite. We had salvaged what we could of the dried foodstuffs from *Sea Sprite*'s hold, and my belly was pleasantly full. I had managed to retrieve my pack from the hold as well, and I tucked it under my head as a makeshift pillow. The night sky was clear, and though the air was still cold, the fire kept me warm, especially with Perrault's magical cloak wrapped tightly around me.

Still, I slept poorly that night. Perrault danced across my vision, sometimes alone, sometimes arm in arm with the woman in the obsidian mask. Dark shapes circled above us—ravens keeping watch over their prize. Again and again flashes of light filled the sky, each illuminating a different scene. I wavered in and out of sleep, and I could not tell what was real and what was dream.

But awake or asleep, I felt the same unease.

None of *Sea Sprite*'s crew would even look at me. They could not bear the guilt, I figured, knowing they were abandoning me. Joen had returned to her crew and slept among them several yards up the shoreline, at a campfire of their own. She had not spoken another word to me, and I did not dare approach her.

Sea Sprite had not even left the island. And already I was all alone.

My eyes flew open. I pulled myself to my feet, and I began walking down the beach.

I didn't know where I would go. But I couldn't stand waiting any longer. Soon the crews would begin to rebuild the ship so they could sail out to sea, without me. I could help with the repairs, perhaps, but would they even want me near them? And even if they did, why should I help them?

I felt my anger rising. It pushed my legs faster, quickened my pace until I broke into a jog.

I skirted the shoreline, just at the water's edge, my bare feet kicking up icy spray with every step. The beach was dotted with small fading campfires, with everyone around them peacefully asleep. I came to the edge of the camp, where flames roared around a large pile of driftwood. I saw Captain Deudermont, Robillard, and a few of *Sea Sprite*'s men, fast asleep.

I ducked my head, hoping none would waken as I passed. I could not bear to look at Deudermont's face, even his sleeping face. My mind rolled through all the interactions I'd had with the captain over the past months: the first meeting, where he had offered me a job on his ship. Calimport, where he had agreed to help me find a certain dark elf. Waterdeep, where he had agreed, against his wishes, to sail into the wintry sea on my hunch.

He had always seemed so genuinely friendly, if a bit distant. I thought I could trust him. But he had betrayed me.

Just like every one of my fellow crew members. My hands curled into fists as I pushed harder down the beach. When the Circle presented their terms, had any of my crew stood up for me? They had stood there in silence. They would rather just leave me to my fate.

I rounded a rocky spur to find another open stretch of beach. Large blubbery walruses, grey-furred, with broad flippers and tusks as long as my arm lounged there, sleeping quietly. Any of them could surely have killed me, or at least hurt me badly, but in my anger I didn't care.

I picked my way through the crowd of the great beasts—there must have been several hundred of them, each longer than I was tall, and probably half a ton apiece.

In the darkness I couldn't help but step on a flipper every so often. But even when I did, the walruses didn't seem to notice, too content in their dreams to waken.

Content, like the crew back at the camp. Even the crew of *Lady Luck* slept soundly, knowing they would soon be heading home. Didn't they owe me a debt of gratitude? I thought bitterly. Had I not been the one who negotiated with Deudermont, to allow them passage home instead of slaughtering them all on that field? Yet none of them had stood up for me, either. None of them had shown the slightest recognition of what Joen and I had done for them.

Joen . . .

My mind flashed red with pure anger too primal to put into words. I let out a roar, a scream of hate and anguish that I hoped would echo all the way back to the camp, where she would hear it and know what I felt.

All it did was rouse the walruses around me. They responded with roars of their own, great barking noises like some perverse giant dog with a sore throat.

One barked out above all the others, a ferocious sound that made my blood freeze in my veins. The commotion died instantly. The walruses settled. Except that those nearest me shifted away, forming a clear path to the largest of them all, who was slowly moving toward me. It moved like a man wounded in the legs, I thought, pulling itself forward on its front flippers, its tail dragging behind him. But it was not graceless—far from it: the creature had practiced that movement for decades, I knew. It was in complete control of its body, unwieldy and massive though it was. Its great tusked and whiskered head bobbed up and down as it approached. Each time its head rose, it issued a bark. It growled each time its head fell.

It had to be the pack's leader, I thought. Like the wolves of my childhood in the High Forest, the walruses must fight each other to determine who would stand as the greatest of the group. That bull showed the signs of many battles—its left tusk was cracked, its tip splintered away. Its body was not a solid gray, like most of the others, but was streaked with scars. And the worst of the scars crossed his face, just below his right eye—a great patch of black on its wrinkled, ancient face.

It was barking a challenge, I realized. I was an intruder, a threat, and it was demanding that I face it in combat or surrender. The choice was not a difficult one, given that it was no less than ten times my weight, with a thick hide and vicious weapons.

I bent low to the ground in a sort of bow, lowering my head deferentially, and retreated a few shuffling steps.

It stopped for a moment, staring at me, then raised its head in what I took to be a victorious motion, and let out a long roar. The crowd of walruses joined in, bobbing their heads and barking a deafening chorus. I kept my head down and slowly backed through the crowd and out onto the clear beach beyond.

"You always were so good with animals," said a quiet voice behind me, a voice I recognized.

I spun around, pulling my stiletto from its sheath, to face the masked woman I had met in Memnon.

But she was no longer masked. And even in the dim light of the half moon, I saw her face clearly. My dagger fell from my hand, thudding softly on the sand.

My mind whirled back across the years, back to my earliest childhood. Back to a small cave in an ancient forest, to the summer nights beneath the boughs, to the forest animals, to the only time in my life I had ever stayed in one place longer than a few months.

To the first time I had met Asbeel, that dark midsummer night. To the bolt of lightning, guided by a friendly hand into my cave, to scare off the demon.

To the fires in the forest. To the last time I had ever seen the only mother I had ever known.

"You died," I whispered.

Elbeth shook her head slowly, wearing the slightest of smiles on her ageless face. "You've grown," she said quietly.

"Tried not to; didn't work." I shrugged.

She laughed slightly. "I've watched you from afar, but I hadn't realized how strong you've become."

"I can't believe you're here." I rushed forward and buried my head in her arms.

But after only a moment, she pulled away. "We haven't much time, child," she said, glancing quickly over her shoulder. "I must leave soon."

"Leave? Why?" I asked. The growl that escaped my lips did not seem my own. My anger had a new target, and it was right before me.

Elbeth sighed. "I do what has to be done, child. As I ever have."

"What has to be done?" I took a step back. "You had to let a five-year-old boy think his mother had died?"

"I am not your mother."

"You were close enough!"

Elbeth gave me a curious look. I swallowed. Was what she had been close enough? I had had a real mother, after all. And a real father too. What would life have been like if they had not died? If I had never gone to live in the forest with Elbeth? I took in a breath as a new thought crossed my mind.

"Did they really die?" I asked quietly.

Elbeth nodded, and I knew she understood whom I was talking about.

"I never hated them for it." I sighed and stared at the sand. "And I never hated you for dying, either." I looked back at her, my eyes filling with tears. "But now how can I not hate you, now that I know the truth?"

"You can hate me as much as you want. But I didn't abandon you, truly, did I? I left you with Perrault."

"You left me *for* Perrault," I corrected. "And hoped he would find me."

She shook her head. "Perrault had found you once before, lying beside your murdered mother. I made certain that he would find you again." Elbeth stepped forward and took my chin in her hand. "Tell me, child. Do you regret your time with him?"

The memories were painful, but I could not keep them from coming. Perrault had shown me the mountains, the great rivers, forests nestled in snowy valleys, and oases in arid deserts. With him I had seen much of western Faerûn, wonders no child my age could hope to witness.

And the stories, told and read, of battles won and lost and legends of old. Dragons buried beneath the hills, monsters slain on the top of mountains, and true heroes journeying into the fires of the Abyss.

And all that still could not begin to describe what Perrault had meant to me, the person behind the stories and the journeys. He had never been very warm, but he had always been there, always guiding me. Whenever I had a question, Perrault would not answer directly but would lead me through a series of other questions, showing me the way to the answer.

Elbeth stood before me, a look of the deepest understanding on her face.

"I can't regret Perrault," I said at last. "But why couldn't he have lived with us, in the forest?"

She laughed. "Perrault, hidden away in a forest? Perhaps he could have, but never would he have!"

"Then why couldn't you have traveled with us?" I asked.

She shook her head. "Your time with Perrault was special because it was you and him."

I swallowed. "He's dead too, now, you know."

She took my hand and squeezed it. "We have spoken enough of the past. We have more immediate matters to discuss. I'm sure you are wondering why we are here."

I nodded, my mind still reeling at the sight of her.

"I am here," she said, "because my duties have brought me here, to join this Circle for the time being. You are here because the stone you are bound to is here."

I felt like she had punched me in the gut. "The stone is here?"

"Haven't you felt better as you grew closer? The illness that had afflicted you since your separation—isn't it gone?"

Reflexively, I flexed my left hand. Indeed the numbness that had crippled me had faded the moment we set sail to the west, heading toward the island. It was just a vague memory.

"When we took the stone from you, we did not know how you would react. We hoped you would suffer no physical ailment, if only we brought the stone far enough from you."

"When you stole the stone, you mean," I said.

"I volunteered for that, child. Because I knew I could not only get the stone, but could prevent the others who sought it from harming you. And I was correct, as it turns out."

"I could have fought Asbeel." I would not concede that she'd helped me at all. Elbeth had stolen the stone. All I could think of was that betrayal. She had betrayed me just like everyone else. "I didn't need your help."

"Be not such a fool. The demon would have killed you."

"So you saved me from him," I said sarcastically, "then took the stone from me. And being away from the stone caused illness. So you almost killed me anyway."

"I am sorry for that." She put her hand on my shoulder. "I know now it was a mistake. But then it was not my decision to give you the stone in the first place."

"Don't try to put this on him!" I yelled and shrugged away her hand. A chorus of barks erupted behind me again.

"I am not. But think back. Would things not have been better had you never touched the stone?"

"Perrault said I was old enough to have back what was mine." I glared at her. "The stone is my birthright. He said it was tied to me already."

"I believe that things could have turned out differently." She looked behind me at the distant waves. "Your soul grows full as you mature. It may well have scarred over the missing part where the stone should have been." She sighed and turned back to meet my gaze. "But now I realize, it's too late. All we know is you can't be separated from it, or else you will fall terribly ill. That is why I insisted the Circle bring you here, where you will be near it again."

"You brought me back here to keep me near the stone," I said. "As a prisoner."

"That was the Circle's goal, yes."

"But why?"

"The story is far too long to explain." Elbeth glanced quickly over her shoulder. "And I mustn't be gone for much longer, or they will start to suspect. Suffice it to say if Tymora's stone is active, at this time, on Toril, then it creates a great imbalance. Good luck for one means bad for another, and the stone had given you undue luck. The circle exists to prevent such imbalances."

"So I have to suffer in the name of balance? That hardly seems fair."

"It is not indeed. But, as I said, it is the Circle's goal."

"The Circle's goal," I repeated. I looked deep into her eyes. "But not yours?"

She shook her head solemnly. "The Circle intends to keep you prisoner. But I cannot bear to see you held against your will. I know now this is not your fate." She spoke faster, her voice a low growl. "The stone is hidden in a cave. The cave lies beneath the water there," she said, pointing at the rocky outcropping at the end of the beach, back toward the sailors' camp. "At low tide, the cave will be exposed."

I looked at her, my eyes wide. "So you want me to go in and steal the stone? Why can't you just give it back to me?"

"It is not my place to return it to you," she said. "But since the stone belongs to you, your taking it is not theft." She took in a deep breath. "I must warn you, this task is not simple. A great guardian of the sea lives in that cave. Be careful that you do not wake him. Even goodly dragons are cranky when they wake, especially if they wake to find a thief in their den."

I barely heard a word past "dragon." My head was spinning. I had always been most fascinated by tales of dragons, the rarest and mightiest of the creatures of the Realms. I found them brilliant and awe-inspiring and ultimately deadly and had always hoped to see one some day. But under these particular circumstances?

"Wait until the ship is repaired," Elbeth continued, not oblivious to my suddenly wobbly knees. "Get the stone, and get back to the ship just as it pushes out to sea."

"What about the Circle?" I asked. "What about Deudermont? He said he—"

Elbeth waved her hand in front of me. "You need not worry about Deudermont. You have a place on his ship. And I will take care of the Circle to give you enough time to escape."

"You'll stop them one against eight?" I asked.

"For as long as I can," she said. She gave me a wide, warm smile. "Which may not be long at all."

"And then what?"

Elbeth picked up my fallen dagger and pressed it into my hand. "You must find a way to restore the balance."

I nodded, trying to think of something to say. The whole plan sounded very dangerous for both of us, but I could think of no better alternative. I had no intention of staying on the island for the rest of my life, certainly not in the name of preserving some mystical balance. So I would face the dragon, and she would face her compatriots, and we would have to hope for the best.

With a heavy heart, I turned and began the long walk back to the camp.

"Who is she?" Elbeth called after me, her voice light, almost happy, despite the gravity of the plan we'd just laid.

"Who is who?" I asked, turning back to face her.

"The girl, the blonde," she said. "She followed you out of the camp, you know, but got spooked by the walruses. She's awake, waiting for you, right now."

I opened my mouth to respond, but nothing came out. I turned on my heel and sprinted off as fast as I could.

CHAPTER 54

I T FELT NEAR A MILE BEFORE THE DIM LIGHT OF THE CAMPFIRES CAME INTO VIEW, AND
another half mile before I saw the camp. Joen sat at its edge, against a log, facing out
from one of the larger fires. I quietly approached. My heart beat faster. I didn't quite know
what I would say.

But as I got closer I saw she had fallen asleep. I didn't want to disturb her. Instead
I crept around the camp and moved in near the other fire, which had burned down to
embers, and found a spot to curl up.

Sunrise was no more than an hour away, and I didn't manage to fall asleep at all.
When the crew rose to begin repairs, I rose with them, thoroughly exhausted.

Sea Sprite had, thankfully, not taken heavy damage, with the exception of the mainmast. And the mast itself was mostly intact; it had only ripped the deck up around it,
pulling up from its anchored points below decks. It had miraculously not snapped.

The work, then, was mostly cleanup: the lower decks had been destroyed by the
moving mast; the top deck had the debris of the storm, plus more than a few broken
boards. But once we cleared the debris, we could reset the mast, then rebuild the deck
with salvaged boards from *Lady Luck*—which had come to rest tightly against a formation of rocks, and showed no desire to move ever again. We'd use her salvaged lines and
riggers to fix the rigging. All in all, Captain Deudermont expected it would take ten days
of hard physical work.

Captain Deudermont showed no sign of refusing my help, and I no longer felt reluc-
tant to pitch in, given my plan. He made no distinction between his crew and *Lady
Luck*'s, nor did he discern based on age. I volunteered to help find lines and whatever food
and supplies might have survived aboard the wreck when *Lady Luck* showed herself at low
tide. Joen volunteered to join me. Soon we were both sifting through the debris in *Lady
Luck*'s dark, half-sunken hold.

For a long while we worked in silence. I lifted a rope covered in seaweed out of a
puddle and wrapped it into a coil, keeping my eyes down at all times. I was terrified of
making eye contact. Dozens of questions and observations—even jokes—ran through my
head. But I was too nervous to say them aloud.

At last Joen had the courage to break the silence. "Where'd ya go, then?" she asked.
Her voice was quiet, but friendly.

I cleared my throat. "Nowhere. I just walked."

"Walked a long time, eh?"

"How would you know?" I said. I picked up a small box of rusting nails and stuffed it in my sack, still looking down, still afraid to make eye contact.

"I followed you. But you already knew that."

"Someone told me you followed me. I didn't believe her until I got back to the camp and saw you, waiting."

"So why didn't you talk to me?"

"Why didn't you stand up for me?" I asked, glancing up at her at last. When I saw her face, I silently cursed. I hadn't meant to ask the question so plainly, or so soon.

She frowned slightly. "I heard a voice, you know? Said, don't say anything now, there'll be time later."

I cocked my head. "A voice in your head? That's not normal, you know."

Her frown deepened. "No, it ain't. But it weren't in my head, either. Was in my ear. Like someone whispering to me, but there weren't nobody there. I dunno, maybe the wind caught someone else's words and carried 'em to me, eh?"

Suddenly I thought of Perrault, standing on the rail of a ship, whispering into the wind, his voice carried over the miles, all the way to the captain of another ship.

My heart leaped. Perhaps his fate had been similar to Elbeth's? Perhaps . . .

"What did he sound like?" I asked tentatively.

"She," Joen replied, and my heart sank once again. "She sounded, I dunno, calm. Comforting, you know? Oi, what's the matter then?"

A single tear had formed and dropped from my eye. I tried to speak past the lump in my throat, but no words would come.

"What, you think I'm going mad and it makes you sad?" she teased.

"Going?" I said.

She punched me in the arm, not hard, but enough to leave a bruise. I pulled away, and she followed, a wicked grin on her face, her hand cocked for another punch.

"Stop, stop!" I said, laughing, surprised that I could manage a laugh. "You aren't mad, and you aren't going mad either. It was magic, I think. I've seen it used before."

"Figured as much. I ain't crazy, you know? But who was it?"

Of course it had been Elbeth. That's why she hadn't spoken when the Circle presented their demands to Deudermont. She had been whispering a message on the wind, her face hidden behind her mask.

Suddenly I remembered Deudermont's vacant stare, as if he weren't listening to the leader of the Circle at all. Could it be that Elbeth had sent him a message as well?

"Well?" Joen asked impatiently. "You gonna tell me who it was, or do I have to beat it out of you?" She cocked her arm and balled her fist.

"It was a friend," I said. "She's going to help me escape, but I have to do something first."

"Oi, how original," Joen said, rolling her eyes. "What's she makin' you do?"

"It's not for her," I said, considering how much I could tell Joen. "The Circle stole something from me, and she told me where it's hidden."

"Great. So, we wait 'til the repairs are done, then we go get it, eh?"

"We?"

"You're only telling me 'cause you want me to come with. Don't deny it, you know it's true too."

I hesitated. "It's too dangerous," I said.

"All the more reason I should come. Someone's gotta have your back."

"Would you have had my back out on the beach, if you hadn't heard the whisper?" I tried, but failed, to keep accusation out of my voice.

She reached out and grasped my hand in hers. I turned to face her directly, to look straight into her emerald eyes, shining in the dim light. I felt suddenly guilty for questioning her, for ever being angry with her. My palm grew sweaty in her strong grasp. There was so little distance between us, so little . . .

The hatch above swung open. We dropped our hands.

A voice called down: "Lunch at the campsite. Make yer way to the shore!"

Joen skipped lightly for the ladder, not once looking over her shoulder at me. I waited a long moment, replaying our conversation in my head, before I started off for the lunch table.

CHAPTER 55

THE DAYS PASSED SLOWLY, FILLED AS THEY WERE WITH HARD WORK, POOR SHELTER, AND worse food. The weather stayed calm and relatively warm—the sun shone by day and the moon grew toward full, illuminating the night. Each evening Robillard would magically start new fires to keep us warm, and we would settle down to sleep. Deudermont posted a watch, unnecessary though it seemed. Certainly no external threat would rear its head, and it seemed unlikely to me that the crew of *Lady Luck* would try to cause any trouble.

Still, the two crews slept apart, each around their own fires. Joen remained loyal to her ship and slept among them. I still considered most of them pirates, evil men who would hurt me given the chance, so I avoided them.

But during the days we often found ourselves alone in the hold, sifting through the waterlogged supplies for anything useful. During high tide, we sat on the beach with the few crewmen who were still injured, since none of us were much use with the manual labor on board.

We talked about the past—about both our pasts. She told me of her parents, who died when she was young. She grew up in Luskan, alone on the streets, making her own way by picking pockets. When she turned nine, she took on with a ship, posing as a boy that she might be offered a job as cabin boy. I told her about my own past, from Elbeth to the present, mostly truthfully. I glossed over some parts, in particular not telling her that Elbeth was on the island.

We only occasionally discussed our plan. After all, it was very simple in theory: on the day *Sea Sprite* was ready to sail, we would go to the cave, take the stone, run back to the ship, and leave. But something still worried me.

Late on the night of the sixth day, I jostled Joen awake.

"Joen, I need to tell you something," I said. The sun had long since set; the midnight hour was past.

"Later," she said, closing her eyes and rolling over. "I'm busy."

"It's about the mission," I said, keeping my voice hushed. "When we get there, you can't go into the cave."

"Haven't we been over this, then?" She lifted herself onto her elbows and peered up at me. "It's dangerous, it's something you have to do, blah blah. I told you: you need someone to watch your back, and that's me."

"It's too dangerous."

She rolled her eyes at me. "You don't listen, do you? I know it's dangerous, I'm coming anyway. What is it, anyway, a dragon or something?"

She laughed, but I did not join her. After a moment she caught my solemn expression and stared at me in disbelief.

"Seriously?" she asked, her voice a hushed whisper.

I nodded.

She looked at me long and hard, her mouth slightly open. I figured she was trying to read my face, to know that I was telling the truth. After a moment, though, her lips curled into that smile again.

"I've always wanted to see a dragon," she said lightly. "This should be fun, eh?"

"Fun?" I said in disbelief. "Are you insane?"

"Maybe," she said, smiling. "But what's the worst that could happen?"

Images of her tiny corpse danced through my mind, ripped to shreds, charred to ash. I could not express in words what I saw, the worst that could happen. But I did not argue.

"That's settled then, eh?" She flopped back down and pulled her blanket over her head. "Now leave me alone."

On the seventh day, the mast had been reset and the deck around it rebuilt, and it was time to start resetting the rigging. Suddenly Joen and I found ourselves the most-worked members of the crew, as we were the two best able to get to the very top of the mast or the farthest out on the wings above the sails. We had no time to talk, and when our long days ended we were both so exhausted we would go to sleep without any words exchanged.

Then finally on the tenth day, the last lines were tied, and Captain Deudermont declared *Sea Sprite* to be seaworthy. The tide was going out, so she was mostly on the beach. At the next high tide, the crew would put her in the water, then be off as the waves began to recede.

It was time.

An hour before dawn, I quietly packed my gear and slipped into my boots—the magical boots that Sali Dalib had "loaned" me what seemed like a thousand years before. Careful not to wake anyone, I snuck out of camp, alone. The lookouts weren't paying much attention—as usual—so it was easy to get out unseen. But I wanted to take every precaution anyway. Not long after, Joen came skipping up the beach.

Her hair was pale in the moonlight. It almost shimmered as it bounced up and down in time with her skip. She was heading off to her doom, to face a dragon, to steal from a dragon, and she was doing so with a light step and a smile on her face.

Perhaps I had been wrong before; perhaps she was indeed insane.

But was I any less crazy?

All too soon, the rocky outcropping where Elbeth said the cave would be was right in front of us.

It was a two-tiered natural rock formation. A stone cliff rose perhaps twenty feet up on the left. A similar face dropped another ten feet to the right. A narrow path snaked between the two. At high tide, the lower rock would be completely covered by the sea. But the tide was nearly out, and fully seven feet of dark, jagged rock was clearly visible.

The jags made fine handholds, and I had no trouble at all climbing down. The water was still several feet deep at the base, but just above the lapping waves I saw a dark slit—the top of a cave.

"What do you see?" Joen called down.

"We're gonna have to get wet," I yelled back.

"Oi, on with it, then," she said, pulling herself over the lip and starting the short climb down.

I blew a sigh under my breath, wishing I could gather the courage to tell her, once and for all, that she could not come in, that I could not let her risk her own safety for my sake. But I had no such courage, so I dropped into the water instead.

I paddled forward. From my vantage point the whole mouth of the cave was visible. I drew out my stiletto, ignited the blue flame, and held it into the opening; just past the cave mouth, a narrow tunnel sloped upward. I swam for the edge, and scrambled out, happy to be out of the ice-cold water.

A splash behind me told me Joen had dropped into the water, and she quickly joined me in the cave. Together we slipped into the tunnel.

The roof scraped against my back, though I crawled flat on my belly. The rocks were wet and slick for the first dozen yards, but they rose steadily, soon clearing the highest water levels of high tide. The air there was much warmer—a blessing: my wet clothes would not freeze.

The tunnel flattened out and gained enough height that we could walk upright. I tried to illuminate the ground in front of us, but the light cast by my flaming stiletto was meager, and many times each we tripped over a jag or a crack in the stone passage.

We walked for what seemed like an hour in silence before the landscape changed. There was no gradual widening of the tunnel, no growth of the cave into a cavern. All of a sudden, the walls and ceiling just disappeared, stretching out around a massive chamber. My light seemed tiny indeed, a pinprick of blue on a great black tapestry.

I thought I heard a sound: a low rumble, rhythmic, and slow. I held out my hand. "Wait!" I whispered. "I think I hear something."

But after a few moments of standing there, I felt only a deep dark silence.

"Don't be a baby. The dragon's out hunting or fast asleep." Joen pushed my shoulder. "On with it, eh?"

Not wanting to seem the coward, I stepped deliberately into the cavern, one step, two, three . . . I saw a glint ahead and moved toward it.

Suddenly the darkness was gone. The light from my magical dagger caught the thing I had seen ahead: a strange sphere with many glassy mirrored facets. The sphere seemed to grab at the light, then project it out from each of those mirrors, amplified ten times over. The whole of the room filled with a pale blue glow.

With my heart in my throat, I quickly scanned the room. There were piles of gold coins, sapphires and emeralds, silver necklaces dotted with rubies. Shortswords and longswords and scale armor, masterfully crafted and probably enchanted. Against one wall stood what looked like an ancient desk and delicately carved bookshelves, filled with leather bound books and scrolls and vials of blue and green liquid.

But I could see no sign of a dragon.

I blew out a low sigh. Joen skipped past me, smiling broadly, practically dancing her way into the treasure. She bent low to scoop up a handful of coins, then let most of it trickle through her fingers as she laughed. A few coins she pocketed, then made to repeat the action.

"No," I whispered harshly. "We're here for something specific, remember?"

"Oi, right, sure," she said, still staring at the coins. "What's it look like, then?"

"It's a leather sash with a large pouch on the front," I said. "The pouch should hold something heavy."

"Right," she said. "We should split the search. You go that way,"—she pointed to the wall with the books and magical equipment—"and I'll go this way." She moved off into the largest piles of treasure, giggling like the silly girl I knew she wasn't.

I moved off toward the wall, not wanting to argue. Besides, the stone could well be that way, and even if it wasn't, I wouldn't mind a chance to look through the ancient books. I had just picked one up when I heard Joen call out to me.

"Oi, this it, then?" she said, and I looked back to see her holding up a leather sash— my leather sash.

"That's it!" I called. "Is the stone in it?"

"Some kind of stone, yeah. Big and black. That's what you're after, eh? The stone?"

"That's right," I said, walking toward her. I had hated the burden of the stone when I had carried it, but all I could think about was holding it again.

"Oi, and look at this!" she shrieked, holding up a jewel-studded belt. "Was lying there, right next to yours! And look, it's got some matching knives on it too. I could use a new pair, you know, ever since your captain took mine."

"Put it back," I said forcefully.

"What, you get to steal from the dragon but I don't?"

"I'm not stealing. I'm reclaiming what's mine."

"You think he's gonna see it that way?" Defiantly, she strapped the belt to her waist. "What, he shows up you gonna say, 'hey mister dragon, this was mine before, I'm just taking it back,' and he's gonna let you go?"

"No," growled a voice, deep as thunder and echoing about the cave endlessly. "I will not."

CHAPTER 56

THE PILE BENEATH JOEN'S FEET CHURNED AND ROSE SEVERAL FEET. THE TOPMOST COINS rolled and slid down, and Joen nearly followed with them. She held her balance, but a moment later we both wished she had slipped.

A great head rose up right in front of her, sporting horns longer than I was tall and a mouth large enough to swallow us both at the same time. Up, up, up stretched its great serpentine neck—ten feet long, twenty, and still it rose. Bronze scales glistened in the pale light.

I had read about the many types of dragons on Toril, and though the light was poor, I was certain it was a bronze dragon. I recounted the passage from Volo in my head, trying to steady my racing pulse: A *reclusive sea-dwelling dragon, the bronze dragon is not evil, but it is paranoid and protective of its treasures.*

Still, paranoid and protective was far superior to many of the other possibilities. Had the dragon been a red, we would already be dead.

The dragon's slitted eyes narrowed at each of us in turn.

"Hardly a meal worth eating," it growled. "If you weren't stealing, I might have let you go."

Joen stood frozen right behind its head. If it had a mind to kill her, it wouldn't take but a moment.

"The Circle sent me!" I blurted out. I glared at Joen meaningfully, hoping to distract the dragon long enough that she could get to the exit. "They gave you something to guard, right? They want it back!"

"You are speaking of the stone, I presume?" the dragon said as it stretched its long neck down to me, its snakelike eyes staring unblinking into my own. "It is not theirs to reclaim. And the Circle knows it, whelp. You are a thief, and a liar."

"No!" I said. "I am no thief." I glared at Joen. Why was she not moving?

"But a liar, you admit to?" the beast said. I had no idea dragons could laugh, but it seemed to be laughing at me.

"No, because the stone is mine to reclaim," I said. Behind the dragon, Joen finally snapped from her stupor and began to pick her way down the loose slope of coins, careful not to make a sound. "If the Circle hadn't told me where to find the stone, how would I have known to come here?"

The dragon blinked for the first time, staring at me curiously. "That may be so," it said, sounding unsure. I got the distinct impression it was trying to sort through the circumstances that had brought the stone to its possession.

"It is!" I said. "The Circle stole the stone from me. And now they want me to have it back. I am here to reclaim what is rightfully mine." Joen had reached the base of the pile, and was moving quickly to the narrow cave entrance we'd used to enter.

The dragon sniffed at the air, its eyes growing wide. "Thieves!" it bellowed. "Thieves and liars! You'll not leave this place, fools!" Its head shot around to where Joen had been standing, crashing against the pile, sending gold and silver and gems flying everywhere.

I took off running, racing Joen to the exit. Sali Dalib's boots hastened my step, but I wasn't quite fast enough. The dragon's head turned on me once again, and I heard the beast's sharp intake of breath. I reached the tunnel just as it exhaled.

The air around me tingled with energy, an electric charge building for just one brief moment. Something slammed against my back, with the force of a thunderstroke and a sound to match. I flew through the air, crashing against Joen. We both tumbled into the narrow passage.

She scrambled to her feet, half-sobbing, her limp hand around my arm. I pulled myself up beside her, bruised but mostly unhurt. The look on her face was a mix of horror and confusion.

"You . . ." she whispered, her voice quivering. "Your . . ." I thought I saw a tear drip down her cheek, but she brushed it aside and shook her head vigorously. "Your cloak," she said, her voice normal again. "It looks a bit worse for the wear, eh?"

I pulled my cloak over my shoulder. Indeed it looked worse: the brilliant royal blue was marked with a great black scar, with small red veins running the length of it.

An image of Perrault leaped into my mind: galloping atop his white steed Haze with the cloak flowing out behind him.

I shook my head, trying to suppress the sick feeling in my gut. "No time to waste, we have to move," I said.

It had seemed an hour getting to the treasure. But it felt like a mere minute before we were crawling down the narrow sloped tunnel toward freedom. Somewhere along the way, I had taken the sash from Joen and placed it over my head. Though it was on top of my shirt, not under it as I used to wear it, its familiar weight felt good against my chest. It was like it was inside my chest, inside my very being. Even through the illness it had caused, I had not noticed how much I had missed the stone until the moment I finally had it back.

We scrambled out of the cave into the predawn light. The tide had gone out further, and there was less than a foot of water beneath our feet. We stopped to catch our breath before starting the short climb and long walk back to the camp.

"How do you suppose the dragon got in there?" Joen asked me. "You think it crawled in when it was tiny, and just outgrew the entrance?"

"Then how would it have all that treasure?" I said. "And what did it eat to grow so large?"

"I dunno, maybe the Circle feeds it and brings it gifts." She shrugged.

"Or maybe there's another, larger, entrance," I said.

Her response was cut short by a loud splashing noise. A few hundred yards out to sea, the water bubbled, and a great reptilian head emerged, followed by the rest of the dragon, wings spread wide, a hundred feet long, wingspan twice that across.

It let loose a roar so loud the rock shook beneath our feet. The mighty beast beat its wings against the air, and turned to the shore—to us.

"Time to go," I said quietly. But Joen was no longer standing beside me; she was halfway up the cliff and climbing fast.

I followed her, quick as I could, thankful for the easy handholds. My palms were sweaty, and my fingers trembled. I doubted I could have navigated a more difficult cliff.

When I crested the rise, my heart beat even faster.

Joen stood, her daggers drawn, her feet set in a defensive stance. Behind her stood a figure with black boots and pants and a white silk shirt stretched over a broad red chest. The twisted metal hilt of a horrible demonic sword rose up beside the wicked, angular face.

"Impressive," Asbeel said with feigned friendliness. "I half expected you'd never return from that cave. Then again, you did have some luck,"—he looked pointedly at the sash across my chest—"on your side."

CHAPTER 57

ONE, TWO, THREE TIMES I SLASHED AT ASBEEL, LEFT TO RIGHT. AFTER ALL THAT TRAIN-ing with the masters of Waterdeep, my swordwork had vastly improved since the last time Asbeel and I had crossed swords. But against Asbeel, it didn't seem to make much difference.

Each time, I struck out at him, his own massive sword was in line for the block.

Joen crouched low to my right. Her heels dangled off the cliff, as she stabbed out with her newly stolen daggers.

Asbeel brought his sword around quickly, aiming a swing at her head. But Joen darted to her left.

I stepped forward, my saber leading. Asbeel had to cut his swing short and retreat another step.

I kept glancing over my shoulder, expecting the dragon to descend upon us. But the dragon seemed to have disappeared.

With each motion Joen and I were more in tune. My first instinct had been to protect her, to keep myself between the demon and Joen. Though I knew firsthand that she could fight, the thought of Asbeel hurting her made me nauseous. But on the narrow ledge overlooking the dragon's cave, I had no way to stand between them.

And so we fought as one.

The demon rushed forward. I stepped to the side. Then Joen darted in, stabbing at his exposed side. Again and again we repeated the maneuver, until we had turned Asbeel in a full circle.

"I'm done playing with you, children." With murder in his eyes, Asbeel lifted his sword for a final attack.

But another, larger, form rose up behind him.

The bull walrus raised its head and let loose a mighty barking roar. Then it brought its wicked tusks, one broken but the other sharp, down at the demon's back. Asbeel tumbled to the ground.

The demon rolled over quickly, bringing his wicked jagged sword to bear against the walrus. The walrus raised its head and let out another bark. Its sharp tusk glinted in the sunrise.

"Come on," Joen said, grabbing my arm and pulling me. "We've got more important things to do than sit here watching, eh?"

I didn't argue. Off we ran, down the beach to *Sea Sprite* and the two crews. At first Joen led, but soon I had passed her, running so fast with my boots, pulling her along behind. I said a silent thanks to the bull walrus. It wouldn't last long against the likes of Asbeel.

The sun had crested the eastern horizon, and its brilliant light sparkled on the ocean. I looked up to the sky above it. The dragon soared there in a wide arc, exultant in the cold air. It seemed to have lost any concern with us; instead, it swept over the ocean.

"Where do you think he's going?" I asked no one in particular.

"She," Joen responded. "And I think she's headed for the ships. Dragons are smart, you know? Maybe she knows we can't get off the island without a ship."

"Yeah, that makes sense," I said. "We should probably run faster then, don't you think?"

"Oi, sounds like a plan."

The wind went from still to gale in an instant. The new dawn was swept away by the black clouds of an oncoming storm.

We rounded the last bend and saw *Sea Sprite* at the edge of the water. Dozens of sailors scrambled over her, trying to get her into the water. On deck at the stern rail, Captain Deudermont called out his orders. Lightning flashed behind him, casting him in silhouette.

With that captain at the helm, *Sea Sprite* would be ready to go, I knew, and no hail nor gale nor thunder would stop her.

The dragon's wide arc brought it back toward land, making a straight line for the still-beached ship.

The air was suddenly lit, but not by lightning. Out of nowhere, a great ball of fire exploded, high up in the dragon's face.

Its roar took on a deeper timbre, of rage and agony mingled. It let loose its breath, a blast of electrical energy to rival the storm above.

But its aim was not good, and the thunderstroke hit nothing but the beach, throwing up only sand and stone.

"Nice one, kids," called Robillard, standing calmly at the edge of the camp, casting another fireball as we ran by. "Felt the need to wake a dragon, did you? Not saying I've never had that urge myself, but this really doesn't seem the best time for it."

Joen laughed. "Once in a lifetime opportunity, you know? She was there. How could we pass up the chance?"

"A fair point," Robillard conceded. He muttered an arcane incantation, moved his hands about in some odd gestures, and again a great blast of fire filled the sky, right in the dragon's path.

"And I see you've decided to rile it up even more," I said sarcastically.

"Just making it ready for our friends," he said.

"Friends?"

At the next flash of lightning, Robillard pointed to some smaller shapes flying toward the dragon. Ravens.

"Oi, nice idea!" Joen said.

"Get to the ship already, would you?" Robillard said dryly, and again he fell into spellcasting.

We didn't need to be told twice. The ship had caught a wind-whipped wave and was floating. The crew who had not yet reached the deck were climbing lines.

Suddenly, a wall of fire shot up between us and the ship, cutting across the beach from sea to cliff. I turned behind me. Another fire wall sprang up, blocking our retreat.

Asbeel ambled through the tunnel of fire, looking none the worse for his encounter with the walrus.

"Enough of this," he said. "You will come with me."

CHAPTER 58

I HEARD ASBEEL'S WORDS ECHOING IN THE BACK OF MY HEAD, COMPELLING ME TO OBEY. I strained against them, trying to call up happier times with Perrault, Elbeth, Joen. Anything to get Asbeel's voice out of my mind. But still I found my feet moving, one shuffling step, then another.

"Let him go," Joen said, stepping in front of me, her daggers drawn.

"Let him go," Asbeel repeated in a mocking high-pitched voice.

With a snarl, Joen leaped at him, ignoring the heat of the fiery walls, ignoring that wicked sword, long and curved and jagged and ablaze with demonic red fire.

In a blink, Asbeel's sword was swinging, and Joen was falling away.

My trance broken, I charged at Asbeel with my sword drawn.

Red and blue flame crashed against each other again and again, each contact hissing and throwing off a burst of steam.

Asbeel gave ground willingly, retreating directly toward one of the fire walls. The heat grew as we approached the sheet of flame, and though Asbeel seemed entirely unaffected, I had to halt my advance and fall back.

"Come on then," I snarled, settling into a defensive stance.

"Yeah, bring it, eh?" Joen said, gathering herself up from the ground. I looked at her, stunned. Asbeel's swing had struck her, I was sure of it. But there she was, standing up unhurt, with only a slight tear in her leather tunic.

She saw my look and threw me a wink—all the answer I would get, as the demon was advancing again.

Joen dropped into a low crouch and moved to her right. I moved to the left. Asbeel shadowed me, moving slowly and deliberately, never exposing more than his side to Joen. He reached out with his sword, a surprisingly tentative strike for such a typically cocky foe. I parried solidly, pushing his sword away.

Again he lunged out lazily, and again I parried. He followed with a quick, shortened horizontal swipe that probably would not have reached me anyway. Still, I tapped the top of his sword with my own and drove the blade down.

I realized my mistake as soon as steel hit steel. He let his blade drop, pulled it down even, and rushed forward. With no resistance, my parry had gone farther than I wanted, and I could not bring my blade to bear. Neither could he, but he had other weapons at his disposal—foremost among them, his own weight.

I tried to step back, but the demon pushed against me, pressing me backward, driving me toward the second wall of fire.

Joen came in hard on his flank, her left dagger up defensively, her right jabbing hard. The demon tried to dodge, but I used my position to my advantage, locking my leg against his, preventing him from taking a step.

Joen's dagger drove into the demon's side. He howled in pain, shoved off me hard, throwing me backward. In a flash, his sword was back in his hand, and he was whipping around. His inhuman strength was on clear display, his sword pummeling through Joen's defenses, sending her tumbling.

My heart dropped, but only for a second. Somehow she came to her feet, apparently unhurt and still holding both daggers.

Asbeel's position had suddenly worsened dramatically. He no longer had a wall of fire to his back; instead he had the two of us on opposite sides, both unhurt.

I moved in, cautiously executing a simple attack routine. Asbeel's sword was there to block each attack, but as Joen moved in from the other side, he had to whip his sword around. Again his strength served him well, and he had the sword around in time, but only just. Joen ducked under his wild swing and fell back.

Which left him defenseless from my side. I lunged in, aiming for a killing blow.

But Asbeel jumped, beating his great black wings once. He was above us, floating over us.

He lashed out with his foot, aiming for my head, but I ducked under the blow.

Joen leaped at him, digging her dagger into his ankle. The demon howled in pain, and kicked out at her. She tumbled away. I couldn't tell whether she had been hit, or had let go on her own. Either way, she landed gracefully, rolling to her feet, her daggers at the ready once more.

The demon beat his wings again, floating over Joen's head, and dropped to the ground.

Joen and I met him in coordinated attack. Each time I attacked, Joen followed suit, her movements a perfect complement to my own. It felt as though I were leading her in a slow dance.

I swept in from Asbeel's right, swinging high; Joen came in from his left, crouched low, her daggers jabbing in unison.

Asbeel ducked under my swing and brought his sword across to defeat Joen's attack. But as I retracted, Asbeel continued his motion, sweeping his and Joen's blades out to the side, bringing around the hilt of his sword.

The hilt: that wicked mass of twisted metal, that same vicious weapon that had struck Perrault months before, that had caused the wound that had killed him.

And it leaped for Joen.

When Perrault was wounded, I had stood behind him, afraid or unable to fight. I would not let that happen again. I would not watch the demon kill another who fought with me, who fought for me.

I screamed as I lunged, throwing my off-balance body not at Asbeel, but at his arm.

My aim was true, my sword diving straight for the sinewy forearm. But the demon's arm was not there—he had released the grip on his sword; his whole move had been a feint. His hand found my throat. Asbeel spread his wings and jumped, letting the gale lift us.

Joen fell to her back, not hurt, but too far away to strike.

Then a silvery glint caught my eye, speeding up toward us from her prone form. It was one of her daggers, cutting through the wind toward its target.

I felt the impact as the dagger drove into Asbeel's back. I heard his anguished scream. Then suddenly I was falling.

Straight for one of the walls of fire.

CHAPTER 59

Waves of heat radiated from the wall as I fell toward it. I grasped at Perrault's cloak, trying in vain to wrap it around me, hoping it would protect me as it had always done. But I could not hold it in the gale.

I closed my eyes. I smelled my hair singeing. I felt my flesh burning. Somewhere I heard Joen scream.

Then the heat was gone. The pain was gone. The scream was gone.

All I heard was the crash of the waves and the howl of the wind.

I opened my eyes and lifted my head from the sand, to find someone standing over me.

"Not satisfied with just a dragon, huh?" Robillard said sarcastically.

"Took you long enough," I heard Joen say, but her words ended in a groan. Asbeel held her aloft, his strong hand around her wrists. Her daggers lay on the ground, both bloody but both useless.

"Release her," Robillard said.

Asbeel laughed. "Come get her."

Robillard said a quick chant and pointed a hand at Asbeel, all five fingers pointing at him. A bolt of red energy leaped from each, darting through the air to burn into Asbeel's flesh.

The demon grimaced briefly, then started laughing again. "The great wizard comes to the rescue, and that's all he can manage?" he said. "What is it, wizard? Are you afraid to harm the girl, or are you just . . . spent?"

Another five bolts leaped at the demon, but again he just laughed.

Overhead, nine ravens circled, descending slowly. *Sea Sprite* drifted away from shore, her sails still furled, waiting for us.

"I think I've worn out my welcome," Asbeel said. "Pity, I was growing quite fond of the worthless rock. Ah, well, I suppose I'll have to take something to remember it by." He beat his wings, catching the wind—which was blowing directly out from the island—and lifted off, still holding Joen by the wrists. "Perhaps you'll come visit me some time, boy?" he chided.

Without thinking, I sprinted down the beach toward him. Loose sand sucked at my feet, yet my pace was ever so fast. I felt a stone beneath my foot, a solid point to push off from.

And I leaped.

An impossible leap, twenty feet into the air, thirty, my sword leading the whole way. Propelled by my magical boots, I caught the demon mid-flight, drove my sword into his flesh just above the hip, into and through. His scream rent the air. He twisted away from me, wrenching Perrault's sword from my grasp.

Down I fell. Joen fell after me, plummeting into the surf thirty feet below.

I plunged into the sea, then emerged choking.

The waves grabbed me, threatening to pull me out to sea, but I paddled furiously and looked up.

Off Asbeel flew, his wings beating awkwardly once, twice, and again. Lightning flashed, and the wings missed a beat. His black form hung in the air for just a moment, then dropped from the sky into the raging seas.

With hardly a sound, my great tormenter disappeared beneath the waves. But it was not without a pang of sadness that I saw him go.

After all, the sword still stuck in his side had served me well.

But then, that sword had only ever had one true mission: to avenge Perrault, its true master. With that accomplished, I supposed, the sword deserved its rest.

A wave washed me up on the shore, depositing me face-first into the sand.

"Nice one, eh," Joen said, spitting seawater and pulling herself up beside me. "Thanks a bunch."

"There'll be time for that later," Robillard said, jogging down the beach to meet us then right out into the surf. "We've got a ship to catch." He held out a hand to each of us. As I took his hand, I shot up to the surface of the water, feeling it hold me as if it were firm ground.

We reached *Sea Sprite* a few minutes later. The storm still raged, but the wind was pushing us away from the island, not trapping us there.

That would be Elbeth's doing, I knew, and I offered a quick thank you to the wind.

CHAPTER 60

SEA *SPRITE* CUT THROUGH THE STORM-TOSSED WATERS WITH GRACEFUL EASE, HER TAT-
tered sails full of wind, her repaired mast straining but holding fast. For an hour
she sailed, putting miles between us and the island, between us and the Circle, and the
dragon, and Asbeel.

Joen and I sat huddled in the crow's nest together. It felt an odd sort of homecoming.
That place had been so important the first time I'd met her. The gull's nest, she'd called
it. But today there were no gulls; the birds we watched for were ravens. And they did not
show their faces. Or beaks, as it were.

The sun had not reached halfway into the sky when we broke clear of the storm.
Beyond the edge of the storm, the day was bright and clear.

A broad smile stretched across Joen's face. She could not stay seated. She gripped the
mast in both hands, letting her weight fall left, then right, a graceful swinging motion.
Her arms were bare to the shoulder, revealing several cuts and a few ugly bruises. I sighed
deeply and stared at my hands.

"Do you think they'll follow us? Any of them?" she asked, for the fourth time.

"Hope not," I said, resting my head against the side of the crow's nest.

"Me too, eh? Wouldn't be so good to get caught out here, eh?"

"Not good, nope."

"Oi, what is it, then?" she said harshly.

"What is what?"

"This doom and gloom thing you're doing. Didn't you notice, we won?"

"Yeah. Sorry."

"So why so down, eh?"

I looked at her for a long time, studying her face, her forgiving eyes, the smile that
had not faded from her features. "I lost my sword, and my cloak is broken," I said.

"Oi, how can you break a cloak?" she said with a laugh.

"Look at it!"

"Already seen it. I think it looks prettier now, anyway. Sorry 'bout the sword, though.
Did its job, didn't it, eh?"

"It's more than that. The cloak, the sword, they belonged to Perrault."

"I know," she said as she leaned in. "Just because you lost the sword doesn't mean you
lost him. Remember that. He'd be proud of you, don't you think?"

"One of the Circle was someone I knew," I blurted. "Someone I thought was dead."

Joen stopped her swinging and sat down, right beside me, her arm brushing against my own. "The one who whispered to me?"

"Yeah, I think so."

"So she's the one who helped us escape, then? Good thing she was there." She laughed.

"Yeah, definitely. But I just wish . . ." I looked back at my hands. "I don't know."

"Yes you do. You wish she'd gotten off the island with us. That you would've had more time with her. Right?"

I nodded.

"But aren't you glad to know she isn't dead, at least?"

Again I nodded. I hadn't thought of it like that before.

"And you got the stone, right? Wasn't that the plan?"

"It's also the cause. The stone cost me Perrault, and it cost me his sword, and it's the reason I can't spend more time with Elbeth. It's such a small thing, but it costs me so much."

"It hasn't cost you me," she said, resting her head on my shoulder.

"Yet."

Her head shot back up. "Don't talk like that, eh?" she said sharply.

Below us, on the deck, the two crews worked together with remarkable efficiency. The captain stood at the helm, calling out his orders. The crew moved about, the slow waltz of a seasoned crew, not brothers in arms but brothers in the same goal, their grudges laid aside for a common aim, for a journey home. A fog was rising over the water, over the ship, but Deudermont didn't change course.

I closed my eyes, letting the rhythm of the ocean wash over me.

"Feeling better?" Joen asked, her voice a whisper.

I turned to her, to say yes. But she was so close, too close, not a foot between us. I could feel the heat of her breath, could smell the salt of her hair, could see her half-closed eyes.

The fog crept up into the crow's nest. A part of me wished to pull away, but a much greater part would not, could not.

Her lips were on mine, and all other sensation was gone. All that mattered was the softness of her lips, the—

"Wait," she said, pushing me away.

I blushed. "I'm sorry. I shouldn't have—"

"I know this fog," she cut in, leaning out of the crow's nest. "Listen."

I shook my head. "Listen? For what?" I perked up my ears, trying to focus past the rolling waves and the breeze.

And there it was, unmistakable.

Hoofbeats, familiar hoofbeats, echoed across the water.

PART VII

Thirteen thousand eight hundred and sixty-eight. Thirteen thousand eight hundred and sixty-nine.

The darkness was absolute. My pirate captors had left me no torch, and the sun had set long ago.

Thirteen thousand nine hundred twenty-four. Thirteen thousand nine hundred twenty-five.

The flicker of their campfire had traced its way down the short, east-facing tunnel to the locked door to a tiny chamber, my cell. The light had been brighter this night than the previous few nights, and the uneven crack at the bottom of the door had allowed plenty of light in. But that light, too, had finally gone out.

Fourteen thousand and seven. Heartbeats, that is, since the light had gone out.

I kept my legs crossed, sitting as comfortably as I could in the cramped cave. I held my breathing steady, keeping count as precisely as I could. Of course my count would be inexact, but that was hardly the point.

The pirates had been drinking heavily, like every night. Most or all of them had surely passed out. Still, I figured to play it safe I'd give them three hours so the last stragglers could drift off to sleep.

Fourteen thousand eighty-eight.

Three hours, fourteen thousand four hundred heartbeats. Soon.

Neither my hands nor my feet were bound. I had gained the pirate captain's trust. Or, more to the point, I had convinced him that he wouldn't hear the rest of my story if he didn't treat me better. And how he had wanted to hear my story!

But I had no intention of letting him hear the rest of it. I had no intention of spending another day here at all.

Fourteen thousand one hundred fifty-six.

The door lock would pose little challenge. I'd been saving some bones from my meals, and as I mostly got scraps, bones were in plentiful supply. I selected two, thin enough to fit in the lock, firm but not rigid, less likely to snap. They would be my lock picks, my key.

Fourteen thousand two hundred thirty-seven.

There could be guards posted at the entrance. I might be able to sneak past them. Maybe I'd have to fight my way out. Either way, I figured I could handle it. I had to, after all.

Fourteen thousand three hundred and five.

My story would have come to an end eventually. And when that happens, the pirates would kill me, of that I had no doubt. So maybe they'd kill me as I tried to escape, but at least I'd die doing something. I had little dread left of the prospect of the end. It was the prospect of the end on someone else's terms that really frightened me.

And I would not let that happen.

Fourteen thousand four hundred. Time to go.

The door made hardly a sound, and my footsteps made even less. My assumption was correct: two guards sat at the end of the tunnel. But they'd been drinking and were snoring loudly. I took a cutlass from one of them, feeling much better with a sword in my hand, even that unwieldy piece of metal. Then I crept past onto the narrow, sandy beach.

The moon was nearly full, the sky clear, and the view was better than I'd hoped it would be. I knew from observing the sunlight that the cave faced east. What I didn't know was that the mainland was visible from the beach.

Pirates lay strewn about wherever they'd passed out, empty bottles and half-eaten food lying next to many of them. It seemed they'd made no attempt whatsoever to find even a comfortable place to lie down. They were sprawled across rocks, flotsam, the various wreckage of and loot from ships.

To my left, the beach extended out of sight. The debris, including the hulks of many wrecked ships, stretched far. A quick glance out to sea revealed the reason for the wrecks: not a quarter mile offshore, several huge rocks jutted out of the water. The tide was low, almost at its lowest point. At high tide, those rocks would be invisible, the strait treacherous to anyone not intimately familiar with those rocks.

To my right, the beach wrapped around a rocky jut. The pirate ship would be there, I figured. A fine hiding place the island made for pirates.

It also made it tough for me to get out of there. No boats rested along the beach. I would either have to take some of the flotsam and use it as a raft or head for the ship itself and try to steal a launch. And the ship would be better guarded than some desolate stretch of drunk- and debris-laden beach.

I moved down the beach, looking for a promising piece of driftwood, but nothing stood out. I decided I would have to risk the pirate ship, so I headed for the rocky spur.

A cave dug into the side of it—perhaps a passage through? It was worth a look, so I crept closer.

A light flared within, and I ducked out of sight. A figure emerged from the cave, carrying a torch. Another followed him, and another after that.

"Impressive," the third figure said. He didn't look directly at me, but I knew he was addressing me. "Or, it woulda been impressive if it warn't a setup."

I recognized the voice—it was the pirate captain. He couldn't have seen me, I figured, so I stayed quiet.

But the beach behind me was suddenly filled with light. Torches flared wherever I'd seen a pirate passed out.

Soon, all those lights moved my way. They'd been watching me through their half-closed eyes. They knew where I was, so I stepped out into the light.

"Fine, then," I said. "Which of you should I kill first?"

The pirate captain laughed. "None, I think," he said. "I think ye should sit down an' tell us more o' yer story."

"And why would I do that when you'll just kill me at the end?"

"Aye, we might, a' tha'," he said. "But we'll kill ye just th' same if ye don't speak as if ye do. An' if ye speak, then at the least someone will know yer story."

The pirates gathered around, all holding torches, all but one brandishing a weapon. I held up my stolen cutlass to the unarmed pirate, and he laughed at me. His fellows soon joined him.

"Why the setup?" I asked. "Why let me get past the guards at all?"

"I wanted ter know if ye really were capable o' what ye been saying," he said. "Ye tell a fine tale, but tha' don' make it true. What we seen t'night, though, tha' makes me think ye ain't lying."

I thought for a moment. "Fine," I said. "Where did we leave off?"

"On a ship, leaving an island," the captain replied. He motioned to the crew. Some of the pirates took seats on rocks. Others brought bits of flotsam and jetsam and made a pile nearby. One dropped a torch into the pile, and soon we had a roaring fire. "Ye'd found yer lost stone, watched that demon Asbeel plunge into the sea, and ye were sailing away."

"Sailing away on a ship, with no wind, and hoofbeats approaching," I said. "Indeed . . ."

CHAPTER 61

"W HO GOES THERE? AND . . . HOW?" THE SAILOR AT THE RAIL MEEKLY CALLED. He stared down from the rail into the dense fog and saw what I saw: the silhouette of a woman riding a horse at the center of a strange mist.

"Permission to come aboard," the woman's voice rang out.

From my high vantage point in the crow's nest, I could almost see the murmur that rolled across *Sea Sprite*'s deck.

"I . . . we . . . I don't . . .," the sailor stammered.

"Permission granted," Captain Deudermont called from the middeck.

The captain approached the rail, his stern gaze forcing the sailors back to their posts. But those who had no immediate duties lined the rail, trying to get a glimpse of the mysterious rider. Joen, the girl beside me in the crow's nest, stepped lightly onto the top peg of the ladder.

"Wait," I said to her. "I have something I need to ask you."

She smiled at me and dropped from view, descending rapidly to the deck. I rolled my eyes and followed her.

The fog had cleared by the time I reached the deck, and even Deudermont's pirate prisoners stood idly by, watching. He'd allowed them to move freely about the decks because we needed help with the ship—and there was nowhere they could run to in any case, given how far we were out to sea. The great mass of sailors and their pirate captives were united in their desire to know how someone had reached us this far out without a boat. I knew the horse was Haze, so I was more concerned with who was riding her. I had only ever seen one other person ride Haze, and he was dead.

"I am an emissary from the Lady's Hall, the temple of Tymora in Baldur's Gate," a voice said. It was a beautiful voice, high and strong at the same time, like music. It was a voice I knew well.

It was Jaide, a beautiful elf, a priestess of Tymora, and friend of my mentor, Perrault.

I sprinted to the rail, nearly losing my balance as my feet slipped on the wet deck. I grasped at the rail for support and slid hard into it. And it's a good thing *Sea Sprite* still had some strength in her or I would have busted right through and gone for a swim. Under normal circumstances, the sailors would surely have laughed at my clumsiness—I was used to that—but all eyes were focused on the two forms standing calmly and casually on the surface of the water.

I had not seen Haze since I left her in Baldur's Gate after a long, fast run, trying desperately to save Perrault. A part of me had feared the horse dead—or rather, that she

R.A. & GENO SALVATORE
223

had left this plane of existence, for I doubted such a magical creature could truly die. But there she stood, tall and strong, her white coat sparkling with salt spray. She must have been tired. We were far out to sea, and walking on water quickly exhausted her, but she didn't show it—nor did the figure seated on her bare back.

Jaide seemed to radiate white light, like a beacon through the thick fog. Her head was turned to the stern of the ship, showing me only her profile: her sharp elf features and her long raven hair. I couldn't see her eyes, but I knew from past experience that they would be the brightest, most brilliant of orbs.

Joen's hand, petite but strong and callused from long days of work, grasped the rail, resting beside my hand. She let out a gasp of disbelief.

Tonnid, a sailor and my friend, chuckled and turned to Joen. "Amazin', ain't it? A horse all th' way out 'ere! Some mighty magic, I s'pose," he said.

Joen nodded, but I knew she didn't share his wonder. She had been on the first ship I'd ridden Haze to, so she knew well the horse's power. And she must have known the source of the commotion before she even got to the rail, as I had. What, then, had surprised her so?

And there was something else in Joen's look, something more than simple shock. Her eyes were narrowed, her gaze fixed and intent. She looked angry.

"What's wrong?" I asked her, and she turned a cold gaze my way.

"Your ride is here," she said, her lips twisting, her eyes strangely wet.

"My—?" I started, but was interrupted when Captain Deudermont's kingly voice split the silent air.

"Well met, priestess," said the captain. "But what can we do for you out here?"

If Deudermont was surprised at all by the presence of horse and rider on the rolling waves, he showed it not at all. Then again, he had listened to my whole tale to that point, so he knew of Haze already, and I'd guess that a man such as Deudermont had seen stranger things in his life.

"What do you mean, my 'ride'?" I whispered to Joen, who looked back at me as though I'd done something wrong.

"I have come to speak with you, Captain Deudermont," Jaide said, and the fact that she knew the captain's name got the attention of the sailors around her. "I have come with a warning."

I'm pretty sure she glanced at me just then, but I couldn't be sure—the priestess seemed to be ignoring me, though she must have seen me there at the rail. I was just about to call her name when Captain Deudermont said to her, "Bring your horse to our stern, and my men will hoist you both up on the launch. Unless there's something terrible descending on us in the next few moments, we'll get you warm and get you fed. Then we can speak at length of this dire warning."

"Haze will find her way to the deck," the elf said, patting the mare's muscled neck. "But I would speak with you sooner."

"My men will throw you a rope, then," he said, turning away from the rail.

"That won't be necessary," she replied, and the light that was Jaide disappeared in an instant then reappeared on the deck.

If Deudermont was fazed at all, he didn't show it. He extended his arm, which she took, and he led her to his cabin.

"Joen?" I asked, but all she could do was stare after Jaide and the captain. If I didn't know any better, I would have said she was jealous.

"I don't know why she's here," I told Joen.

She looked at me funny and stalked off to her duties.

I moved toward the ladder to the crow's nest and my post. The sailors were lowering a gangplank to help Haze aboard. I wasn't strong enough, and only so many hands could fit around the platform, so I left that for burlier men. But the chill north wind was blowing again. Freezing up in the crow's nest for no good purpose seemed a bad idea, and I was a little confused still by Joen's reaction to the appearance of Jaide, so I stayed on deck. That, and I was curious about the elf woman's warning—I couldn't help feeling I had something to do with it. Or more accurately, that the Stone of Tymora had something to do with it.

Excitement still rippled through the crew. The sailors seemed to pay little attention to anything but their own tasks and their hushed conversations with the men standing next to them. Not a soul even looked at me.

Jaide hadn't seemed to notice me, and I have to admit I was feeling more than a bit left out. But with the crew distracted, it wasn't too hard for me to pretend to work a little here, make like I was tying a knot there, and check the rigging a few steps farther until I found an out-of-the-way place right next to the door to the captain's quarters. I pressed my ear against the door and listened.

I heard only Captain Deudermont's voice inside, laying out the events of the past couple tendays. He told her about how his ship had been commissioned a pirate hunter by the Lords of Waterdeep. In Waterdeep, I'd overheard the pirate Chrysaor plotting to locate the Stone of Tymora—my stone. I, along with the crew, convinced Deudermont to sail his ship to catch the pirate, only to find out we'd been led into a trap. A group called the Circle had used Chrysaor to lure our ship onto the island where they'd hidden the stone, and where they planned to hold me along with it. With the help of Joen, I managed to scuttle their plans and recover the stone, and we'd made a hasty escape aboard *Sea Sprite*. He told the story so well, I found myself lost in his voice. It took me a long while to pull out of that trance, to remember that I had, in fact, been along for that adventure, that the story included me, often even focused on me. I had never heard Deudermont spin a yarn before, and hadn't realized he was possessed of such a talent, so much like Perrault. He even had me holding my breath when he spoke of *Sea Sprite*'s collision with Chrysaor's ship, *Lady Luck*, with the tumbling mast and all, as if I were afraid he'd rewrite the story to say we'd all sank and drowned, and as if his saying it would have made it come true.

After a while, Deudermont came to the end of his tale. "Will you now humor me with your own tale?" he asked the priestess. "You were going to tell me how Maimun's presence aboard *Sea Sprite* endangers my crew."

I blinked. What did he say? I could feel it—more bad news was on the way.

"I shall indeed, Captain," Jaide replied. "But first I must take care of something."

I heard footsteps so light it took me a moment to realize they were headed my way. I pulled back from the door just as Jaide yanked it open. She smiled, but behind her, Deudermont looked something bordering on furious. It wasn't the first time the captain had looked at me like that—and it was always hard to bear. Jaide motioned subtly away, indicating that I should leave, and at once.

"Listen, I—," I began.

"Leave," she all but growled at me.

"But I—"

"I'll not ask again," she said. But as she spoke the words aloud, I heard her voice even more clearly, whispering in my head: *This is twice you have eavesdropped on me,* her voice echoed. *Patience, dear child. All will be revealed in due time.*

I rolled my eyes and turned away.

Don't be rude, she said without speaking.

Why not? I replied mentally. *You knew I was there, but you said nothing. You let me waste my time, but you won't let me hear why you think Captain Deudermont should be afraid of me—not that I don't know full well that what gives me luck takes it from those around me. Why am I always a danger to everyone who—?*

I saw no harm in letting you hear a story you knew. By this time she had shut the door and I could hear her real voice beginning her tale inside the cabin. But she didn't break off the mental link. *Go see to Haze. She'll be happy to see you.*

Unlike you, apparently, I answered, but Jaide didn't respond.

Not sure if she'd even received my last communication, I walked away, however reluctantly. Had I'd gotten the last word or not, and what new danger was coming *Sea Spite's* way because of me?

I found Haze standing on the forward deck of the ship, holding steady against the bucking of the waves. She turned her head to look at me as I approached and she nickered softly in recognition. Joen, who was busily grooming the beautiful mare, didn't even bother to look up.

I put my hand on Haze's muscular neck, gently stroking her soft hair. It was so sleek with the dampness of the foggy night. She seemed to appreciate my touch, but she wanted more. Half a step brought her body against mine, nearly knocking me from my feet. She wasn't trying to hurt me, she was trying to hug me, the way horses do. I gladly accepted, wrapping my arms around her.

"Listen, I have to ask you something," I said to Joen.

She didn't answer, and I hesitated.

"I can tell you don't like her," I said.

She looked at me, puzzled. "Oi, why wouldn't I like the horse?" she asked.

"No, I meant Jaide."

She scowled. "You came to tell me I don't like the elf?"

"You've been angry with me from the moment she appeared," I said. "Either you don't like her, or I've done something wrong. Or both."

I felt something sharp against my arm—Joen's brush. "You're in my way," she said, roughly prodding with the sharp-bristled thing until I pulled back.

She went back to her grooming, running the brush through Haze's fine mane, though the hair wasn't tangled at all. It was not a horse brush—there wasn't one anywhere to be found on the ship, after all. It must have been Joen's own personal brush, though where she'd gotten it I had no idea. Had she found time to recover it from the wreck of *Lady Luck?* Joen had been one of Chrysaor's crew and their ship, *Lady Luck,* had been lost on the shores of the Moonshaes, in the same crash that had almost scuttled *Sea Sprite* for good. Our ship had survived, but the pirate ship had not been so lucky, in spite of its name.

That she'd use her own brush to groom the horse seemed fitting to me somehow, particularly given the loving manner in which she performed the task.

Too loving and intent, maybe. I got the feeling that Joen fell into her work to distract her from something else, something not so good.

"Have you met Jaide before?" I asked.

Jaide had lived in seclusion in her temple, and though for exactly how long, I was uncertain. I assumed it had been some time. But I didn't know enough of Joen's history to be certain she hadn't somehow met the elf during her time in Baldur's Gate.

Joen shook her head.

"She's a priestess," I said. "She was a friend of Perrault and Alviss, and—"

"Did I ask?" she snapped, scowling at me.

I returned her sour look with a glare. "Did I do something to make you angry?" I asked.

She shook her head again.

"Then why are you yelling at me?"

"I don't know, eh?" She hesitated a moment before continuing. "There's just something about her, you know?" She shook her head again, mad—at herself, it seemed—and confused. "I guess I just thought we would see some of the world, you and I, and leave all this Tymora business behind us. But she came here for you, didn't she? It's still all about that stone."

"Jaide's a friend," I told her. "And the stone has got to be destroyed."

"Oi, I see how it is." I thought for a fleeting moment that I detected a hint of jealousy in her voice, but that didn't make sense. "She's a friend to you." Something about the way she said the word "friend" made it sound like an insult.

"And so are you," I said.

Joen didn't answer at first. She went back to gently brushing Haze's hair.

"She's beautiful, isn't she?" Joen said after a moment.

"She's an elf. They're all beautiful," I replied.

Joen looked up at me, rolling her eyes. "I meant the horse."

"Oh. Um, yeah, she's really pretty. Especially her eyes." I cringed, and a cold sweat broke out on my forehead. Haze's pale orbs were something to behold, but they had nothing on the emeralds flashing from beneath Joen's tousled hair. "Like yours."

Joen took the compliment with a smile, the first smile on her I'd seen since Jaide's arrival. Again Joen quickly turned back to the horse, running the brush gently through her mane.

I stayed with Joen and Haze for a long while, gently patting the mare. Neither Joen nor I said another word, and the events of the day played through my head—most especially the moment before Haze and Jaide had appeared, as the fog was rolling in, hoofbeats on the wind, when I had shared a kiss with this pretty girl. It had been unexpected and awkward, at once too long and far too short. Perfectly imperfect, it stuck in my head, replayed over and over again. I wanted nothing more than to rush over and embrace Joen, to kiss her again, but at the same time I was petrified at the thought of it. She had essentially ambushed me, caught me off guard. Given any time to think about it beforehand, I never would have been able to muster the guts to approach her, let alone kiss her.

Joen kept her focus on the horse, but tossed me the occasional glance. I could see her coldness from earlier fading, the light returning to her eyes. But after one such glance, her gaze stopped, held. Her eyes narrowed and her expression dropped into a scowl. Without a word, she turned and stormed away.

"She's yours now, you know," said a voice—Jaide—from behind me. It took me a long moment to realize which "she" Jaide was talking about, and my face flushed red when I realized the road my confused thoughts had wandered down.

"But won't you need her to get . . . wherever it is you're going?" I asked.

"I'm not far now," she replied. Something about her tone, her smile, or her posture seemed wrong to me. I felt for sure she wasn't telling me the truth, or at least not the whole truth. Asbeel was dead. What had changed to bring Jaide all the way out here? The horse was surely tired from the run, though she didn't show it. It was the farthest I'd heard of Haze traveling out to sea, and if Jaide hadn't found the ship in the wide, cold sea, they both could well have died.

"Listen," I said. "I need to ask you something."

"Not right now, Maimun," Jaide replied.

"Stop doing that!" I said, getting angry.

"Doing what?"

"Evading my questions!" I realized as soon as I said it that I had made a mistake. "I mean, not you, specifically. You know. People in general. No one wants to answer my questions today."

Jaide laughed. "No one ever wants to answer questions, child, especially questions as difficult as the one you wish to ask me."

"I need your help, your advice."

"I cannot advise, but I have come to help."

"I need—"

"I know what you need, and what you will need in the days ahead. So I have brought Haze for you. Trust in her. She will not fail you."

"That's all?" I asked. "You came all the way out here just to deliver this horse to me? So I could ride her—where?"

"I rode all the way out here to deliver a horse," she answered with a cryptic smile. "And you know what you need to do, and you know you can't do it out here on this ship. You'll need magic, Maimun. Powerful magic."

Something made me think, just then, of the last time I had seen the dark elf Drizzt. He had told me the name of a wizard who he thought might be able to help me: Malchor Harpell. I was about to ask Jaide about that, but before I could, she said, "Now I must be off. I have my own business to attend to."

And before I could ask anything more, Jaide's smile stopped me cold. She stepped onto the rail and stood tall, graceful, her hair blowing in the wind. A mighty gust blew, and Jaide leaped into the air, her white gown catching the wind and billowing like a sail, her beautiful form drifting out to sea. The gust continued, powerful wind blowing both west and south, straining the already damaged rigging of the ship. Jaide rode the wind like a gull, soaring fast and far across the tops of the waves.

Then, as suddenly as the wind had blown in, it stopped, and she was gone.

CHAPTER 62

F OR THREE DAYS THERE HAD NOT BEEN A BREATH OF WIND. CAPTAIN DEUDERMONT HAD managed to keep the crew members at their posts the whole time, a testament to his reputation and stature, given the troubling circumstances.

The air had seemed to grow colder each day, and each morning we awoke to find the ship covered in ice, which had presented great challenges and greater danger. The ice had needed to be smashed and chipped and tossed overboard, else its staggering weight would have threatened to bring the whole ship down. Worse, as our ship had only recently been repaired, moisture kept getting into the imperfectly sealed boards of the deck and hull. When it had frozen there, it expanded, pushing the boards farther and farther apart, further degrading *Sea Sprite*'s seaworthiness. How she had creaked and groaned in protests those cold days, as if she were in pain. And given the damage *Sea Sprite* had taken in the collision with *Lady Luck*, she probably had been! I had remained in awe that the ship was still afloat at all after having had her mast torn so, taking pieces of deck with it.

To make matters even more miserable, we had lost much of our supplies in the initial wreck. We now carried twice as many people as when we'd set out from Waterdeep, what with *Lady Luck*'s crew aboard.

It was that fact that the crew seemed most unhappy about. There could never be a mutiny on Captain Deudermont's ship. The crew knew all too well that none among them could sail her better. And this crew was wise and experienced, and surely wouldn't blame their beloved captain for the failure of the wind, especially not when we'd just escaped an island wherein resided a group of druids who claimed to control the weather. Most of the muttering those long days had been about those druids, rumors and speculation that they were planning to starve us out until we gave back what they wanted.

That prospect frightened me greatly. I was, after all, what they wanted.

I couldn't help but think Jaide had been right, that my presence—the presence of the stone—endangered *Sea Sprite*'s crew. Not druids, not pirates, but me. So what? So then, I should leave? I had Haze. I could ride off any time. Lucky for me. But what about Joen?

I had known that the longer *Sea Sprite* sat adrift, the more the crew would come to resent its pirate captives—Joen among them. I had tried time and again to talk to her, but she seemed to act as if I had already left. She had made it clear I had chosen my desire to destroy the stone over . . . what? *Sea Sprite*? A life at sea?

Her?

There was more to consider than that. Jaide had told me I'd need powerful magic to destroy the stone—magic I couldn't find aboard *Sea Sprite*. But where to find that magic—Malchor Harpell? How would I find him when I knew nothing of him, save his name? Should I leave to find him? Or stay here with Joen?

Though my mind had raced with one plan after another for the last three days, I had stayed at my duties, unable to decide what to do. Since I'd been at sea, the magical cloak I inherited from Perrault had protected me from the wind and the rain, the cold of the northern seas and the baking sun of the southern waters. But no longer. My watches in the crow's nest had been hours spent freezing, the deepest of chills that had numbed my fingers and toes in heartbeats and had settled deep into my bones. It would then have taken several hours in the relative warmth belowdecks to drive that cold from me, and somehow I had felt that each time it had taken longer to recover, and that my fingers and toes had permanently lost just a little more feeling.

I still wore the cloak, though its perfect blue had been marred by a great red scar. The amazing magical cloak had stopped the breath of a dragon, had protected me so fully I hadn't even quite realized what had happened—until I'd happened to glance at the cloak and the scar, and the destruction the breath had wrought.

I carried also a new addition to my kit: a sword. The saber had belonged to one of the pirate crew who'd fallen in battle. It was a simple thing, a long thin sword that curved slightly at the end, and it was in size and shape similar to my old sword, except that lost magical weapon disguised itself as a stiletto, making it far easier to carry around. I constantly found the new blade, which was nearly half my height, tangled in a line, or in my legs, or in someone else's. My old blade was much lighter, even in its sword form, than this hunk of beaten steel.

And that old sword, sorely missed, could burst into magical blue flame at my mental command.

But alas, that sword had been lost to me, embedded in the flesh of the demon Asbeel, who was somewhere at the bottom of the vast ocean by now. I could lament not having the sword, of course, but I surely didn't lament the manner in which I had lost it. It had been beyond fitting that Perrault's sword would claim but one life while in my possession, and that life would be of the beast that had mortally wounded him so long ago.

So long ago—just this past midsummer, less than a year past.

And so it was that I descended from the crow's nest in the evening of the fourth day, lost in my quiet contemplations, rubbing my fingers in a futile attempt to restore circulation, trying not to trip over my own sword.

I caught up to Joen belowdecks, just as she descended the ladder into the hold.

"Hold up," I called, hopping down the ladder three rungs at a time. My showing off backfired, though, when my numbed feet missed the third-to-bottom rung and I dropped the last few feet, landing ungracefully on my rump. I jumped back up and resisted the urge to rub my aching behind, trying to save some face, but I knew by Joen's look that I had failed.

"Ladder's slippery when it's wet, eh?" Joen said, that familiar edge of sarcasm in her voice.

"It's not wet," I said before I realized what that would imply.

"So you're just a drunkard without a drink, then." Joen chortled loudly, turned, and walked across the almost empty hold. I could see immediately where she was heading: in one corner, a pile of crates and a few blankets formed a makeshift fort.

"Arranged a cabin for yourself, I see," I joked, but she didn't laugh.

"Wind hasn't been blowing much since we cleared the island, eh?" She crouched low, sat down on the deck, and slid herself effortlessly into the rickety construction.

"That can't last forever," I said, approaching the fort's entrance. I moved to follow her, but she glared at me from within.

"Oi, room for just one, an' I'm the one, eh?" She pulled a stained old remnant of a sail over her makeshift cabin, closing herself inside.

"Gods, what's eating you?" I said, maybe a bit too harshly.

"Go away, eh?" she replied, her voice muffled behind the canvas.

I took a few steps back toward the ladder, but stopped short. "No," I said.

Joen didn't answer.

I raised my voice. "No!"

Again, no answer.

I went back to her little hut. "I won't go away. Not this time."

"Oi!" she yelled, sliding out from behind the canvas and rising quickly to her feet. "You'll go away or I'll make you go away, eh?" She rushed forward, finger leading, ready to poke me in the chest.

At the last moment, I noticed a glint of steel in her hand. She led not with her finger, but with one of her daggers.

I stumbled back, shocked, nearly tripping over my own feet. I searched for words, for something to say to stop her maddened rush, but only a frightened yelp escaped my lips. I scrambled back, back, Joen's dagger dancing a few inches from my chest, shadowing my every move.

I crashed hard into the ladder, knocking the air from my lungs. The dagger rushed forward, coming to rest in the hollow of my chest. I half expected Joen to complete the thrust, to drive that finely crafted weapon into my heart. But she stayed her hand.

"What are you doing?" I asked once I'd regained some breath.

"Your mouth's moving," she said harshly, "but your legs should be, eh?" She pressed the dagger just a little bit harder, its fine edge creasing my tunic.

"Why—?"

"Because you ain't listening to me!" she interrupted.

Trying to keep my voice calm, I finished my thought. *"Why* are you so angry?"

Her face twisted, and suddenly Joen's hand held my throat. I could barely breathe, let alone speak. She pushed me upward, up the ladder. She was strong, and I had no choice but to oblige. I raised a foot up on the first rung then the next, and Joen followed. Her arms weren't long enough to keep her hand at my throat, nor could she keep the dagger against my chest. Instead, the blade slid down the front of my tunic to my belly, then lower.

I climbed the ladder in a hurry.

The crew was highly disciplined, but three days in the doldrums had begun to wear on them. Men were at their posts, but leaned on the rail or sat on makeshift seats—empty barrels and crates—or hammocks taken from below. Only Captain Deudermont, who was at the helm stood tall. But he barked no commands, said nothing at all. He just stared off into the distance. Beside him, the wizard Robillard sat cross-legged on a floating disk of faint blue light.

So the scene that had unfolded at middeck—me scrambling out from the hold, followed by the yellow-haired pirate girl brandishing a dagger—had surely stood out. But still, no one seemed to take any heed.

"What is it about Jaide that—," I started to ask.

"It's not about her," Joen said as she emerged onto the middeck. She still had her dagger, but she didn't press the attack this time. "The wind died when she got here, and I don't even know her, eh?"

"The wind died when she left."

"Oi, then maybe I'm angry she left!"

"I thought you said it wasn't about her."

"It's not about your elf woman!" Joen was practically yelling. "It's about the wind! You and that stone of yours . . . You can ride out of here any time you like, leaving bad luck behind for us. See there, see the empty sails?" She pointed her dagger at the mainsail, raised to full but slack in the still air. "Soon we'll run out of food, eh? And our bellies will be empty as that bloody sail."

"What would you have me do about it?"

"What, you mean you can't make the wind blow?" she shouted, sarcasm dripping from every syllable. "Why are you even here anymore? I thought your elf priestess gave you new orders. I thought you were done with m—"

She looked as if she wanted to continue, but a sudden commotion on the deck interrupted her.

The sailors had suddenly stood up, stood straight. And they were all staring, but not at us. I followed the gaze of the nearest man up to the mainsail.

The canvas rippled with the last breath of a gust of wind. We all stared for a few long moments, but another gust didn't follow.

Joen's whisper broke the silence. "Did you do that?"

"I think *you* did," I whispered back.

"Oi, I didn't do nothing!" she said. "I just said, 'You can't make the wind blow?' "

We looked up at the sail, but nothing happened.

She raised her dagger again, blade pointing at the sail. A gust of wind rose up around her, tousling her short blonde hair, filling the sail. The dagger slipped from her hand, dropped, spinning over once before digging point first into the wood. The fine blade cut deep into the deck, sinking nearly halfway down the eight-inch blade. I stared at it for a moment, trying to make sense of it. Not even a magical dagger should have slid so deeply into *Sea Sprite*'s strong planks.

Joen backed up a step, staring at the quivering dagger. I followed suit.

"That dagger," she said softly. "I took it from the dragon."

"I know," I replied.

"Think it's magical, eh?"

"Looks that way."

She paused for a moment. "God's favor, then," she said at last, stepping forward, reaching out to take the dagger.

A hand caught her wrist before she touched the hilt. "It's not the dagger," said Robillard.

Joen and I looked up to see both the wizard and the captain standing over us, staring at us with stern faces. I became aware of other eyes upon us too—every set of eyes on the deck. The action had shaken the sailors from their collective stupor.

"It's not the dagger," said Robillard, pulling Joen's hand up toward his narrowed eyes. "Where did you get that ring?"

"Same place I got the dagger, eh?" Joen replied. "Oi, let go, you're hurting my arm!"

Robillard grabbed her hand and tugged at the ring. By the grimace on her face, I figured the ring didn't want to leave her finger, but after a moment Robillard pulled it free. Joen stumbled back with a yelp, crashing against me and nearly knocking both of us to the ground. A trickle of blood dripped from her hand, from the cut on her knuckle where the wizard had torn the ring away.

"This is powerful magic, child," Robillard said, his voice hushed. "I ask again: where did you get it?"

"I took it from a dragon," she said. "It looked pretty, eh?"

Captain Deudermont interjected, "You stole from the dragon? Small wonder he attacked us, then. That was a foolish thing to do indeed."

I gently patted my chest, or more particularly patted the pouch set against my chest. The bag held the magical stone I had also stolen from the dragon. Though in fairness, the stone had been mine to begin with.

"You will relinquish your daggers, young miss," Deudermont continued, paying me no heed. "And then you will go below."

"Hey . . .," I started to argue, but Captain Deudermont cut me off.

"And you, Mister Maimun, will take your post in the crow's nest." He raised his voice so that the whole crew could hear. "We have our wind."

A cheer went up across the deck, muted and muffled at first. Then Robillard, now wearing the ring he'd taken from Joen, his eyes glittering with glee as he stared at it, waved his hand at the sails and a billowing gust rose around him and filled the mainsail. The cheer grew louder.

CHAPTER 63

"L AND HO!" I CALLED FROM THE CROW'S NEST. "BEHOLD THE WALLS OF WATERDEEP!"

We had sailed three days under the power of Joen's—now Robillard's—ring before a natural wind had come up from the northwest, perfect for filling our sails on our eastward voyage. Four more days after that, the same steady north breeze chilling my bones, I finally caught sight of Waterdeep, of a safe port and perhaps a warm bed.

A commotion on the deck caught my attention. I peered down from my tiny bucket, trying to comprehend what I was seeing. All the sailors of Deudermont's crew suddenly left their posts. About half headed toward the hold, while the other half gathered around the pirates who'd been given deck assignments for the day. The sailors moved with the precision of a trained fighting force—a trained, well-armed fighting force, I realized, as their weapons slid free of their sheaths.

"Hey!" I called down. "What's going on down there?"

Robillard, watching events from the sterncastle, called back, "Just stay put. It'll be over soon."

I was already setting my feet to the top rung of the ladder as he spoke and wasn't about to stop, but his words proved nonetheless true. By the time I set foot on the deck, the pirates on deck had been subdued, surrounded by sailors.

I headed below.

But I was, again, too late. I found the remaining pirate crew similarly rounded up and locked in the brig. The single cell was too tiny to hold even half the pirate crew, but once those captured above were brought in, surely the brig would be dangerously tight.

I scanned the captives, holding out some impossible hope that Joen had managed to elude the crew. But alas, her emerald eyes bore into me, peering back at me from the crowd.

"Maimun, I—," she started to say, but Captain Deudermont's voice cut her off.

"I did what I had to," the captain said, striding into the room.

Joen turned her gaze to Deudermont and her eyes narrowed to angry slits. "You lied to us," she said, and several others took up an echoing chorus of protest.

"A tenday in this tiny cell would have been unmerciful, and indeed might have been the last for many of you," he replied. "I have no desire to inflict such needless suffering."

"Oi, but he means 'e needed us to crack the ice and tie the sails," one pirate growled.

"I could have lawfully put you to the deeps and fed my crew far better," Deudermont reminded them.

"Ye've had to fight us first, what," said one. "Ye lying dog!"

"I have no desire to kill you, sir. Even now," Deudermont replied.

"Only to turn us over to them as will, eh?" Joen retorted.

"If you're found guilty of piracy, then yes."

I could hardly believe what I was hearing. How could I have judged Captain Deudermont so badly? I took him at his word, and every indication over the last tenday was that he meant to keep that word. Until now.

"But enough of this," he said, and turned to leave, then stopped to stare down at me. "Mister Maimun, you have duties to attend."

I squared my shoulders—not an easy thing to do under the glare of Captain Deudermont. I had always thought of Deudermont as regal, kingly, deserving of respect, even when I disagreed with him. Even when he had betrayed me—or, rather, I had thought he was betraying me, though events would prove otherwise—he had always appeared in command, and it had always seemed as if he *should* be in command.

But not now. His face was pale in the meager light, and his eyes, usually so confident, looked weary. His jaw was clenched too tightly, his arms crossed defensively over his chest. He was as imposing as always, but he also looked unsure, unhappy.

I wanted to confront the captain right then and there, try to make him see the error of his ways. But there were too many people around us—crewmen and pirates—and he would never concede in front of them.

I bit my tongue and walked past him, out of the room. I could feel Joen's eyes on my back, could hear her whisper, again, "Maimun, I . . ."

I found the captain alone an hour later and dared to follow him into his private quarters. I begged his pardon a dozen times before he even acknowledged my presence.

"The pirates are not your concern," he finally said to me. He sat down at his desk and did not motion to any of the comfortable chairs in the outer room of his quarters. His stare bored into me.

"N-not . . . most, no," I stammered, and only in hearing my own voice did I even realize how scared I was at that moment. Until then, perhaps I hadn't considered how much I had to lose.

"Yet you come to lecture me?"

"Your pardon, Captain, but you gave them your word." There, I said it. And to my surprise, merely speaking the truth lent strength to me—strength I sorely needed in that moment. "Out in the fight, when the sails all tangled, you made a deal, and a good one, but now you're—"

"You're a young man, Maimun," Deudermont interrupted. "Is it not just to serve the common good? There is an old saying that the means do not justify the end."

I thought I understood his meaning enough to agree with that old saying, and my nodding head did just that.

"In most cases, I would agree," Deudermont explained.

There was something in his voice that rang hollow to me.

"Our situation was desperate," he went on. "For both crews. A fight would have left all your pirate friends—"

"They aren't . . . all . . . my friends!"

I didn't like his responding smile.

"They would *all* have died out there on the cold waters," he said. "Or, what few might have escaped the blade would have spent the rest of the time miserable in the brig—and we'd not have fed them nearly as well. Instead, they enjoyed days of hope and honest work—no small thing—and something I will tell the magistrates on their behalf."

"Right before the magistrates hang them, you mean."

"The course they chose portended harsh justice, Maimun," he said, his voice cold enough to send a chill down my spine.

"And so they'll all hang for it," I said with as much sarcasm as my lack of breath allowed.

"Not all," he said, and I found myself believing his smile, but not his words. "There is little doubt of their piracy, but only the most hardened will be hanged. And not likely your little friend."

"Who'll spend the rest of her life in a dungeon, then?"

He shrugged—shrugged!—and oh, but I could have put my clumsy saber through his heart at that moment.

"They chose their flag," he said. "What would you have me do?"

"Keep your word!"

"I cannot."

"Then let Joen go!" I blurted, and didn't even care about the desperation in my voice or the tear in my eye.

"It is not my province to make such indiscriminate decisions. I am not a magistrate."

"At sea," I argued, "the captain is judge and jury."

"Harbor, ho!" someone cried from out on the deck.

"The harbormaster has spotted us and signaled us in," Deudermont said. "We're no longer at sea. Is there anything else, Mister Maimun?"

So much had been confusing in my strange journey, my life, but nothing more so than that strange conversation with a man I had thought was one thing, but was proving to be another. To claim that we were no longer at sea? A man like Captain Deudermont did not abide, did not govern, that kind of a cheap dodge. It made no sense to me—not the breaking of his word, not that this was his plan from the beginning, and not his refusal to free Joen. What threat was she to him or to the Sword Coast? She was just a girl, a kid like me.

There was nothing more to say, though, and like a good sailor, I took my post. I would be needed in the crow's nest to help guide the ship into port. At this time of year, the ice floes had receded to the north, but the occasional berg could still drift down this far south. I would be the ship's eyes this one last time.

I had learned well never to count on anyone but myself, and if Captain Deudermont wouldn't help me, then I had to make my own way. I had the stone, I had a purpose, and I had Haze, but I was missing something—something I couldn't leave *Sea Sprite* without.

The stone had brought all this down upon me, upon us. The stone had brought Joen out to sea with Chrysaor, the genasi pirate. The stone had put Deudermont and his sailors on Chrysaor's tail. Every event that had led to Joen's capture had been brought about by this cursed object, this weight around my chest—around my entire life. Maybe the stone had been working on Captain Deudermont, turning him back on his own word?

Maybe not, but it didn't matter. I knew what Deudermont had promised the pirates—a way back to Waterdeep in exchange for their help in restoring the ship—and I knew that their side of that bargain had been fairly delivered. I knew what was right, and I knew now what to do.

CHAPTER 64

HEY, TONNID, YOU MIND HELPING ME WITH SOMETHING?"

The man the crew called "Tin Head" looked up from his task. He was securing some lines near the port rail, standing a few yards from the nearest sailor.

"Whaddya need, Lucky Lucky?" His voice was low and ponderous as he whispered his nickname for me.

"Look, Tin," I said, "I don't think I'm gonna be here much longer, and there's something I want to give you before I go." Tonnid and his buddy Lucky were the closest things I had to friends on this ship—besides Joen—and I hoped my bluff would make enough sense to pry him from his duties. Thankfully his assignment was nonessential, and though he could certainly catch trouble from the captain if Deudermont knew he was leaving his post, the big sailor nodded.

"I left it near my bunk," I said, leading the way stealthily to the ladder below. A few other crewmen took note, but only in passing. They had their own duties to attend to.

The crew's quarters belowdecks were in some disarray. The crew—those who hadn't been on deck for the past six hours—had been celebrating the end to a successful voyage. Cards, crude bone dice, weighted clay mugs, and stale bread were scattered about on the few makeshift tables thrown together from empty crates and barrels. About the only thing anyone had done to clean up was to blow out the candles.

I took a seat on a bunk near an abandoned card game. Tonnid sat across from me.

"Look, Tin, I'm sorry," I began.

"You ain't here to gimme anything, are you?" he concluded.

"No, I'm not."

"You wanna take something."

"You know, you aren't as dumb as people think," I said with a chuckle.

"Nope, I ain't. But I don't mind 'em thinkin' it." He rose slowly. "But I can't just give you the key, y'know."

There it was. In that moment, in that admission, I knew that I wasn't the only one angry about Captain Deudermont's betrayal. Many of the crew of *Sea Sprite* had served aboard pirate ships as well, and in the long and dangerous days at sea, friendships had been forged between the crews. We had all worked for the common good, after all. These sailors knew redemption, and since a man's word was about the only thing a sailor had to hold onto during the trying days at sea, Deudermont's betrayal had stung them profoundly.

"I'm sorry, Tonnid," I said again. I stood and snatched one of the weighted clay mugs, still filled with a bit of ale, from the table. I leaped at Tonnid, swinging the mug at his head. The man, much larger than I, didn't even flinch. He bowed his head, catching the mug full in the brow.

Tonnid tumbled over backward, landing heavily, but on a bunk. Not that the ship's bunks were particularly soft, but anything was better than the hard wooden deck.

I went to the fallen man. He was still breathing, but out cold. His face was twisted somewhere between a grimace and a smile. I could see that his injury was superficial—I wasn't even certain if I had truly knocked him unconscious.

I grabbed the key ring hanging from his belt. Half a dozen keys of various shapes and sizes jangled on a large iron ring.

"Probably should have asked you which one it was," I lamented. I checked one last time to make sure he wasn't seriously hurt, then I sprinted off to the brig.

Two sailors guarded the prisoners. I knew neither of them particularly well, but they hardly looked surprised to see me.

"Captain wants me to relieve you," I said, facing the taller of the two, a man named Wart.

"No, he doesn't," Wart replied.

"He said we hold the brig till he comes himself," said the other, a toad-faced man called Vil.

"Which means, he didn't send you," said Wart.

"And that means you shouldn't be here."

"So why don't you just turn 'round and go away?"

Each followed the other's thoughts easily. They were friends and had probably fought together as effectively as they conversed.

But I had no choice.

The two flanked a wooden door beyond which was a small antechamber with the iron-barred cell that held the pirates—and Joen.

I rushed to my right, toward Vil, trying to snap my sword from its sheath as I went. But I was unaccustomed to the longer blade of my saber. It wasn't all the way out of its sheath when I reached the sailor, so I settled for throwing my shoulder into him, hoping to shove him aside in a moment of surprise.

But he was much stronger than I, and even with my momentum I barely moved him.

I fell back a step as Wart approached. He and his companion drew cutlasses. I finally got my saber free, and fell into a defensive stance. Two against one, and they were both bigger, stronger, and probably better trained than I.

But I had to get through that door.

I skipped away from Vil, closing the distance to Wart in a single stride, and lashed out with my blade. One, two, three times my sword cut through the air, but each time Wart's cutlass parried cleanly. He made no attempt to retaliate, but neither did he give ground. He was waiting for his friend to engage.

I darted back a step, pivoted, and brought by sword around in a wicked cut aimed for Vil's head. He had followed, as I figured, and my aim was true. But like his friend he was ready for the attack, and his sword stopped my own.

My attack had left my back exposed, an opportunity Wart didn't ignore. He stepped up, chopping his sword down at my head. I dived aside to my left, barely missing the blade. My own sword came up just in time to pick off Vil's attack, a horizontal slice from his right—directly against the momentum of my dodge.

By sheer luck, my blade stopped his, but the force of the blow made my arm tingle.

I had no time to recover as Wart cut in, his blade swinging at my shoulder. I couldn't bring my sword around fast enough to stop it, so I brought my empty hand up instead, hoping somehow to deflect the attack.

But my hand wasn't empty. It held Tonnid's key ring, gripped firmly in my fist, the iron circle across my knuckles.

The sword bit deep into the iron, nearly cutting through, but the ring held. I slid back a step, and the two sailors followed. I slid another step, and they paced me. Then I dropped my right foot behind me, as if I were going to step back again, and they moved forward once more, swords at the ready.

But instead of stepping back, I dived forward. They weren't expecting that, and each brought his sword in close, defensively. But my target was not either of them. Instead I aimed for the space between.

I went into a diving roll right between the startled sailors. I came to my feet a stride past them and let my momentum carry me forward beyond the reach of their swords, right into the wooden door.

I put my shoulder down and slammed into the door, hoping it wasn't locked.

Luck was with me. The door was locked, but the jam was a bit warped, having been damaged in the wreck. My shoulder stung from the impact and I couldn't keep my balance, but I slammed right through the door, bursting into the antechamber of the brig. I stumbled forward and fell unceremoniously on the floor.

The pirates, thirty strong, burst out in laughter.

I held up my hand, showing them the key ring.

The laughter stopped.

"You kill none of *Sea Sprite*'s crew!" I demanded.

No one answered.

"Promise! All of you!"

A chorus of "aye" came back at me, and figuring I didn't have time to poll them all, I knew it would have to do. A thin but strong hand reached out from the cage, near the door. I tossed the key to Joen and spun around, sword at the ready, preparing to defend myself once more.

But Wart and Vil had stopped in their tracks, just on the far side of the door. Their eyes were wide, their faces pale. I took a step toward them, and they turned and ran.

Behind me, the metal door swung open with a creak, and a stampede of unwashed bodies swept over me, pushed me aside and to the ground, very nearly trampling me.

It seemed like a long time—too long—before the crowd passed, though it was likely just a few heartbeats. And once they had gone, that same strong, thin hand grasped my shoulder and pulled me to my feet.

"I didn't betray you," I said to her.

"Oi, never said ye did," Joen replied, and her smile was genuine.

Before I could say anything else, she'd turned to run, and I followed her to the ladder.

By the time we reached the deck, the ruckus was in full swing. The pirates, though unarmed, had apparently caught the crew by surprise, and they'd pushed all the way to the gangplanks. They weren't trying to fight, after all, but were simply trying to get off the ship and out along the docks. The sailors had regrouped around them and were forcing the pirates toward the planks, out onto the long wharf. But the ship wasn't fully tied off, and the rocking of the deck made the crossing difficult. For each pirate who made it to the dock, another fell into the icy water below.

But I had a different plan, a different destination. I took Joen's hand and steered her to the captain's quarters.

"Try and find—," I started.

"The captain's key?" she finished, holding up the key ring, an ornate brass key singled out from the others. "This one looks to be the fanciest. Ye think it's the one?"

"Good a guess as any."

We reached the door apparently unnoticed, and Joen inserted the key. But it didn't turn.

"Guess that ain't it, eh?" she said, pulling up another key.

"Come on," I said. "If anyone notices us, we're dead."

"Nah, if we get caught, we're fighting," she said, discarding her second attempt and pulling up a third. "We ain't dead till we get killed, you know? And we ain't nothing if we ain't tough to kill."

The third key turned with a *click,* and we pushed through into the outer room of the captain's cabin. The room was, as I'd hoped, occupied. Valuable commodities were safest in the only locked room on the ship, and a magical horse was valuable indeed.

Haze lifted her beautiful head, shaking out her white mane. She peered at me with recognition. I imagined she was smiling.

"So that's the big plan, eh?" Joen asked.

"Good one, isn't it?" I said, moving to untie the mare.

"I don't see her saddle."

"She doesn't need one. Trust me."

"I do."

I stopped and looked at her, hoping to catch her gaze, wanting to ask what she meant, wanting to ask so many questions. She had been so cold to me since we left the isle where our two ships had crashed—no, since Jaide had arrived on the ship—but here she was, saying she trusted me.

Well, I guess I had just broken her out of the brig and was saving her from a noose or a dungeon cell in Waterdeep.

"I trust you too," I said.

She gave a little laugh. "I know," she said.

She was staring right at me, so close, just as we'd been in the crow's nest a tenday earlier—just as we'd been when she'd kissed me.

I wasn't sure of much at that moment, but I was sure I wanted to kiss her again. I gathered my courage, took a deep breath, and leaned in.

But she pulled back and shook her head.

"No?" I asked past the sudden clench in my gut.

She shook her head again. "Just friends," she said. "We gotta be just friends."

"But, in the crow's nest . . ."

She took a long pause, searching for an answer. "We'd just got off the island, you know? With the demon and the dragon and the druids and all that. I was just, you know, happy to be alive."

"So you're saying it was a mistake?"

"It wasn't a mistake. It was . . . ooh."

" 'Ooh'?"

But she didn't answer—she wasn't looking at me. She was staring at an ornate oak chest bound in brass and trimmed in silver and gold.

"Leave it," I said.

"Can't do that. Get Haze untied."

"It's probably locked, anyway," I warned her.

She held up the brass key that had failed to open the captain's door. "Oi, I'd expect so," she said with a laugh.

I dropped what I was doing and sprinted across the room. But Joen had already put the key in the lock and turned it before I could stop her.

The top of the chest popped open. A modest sum of gold stared back at us, as well as a few sparkling gems, some pieces of parchment, and a belt with two ornate, jewel-hilted daggers.

"We can't steal from Captain Deudermont," I said.

"Oi, why not? He wanted to kill me."

I stumbled for an answer but could find none. But to my relief, Joen grabbed her daggers and nothing more.

"These are mine anyway, eh? So I ain't technically stealing. All right?"

"All right." I turned back to Haze.

"And I'm taking one of these shines," Joen said, snatching a small blue gem from the chest. "For the ring that wizard stole."

I let out a long sigh. It wasn't worth an argument.

I untied Haze then poked my head out onto the deck, looking for some sign of pursuit. But no one seemed to notice me. They were all preoccupied with the melee raging across the deck. I took Haze by the mane and led her out onto the deck, Joen at her heels.

"Maimun!" a stern voice roared across the deck at me.

The hair on the back of my neck stood up and my knees actually started shaking. It was Captain Deudermont.

"Just get on!" Joen said, her voice cracking a little.

"Maimun!" Deudermont shouted again. "Hold right there, boy! Is this your d—"

Whumph!

Now I had to turn and look at him. The captain had been knocked on his rump by one of the pirates, and though the captain was red faced with anger and embarrassment, he was unhurt. The pirate who'd knocked him down got one of the captain's boots between his legs, a boot that lifted him right up and over the rail.

The situation wasn't much better for the rest of the pirate crew. As Joen tried to pull me up onto Haze's back, I watched the last group turn and try to cross the gangplank. But as soon as the last of them set foot on it, the whole thing simply vanished into thin air, and the pirates plummeted out of sight. I looked up to the sterncastle, directly above me, where Robillard stood laughing. He looked down, reached out, and helped the blustering captain to his feet.

I looked back at the gangplank and saw a magical net—woven strands of blue energy—rising of its own accord up over the rail and onto the deck. Nearly a score of pirates was tangled among the web.

The remaining dozen were on the long wharf, but the end was sealed off by armed and armored Waterdhavian guards. They had no place left to run.

"Oi, you have a plan, yeah?" Joen said. "Cuz if ye don't, we're next."

As if on cue, I heard Captain Deudermont say, "Robillard, the boy!"

"Of course," I replied, and hopped up on Haze's back, behind Joen.

I reached my arms around her and grasped Haze's mane. The horse apparently didn't need my guidance. She saw her escape route as clearly as I did.

In three strides, she was at full speed. In four, she was at the starboard rail—the seaward rail. Then she was airborne, Joen and I clinging for our lives. Something bright and cold and made of greenish-yellow light flashed just over our heads—something conjured by the wizard Robillard.

Haze fell below the arc of the wizard's spell but didn't splash into the water below. She landed with a jolt that almost knocked Joen and me off her back, but her hooves barely left an impression on the water. As the magical creature ran out a few yards then turned left toward the eastern edges of Waterdeep Harbor, I heard Captain Deudermont call my name one more time, but no more spells were cast our way.

I glanced back at *Sea Sprite*, the ship that had been the nearest thing to a home for me for the past months. Some of the crew lined the rail and I imagined they were bidding me a fond farewell—and maybe a few of them were—but in all likelihood, most of them were cursing me and all the trouble I'd brought.

I could hardly fault them for that.

And standing tall above them, his fine hat clinging to his head despite the wind, stood the captain. He didn't look as angry as I'd expected. From a distance, I couldn't see any rage in his burning eyes.

Only disappointment.

CHAPTER 65

A FEW LONG MONTHS AGO—AN ETERNITY AGO—HAZE HAD RUN TWO DAYS STRAIGHT, full gallop, without a rest. There seemed something eternal about the horse, magical and beyond the limitations of the flesh, or so I had thought.

But as we rode toward the imposing structure of East Torch Tower at the far southeast corner of the sprawling city, she could barely hold her gallop. By the time we rounded the sea wall and made landfall south of the city limits, she refused to run, and she was breathing hard.

Joen and I dismounted and did our best to examine the horse, but other than her obvious fatigue, Haze seemed fine. We both wondered if Robillard's spell had come closer to the animal than we'd thought. Neither of us could dismiss that the wizard might have worked some debilitating magic on the regal creature, but if that was the case, all either of us could do was hope it eventually wore off.

In some ways, though, her fatigue kept our pace slow, appearing casual to the many people who wandered the snow-lined roads on the outskirts of the great city. No one gave us a second look.

We had no provisions and traveled as quickly as we could manage. Haze needed to rest often, and we took that time to forage what bits of food we might find—berries, roots, and such, but it was always too little.

"Maybe she needs more food," Joen wondered, patting the horse's mane as we rode along a narrow dirt track.

I shrugged and replied, "Maybe. *Sea Sprite* didn't have much in her stores to offer a horse, and the grass here is still dead and frozen."

In some ways hoping we were right, in other ways fearing the beautiful horse was starving to death, we avoided the subject like we avoided the main road. But by the third long, cold, hungry day, our stomachs were rumbling loudly, and it became obvious that we needed to find a town—or at least a homestead—soon, or we'd all perish.

An early spring storm came up, cold rain blowing hard. I wrapped my formerly magical cloak as tightly as I could around the two of us. Before it had lost its magic, the cloak would have expanded to easily cover us both, but now each gust of wind pulled up its edges, threatening to throw our meager cover off entirely.

Despite her continued exhaustion, Haze trotted down the muddy road with barely a bump, every movement fluid. The same magic that allowed her to run across open water kept her from digging in too deeply in the mud. I wrapped my arms around Joen and grasped Haze's mane tightly. I ducked my head beneath the cowl of my cloak and closed my eyes.

Haze will keep the road, I trusted. She's smart.

A sharp elbow to the chest jarred me.

"What was that for?" I asked.

"Gotta stay awake, eh?" Joen said.

"No, I don't gotta," I answered.

"It's how you freeze, y'know? You fall asleep and then you don't wake up."

"I'm not about to freeze to death."

"How do I know that, eh?" Joen turned in her seat to look at me, her eyes full of concern.

"I just told you."

"Oi, but ain't that exactly what someone would say if they were freezing?" She smiled and laughed.

Smiled and laughed—out here in the increasingly wild North, in the freezing cold, starving and miserable. I looked at her, searching for some sign that she was just putting on a brave face to keep my spirits up, but her mood appeared genuine.

Another gust of wind blew in, lifting the cloak and tossing Joen's blonde locks in front of her face. Her hair was shorter than it had been when I'd first met her. Then, her wheat-colored tresses had reached most of the way down her back, but now the jagged edges where she'd taken dagger to lock barely touched her shoulders.

But the look certainly suited her, and I wanted to tell her that but I couldn't find the words.

She turned away from me, pulled the hair back from her face, and shook her head vigorously. If I weren't already soaked to the bone, the sudden wave of water her hair threw into my face might have startled me.

I retrieved the corners of my cloak, fluttering around us in the breeze, and pulled them forward, once again wrapping the tattered thing around myself and Joen. I dropped my head to her shoulder, planning to ignore her warning and take a nap.

But something off a few hundred yards up the road and a few hundred to the side caught my eye.

"Is that . . .?" I began, staring into the distance.

"Torchlight," Joen said.

Though we were three days east of Waterdeep, there were still farmsteads and tilled fields, a few abandoned buildings and crumbling watchtowers, and scattered copses of bare trees. The hills looked like frozen waves, and the heavy rain was melting snow and ice and creating little fast-running streams all around us. The sound of the rain was practically deafening, and the clouds were so heavy it was almost as dark as night. The torchlight, however distant, was unmistakable.

"Could be a patrol from Waterdeep looking for us," I said, hoping it wasn't true.

"They wouldn't waste their time," Joen said, "especially in this weather."

"Bandits, then?"

"Could be. Think they'd have some food, eh?" she chuckled.

"I doubt they'd share."

"C'mon, it ain't bandits. You just don't wanna get your hopes up, right?"

"What do you mean?"

"It's a hamlet," she said. "But if you say, 'It's a hamlet' and it ain't, it means you got hopeful too early."

"It could be a hamlet," I said. "But way out there?"

"It's a hamlet, or a farm at least, and we're going there, eh? What's the worst that could happen?"

"Could be an orc war party," I joked, but even as I said it, the thought made me shiver.

"All right, sure. But what's the *best* that could happen?"

"It could be Malchor Harpell," I said.

"Oi, who?"

"He's a wizard, I think. I was going to look for him last autumn, but then I found Chrysaor in Waterdee—"

Joen's angry growl cut me off. "Chrysaor. Yeah, that's the best case right there," she said.

"Best?" I asked, confused.

"Chrysaor's the one carrying that torch, and we find him, and I kill him dead, eh?" she said. The anger had left her voice as quickly as it had come, replaced with a chilling flatness.

"It's probably just bandits," I said, trying to change the subject.

We both laughed and Joen patted Haze on the side of her neck, teasing her in the direction of the torch. The horse turned—and stumbled. Joen and I both jerked forward, and my forehead hit the back of her head hard enough that I saw stars and she gasped in pain. Haze's head dipped forward, and we both slid off her back for fear we'd tumbled forward over her head.

When our weight was off her, Haze seemed to feel better, but not much better.

"She's never stumbled like that before," I said.

Joen's brow was furrowed and her jaw tight as she patted her hands gently along the horse's flank. We were all dripping wet and our breath came in puffs of white steam— Haze's bigger and faster than ours.

"She needs rest," Joen said to me, then to Haze, "Don't you, my fine girl?"

I looked around and there was no other sign of life, not even an abandoned barn or a stand of evergreens that might have sheltered us. There was just that torchlight.

"Maybe you can trust in that luck of yours, eh?" Joen said, and her voice was tight, strained.

I shook my head at first, but when her face fell, I nodded instead.

Looking back at the torchlight, I said, "Whoever it is, we should try, while Haze can still walk at all."

CHAPTER 66

I 'M NEVER GOING TO HEAR THE END OF THIS, AM I?" I ASKED WITH A SIGH.

"Not for a long time, at the least, eh?" Joen said.

The torchlight we'd seen from the road turned out not to be a torch at all, but the diffuse glow of a fire in a fireplace. The light emanated from the window of a small house that was itself part of a small collection of buildings.

It was a hamlet.

"You folks look cold an' wet," a man called out to us as we trotted into the tiny town. He seemed like a nice enough sort, with a full, busy brown beard and the sturdy wool and leather clothes of a frontier farmer.

"Well met, good sir," Joen said, sounding uncharacteristically friendly. "You know where we can get warmed up?"

"Ayuh, I do at that," the man said. "I got a warm fire and good food if ye'll come inside."

"Very kind of you to offer," I said.

"Comes with a price, though," he continued, ignoring me.

"We have no coin," I said.

"Don't have to be coin, then," the man offered.

I looked around at the tiny cluster of houses. The village was altogether only half a dozen buildings clustered close together and circled by sturdy fences. In some ways it was almost more a fort than a town, but then we were far from any city and the reach of armed patrols. The folk out this far had to fend for themselves and had built this village—little more than a meeting place for scattered farmsteads—to keep someone, or some*thing*, at arm's length. Still, that fire looked warm, and I could see a stable where Haze could get some rest.

Joen nudged me, showing me the gem she'd taken from Deudermont's cabin.

I lowered my voice to a whisper and said to her, "That's worth more than a meal and a night in the stables." I shook my head then called back to the man. "What did you have in mind?"

"Oh, nothin' much. The horse'll do," He flashed a near-toothless smile.

Before I could stop her, Joen stepped away from the ailing horse. The man took a step closer, thinking she had accepted his offer. I knew better. I tried to hold her back, but lost my balance, falling unceremoniously into the mud, pulling Joen down with me.

"Oh ho, now ye'll need a bath too," the man cackled.

"Joen, put the daggers away," I whispered. "Ignore him. We'll move on."

"He wants Haze bad enough, maybe we go to sleep tonight and don't wake up in the morning, eh?" she said, her voice colder than the driving rain. "I'll give him a few good, painful memories, and then we can have all the food and warmth we need."

"We're not killers," I reminded her, "and we aren't bandits."

"Not yet, anyway."

"Joen . . .," I whispered.

She looked at me for a long moment. "Fine," she said at last. "But if no one else will help, we come back and take what we need here, eh?" She took my arm.

"Agreed," I said, pulling her to her feet. Together we turned toward the rest of the town.

We'd taken only a few steps when the man called after us. "Change your mind, did ye?"

"Oi, hold your tongue or I'll cut it out," Joen snapped at him.

"If I can't have the horse, lad," the man said with a cackle, "maybe you could leave me the lass. I could use someone to do the cookin' and washin' up."

Joen stopped dead in her tracks, but before she could turn and take a step, I wrapped my arm around her waist, trying to pull her along. I managed only to tackle her once more into the mud. The man behind us cackled away.

Across the way, the door to another house swung open. A bit of light trickled out into the street—not so warm and inviting as the first man's house, but light nonetheless. The hunched silhouette of an old woman stepped through the door.

"You dearies just ignore that old codger," she called out to us.

"We're lost," Joen and I replied at the same time.

"Well, that's a shame. Come on now. I've got warm food and a spare room."

We both rose from the mud—again—and walked toward the woman. Joen cast one last deadly glare over her shoulder at the toothless man, who was still laughing wildly.

"Room's been empty since my son left," the woman said as we approached the quaint little cabin. "Left it ready in case he comes back to visit, but he never does. Well, I ain't got proper stables for your horse, but I can put him in with the pigs, if you want."

"She," I said. "And I think she'll be grateful for any shelter at all."

"All right, dearie. You two can head in, leave your wet things by the fire. I'll put your horse up and be back shortly." She reached up to pat Haze's strong neck, and the horse, a good judge of character, didn't shy away.

It had been so long since I'd had a warm meal, I had nearly forgotten just how good it can be. And the old woman, Tessa, proved to be a fine cook.

Dinner conversation was light, as Joen and I each had food in our mouths for the whole of the hour. I had once read that following a period of starvation, it's a bad idea to eat too much too quickly, but when presented with food after three days without, no amount of logic would keep me from stuffing my face as thoroughly as I could manage.

We did get a few words in between bites, relating only the barest essentials of our story to Tessa: we'd been sailors but had quit the crew, and now we journeyed east. And it wasn't until then that I really stopped to wonder where we were heading, after all. At first we'd just had to get away from Waterdeep, for fear that Captain Deudermont had set the Watch on us. But now . . .

"And how about you, ma'am?" I asked Tessa after I'd finished chewing the last bite of my fourth plate of food. "How did you come to live out here?"

"Most of them that live in these villages were born to 'em, I expect," Tessa replied. Her voice was as warm and as welcoming as the fire dancing in her hearth. "But I was a city girl once, long ago. Lived in a place far to the south, called Baldur's Gate. You ever been that way?"

"We've both been there, aye," Joen said. "We met for th' first time on a ship just out of the Gate, last summer, you remember?"

"I remember the meeting, but the ship's name escapes me," I said.

"Doesn't matter now, eh? She's at the bottom of the sea." She shot me a glance somewhere between anger and laughter.

I winced at the memory. My mentor had called pirates on my behalf to take that ship. I had thought by now Joen would have let that go, but apparently not.

"So, why did you leave the Gate?" I asked Tessa, trying to change the subject.

"Not unlike you, I'm guessin'," she said, "I was runnin' from someone. Took my son and left the city, came to where the towns ain't even got a name. Farmers and trappers 'round here just call it 'Town.' Better place to raise a young boy, anyway, out where there's room to play and grow."

A flash of a forest entered my mind. Yes, growing up in the wilder world had been good for me. "I lived in the countryside when I was young," I said, embellishing my story a bit to make it fit. "But I longed to see the cities."

"Well, so did my son, at that!" the woman said with a laugh. "He turned his twentieth and he met a girl, and off they went to live in the city, and I've been alone since. But I bet your'n parents still live out in the country, don't they? And they're just waitin' for you to come home and visit, like a good boy should."

I winced. Apparently noticeably, as Tessa's expression dropped a bit.

Joen spoke for me. "We're both orphans," she said, her voice toneless, matter-of-fact, as though being an orphan was nothing to worry about.

"Oh, dearies, I'm sorry. And here I am bringing up memories you probably don't want to be seeing. Oh, I'm so sorry."

You're half right, I thought. Plenty of memories, but I'd rather remember than forget.

"Well, anyhow, dearies, it looks like you've had enough of my cooking for now," Tessa said after a pause.

"Yes, and it was wonderful," I said.

"Oi, delicious," Joen agreed.

"Well, thank you for saying. Now, as I said, there's an open room and the bed's all clean and made and ready. I expect you two could use a good long sleep, yes?"

I nodded emphatically, rising to my feet. Joen followed suit.

"Well, it's right through there." She motioned to one of the plain doors in the plain walls of the plain room. "I'll just clean this up. You two can head for bed. I'll wake you for breakfast in the morn."

I would have helped with the cleaning, but after three long days on the road, the thought of bed was simply too enticing. Joen, I could see, agreed, based on the way she pulled her feet behind her. Usually she walked with such a light step, practically a skip.

Of course, once we got into the guest room, one more problem became obvious. There was only a single bed, and it was rather small. Joen didn't seem to mind—or even notice. She simply moved to the bed and plopped down.

"I suppose I'll sleep on the floor, then," I said. "Toss me a pillow, would you?"

Joen looked at me for a moment, puzzled, then burst out laughing.

"What, you're afraid to share a bed with a girl, eh?" she said, her voice low, mocking.

I took a little wooden carving of a horse off a shelf and turned it over in my hands, pretending to be interested in one of Tessa's son's childhood toys. "I . . . um . . . I don't . . . What?"

"Relax, *kid,*" she said, emphasizing the last word as if she were so much older than I. "Look, it's simple." She took one of the pillows and laid it down the center of the bed, which was clearly delineated by the simple pattern of the homespun quilt. "This is the line. You cross the line, I'll stab you really really hard with my daggers. You got it?"

I put the horse back on the shelf and reached for the little wooden pig next to it. "These are . . .," I said, searching for a word, any word, ". . . fun."

"You shut up and go to bed already, eh?"

The storm passed in the night, and I awoke to sunlight streaming in through the bedroom window. Joen had apparently risen before me, and the room was empty, the bed warm and comfortable. I wrapped myself in the blankets and watched the morning light, which was shining through the dusty glass, trace its way across the floor ever so slowly.

The door burst open and I sat up, startled.

"Wake up, lazy," Joen said as she entered. Her hair was damp, pulled back from her face. Her clothes were clean—or, at least, cleaner than they'd been the day before.

"I'm not lazy," I said, rolling out of bed. My foot caught on a rug I hadn't noticed the previous night. The rug slipped out from under me and I stumbled, nearly crashing to the floor.

"Oi, you're clumsy, though," Joen chuckled.

I shrugged, hardly in any position to argue.

"Well, the washroom's open, eh? And Tessa's cooking breakfast."

"Sounds like a plan," I said.

"No, it really doesn't," Joen answered. "Do we have a plan?"

"Sort of," I said, moving toward the door.

But Joen stepped in front of me. " 'Sort of' ain't good enough right now, eh?" she said.

"I have a name," I said. "The dark elf told me: Malchor Harpell. When we find him, I think he can help us destroy the stone."

"Oi, you mean the stone that got me free of *Sea Sprite*'s brig, that made good our escape, that cold and wet as we were got us to Tessa? That's the stone you want to destroy? The one you almost killed me and my shipmates to get? I say we follow Tymora's good fortune wherever she leads us, and—"

She was interrupted by the clatter of clay plates as Tessa set the table just outside the door. The smell of freshly cooked eggs wafted in, and my stomach rumbled a bit.

Again I moved toward the door, and again Joen stepped in front of me. "I don't want it," I told her as plainly as I could.

"And you can't toss it away, or give it away?" she asked.

"Can't you just trust me that this is important?"

"Can't you trust me enough to tell me what I'm out here risking my life for?" Joen's expression was soft, gentle. I had not seen such a look on her face often, but it seemed to fit. "Oi, didn't we just face a dragon to get the thing back?"

"I can't just toss it away," I said. "If I get too far away from it, I die."

Joen's eyes widened and she backed a step away from me. She was about to say something when there came a sharp rap on the front door of the cottage. I heard Tessa move to the door, humming a soft tune. "And this . . . Malker Horple?"

"Malchor Harpell."

"Can take care of that for you?" she asked. A look of desperation crossed her face and made my heart sink. "He can free you of it?"

"Before I found you in Waterdeep," I said, "I had a guide, a friend. He gave me that name. I don't know any more than that he might be able to help," I said, crossing to the door and pulling it open. "I have to find Malchor Harpell."

I stopped in my tracks. The front door to the house was ajar. A man had entered. He had apparently been speaking to Tessa, but now he turned to look at me.

"Well now," Chrysaor said, his voice deep, his bluish skin shining in the morning sunlight. "That's an interesting name for a child to know."

CHAPTER 67

ALWAYS BEFORE, JOEN'S MOVEMENTS IN BATTLE HAD BEEN GRACEFUL, EACH MOTION leading naturally to the next. But not this time.

All grace had left her, replaced by pure rage. She leaped forward, stabbing out with both her daggers.

I looked at Tessa. Her jaw hung open, and her face was pale.

"How do you know him?" I asked her.

"Don't, dearie," she said. "He just showed up. I was gonna ask him to join us for breakfast."

Chrysaor fell back a step, out of Joen's reach, and she pursued, step for step, withdrawing her blades and stabbing out again.

"I don't think he's here for breakfast," I said.

Joen slashed at him, a wild roundabout swing that came up short.

"No," the old lady replied. "I suppose not."

But even as Joen's dagger flashed harmlessly by, she charged in behind it, stabbing with her other hand, an awkward and off-balance movement that conveyed her blind rage.

The pirate's sword finally left its sheath. Though it was a fine metal blade, straight and narrow, it seemed almost dull in comparison to Joen's flashing daggers. Each ray of the morning light glinted off the twin weapons, reflected a dozen times, shining as bright as the sun itself.

Chrysaor held his sword vertically, and swept it across his body, driving both of Joen's daggers to the side. She retracted, leaving an obvious opening in her defenses, but Chrysaor didn't attack, and Joen quickly righted her blades.

The blue-skinned pirate captain risked a glance my way and said, "Your friend wants me dead."

"I tend to agree with her," I answered.

"You shouldn't."

Joen jumped ahead again, and once more, Chrysaor deflected her attack. Metal rang against metal, and Chrysaor sidestepped another brutal thrust.

Joen rushed forward again, but this time Chrysaor moved to meet her. He parried one thrusting dagger, sidestepped the other, and for the first time made an attack of his own. He punched out with the pommel of his sword.

Joen didn't even begin to dodge the attack. Chrysaor's weapon collided heavily with her shoulder, sending her staggering back several steps. The genasi followed her, kicking out at her ankles, trying to trip her. She skipped back a few steps, holding her balance, but barely.

"You know," I said to Tessa, "I should probably help her."

"Might be a good idea, dearie."

I dashed into the guestroom, where my sword belt lay beside the bed. I scooped it up, strapping it to my hip as I rushed back to the battle.

By now, Joen had pushed Chrysaor back from the cottage door and out into the single muddy street around which the tiny hamlet was built. And the battle had attracted attention. Every door in town had opened, with at least one person standing in each doorway, watching in something between shock and amusement. Directly across the lane, the old man from the night before hooted and cheered—but I couldn't tell which side he was on.

"Come on, little girl," Chrysaor taunted, beckoning her to him with his free hand.

"I'm no little girl," Joen hissed, leaping forward again.

She stabbed ahead with her left dagger, but Chrysaor picked the attack off cleanly with his sword. She stepped forward, cutting across brutally with her right. He fell back a step, out of reach. Joen planted her foot, thrusting her right-hand dagger ahead. His only escape was to her left, rolling his body away from the jab.

Or, I noted, he could have come straight ahead and attacked her too-aggressive posture, using his longer blade to keep her at bay. But once again, he chose not to attack, only to defend, and I knew that he was too fine a fighter to unwittingly let so many obvious opportunities pass.

"I could have killed you as you slept, if I had a mind to kill you at all," Chrysaor said.

"If you don't want us dead," I cut in before Joen could respond, "then why are you here?"

"Ah, a question at last," he replied. "I was sent to watch you, of course. To follow you and report on your progress."

Joen continued to press her attacks, daggers cutting and thrusting, but Chrysaor was always one step ahead, his defenses always in place. Joen seemed not to have tired at all—remarkable in and of itself—but she hadn't wearied her target either.

But now I was more interested in what the genasi had to say than in trying to kill him—that had always been Joen's fight, the same way the stone was mine.

"Report to whom?" I asked him. "Your master is dead."

Chrysaor laughed. "Surely you know better than that," he said. "A demon as my master? Please."

At last, I fumbled the buckle of my sword belt closed and tried to draw my sword as I ran to Joen's side, but once again the long blade failed to come out cleanly. Instead, the dangling scabbard, moved by the withdrawing blade, tangled in my legs. In the already slippery footing of the muddy "street," my boot slid out from under me, and I fell with a splash into the muck.

"Oi, you work for the Circle, then," Joen snarled. "You've been working for them since the start."

"Pretty," Chrysaor said with an infuriatingly smug smile, "but not so smart. I see why you like this one, kid."

Irritated by that last crack, I pulled myself up quickly, trying not to look any more foolish in the process, but no one was looking at me.

Of course they weren't. They were focused on the fight raging not a dozen feet from me.

I extracted my sword, more carefully this time, and finally took my place at Joen's side.

Joen stepped forward, her face a twisted scowl. "You shut up," she said. "You betrayed your crew and got 'em killed."

I moved around Joen, looking for an opening, for a way to help. But Chrysaor moved with me, rotating around Joen as if she were the center of a wheel, and we two were the spokes. However I moved, he kept her between us.

"I warned you all of the dangers," the pirate argued.

Joen let out a low growl, pushing ahead ever more furiously. Left, right, left her daggers cut, and one wild sidelong slash nearly clipped me as the blade came around! Chrysaor parried the first, then the second swing, and stepped back from the third, and the slash.

"Oi, 'In my employ you shall find only the greatest gain,' eh?" Joen shot back at him. "Isn't that what you said back when I joined *Lady Luck*'s crew?"

Joen pressed the assault. She stabbed out with her right hand, and Chrysaor stepped back. She followed with a left. He stepped back again. She leaped forward, punching out with both daggers. Chrysaor fell into a backward roll, falling beneath the cut of her blades, and came to his feet a few strides away, a bit muddy but unharmed.

"And where did you get those fine, shining daggers, child?"

Joen hesitated.

"Took them from a dragon's hoard, isn't that right?" the genasi went on. "A dragon's hoard you never would have found had you not sailed with me?"

She charged ahead, cutting with both daggers. Chrysaor brought his sword in for the parry, but Joen's attack was a feint. She withdrew both blades, letting the sword slip harmlessly past. She brought one dagger up quickly, snapping it against Chrysaor's blade, forcing it farther out to his side. With the other, she plunged ahead.

The pirate stepped back, out of her shortened reach, and brought both hands to the handle of his sword. With a burst of strength, he shoved back against Joen's pressing dagger. He was much stronger than she, and her footing was slick. She skidded back a few feet. Joen held her balance, bringing her daggers up in a defensive cross in front of her, but Chrysaor did not press the attack.

"You led us out there," I said as Joen circled him, looking for an opening. "You wanted me to pursue you, to be captured by the druids."

"And I knew Captain Deudermont was honorable enough to give you the chance," he said with a wry smile.

I snorted at the thought. "Deudermont said no," I told him. "It was *Sea Sprite*'s crew that changed his mind."

"And it doesn't excuse you using your own crew like that," Joen added.

"I need no excuses for my actions."

"Oi, I think you do, at that."

Then I saw the pirate's arm twitch—just the slightest jerk of his elbow.

"Joen, duck!" I cried out.

Her defenses weren't set. She thought of nothing but trying to kill him, unconcerned for her safety. But he had been fighting purely defensively, letting her attacks play out. He had tricked her, had goaded her into his trap.

He had tricked us both, I realized. I could have kept pace, could have been there to pick off the attack. But I wanted to hear what the pirate had to say.

The flat of Chrysaor's blade struck Joen's left ear, rolled up and over her head, and tapped her right temple. His empty left hand caught Joen's wrist and he pulled her past him. He planted a boot on the small of her back as she stumbled past. Kicking out, he launched her skidding to the ground several feet away.

"Are we done playing yet, children?" Chrysaor asked.

"I'm not playing," Joen snarled, spitting out mud.

"Not very well, at least."

Joen rose to her feet and stalked toward Chrysaor.

"I could have killed you right there," he said.

"I will kill you right now," Joen answered.

"Stop, Joen," I said. He was right. He could have killed her a long time ago. He could have killed us both, but he hadn't. He had something to say.

Joen shrugged me off but hesitated, looking for an opening in the pirate's defenses that wasn't there.

"All irrelevant, all of this," Chrysaor said, waving his arms as if to chase away the conversation. "There's a more important question you want to ask of me. There's someone you'll like to meet."

"I don't think there's—," Joen began.

"Malchor Harpell," I said, cutting her off, but lowering my voice so the villagers wouldn't hear.

Chrysaor pointed a finger to me, nodding. "And there it is. I know much of him, as most learned folk of the North should."

"We don't care," Joen cut in.

"I care," I said, and Joen glared at me.

She walked over to me and said in a whisper, "Nothing he says can be trusted. We should kill him and be done with it."

"I don't trust him," I replied. "But he buried his lie in truth last time, didn't he? He did lead you to a treasure hoard."

"Guarded by a dragon, after we were caught by a pirate hunter and wrecked in a blizzard."

"So maybe we'll have to fight a dragon to get to Malchor Harpell."

"Or this wizard of yours is dead, or this time Chrysaor's just lying and it's a trap."

"Or," Chrysaor said, "my task is not to get you killed, and I have no particular reason to keep you away from Malchor Harpell, so I'll tell you truthfully what I know."

"I doubt that," Joen said.

"But say it anyway," I finished.

Chrysaor nodded. "The Harpell clan are wizards, nearly to a one," he said. "Most of them live in the town of Longsaddle, a tenday's ride to the northeast of here. But Malchor no longer dwells there. He instead resides in his own private tower, the Tower of Twilight."

"And where is this tower?" I asked.

"I'll have to show you."

"No." Joen spoke before I could, but my answer would have been the same.

"The tower is magically hidden. You'll not find it without my help."

"We'll take our chances," Joen said.

"No," I cut in, my voice low, quiet. "We won't."

She stared at me in disbelief. "You want to take him along?"

"I want him to show us to the tower. That's all." I looked back at the pirate and said, "If you never served Asbeel and aren't reporting to the Circle, who is it, then, that's so interested in helping me find this wizard?"

The pirate smiled at me in a way that made it clear he thought I should know the answer to that.

"Elbeth," I said before I even realized I was thinking of the woman who had raised me as her own child.

"Quite a lady," the pirate said with a chuckle, "isn't she?"

"Oi, you believe that?" Joen asked me, and her voice made it plain that she didn't.

"I don't know," I answered, "but I need to find Malchor Harpell, so I need him."

She scowled at me. "What if I tell you it's him or me, then?"

"I'll choose you," I said without hesitation. "But please, please, don't. I know it could be a trap. I know Malchor Harpell could be of no help. I know this pirate might be leading us into the gods alone know what. But I need to learn the truth, and I won't find it in this one-mule hamlet." I glanced around at Tessa and said with a shrug, "Sorry."

"No worries, lad," the old lady replied. "We really only do have that one mule, and you've given us more excitement than we've had since that dragon flew over in the Year of the Bloodbird."

I looked back at Chrysaor then to Joen, and asked, "So?"

Her scowl softened a bit. After a few moments, she nodded her assent.

"We're agreed, then," Chrysaor said jovially. "We should be off at once, unless you have other plans."

"Lead on," Joen said, but she wasn't the slightest bit happy about it.

CHAPTER 68

WELL, THIS IS EXCITING, EH?" JOEN SAID OVER THE CRACKLE OF THE FIRE AND THE howl of the wind. She did little to hide the sarcasm in her voice.

We had set up our camp in the midst of a small grove of pines that sheltered us from the wind still blowing hard from the north. At the edge of Neverwinter Wood, a tenday and a half's journey north of Tessa's village, we had finally come to the Tower of Twilight.

Or, rather, we'd come to a small pond with a tiny, empty island bordered by the grove of pines. Winter had not yet relinquished its grip here, and patches of snow dotted the area. The journey had been arduous, the road a mix of mud and snow, the wind often biting. But the sky had been bright, the clouds few, and on some days, we'd even been warm.

We had journeyed more slowly than I was used to, partly because Chrysaor had walked ahead of us—a good ways ahead, by Joen's insistence—but partly because Haze had still seemed weak. We had stopped well before nightfall each day, and had risen after daybreak. I had said it was to avoid having to make or break camp during the cold, dark, northern spring nights, but really I had just wanted to let Haze rest. It had struck me how greatly Haze's stamina had lessened, and I had feared that maybe the magic that had allowed her to run so swiftly, even across water, had come at a greater price than I'd imagined.

The nights had been cold, but Tessa had given us some warm blankets before we left—they'd been her son's, and she had no longer needed them. In payment, she had requested that we visit if ever we were in the area again, a request Joen and I heartily agreed to.

But today had dawned cold, and it had stayed cold. Clouds had hovered low over the land, and the wind had blown fiercely. It had been barely past midday when Chrysaor stopped his march and had called for us to set camp here in the trees. When he had told us we'd arrived, I had laughed at first—Joen hadn't, she had simply scowled. But now, after a few hours, I came to realize the blue-skinned pirate had been serious.

"His friends ain't on time, I guess," Joen said.

"That, or he's lost his mind," I replied.

"Oi, he never had one to begin with."

I laughed as a light snow blew up on the wind—the beginnings of a late-season snowstorm. The sun, masked behind the clouds, touched the southwestern horizon.

"Nothing to do now," I said. "It's late, it's snowing, and this is as good a place to camp as any."

"No," said Chrysaor, approaching the fire, the light reflecting weirdly off his blue skin, tinting him a deep violet. "It's as good as any place under the open sky. But tonight, you will sleep in beds, I assure you. It won't be much longer now."

"Before what, eh?" Joen said. "Before your crew shows up to kill us?"

Chrysaor shook his head. "Patience is a virtue you should learn, little lady," he said with a wry grin.

"Call me 'little lady' ever again," Joen snarled, "and I'll cut you just right so you can take the nickname as your own."

It took me a moment to sort out what she meant, but when I did, I found myself turning my hips away from her and crossing my legs.

"What do you prefer, then?" Chrysaor asked. "I've been calling you 'child,' and you've yet to protest."

"I'd prefer you not talk to me at all," she said.

The pirate nodded, bowed low, and turned back to the pond.

Or, rather, to the shimmering image floating above the pond.

As the sun disappeared beneath the horizon, the very last ray of light traced its way up an object, a tower, standing on the tiny island. Its twin spires reached skyward, twisting into the night sky, each point sparkling like starlight. The whole structure was emerald green, brilliant as Joen's eyes.

A beam of green light traced out from the base of the tower, across the pond to the near shore, forming a sort of bridge of light. I approached tentatively, Joen and Haze following. Chrysaor did not move.

"I lead no farther," he said. "I have shown you to the tower, but I have no place here."

"Why not?" I asked, a bit surprised.

"Oi, don't ask him that," Joen said. "He might change his mind."

"No, child, I will not," Chrysaor said. "But this is not my quest."

"Your quest is to follow me," I said. "But you won't follow me inside?"

"Don't worry," Chrysaor said with a laugh. "I'll be fine without you." He bowed low, sweeping off his hat. "Farewell, and good luck."

The blue pirate, the man who had twice tried to kidnap me, turned on his heel and walked away, disappearing into the grove of pines.

I stared after him for a long time. I hadn't expected that.

Joen just shrugged and walked past me to the bank of the pond and the green light.

"D'you think it's a bridge?" Joen asked.

I stepped closer to the beam of light, though looking at it made me dizzy. It was like a rainbow, but I could clearly see the ends of it—one right in front of me, the other at the foot of the strange tower.

"I don't know," I said, shaking my head. "We could swim across."

"Why go to all this trouble to make us think it's a bridge if we only end up falling in the water anyway, eh?" Joen said as she stretched out her foot, gingerly touching the light.

I reached out to pull her back, afraid of . . . I don't know what. But before I touched her, her toe touched the light. She seemed fine.

"So?" I asked. "What is it?"

She looked at me, smiled, and stepped forward. She looked quite strange, standing on a beam of light, hovering a few feet above the still water.

"C'mon, then," she said with a smile. "Let's see what's here, eh?" She laughed and ran off across the bridge, then around the base of the tower and out of sight.

Haze and I followed, reaching the island just as Joen completed her lap of the structure. "No door," she said, but she was still smiling.

"You think it's magically hidden, maybe?" I asked.

"Oi, I sure hope so!" Joen said.

"You like magic," I noted.

Joen nodded enthusiastically.

"A bit too much, I think," I said, looking up at the seemingly impenetrable tower.

She scoffed and said, "Hey, this was all your idea. And besides, ain't no such thing as liking something too much."

"That, my dear girl," said a voice, "is simply not true."

A man strode out from the wall—directly through the wall, not through some concealed door—as if he were some sort of apparition, some ghost. Joen jumped a bit, startled. Her eyes went wide, her mouth dropped open, and I thought she was about to scream.

She laughed instead, a deep, heartfelt, truly joyous laugh. Something about it seemed weird to me—unlike her.

"Charming," the man said with a mysterious smile. He stood tall, with neatly trimmed salt-and-pepper hair. His clothing was plain—simple breeches and a tunic—but it looked finely tailored and probably expensive.

"You would be Malchor Harpell," I said. "I'm Maimun, and this is Joen. We've been looking for you."

"Obviously," he said. "Those who aren't looking for me rarely find me. It's one of the many benefits of living in a mystical tower, you see. The question, then, is not whether you are looking for me, it is why you are looking for me."

Joen skipped lightly over to the tall man. "We need some help," she said, her voice rising and falling as if in song. "Someone said you can help us, and we need some help."

She seemed way too giddy. "Joen . . .," I started to say.

Malchor Harpell laughed. "Well, that begs two questions: what do you need help with, and who told you I could help you?"

"Drizzt Do'Urden," I answered.

"If you need help with him, I cannot assist you," he said, his voice suddenly darker, and Joen abruptly stopped laughing.

"No," I said, looking at Joen, who seemed at once angry and confused. "It was Drizzt who sent us."

"Drizzt sent you," Joen said, blinking and rubbing her eyes. "I never met him, though. I just followed along." She looked up at the tower, the magnificent structure rising to catch the very last rays of the sun, and the very first light of the stars, twinkling in the night sky. "Oi, but I'm glad I did!"

"Joen, what's wrong with you?" I snapped.

She shook her head, but it was Malchor Harpell who answered, "That was me." He winked and passed a single finger in front of Joen's face. Joen blinked back and shook her head as though she had just awakened from a deep sleep. "The bridge doesn't last all night, I'm afraid, and you seemed . . . cautious."

"Was that some kind of sp—?" Joen started, but seemed afraid to say the word "spell." A chill ran down my spine, but Joen seemed no worse for wear.

"If Drizzt sent you," Malchor Harpell went on, "then surely you can tell me who he travels with."

"Wulfgar," I said. "A giant man of the North. And a dwarf called Bruenor, and a woman named Catti-brie. Oh, and there's a halfling, what's his name? Regis, I think."

Malchor nodded. "And what did he think I could do for you?"

"Information," I said. "About this."

I unfastened the top few buttons of my shirt, reached in and withdrew the magical stone from its pouch. It was heavy, perfectly smooth, and black. I held it up for Malchor to see.

The wizard's eyes widened.

"It's the Stone of—," I began.

"I know what it is," he said, quickly regaining his composure. "May I?" He held out his hand to take it, but I hesitated.

Malchor took a step back and waved his hand to indicate the sparkling emerald tower.

"Where are my manners?" he said. "Please, come inside and be welcome."

He reached out to the shimmering wall and traced the vague outline of a door. Even before he finished, a door appeared in the place he'd outlined, emerging into being and swinging open at the same time.

Joen stepped back one step. I stepped back two.

"A friend sent you to me," the wizard said. "If you need information, you must let me examine the object."

"You just said you know what it is," I said.

"I also know it is bound to its bearer," he replied, "so there is no point in my stealing it. As I said, if you need information, you must trust me."

"Oi, if he wanted to just take it, he could have, you know?" Joen piped in, taking two steps toward the door. "I mean, look at this place, right? If he can make this, you think you can stop him?"

"Wise words, if a bit misguided," Malchor said. "I helped create the tower, 'tis true, but I did not make it alone. Please . . ."

He motioned to the door again, and Joen brushed past me to step into the dim green light beyond, winking at me as she passed. I thought of the spell that had made her giddy and adventurous. Was she under its influence again? And if so, why wasn't I?

"You could take the stone from me any time you want to," I said, and the wizard nodded. "But you want me to hand it to you."

"I am not your enemy, young Maimun."

"How do you know my name?"

"I know many things, many things that may help you, but first . . . ." He held out his hand.

I thought for a moment, then placed the stone in his palm.

"Good," he said. "Now, let us go in out of this chill wind and brewing storm. You can tell me your tale, and I will see if I can help you."

Malchor turned and walked back into the tower before I could finish.

I gently grabbed Haze's mane, expecting resistance from the horse, but she walked through the shimmering door ahead of me. I followed quickly.

I found myself in a mostly empty circular stone room. There were two other exits: a large wooden door and an open archway leading to a stone staircase. The door had disappeared behind me even as I stepped through it. Malchor stood at the archway and Joen skipped over to him.

"What of Haze?" I asked, finishing my previous thought.

"A fine name for a fine horse," Malchor said. "She'll find her own way to the stables, I think."

"Stables?" I asked, looking around doubtfully. "The tower's not that big."

"It's bigger than you think," Malchor assured me with a sly wink.

Haze let out a soft snort and walked to the wooden doors, which swung open at her approach.

"She'll find fresh food and a soft bed of hay awaiting her," Malchor said. "Now, come, let us find more comfortable surroundings for ourselves." He turned and walked to the stairs, Joen right behind him.

I followed them up what seemed a dozen sets of winding stairs, past doors open and closed, rooms and side passages, until finally we entered Malchor Harpell's great hall. The room seemed at once huge and cozy. The table was grand, stretching a dozen yards, but there were only three chairs, all set neatly around one end of the table. Malchor took one chair, motioning for Joen and me to take the others.

"Now, you can tell me your tale in full," he said. "And when you're finished, we will have a meal and discuss what comes next."

Back at the village, Tessa had set us a wonderful meal—cozy, friendly, with plenty of good food and good conversation. It had been a welcome break from a rough road.

But it paled in comparison to the feast laid out by Malchor Harpell. The meal covered only a small portion of his great table, but the food was piled high, and though we pulled hungrily from the pile, it never seemed to diminish. The whole crew of *Sea Sprite* could have eaten here without trouble until they were full to bursting.

Joen and I, for our part, stuffed ourselves. Malchor ate as well, though not nearly so much. He could feast like this every day if he wanted to, I supposed, but we travelers had eaten only dry bread and salted meats for the last tenday and a half.

Malchor kept silent throughout the meal, and neither Joen nor I took enough time between bites to say much. After what seemed hours, I pushed my chair back from the table, full and satisfied. A few moments later, Joen followed suit.

Malchor stared at us for a long while. I wondered whether he was waiting for something, waiting for me to speak up. But I had no idea what to say, so I stayed quiet.

"I can help you," Malchor said at last, taking the stone from a pocket and placing it on the table. "I do have some information and a good idea where you could find more."

"That's great," I said, beaming.

Joen put her hand on my shoulder and opened her mouth to give congratulations, but only a belch came out. Her hand shot to her mouth and she blushed, but the wizard didn't seem to notice.

"However, information is a valuable thing," he continued.

"We have no coin to pay you," I replied.

"No, but we have this, eh?" Joen said, pulling the sparkling sapphire from her pocket and placing it on the table.

"I don't care to put a merchant's price on knowledge," Malchor said. "I seek something else."

"And what is that?" I asked.

"Two things: First, trust. You've already demonstrated that by turning over the stone when I asked. But second, and more important, discipline."

I waited for him to continue, but he said nothing. "I don't understand," I said at last.

"I'll explain, then. I require first that you trust in me, that you believe I can and will help you."

"We do trust that," I said. "Drizzt trusts you, so I trust you."

"That you trust the dark elf is wise of you," he said. "But as I said, the second price is more important."

"Discipline," I said. "What kind of discipline?"

"The kind of discipline it takes to resist asking that very question," he replied.

"I've traveled up and down the Sword Coast, fighting all sorts of monsters. I'm bound to that stone magically. And you don't think I deserve some information about it?"

"I don't think you're ready for it, no," the wizard said. "You're a child, Maimun, and I am deeply sorry for whatever has caused you to come into contact with an artifact of this immense importance. How it bound itself to you, at your age, is a question I will puzzle over for some time, I'm sure. Now, if you do not trust my judgment, take the stone back and leave. Otherwise, follow me."

The wizard rose to his feet. With some difficulty, I rose too, and Joen did likewise.

"I didn't come here to—"

The wizard turned on me and I almost choked trying to stop talking. His eyes were so cold, but when I took a deep breath, his expression warmed and he said, "Discipline," once more.

"Discipline," Joen repeated, and I wasn't sure if she was making fun of me or Malchor Harpell. For her sake, I hoped it was me. The wizard didn't even notice.

We climbed two more sets of stairs, crossed through an ornate set of double doors, and went down a long, winding, narrow passage. The whole way, no one spoke a word. The only sound was the *clomp* of our booted feet on the hard stone.

Finally we stopped at a single plain wooden door. Malchor pushed it open, revealing a large circular chamber with a low-ceiling and the walls lined with bookshelves. Two more doors, also plain wood, opened out from the room, one to the left, the other to the right. In the center of the room stood a strange contraption that I could not identify, but that looked sort of like an ornate pillar.

"Welcome to the Martial Hall," Malchor said, striding purposefully into the room. Joen and I followed. "Herein you will prove your discipline."

"How?" I asked, but Malchor motioned for me to be silent.

"Maimun, please come stand over here," Malchor said, motioning me toward one of the doors. "And you, young lady, stand on the opposite side of the room."

We complied, and Malchor walked back to the middle of the room.

"These books contain many secrets of mental discipline and martial prowess. Meditation and sword fighting, willpower and open-hand combat—all the tools you will need to become warriors are within. And this" —he rested his hand on the odd contraption in the room's center, a tall pillar made of several circular stone pieces stacked upon each other, each with many stone protrusions—"will be your sparring partner."

Malchor walked from the pillar to one of the doors and continued, "The doors each lead to a small bedchamber. These will be your quarters for as long as you stay here."

"And how long is that, eh?" Joen asked.

"Until the last snows of winter have receded and the land is in the full bloom of spring," he replied.

"Not so long," Joen said. "We can handle that, I think."

"Seems long to me," I grumbled.

"Until the land blooms . . . next year," Malchor finished.

My words caught in my throat.

"If you can stay here for a year and a month learning what I have to teach you, you might just survive what is ahead for you." He turned to face me directly. "You must release your arrogance, your impertinence. It will only hold you back. Force your ego down into yourself, hold it at bay, and you will have proven your discipline sufficient, and I shall answer your questions." He walked back to the threshold of the door we'd entered from. "I have to know if you carry the stone, or if the stone carries you."

That sent a chill down my spine, but still I said, "We can't stay a year."

"Oi, why can't we?" Joen asked. "Warm beds, good food, a roof over our heads? This place is a paradise! I could stay here forever, you know?"

I looked at the wizard and asked in as low a voice as I could, hoping Joen wouldn't hear, "Are you making her say that?"

"Oi, what?" she said. She'd heard me and was not happy.

Malchor smiled and shook his head, and I believed him.

Glancing between Joen and Malchor, I could hardly find words. "But, we're going to . . . we have to . . ."

"To destroy the Stone of Tymora"—Malchor held up the fist-sized object—"an artifact of no minor power, and thus a task of no small difficulty." He tossed it to me, and I caught it easily. "And tell me, where do you plan to go from here?"

I pondered a moment. "I'll find Drizzt," I said finally. "He'll help me."

"Drizzt Do'Urden is currently engaged in preparations for a war," Malchor said. "He'll be too distracted with his own troubles to offer you help. I am the only one who can help you now."

I thought a long while, trying to find some alternative, some way out. But Malchor was right. This was the only place I knew to look. If I got nothing from Malchor, I would have no direction at all. And somehow, I doubted the luck imparted by the mystical artifact would aid me much in finding the means to destroy it.

After several long moments, I nodded my assent.

"It's settled then," Malchor said. Across the room from me, Joen was practically beaming. She'd never had a home at all, I realized. An orphan child, the closest thing to a home she'd ever known were those ships she'd crewed. Then again, I hadn't had a true home since my time back in the High Forest with Elbeth, which had ended when I was but six years old.

"You'll find clean clothes and weapons waiting for you in your bedrooms," Malchor said. "You will not leave this room and its adjoining areas except when I gather you for meals."

Joen's smile disappeared in a flash.

"Discipline," he reminded. She grimaced, but nodded.

Malchor gave a curt bow and spun on his heel. The door slammed shut behind him.

"Oi, he wasn't serious about not being able to leave this room except for meals, was he?" Joen asked me.

It was going to be a long year.

PART VIII

"So ye got yerself stuck on land fer a year?" the pirate captain asked. "Sounds like a prison sentence, yar?"

Most of the pirates had taken seats on the soft sand. Weapons had long since been put away. I perched on a rock, sitting above the crowd, speaking down to them as though I were the smallest person in the crowd. My own cutlass—rather, the one I'd stolen from one of the pirates—lay across my lap.

The only person still standing was the pirate captain himself. Despite his wooden leg, he stood tall and firm as I spoke.

"More like a boarding school," I said.

"It could've been worse, then, eh?" the captain offered.

"Yeah, I could have been stuck here for a year."

"Aye, that'd be worse by far!" he said. "It be summer now, but ye should see th' place in th' winter!"

"How far north are we?" I asked. "I was adrift for a while before you picked me up."

"And asleep for a good while after that," the pirate agreed. "The shore across the narrows, tha' be near Neverwinter Wood. So we're pretty near th' same latitude as yer Tower o' Twilight."

"Well, I didn't get much view of the weather that year, winter or otherwise. Actually, I didn't get much view other than the inside of those two rooms, plus the great hall where we took our meals."

"Aye," the captain said, "and ye learnt all about fighting a dummy!"

The whole crew got a long and hearty laugh out of that one.

"Can I get back to my story now?" I asked finally.

"O' course, me boy. But I've a fair wager I know how it ends."

CHAPTER 69

MALCHOR HARPELL HAD CALLED THEM KUO-TOA, BUT I COULD ONLY THINK OF THEM as a shark's worst nightmare.

They stood on two legs, like a man, and had two arms and a head, but that was where any resemblance was overwhelmed by the sheer alienness, the disturbing wrongness of the growling fish-men. Their heads were massive—way too big for their squat but sturdy bodies. Their eyes might have been a beautiful shade of blue on a human, but on them, the orbs were bulging, slimy, wet things the size of dinner plates that goggled from the creatures' green-scaled heads. Their huge mouths, in the shape of an upside down U, were so packed with bony fangs that were so long and sharp the kuo-toa couldn't close their mouths. The sound the creatures made was like water going down a drain.

"This is new," Joen said as her daggers came out of their sheaths and out to her sides, luring in the kuo-toa.

I nodded and drew my cutlass.

I think the one with the trident said something to me, but if the sound it made was a language, it was an insult to all languages everywhere.

The other one came in at Joen, and came in fast. It hadn't occurred to me that something that looked like a fish with legs could move so fast. In its green, scaly hands, it held a dagger whose blade was rippled with deadly barbs, like a knife with needles welded to it.

"Here we go again," I said, and slashed out to my right with my cutlass to keep the rushing creature away from Joen, just like General Gorrann had done in the last battle of the third winter campaign of the Trollflame Wars.

"Oi," Joen exclaimed, "thanks. Trollflame Wars?"

I nodded and fended the kuo-toa, giving Joen a moment to stab down and back up at it—just like we'd read in one of Malchor Harpell's old books.

When we'd first arrived at the Tower of Twilight, I had yearned for the road, my desire to be on with my quest overpowering. I had often tried to pry some information from the wizard, some starting point, so that we could leave this place and abandon his pointless exercises.

But the wizard had remained tight-lipped, and I got nothing useful. After a while, I had given in and had chosen instead to dive into the collection of books Malchor had left us with.

The kuo-toa with the dagger slipped back out of Joen's attack, and I'd swear it smiled at us. That wasn't a good sign.

I heard a crackling noise just before I smelled ozone in the suddenly heavy air of our exercise room. I sidestepped and spun back to the kuo-toa with the trident, and before I saw the lightning—if you can see it, the paladin Lord Richauld of Neverwinter wrote in his *Annals of Martial Development in the Holy Orders*, you're already dead—I jumped. I grabbed the heavy wooden rafter above my head with my free hand and tucked my legs up under me just as a blinding bolt of twisting yellow lightning burst from the kuo-toa's trident to smash into the wall behind me.

Growing up, I had loved my adopted father Perrault's collection of books, both for their practical and informative value, and for the amazing stories they told. Here was much the same—books on swordplay and battle tactics often included detailed accounts of wars and examples of theory put into practice. I would read these stories a dozen times, committing them to memory.

"It's a lash," Joen shouted over to me, and though the lightning bolt had spent itself against the wall, the room was still filled with an almost deafening sound: steel ringing on steel so fast and so sharply, it made my ears ring in harmony. The monster was slashing at Joen so quickly, so feverishly, I could hardly see its wicked weapon, but Joen fended it off with her twin daggers so quickly and thoroughly the kuo-toa took a step back. "And this one's a cutter, I think."

I nodded and dropped back to the floor, already running to close the distance to the kuo-toa lash before it could send another bolt of lightning my way.

Joen liked books about monsters—especially sea monsters. A few months ago, though, Joen had stumbled upon a tome truly after her own heart. It was a translation of a book from the Shou empires of the far east, separated into three volumes. The first was all about mental discipline, of course. The second, tales of Shou and Kozakuran warriors and their combat tactics. It often detailed battles in which small groups stood against overwhelming odds, and culminated with the tale of a warrior who stood alone against a thousand men and emerged victorious. I could have spent a year simply reading and rereading those tales detailed in the second volume.

But Joen barely skimmed those parts I found most interesting. She read and reread the third volume: a detailed manual on the martial techniques of one sect of Shou warrior-priests whose favored weapon were twin daggers.

"So I cut both my daggers down, like this, eh?" Joen said, bringing her arms down, one in front and one behind, her blades catching the kuo-toa cutter's barbed dagger between them. "And I twist, just half a foot, back against myself, see?" She twisted, her daggers moving subtly, and the barbed knife came right out of the monster's hands.

I batted away the lash's trident, its wicked tines still crackling with sparks of lightning. The creature kept gurgling at me, staring at me with those huge, hateful eyes.

Waiting for Joen to continue, I snuck a glance her way and was almost skewered in return. The kuo-toa lash was slipping back on its black-taloned feet, trying to get its long-shafted trident between us. If it got reach on me, I was in trouble, so I did my best to turn the creature around, attacking at its right and sidestepping to my left.

When I moved around enough to see Joen, I was surprised to see that the cutter had somehow retrieved its dagger.

"Fast little bugger," she said. "So I just anticipate its feints, eh?" She was describing a particular defense to be used against a foe with superior speed.

"Then?" I asked. Joen could never just talk straight through, she always needed me to prompt her. I figured it was her way of making sure I was paying attention because she rightly figured I was a lot less interested in her two-dagger style than she. But she had sat through my stories for so long, I felt I should humor her.

"And now I spin back the other way." She brought both her arms in tight, spinning quickly. "And I'm inside its guard!" She thrust out with both arms, her left darting out directly behind her, her right diving forward for the cutter. Her dagger pierced the scaly green skin of the kuo-toa, and I'd no doubt she would drive it right through the slimy thing. But she stopped short, holding the fast-moving fish-man in one spot. Of every part of the move, what impressed me most was her ability to so completely stop the momentum of her dagger. I always knew she was a pretty good fighter, but that level of control over her weapons revealed to me the gains she had made over our thirteen months of training.

"And now you finish it off," I said.

"Yep," she answered, withdrawing her dagger and slashing the other around to slit the kuo-toa's throat.

Twin bolts of lightning flashed out from the lash's trident and I felt every hair on my body stand on end and sort of twist. My teeth clenched and my vision went all different colored blobs. I think I was still standing up. Anyway, I could see the second fork slam into Joen and send her hair out around her head in a perfect sphere, and I was awake just long enough to find it funny that her hit-by-lightning face looked just like her about-to-sneeze face.

"Impressive," Malchor Harpell said when he was reasonably sure I was alive. I wasn't so sure myself.

"Really?" Joen asked, and I could tell she was annoyed, but couldn't tell if she was annoyed with me, Malchor, or the kuo-toa—which stood at attention behind the wizard.

It took us both the better part of an hour to remember how to stand up. I stood there, looking back and forth between Joen and Malchor, waiting for one of them to start yelling at me.

"I have told you that thinking too much about what you're doing while you're doing it," Malchor said, "much less talking about it, can get you killed, haven't I?"

I nodded and started to stagger away to my room, where I intended to sleep for several tendays.

"Not so fast," Malchor said.

I stopped and turned. "Yes?"

"Do you know what the date is?"

I shrugged. "Spring?"

"The date of spring?" Joen needled me, then shook her head, blinking, and smoke came out of her hair. "It's the day before the elventeeth of Monthember third . . ."

"Close enough," Malchor said. "The snows have gone. And with them, your time here." He patted the kuo-toa lash on its slimy green shoulder, and the creature faded into nothingness along with its comrade, replaced by a couple of simple chairs. "Come, sit back down."

My heart raced in my chest. I was shaking more from excitement now than electricity. Quickly I took my seat. My knees felt as though they'd packed off and moved to Waterdeep.

Joen, though, hesitated. I gave her a curious look, and she sighed and crossed the room to sit next to me.

"You have earned the information I possess," Malchor said, his tone heavy. "This last bit aside, you have proven you are capable of discipline and of trust, and you have given all that I asked. So I will keep my end of the bargain and tell you what I know. If, that is, you still desire it."

"We do," I said quickly, forcing my head to clear.

Joen didn't answer, though, and Malchor and I stared at her for a long moment before she finally nodded her assent.

"Very well. The stone you gave me is, as you said, the Stone of Tymora. It grants its wielder the boon of good luck. But such a boon, as all gifts of the gods, must come at a cost.

"As to what precisely the cost is, the legends disagree. Some say it draws luck from the world around it, that the wielder will be lucky but those who travel with him will be unlucky. Others claim it draws its power from the wielder himself, leading to an unnaturally short lifespan. Both those conflicting legends, and your own tale, seem to support both of these theories. Those who bond with the stone, as far as they are known, do tend to die young, as do those with whom they associate."

I put a hand to my chest, where the stone still rested against my heart.

"How is this lucky, exactly?" I asked.

"I, however, do not think this limited lifespan is the result of some magic draining your life-force," Malchor went on, ignoring me. "I suspect it is merely a result of possessing something powerful. That is, possessing something others want and are willing to kill for. Good luck will only get you so far. Eventually, those who seek power at your expense will have it, and they will hurt you in the process."

Joen looked at me funny. I said, "I'm still a little woozy. If you want it, now's your chance."

She almost laughed, but shook her head and looked away instead.

"Something the legends do agree on, however," the wizard continued with hardly a pause, "is that the Stone of Tymora is not truly unique. Luck is not always for the good, and one's good luck often means another's ill fortune. Just as Tymora, goddess of good fortune, created this stone, her sister Beshaba, goddess of ill fate, crafted her own. That stone has not been seen in two centuries, and its current location is unknown."

"Two stones?" I asked. And I thought my head hurt before. My shoulders and knees shook as though I'd just been hit by another lightning bolt. Two stones?

"Tymora and Beshaba, sisters, opposites," Malchor said.

I had to think about that for a moment, and the wizard let me.

"So is the other stone bound to me as well?" I asked. "I mean, in the small things, I've always had good luck, but overall this stone seems to bring more bad than good."

"No," Malchor said. "The Stone of Beshaba is not bound to you. After the two stones were crafted, the goddesses bound each to the soul of a mortal. When that mortal should die, the stone chooses another soul to claim as its own."

"If a goddess can bind it," Joen asked, "can she unbind it?"

"Should we be praying?" I added.

The wizard smiled and shook his head. I knew it wasn't going to be that easy.

"And Lady Luck found me," I sighed.

"The goddesses each claimed a newborn elf," Malchor said, "and these they bound to the stones to watch over the wielders and to make sure that with the mortals' passings, the stones would find their way to their new chosen souls. And these elves they named the Sentinels, and to them they gifted the blessing of ageless immortality, so long as they held to their duties."

"Elbeth," I whispered, and the wizard just shrugged.

I waited for him to continue, but he didn't. "That's it?" I asked after a long moment. "That's the information we had to wait a year for?"

"Oi, a year and a month," Joen corrected.

"There's more," Malchor said, blowing out a long sigh. "But again I ask, are you certain you want to hear this?"

"Yes," I snapped. "And you owe it to us to tell."

Malchor nodded. "As with all artifacts, there is a way to destroy the stone, but it is near impossible. You must have, in the same place, both stones and both Sentinels."

"Oi," Joen gasped. "Yeah, sure."

"The Sentinels themselves are the only ones who know the details of how to be rid of the stones," Malchor went on. "And as their immortality is tied to the existence of the stones, they will not be forthcoming with how to destroy them. So there it is. If you want to destroy the Stone of Tymora, you need to find the Stone of Beshaba and both Sentinels, and convince one of them to tell you how to destroy the stones."

"Great," I said. "So all we need is to find another goddess-crafted artifact stone. Where should we start looking?"

"I suggest the library at Silverymoon," Malchor said. "It has the most thorough records of events historical and magical in this part of the world, and the legends suggest the stones first appeared here in the Silver Marches. If there is any further information to be had, you will likely find it there."

"And if the library can't help us?" I asked.

Malchor only shrugged.

"And we wasted a year," I said, getting angry.

"Wasted?" Malchor asked. "Perhaps. If you cannot put down your ego, your arrogance, after all this time, then it was a year wasted indeed."

"No," Joen said, "we didn't waste it. We had a roof and food and good reading and good company, eh? There's worse ways to spend a year, you know?"

I looked at her, still angry. But I didn't speak.

"Look, I know you wanna destroy the stone," Joen continued. "But if we can't find a way, or if it's too dangerous, can't we just live with it? Summer's coming, and I'd like to see the world some, you know?"

"You heard him," I said. "The wielder of the stone and those around him tend to die young. Do you want to die young?"

"Ain't a short life full of luck better'n a long life without it?"

"A lucky life I don't get to choose is worse than an unlucky one I do," I retorted.

"And what about my choices, eh?" Joen asked.

"You choose whether or not to follow me."

"Same goes for you. You could follow me."

"Yes, but I choose to destroy the stone, whether you follow or not."

She stared at me, and I stared back. There was anger simmering behind those emerald eyes. I could tell she wanted to hit me, and I figured I probably deserved it. But that would not deter me. I knew what I needed to do, and I intended to do it.

The silence remained unbroken while we stared at each other, unblinking.

"All right," she whispered quietly at long last. "I'll follow you to Silverymoon. But if we find nothing there, we give up, at least for now, eh?"

"Fine," I agreed.

"Your horse waits downstairs," Malchor said. "I've given her a light saddle, though she doesn't need one. It makes carrying supplies a good deal easier. She is well rested and long recovered from that enervating spell, so I'm sure you'll find the journey more pleasant. I've also provided you bedrolls, a tent, and a satchel from which you can pull food three times a day every day, of the same quality you've been eating here this past year. And though I'm sure you won't need it, I wish you the best of luck."

"Thank you for your hospitality," I said, rising.

Joen rose beside me, and though the conjured kuo-toa's lightning still fizzled in our skulls and we looked as though we'd been hung from the top of the tower for a month, she followed me downstairs to where Haze waited. Within an hour, we were away, riding east under the midday sun, headed for Silverymoon, and hopefully, some answers.

CHAPTER 70

W E STUCK TO THE MAIN ROAD AS WE TRAVELED, HEADING EAST TOWARD SILVERYMOON. The road was broad and well marked, but the numerous spring storms combined with the thaw had turned it mostly to mud. That mud was creased deeply with the tracks of wagons, horses, and men—the first trade caravans of the season.

The land grew more rugged as we moved farther east. A spur of the mighty Spine of the World mountain range stretched down from the north, and though we wouldn't have to cross it, we would pass nearby. Rolling farmlands and scattered homesteads gave way to hills and forests, and morning dew became morning frost as we climbed higher. But still, each day the season moved closer to summer, the days grew longer, the midday sun a bit brighter.

We passed a few caravans on the road, mostly humans and elves. They were headed from Silverymoon, I figured, to Luskan, Waterdeep, and other points to the west. When necessary, we gave them the road, and we always offered a friendly greeting. But they had their destination and we ours, and so there was little conversation.

I expected that would be the case when on the fifteenth day, as we sat on the side of the road taking our midday meal, another caravan rolled over the next ridge. Three wagons, each pulled by two horses, slogged through the mud. Behind them, another pair of horses walked—spares, in case any of the pulling teams were injured.

"Dwarves," I said, pointing to the squat figures driving the teams.

Joen looked up from her venison stew—our latest hot meal pulled from Malchor's magical satchel. She followed my gaze to the caravan, peering at the approaching wagons. As they neared, it became obvious that my guess was correct, for the wagons were filled with short, stocky people, each wearing armor of some form or another, each with a helmet atop his head and a great bushy beard of black, brown, or gray.

"Oi, I didn't know there were dwarves around here," Joen said.

"Sure," I answered. "In Sundabar or Citadel Adbar, to the east past Silverymoon. But I didn't think they'd be trading this far out."

"Why wouldn't they? "

"Well, it's a long journey, and the roads aren't very safe. There are spring storms, not to mention bandits, and . . ."

My voice trailed off, buried beneath the sudden furious howl of two dozen small, ugly humanoids leaping up from the surrounding rocks and brush.

"Goblins," I finished.

Before I could react, Joen was on her feet and sprinting off toward the dwarves. I stared after her, in awe of her courage. She knew little of dwarves and probably less of goblins, yet the moment danger reared its head, off she went.

I calmly walked back to where we had been resting, unfettered Haze, and climbed into her saddle. The goblin war cry had apparently also startled the horse. She was into a gallop almost before I was settled in my seat.

I overtook Joen several hundred yards from the dwarves, slowing down long enough to help her into the saddle behind me. Together we charged into the brewing melee.

The dwarves, for their part, were obviously battle seasoned and battle ready. As soon as the goblins leaped at them, they formed into a tight square, each of the eight stocky, bearded folk protecting his neighbor with his shield, and fending off goblins with a spear, warhammer, or axe.

The goblins were far from organized, throwing themselves wildly at the dwarves, battering away and being battered. Though they outnumbered the dwarves three to one, their initial assault was a disaster. Three goblins lay dead, the rest pushed back from the phalanx, and not a dwarf had more than a slight scratch on him.

The largest among the goblins—which wasn't saying much, as the spindly little things rarely top four feet—shouted something in a coarse, guttural tongue. He motioned to the dwarves, apparently urging his fellows to attack. But the suddenly demoralized goblins seemed hesitant. They kept glancing around, looking for an escape route, then noticed . . . us.

One of the smaller goblins grabbed its boss's arm. The larger creature smacked the little whelp, turning around angrily.

I brought Haze to a trot, suddenly apprehensive.

The big goblin fixed its eyes on me, opening its mouth in a wicked grin. Again it bellowed something in its guttural tongue. This time the goblins didn't hesitate.

The turned their backs on the dwarves and ran down the road.

Directly at us.

"Oi," Joen said.

The dwarves, for their part, were no cowards. As soon as the goblins turned and fled, six of the eight dwarves leaped into pursuit. The others moved to the back of the wagons, to the tethered horses.

Joen hopped down from Haze, drawing her daggers. I followed, pulling my saber from its sheath and slapping Haze across the rump, sending her running.

"Brace yourself," I said. "The goblins are faster than the dwarves."

"Oi, but not the horses," Joen answered. And indeed, it appeared she was right. Even in the thick mud, the horses easily outpaced the little orange-skinned humanoids.

But the goblins had a head start. The first of the ugly things reached us just as the riders overtook the last rank of goblins.

The first goblin leaped at me with abandon, spear tip leading. I brought my saber around, easily parrying its crude thrust, and rolled my blade up along the shaft. The goblin hardly even tried to slow itself, and my sword cut cleanly through its filthy leather jerkin, gashing its chest and dropping it to the ground.

But two more goblins were right behind.

I darted left, away from Joen, bringing my sword in a horizontal slash aimed at the nearest goblin's head. This one had its sword in line for a parry and knocked my sword high. But before it could recover to attack me, its own companion slammed into its back, pushing it to the ground.

I brought my sword down from on high in a heavy chop. The newest goblin, stunned from its impact against its companion, didn't have time to react before my sword killed it.

Joen, for her part, was a blur of motion, twirling and stabbing, quickly felling the first goblin to attack her then fending off the next three simultaneously. Our time at the Tower of Twilight had not been wasted. Her dance was fluid, perfect, mesmerizing.

But mesmerized was not something I wanted to be at that moment, as the goblin on the ground and two more charging in all lashed out at me.

I fell back, trying in vain to withdraw my sword from the dead goblin. I couldn't move quickly enough to evade the attacks with the fouled weapon, so I let it go, choosing my life over my blade.

A sudden thunder of hoofbeats heralded the arrival of one of the dwarf riders, who had cut a bloody swath through the goblin swarm. His horse shoved aside the two standing goblins that were attacking me. Its hoof dropped onto the prone goblin, landing with a dull thud and the crack of bone.

But the horse stumbled on the creature, throwing its rider. The black-bearded dwarf landed heavily in the mud. I feared the massive impact may have killed him, or at least knocked him out.

Instead, he was back on his feet in a flash, laughing and brandishing an axe. With one light tug, he pulled the sword out of my goblin victim and tossed my sword to me.

The other rider came in behind him from the other side, pushing goblins out of his way with his horse. A few spears reached up at him, prodding at his heavy armor, but he paid them little heed. Joen fell back from her melee, and the goblins didn't pursue. The second rider, a yellow-bearded fellow, joined we three.

The goblins hesitated, but only for a moment. Five more of theirs were dead, but they still had us outnumbered, sixteen against four.

Thrust and parry, parry and thrust. Keeping my thirteen months of training in mind, I worked furiously to hold off the savage assault. The black-bearded dwarf with the axe stood alongside me, his broad shield serving as fine protection for the both of us. Similarly, the yellow-bearded dwarf offered his aid to Joen. But after a moment of furious combat, each of us sported the nicks and cuts of battle, and while our parries and blocks were growing slower as we tired, the goblins' frenzy only seemed to build.

"Ye might want t'brace yerself," the black-bearded dwarf whispered to me. "This'll be int'restin'."

"Define 'int'restin'," I said.

He only laughed. His companion joined him.

And so did the six heavily armored dwarves charging in from the back.

The phalanx crashed against the goblins, and the goblins crashed against us. The sheer weight of the impact shocked me, and I was unable to hold my footing in the loose mud. I dropped flat on my back.

Desperately, I brought my sword up to fend off the inevitable goblin attack. But it never came. The force had knocked me down, but it had also scattered the goblins. Heartbeats after the reinforcements arrived, the remaining creatures were dead or scattered, and my black-bearded friend was helping me to my feet.

I was covered in mud, head to toe. Somehow, Joen seemed to have avoided even getting dirty. Her blonde hair matched that of the other dwarf rider who had come to our rescue, and she stood leaning on the dwarf's shoulder. The two of them tried, and failed, to hold back their laughter at the sight of me. In the meantime, two of the dwarves gathered their horses and rode back up to the caravan. The well-trained pack beasts had already started moving toward us, and the dwarves' wagons were rolling up before the last of the wounded goblins had even been put down.

Curious, I knelt down next to one of the dead goblins and looked over the nasty creature—nasty looking, and nasty smelling. "Bandits?" I asked the dwarves around me.

The leader of the dwarves shrugged and started poking at the goblin with his axe. "An insult to bandits, if ye ask me," he said. But as he prodded at the goblin, I noticed it wore around its neck a little totem made of twigs and bone. Gingerly, not really wanting to touch the thing, I picked up the totem and pulled it off the length of twine it hung from.

"What's that there?" the dwarf asked.

"Some kind of jewelry?" Joen asked.

I shook my head and answered, "Maybe a clan symbol of something."

It was shaped like the antlers of an eight-point buck, and something about it made me shiver.

"Are you from Sundabar or Citadel Adbar?" Joen asked the dwarf leader.

"Neither, girl," answered the black-bearded dwarf. "We be from Mithral Hall, home o' Clan Battlehammer and good King Bruenor Battlehammer."

"Bruenor?" I asked, momentarily forgetting the totem. "You know Bruenor?"

"*King* Bruenor," the dwarf corrected. "An' every dwarf in the Marches knows King Bruenor."

"Big red beard?" I asked. "Travels with two humans and a dark elf?"

The dwarf looked at me curiously. "Few folks in the North ain't heard them stories. Why you ask, boy?"

"I sailed with him, two autumns past," I said. "In the southern seas between Baldur's Gate and Memnon, then back to Waterdeep just before the winter."

"Well, that's int'restin'. Name's Kongvaalar. What're ye called?"

"My name is Maimun, and this is Beshaba," I answered. Joen looked at me funny—they all did. "Wait," I said, looking down at the totem I'd pulled off the dead goblin. My hand shook and I dropped it as though it were a spider about to bite me.

"My name is Joen," Joen told the dwarves, then looked at me and said, "What's the matter with you?"

"*Rites and Practices of the Cults of the Realms,*" I said, quoting the title of one of Malchor Harpell's many books. "The goblins were wearing the symbol of Beshaba." And another chill hit me when I said her name.

"Well," Kongvaalar grunted, "they honored their goddess with their bad luck."

Joen and I exchanged a fearful look. I was starting to have a hard time believing in coincidences. Maybe there was a reason the goblins were so quick to turn away from the dwarves when they saw us.

"Well, any friend o' me king's a friend o' me own," Kongvaalar said. "Pleasure fightin' at yer side, but we needs be off. Things to do, ye know." He gave me a curt nod and turned back to his caravan.

"Wait," I said, and the dwarf obliged. "King Bruenor's drow companion, Drizzt. Do you know him?"

"Aye, we know him."

"Is he at Mithral Hall?" A plan formed in my head—a contingency plan, really. If we couldn't find what we needed in Silverymoon, I would seek Drizzt's counsel. But then I remembered my promise to Joen: if Silverymoon was a bust, we'd stop looking for the time being.

"Some o' the time, he's there," the dwarf answered. "But more often he's in Silverymoon, or on the road between."

I nodded and Kongvaalar turned and started away again.

"Oi, hold a bit," Joen said.

"Oh fer . . .," the surly dwarf grumbled, stopping once more.

"Dwarves like shiny things, right?" asked Joen.

Kongvaalar scowled at her, and behind him, several other dwarves grumbled.

"I mean, gems and the like. Dwarves like to trade in gems, eh?"

"And yer point is?"

She reached into her pocket, withdrawing the sizeable sapphire she'd taken from the dragon's lair.

The dwarf's eyes went wide, just for a moment, then his face went stony again. "That ain't worth much, girl," he said. "Not even worth our time to stop and trade for it."

"Then why haven't you left yet?" I asked.

Kongvaalar's face screwed up a bit. "Since yer friends to King Bruenor, we'll stop 'n trade," he said. "But it's only semiprecious, so it ain't worth much."

"That's not true," Joen said.

Kongvaalar scowled again. "Yer callin' me a liar?" he said, indignant.

"Oi, not really," she answered. "Jus' saying, this is a very valuable little shiny. You're trying to make us think it ain't so we'll sell it for less than it's worth."

"That's the same thing as lyin'," Kongvaalar said, his face sour.

"Not hardly," I interjected. " 'Everything is worth what its buyer will pay for it, and what its seller will sell it for,' " I quoted from another of Malchor's books, penned by a famed dwarf merchant. I hoped the dwarves would catch the reference.

By the softening of Kongvaalar's face, I figured he had. "Aye, that be true," he said. "And you know what they say about the fool and his coin."

"They were lucky to get together in the first place," I finished, again quoting the old dwarven text.

"But we ain't fools," Joen said. "And this is no coin. Though it is worth more'n a few of them, eh?"

"Aye, that it is," the dwarf said with a sigh. He held up a hand to the other driver of the lead wagon, who apparently had already counted out the appropriate number of gold pieces. "A hunnerd in gold," he said, tossing a small bag to me. "That'll last yerselves some, if ye spend it wisely."

Joen skipped up to the wagon and handed the sapphire to the dwarf. He accepted it, but his mouth turned down in a frown. I figured he must not have wanted to pay so much for the stone, though I also figured it had probably been worth even more.

I wasn't about to argue with this fortune, though. I peeked into the bag to see the glint of gold.

Silverymoon was not like any city I'd ever seen. It didn't seem to be a city at all, really. Instead, it appeared as something between a city and a forest, with more than a hint of magic to complete the picture. Whereas other cities, particularly in the wealthier districts, may have tree-lined avenues, here it seemed the avenues lined the trees—roads wound around the trees, which had probably stood since before there was a city here.

The architecture, too, seemed a natural extension of the woods—not the gabled roofs of Waterdeep or Baldur's Gate, nor the squat, square, mud-and-stone houses of Calimport or Memnon. The structures here flowed freely, rising and falling like the surrounding hills. Spires of various shapes and sizes stuck their heads skyward, mingling with the numerous trees.

The city was alive with springtime, the trees blooming, the people enjoying their first opportunity in months to be outside. People—and elves, dwarves, and halflings—wandered about, some aimless, some moving with great purpose. Commoners in plain clothes mingled with wizards in robes and soldiers in shining silver armor. They walked or rode, or floated along on magical creations, or flew on winged steeds. Usually Haze, in her magical beauty, would stand out in a city, but here, she, and we riding her, seemed a normal part of the crowd.

Once we passed the city gates—they were left open, and the guards hardly gave us a passing glance—Joen said barely a word. She was gripping my waist tightly, leaning her head back, gazing skyward at the trees and spires and flying things, taking in the beauty of the place. I envied her some, her ability and willingness to just bask, but I couldn't join her. I had my own purpose, my own task to accomplish. And my own worries.

Who had sent those goblins out after us, and who might still be stalking us? Beshaba's Sentinel? I didn't even know who that was. For all I knew, there were mad cultists around every tree trunk, just waiting for an opportunity to jump us.

Though the streets were often broad, they were always winding, and many times I had to ask directions. The citizens of this beautiful, open city were no less open themselves, and with each inquiry I received a courteous and usually helpful answer. Though it took a fair bit of time, especially since I felt the need to examine everyone we met as closely as I could for some sign or totem of the Maid of Misfortune before I felt safe talking to them, we reached the library without any trouble.

I tried to dismount, only to find Joen still holding me tightly, strongly, keeping me firmly in place. She stared at the structure in front of us, soaking it in, admiring its beauty. And truly the great library at Silverymoon was beautiful. Unlike much of the rest of the city with it myriad of free-flowing forms, the library appeared more structured. It was square, classical, reminiscent of the temples in the walled-off Temple District in Baldur's Gate. Yet, somehow, it seemed it would fit only here in this place. Its roof was high, its windows huge, bright, and grand. Along the front marched a colonnade of tall pillars carved of perfect, unblemished marble.

Again I tried to dismount, anxious to get inside and find the information I sought. But Joen didn't seem to notice me at all.

I cleared my throat, hoping to get her attention. When that didn't work, I pinched her arm instead.

"Oi," she said, looking at me at last. "That hurt!" She punched me in the shoulder, but not very hard.

"We're here," I said.

"Oh. Good." She released her viselike grip, finally letting me dismount.

The antechamber of the library was much like the outside: classical, aged, beautiful. Doors opened left and right, and two more doors stood beyond a desk on the far wall. A woman in a silver robe sat behind the desk, several tomes splayed open before her. She looked up as we entered.

"Public rooms left and right," she said, her tone bored. "Help yourselves, and have a pleasant day." Her head dropped back to her reading.

"Public rooms?" I asked.

"That's what I said," she answered without raising her eyes.

"So not all the books are public?"

Now she looked up. "Of course not," she said. "Not all information is equal, you know."

"Yes, I'm aware," I said. I was acutely aware of the differing value of information—after all, I'd just spent a year and more to obtain but a small piece of what I sought. And that information had basically just been a marker, pointing here. Somehow, I doubted these public rooms would prove especially useful. "How can I see the rest?"

Her expression soured. "You would need permission," she said. "A sponsor from among those the library trusts would be your best bet."

"I don't know anyone in Silverymoon," I said.

"Then you're out of luck."

"Well, maybe you can help me here, then," I said. "I'm looking for information on something."

"If it's in the public rooms, I can help you find it," she said.

I pondered for a long moment whether I should trust this woman, but decided I had no real choice. And after all, this was a library in one of the great cities of the North, a city with a well-earned reputation as dedicated to study, to learning. I doubted she'd have some nefarious motive.

"I'm looking for information on the Stone of Tymora," I said.

Joen cast me a doubtful glance. Apparently she'd been thinking the same thing I had, though perhaps she'd come to a different conclusion on the wisdom of trusting the librarian.

The woman, for her part, seemed unfazed. "That's an unusual request," she said. "But any information on artifacts, assuming we have such information, would be in the restricted section. I'm sorry." She once again looked down to her tomes.

At a loss, I turned and slunk out of the building. Joen followed.

"Well, we tried, eh?" she said, putting her hand on my shoulder.

"We failed," I answered. The beautiful plaza in front of the library seemed so out of place, given my foul mood.

"They might not even have anything, you know?"

"But they might, and I can't even try."

"Well, we can try to find a sponsor, then." I could tell she was just trying to cheer me up, that she didn't really think it particularly plausible, at least for now. She would rather we give up and move on.

I unfettered Haze from the post I'd tied her to outside the library. "Come," I said. "Let's find a room for the evening. We can head back west in the morning."

"Oi, you're giving up?" she asked, shocked.

"Isn't that what you want?"

"Well, um, sort of, I guess," Joen stuttered. "I mean, I want to travel and all, and I . . . I don't know. I don't like seeing you so down, you know?"

I climbed onto the horse and helped Joen up behind me.

I smiled at her. "Well, then you'll be happy to know I'm not done quite yet. I want to go back to the Tower of Twilight. I bet Malchor can get us into the library."

"If he could, why didn't he send word ahead?" she asked.

I shrugged.

"Oi," Joen said after a moment. "What about that elf?"

"What elf?" I asked.

"The one who pointed you to Malchor in the first place. The dark elf."

I pulled the reins sharply, bringing Haze to a halt. Why hadn't I thought of that?

"Hey, you there, guard," I called to a passing man in silver armor.

"Move along, citizen. I'm very busy," the guard answered, continuing on his way. I kicked Haze into a slow walk beside him.

"I'm looking for someone," I said.

"Best of luck finding him," he replied. "Or her, as the case may be."

"Do you know Drizzt Do'Urden?"

The guard stopped and stared at me. "Course," he said. "All the guards here know him. We've been told specifically to let him pass and not bother him. Only one of his kind I know gets that sort of treatment in Silverymoon."

"Is he here now?" I asked. "Is he in the city?"

"Last I heard, aye. He was visiting with the Lady."

"The Lady?" Joen asked.

"Lady Alustriel," the guard said, and he looked confused when we looked confused. "Our protector and greatest heroine, Lady Alustriel of Silverymoon? One of Mystra's blessed Chosen?"

I had indeed heard of the Chosen of the goddess of magic, nearly godlike beings themselves. Drizzt truly had powerful friends.

"Do you know where I could find him?" I asked.

"Ask around," the guard advised with a shrug. "He'll get wind of it soon enough, and find you. But a word of advice . . ."

"Yes?" I asked.

"If you mean him any harm," the guard warned, "I'd give up now and save yourself a couple scimitars to the belly."

CHAPTER 71

W E MANAGED TO FIND A CLEAN STABLE FOR HAZE, THEN SET OUT INTO THE GLORIOUS city in search of Drizzt. By the time night fell, we'd been kicked out of every tavern and inn in town. Almost everyone had seemed to know the drow—they knew of him, at least. But everybody had looked at us as though we were crazy or just a couple of irritating kids. The best we had gotten out of anyone was, "If I run into him, I'll let him know a couple of kids're lookin' for him." We got that about a quarter of the time. The rest of the time was more like, "Get outta here. This ain't no place for kids!"

As we wandered down a particularly dark, winding thoroughfare, Joen asked me, "Well, what now?"

"I think there's another tavern up the street here," I replied. "Maybe if we ask people going in or coming out—"

"No," she interrupted me. "I'm getting tired. We need to find someplace to sleep."

I shrugged but didn't answer. I was too busy being frustrated to be tired.

"I'd be happy to curl up in the hay next to Haze," Joen said, nudging me with her elbow.

I sighed and nodded. "I guess we can try again in the morning."

The stables were the other way, so we stopped in the empty street and turned around. When we did, we seemed to startle a pair of men a few yards behind us on the street. They recovered quickly, but there was something about their manner that worried me, so I nudged Joen again and used my eyes to indicate the two shadowy figures. We'd both spent enough time in the rough and tumble cities of the Sword Coast to be wary of strangers on the street at night, and though we stayed calm, we were ready for anything as we passed.

The two men stopped walking and one leaned against a building. I could tell they were looking at us as we passed, and though they whispered quietly to each other, I was sure I heard one of them say, ". . . the stone and be done with it."

My hand went to my sword, which startled Joen. She stepped away from me and reached for her daggers. On cue, the two men threw back the heavy, black, hooded cloaks they wore and drew wicked slim-bladed daggers of their own.

"Good ears, boy," one of them said.

I brought my cutlass up to protect myself, and Joen did the same with her daggers.

"We don't want any trouble, mates," she said.

The other man smiled, showing a few missing teeth, and said, "Well, girlie, seems as trouble wants you."

I didn't recognize either of them, but their intentions were plain to both of us. When they came on, we were ready. And the closer they got, the better I could see them. The symbols of Beshaba, the goddess of bad luck, that both of them wore glinted in the dim moonlight.

"Who sent y—," I started to ask, but was cut off by a lunging stab from one of the cultists. I knocked his blade away and twisted my sword around and down in the manner of Master Kheene, author of *The Well-Tempered Bladesman*. That three-hundred-year-old advice had stood me in good stead—my blade nicked the man's hand and he hissed and stepped back, bumping into his friend enough that the second man's lunge at Joen was ruined.

Joen skipped back three quick steps and spun her daggers in her hand, faking as if to throw. Both of the cultists dodged the expected attack, but it never came. Instead, the one I'd nicked leaned in to my follow-up attack, and the tip of my cutlass plunged two inches deep into his right biceps. He shouted a word I'd never heard before, and I'd heard a lot of words like it from the sailors of the Sword Coast.

He stepped back, twisting away from me so fast he stumbled. But his friend recovered and lunged at Joen, who slipped to one side fast—but not fast enough. Though she was out of reach of the cultist's knife, the man spun in a fast and sudden kick that hit Joen on the shoulder and drove her to the street.

"Joen!" I called.

"We were to take yer stone, boy," the man I'd stabbed growled at me. "But now I think I'll have to kill you too."

By the cold look on his face, that idea didn't seem to bother him at all, and he slashed at me, running in to try to get too close to me for my cutlass to be of any use.

He succeeded, and had Malchor not drilled us for a full tenday on how to stretch our necks to one side, he would have stabbed me in the eye. Instead, he overreached and I brought my knee up between his legs.

He doubled over with a pained grunt and almost went down to one knee. I pushed against him, trying to knock him down, but he was too heavy.

"Maimun!" Joen called. When I looked up, my blood ran cold. The other man held her right wrist in his free hand and had his dagger at her throat.

"Drop 'em, little sister," the cultist said, and Joen looked at me for a cue as to what to do next.

I hesitated just long enough—barely a heartbeat—for the man I'd kneed to stand up, fast, and bowl me right over. He must have been twice as heavy as I. I grunted when I hit the cobblestones, then gasped when my cutlass clattered out of my hand.

"Now," the man who held Joen said. The other man advanced on me with murder in his eyes, then he lay down on the ground.

I blinked. What just happened?

He screamed, but the sound stopped short, replaced by a feral growl. I blinked again, not sure what I was seeing. It was as though a mammoth shadow had materialized out of the dark night air to press the cultist to the ground.

The man holding Joen said another harsh word, one the crewmen of *Sea Sprite* used to say when Captain Deudermont wasn't around.

"Holy—!" Joen started to say, but stopped with a gasp when the man holding her wrist, holding a dagger to her throat, was yanked away from her and into the impenetrable darkness at the side of the street. There was the sound of a ruckus somewhere out in the darkness, a grunt, and a sound like a heavy bag of rice or flower dropping to the ground.

Joen stepped back from both shadows, confused and frightened, while I scrambled to my feet, backing away from the shadow that still held the cultist to the ground. It wasn't a shadow, but an immense black cat unlike anything I'd seen before.

The man had fainted, or maybe the weight of the terrifying beast that sat on him had rendered him unconscious, making him as helpless as a baby.

"Thank you, Guen," a familiar voice sounded, echoing in the otherwise empty street.

Drizzt Do'Urden emerged from the darkness as the great panther backed away and seemed to merge with the shadows.

Joen let out a startled gasp. "Dr-drow!" she stuttered. She stumbled back and landed in a roll but recovered, coming to her feet gracefully, in perfect balance, daggers in her hands.

"Hold," I said. "He's a friend. This is Drizzt."

Joen looked at me as though she wasn't sure she should believe me.

"Please, put your blades away, young lady," the drow said, his tone gentle but forceful enough to make it clear that he wasn't joking around.

"Please," I said. "He can be trusted."

Joen shifted uncomfortably, even took another step back. She put her daggers back in their sheaths, though her hands stayed on their hilts, and a scowl remained on her face.

I moved to shake Drizzt's hand, and he clasped my wrist firmly.

"Maimun," Drizzt said. "I understand you've been looking for me."

"People actually told you?" I puffed up a bit, excited at the prospect that I had been recognized. "I was sure they were just shining us on."

"A youth, perhaps fourteen, riding a beautiful white mare, wearing a blue cloak," Drizzt said. "Not the typical look for a traveler. And I must admit, I'm surprised to find you so far from the coast. I thought you'd found what you were looking for out there."

"I'm surprised to find you again at all," I answered. "And I did find the stone."

"I'm glad to hear that, but I wasn't referring to the stone. You found a place, a home with Captain Deudermont and his crew, did you not?"

I shook my head. "Captain Deudermont . . ." I wanted to tell him everything that had happened, but Deudermont was Drizzt's friend and had been before I ever met the dark elf. "I loved my time at sea, but it was never home," I answered instead.

He nodded in understanding. As I stared into his piercing lavender eyes, I figured he understood more than I'd said—perhaps even more than I myself understood. He motioned down the street and said, "Let's be on our way. You little friends here will be cross with us when they awaken."

I glanced down at the unconscious cultist laying on the street, and followed Drizzt in a leisurely walk. He behaved as though battling evil cultists in the middle of the street was a nightly occurrence. For him, I suppose, I could imagine it might be.

"Well, now you're looking for me," Drizzt said when we were far enough from the unconscious man that if he did awaken, he wouldn't hear us. "What do you need?"

"Why are you here in Silverymoon?" I asked, not yet comfortable enough to ask for his help.

"Visiting a friend. And you?"

"Your friend, she's Lady Alustriel?"

"Lady Alustriel of Silverymoon, yes. You've not met her, but you've seen her work before."

"I have?"

"Think flaming chariots. They're a specialty of hers." Drizzt and I both smiled at the memory of the first battle I'd witnessed aboard *Sea Sprite*. After all, it's not often one sees a red-bearded dwarf crash a flying chariot of fire onto the deck of a pirate ship.

"Come, my friend, you have a favor to ask. So ask it."

I blew out a long sigh and said, "I need access to the library here in Silverymoon."

"It's open to all," Drizzt replied.

"Not all of it, and what I need is in the restricted collections."

"You seek information on that artifact of yours," Drizzt guessed. "And you've already seen Malchor Harpell?"

"I want to know how to destroy it," I said, resigned.

Drizzt looked at me curiously. "Is it not an artifact of good fortune?"

"So I'm told, but it always seems to bring me bad luck," I said. "Demons and dragons and druids who tried to take it from me or to kill me for it—every bad thing that's ever happened to me has been because of this stone."

"Like our friends back there?" Drizzt said. "But what of all the good things?"

"What do you mean?'

"You grew up in the High Forest with a druid, did you not?"

I nodded. "You remember my story," I said.

"Much of it. And you later traveled the land with a wandering bard, your mentor. Correct?"

"Yes."

"Would they have taken you under their wing if you weren't connected to the stone?"

"No," I said sharply, "because my parents never would have been murdered by some-one looking for it!"

"Perhaps," Drizzt replied. "But do you regret your time in the forest or on the road?"

I hesitated. "No," I answered.

"We must take the good with the bad," he said.

"So you're saying I shouldn't destroy the stone?"

"That is not my business, as you've pointed out. But what I am saying is, think long and hard about your path. About the path you choose. Before, your road had often been chosen for you, but now you make your own way."

"I have thought long on it," I replied.

"All right, then. I'm on my way to the palace. I'll speak with Lady Alustriel, and she'll arrange that you get a look at the books you need. In the meantime, go find a place for the night and stay off the streets before more of those gentlemen, let alone demons and dragons, come looking for you again."

"Thank you," I said, shaking the dark elf's hand once more.

Drizzt offered Joen a curt nod as he departed. Her scowl had lessened somewhat, but her hands remained on the hilts of her weapons until long after he'd gone out of sight.

CHAPTER 72

I T SHOULD BE RIGHT OVER HERE," THE LIBRARIAN SAID. SHE WAS MUCH FRIENDLIER THE second time we'd met her. Receiving instructions from the Lady of Silverymoon to allow us in would do that to a person, I supposed.

She led us down a narrow aisle between two tall bookshelves. Whereas the library was airy and beautiful in the public areas outside, here it more resembled a dungeon. A maze of shelves, tightly packed and full of tomes and scrolls, filled chamber after chamber. There was no organization system that I could discern—though, following the surprisingly fleet-footed librarian, I didn't have time to really try to figure it out. She seemed to know exactly where she was going, though, so Joen and I followed without question.

"And here we are," she said, coming to a halt before an utterly nondescript bookshelf. "Everything on the stones of Tymora and Beshaba are right there." She pointed to a group of tomes and scrolls on the seventh shelf up from the floor.

"How are we supposed to get—?" I started to ask, but the woman was already gone.

Joen and I looked at each other and shrugged.

I looked up at the shelf, which was easily fifteen feet above the floor. We searched around for a ladder, then anything we could make into a ladder, but short of making a precarious pile of valuable tomes, we came up with nothing.

"Oi, I could climb it," Joen offered.

"But if this thing isn't anchored to the floor, it'll fall right over on top of you."

Joen shrugged that off and said, "All right, then, let's just give up and go back to Waterdeep and see if we can sign on to a ship."

I didn't bother to answer that. The twinkle in her eye was enough for me.

"I'll climb it," I said, but before I could grab the first shelf, Joen had already clambered halfway up—and the whole bookcase started to sway.

"Oh," she said, looking down at me with wide eyes, "this is going to be bad."

I pushed back on the bookcase, and though I was nowhere near tall enough or strong enough, I guess I gave it just enough to set it back straight. Joen took a deep breath, then gasped when the bookcase started to gently lean in the other direction. No way could I pull it back.

"Wait! I exclaimed. I had an idea.

"Wait?" Joan asked, surprisingly calm, like the eye of a hurricane. "Are you kidding me?"

I ran as quickly as I could to the other side of the bookcase and jumped up into the first shelf. That slowed its descent just a bit and made it possible for me to clamber up a couple more until I was about as high off the floor as Joen. We couldn't see each other, but I could hear her sigh in relief.

"Whatever you just did," she called, "it worked."

I quickly explained to her that we should carefully climb up the bookcase at the same speed so it stayed balanced. Joen caught on quickly enough and we used some of that discipline we picked up at the Tower of Twilight to carefully ascend the precarious bookcase.

"Here we are," Joen said. "Now what?"

"Well," I started, "now I can . . ."

But the books we wanted were on the other side.

"I can't see them," I said.

"Yeah," Joen answered, "and too bad I'm a total drooling village idiot who can't read or anything."

That made me cringe and I apologized as she gathered up as much as she could carry and still climb. Then together we managed to get back down to the floor without being crushed. We met up again on the other side of the bookcase and I took a couple of the books from Joen.

"We can start with these, and . . . um . . . Do you feel that?" I said.

The floor rumbled. Joen looked around, surprised, then retreated a few steps. The librarian rounded the corner, pushing a great rolling ladder.

"Here we are," she said. "Now, the first scroll on the left up there is an . . ." She spotted the books we were holding, looked up at the shelf, back down at us, then back up at the shelf.

"Thank you," Joen said, sheepish. I just kind of smiled.

". . . index," the librarian went on. "It will tell you what the rest are. You can't take anything from the library. Check in with me on your way out, and please do not climb the bookshelves." She walked away before I could respond.

"Thank you!" I shouted after her, but the sound seemed muted and I wasn't sure if she'd heard me. I moved to the ladder. It was huge and bulky, but it rolled easily.

"Yeah," I said, "that'll come in handy."

"Come on," Joen said. "The sooner we get started, the sooner we can leave."

"I could spend a decade in here," I said, looking up from a scroll and gazing around the cavernous library.

"Oi, reading stories and the like, right? Sounds thrilling," Joen said.

"Yeah, it does," I started, turning to face her. But her posture—and her tone, I then realized—did not fit with her words.

Joen's arms were wrapped tightly around her body and her head was down, her yellow hair—long once more, as she'd not cut it in the past year—draped over her face. Her eyes darted around, barely visible under the shield of her hair, but obviously uncomfortable, nervous even.

"Is something wrong?" I asked.

She looked up at me. "I'm fine," she said. "I just . . . can we be done quick here, please? This place makes me feel . . . odd, you know?"

"I thought you liked books," I said, curious. "You seemed to like Malchor's books, anyway."

"It ain't the books," she said. "It's the place. It's just too . . . closed. I want to see the sky, eh? Feel the wind. And here it's like, there is no sky and there never will be." She shuddered and dropped her head again to an open book on the table in front of her.

"The sky is just above us," I said. "Just past the ceiling."

"Oi, I know," she snapped. "I ain't stupid."

We'd found a free table and piled as many of the books and scrolls on it as we could, then just started reading. The room was so quiet you could hear a pin drop, and we both spoke in hushed tones.

"It's all in Elvish," Joen said, frustrated. "This one too," she added, indicating scroll after scroll. "And this one, and that one . . . all of these."

"Give them to me," I said. "I used to read some Elvish a while back."

"Oi, what do they say, then?"

"I said I used to read it. I haven't had a chance to in years."

Joen growled and slammed closed the tome she was trying to read. "If Malchor knew we were coming here next, why didn't he teach us to read in Elvish?" she asked.

"He was too busy teaching us discipline," I answered.

"By locking us in a room with a bunch of books on discipline, eh? Why couldn't one of those books have been in Elvish?"

I looked to the shelves around us. They were filled to bursting with tomes and scrolls and books of various sorts. "Maybe," I said, thinking aloud, "there's a lexicon somewhere around here."

"A whatsicon?" Joen asked.

"A lexicon. A book written in two languages, to translate from one to the other."

"Oi, that'd be useful. Maybe that librarian woman has one."

"Shhh!"

That sound startled us both. It was the librarian, staring down at us as though we were unclean things that just wiggled our way out from under a rock. I grimaced, but Joen hid a smile.

The woman handed me a little silk pouch. I only glanced away from her for a second and she was gone.

"That's just creepy, ain't it?" Joen whispered. "The way she does that?"

The soft silk pouch felt heavy in my hands. I could feel a single object inside, round and curved. Without hesitation, I opened the drawstring and pulled out the object: a large glass lens.

I peered through the lens, looking at Joen, expecting her to be distorted. But she looked perfectly normal. However, I felt like something was amiss, but I couldn't quite place it.

I pulled the lens away from my eye. My view didn't change.

"Great," she said, "now we can see the words we can't read more close up."

I brought the lens back to my eye then withdrew it again. After several more attempts, I finally figured out what I was seeing.

Without the lens, the words on the spine of the tome on the shelf behind Joen was written in Dwarvish. When I brought the lens back to my eye, the words were written, very clearly, in Common.

"Well," I said, "I guess I found our lexicon." I took the big book from Joen and started to read. "It works on Elvish too."

"Well hurray," Joen quipped. She stood up and stretched. "Nature calls."

I waved her off and she went to find a bathroom. I had barely begun to start reading when she tapped me on the shoulder. Still reading, I said, "That was fast."

She leaned down so her lips were very close to my ear and whispered, "Someone's here."

I looked at her out of the corner of my eye and she whispered, "He's writing, but not reading."

Right away, I realized someone was listening to us and writing down everything we said. We were doing research for him too, whoever he was.

The study table had a collection of quills, a communal inkwell, and a small stack of parchment sheets. I took one and wrote: What does he look like?

Joen took the quill from me and wrote: Cloke, hud up. Her penmanship was as bad as her spelling.

I took the quill back. Like last night?

I looked at her and she nodded.

Act normal, I wrote with my left hand and loosened the cutlass from its sheath with my right. But no reading aloud.

She nodded and went a different way to find a bathroom while I tried to read and keep one eye on the lookout. It wasn't easy.

After a bit, she came back and whispered in my ear, "He's gone."

"We should still be quiet," I whispered back, looking around.

She sat across from me, took a quill, and wrote: Wut exakly r we lucking four heer?

"Nice spelling," I whispered and she made a gesture that the sailors used to use.

I took the quill from her hand and wrote: If I can find a book called *How to Destroy the Stone of Tymora*, that would be great, but failing that, anything that will at least point us in the direction of the Stone of Beshaba. We know we need both to destroy one.

She read that and nodded. We both went back to reading.

To save time, we'd pulled down all the documents from the section the librarian had pointed out—there weren't many, maybe half a dozen tomes and two scroll cases, plus the index. A cursory glance at the tomes suggested there would be little information there. Two of the six were regional histories written by the famed traveler Volo. One concerned the history of the High Moor, and was in fact an Elvish translation of a tome my mentor, Perrault, had carried, and had once made me read—or more likely, this was the original tome, and Perrault's was the translation. Another work of Volo detailed the Great Desert, Anauroch. What these had to do with the stones, I couldn't quite fathom. I wondered at first if they'd perhaps been mixed into the collection by accident, but their titles appeared on the index alongside the remaining documents.

The other four tomes detailed histories and mythologies relating to Tymora and Beshaba. Whether they contained any relevant information, we couldn't tell just at a glance. One tome did reference the stones themselves, but the passage in question was a story about the heroic deeds of a past stone bearer and said nothing about how to destroy them, or how to find them, or the identity of the Sentinels, or anything I found particularly useful or interesting.

While Joen made her way slowly through a book of funerary rites, I opened one of the scroll cases, which had huge scorch marks on it as though it had once been set on fire. It wasn't easy to open, and was even harder to get the partially burned scroll out of, but eventually I sat back to read it. Because it was written in some type of Elvish script, I traced the magical lens over the parchment, watching in amazement as the Common-tongue translation appeared behind the curved glass.

"Oi, this's some sort of map," Joen said.

I shushed her and looked up to see her holding a piece of parchment that had been tucked into the pages of the funeral book. She placed the map in the middle of the table so we could both see it. It showed some desert—probably Anauroch—but its labels were not in Common.

She reached over and snatched the lens from my hand.

"Hey!" I exclaimed, and my own voice sounded deafening in my ears.

Joen took great pleasure in shushing me. She gazed through the lens at the map.

"The lens isn't working right," she whispered. "This isn't in Common."

I slid closer to look, and sure enough, as she held the lens over the tags, the words still appeared to be in another language.

"We should ask the librarian about it," she whispered.

I held up a hand to stop her and pointed to a symbol on the map that looked like half a letter.

"Oi, yeah, I see it. Could be an *o*? Maybe a *g*?"

I shrugged and reached out for the lens.

"I don't see how it's gonna matter who holds the lens," she whispered, but gave it to me anyway.

I turned away from her, putting the lens back on my own parchment.

"Hey, give that back!" she shouted angrily, then clapped her hands over her mouth. Trying not to laugh, she grabbed at my shoulder, hoping to turn me back around. When that failed, she tried reaching over me to grab the lens. I just kept reading and trying not to laugh myself.

"Hey now, this one is interesting," I whispered, then motioned her over to look through the lens with me. The scroll was all about the Stone of Beshaba, how it was cre-ated, the first soul given to it, the Sentinel—I almost dropped the lens, I was so surprised.

Joen gasped and we both read: And the Sentinel was an Elf of exceeding Grace. And the Sentinel was called . . .

But it was burned on that edge. We couldn't read it.

Joen pointed to a partial letter and whispered in my ear, "Could be an *a*."

I could only shrug and read on.

It said the Sentinels are connected to their stones and to each other. They always know where the other is and where the stone is, and the soul the stone has chosen. That must be how those cultists had found us.

"Great," Joen whispered.

Though it had been a while since we'd seen the hooded man or anyone else, I took up the quill and wrote: If this scroll case has information on the Stone of Beshaba, maybe the other has information on the Stone of Tymora.

She took the quill and wrote back: And that'd have the name of Timora's Centenal.

And that Sentinel can find the other Sentinel, I answered in writing. And then we'll have both Sentinels, and one can lead us to the other stone!

We looked at each other, then, lunged for the unopened scroll case as one. Joen got there first.

"Careful," I whispered.

"I know! Relax, eh?" she answered, plucking the silver stone cap from the scroll. With shaking hands she withdrew the parchment from inside. She stared at it a moment, then her face dropped into a half frown, half scowl.

I tried to make it clear from my facial expression that I was waiting to hear what it had to say. She turned it around to show me and mouthed, "The scroll is missing. There's just another map."

"No," I whispered, holding up the first map. "It's the same. Look." When we looked at them side by side it was obvious that they were identical, but the lettering was different.

I thought for a bit then took the parchment from Joen's hand. I stacked the two maps, holding them toward a lamp. The parchments were thin, nearly translucent in the light, and I could clearly see the markings of one map through the other. I aligned them, and sure enough, the gaps in the text of one perfectly fit with the other.

"The lens," I whispered, turning to Joen. But of course, she was a step ahead of me. As I turned, I nearly smashed my face into her rising arm.

"Watch it, eh?" she muttered as she shoved me aside and grabbed the stacked maps, bringing the lens up in front of them.

It was Anauroch after all.

"But what's this?" Joen whispered, gesturing at the other word.

There were only two labels on the whole map—the other markings appeared to be short poems scattered around the edges. But Anauroch, the Great Desert, was clearly marked, and along its western edge was a small symbol the lens translated as "Twinspire."

I shook my head and shrugged. Neither of us wanted to say the word aloud lest our "friend," was still skulking about.

She looked at me, her dour mood of the past few hours gone, the twinkle back in her eye. "Hold these," she said, practically shoving the maps and the lens into my hand. I tried very hard not to crumple the parchment scrolls as I caught them, but I was fairly sure there was now a crease or two that hadn't been there before.

I watched in amazement as Joen became a veritable whirlwind of energy. She bounded over to the books, collecting them into one armload, and very nearly ran up the ladder. She piled the books into their compartment haphazardly then leaped back down to the floor. She swept the last parchment up, rolled it quickly and placed it in a scroll case. She put it in the correct case, I noted, but I figured that was more luck than intent. I separated out the maps, moving to hand her the correct fragment. But she ignored me, climbing the ladder again, and placing the scroll case and the index scroll among the tomes.

Down the ladder she came again, grabbing the remaining empty scroll case. She held it out to me expectantly. When I hesitated, she tried to grab the maps. Realizing what she meant to do, I rolled up the parchment sheets, figuring I'd be a lot gentler than she was being. I slipped the maps into the case.

"Wrong case," I said.

"Oi, I don't care," Joen said, popping the cap on the case. "Come on!"

She took off at a near sprint, rounding the corners in the maze of books with such speed I feared she'd career into the shelves and cause a serious disaster. But she'd always been graceful, and the year of training at the Tower of Twilight had only enhanced that, and despite her speed she moved in perfect balance. I followed. The boots I'd procured from Sali Dalib so more than a year ago in Memnon magically allowed me to move so quickly it was easy to match her speed.

On the journey through the library, Joen kept her head down, and I figured she wasn't paying much attention to our route. But, as it turns out, I was wrong. She never hesitated at a turn, but moved with purpose and direction, and only a few moments later we were bursting through a door into the antechamber of the library.

The librarian wasn't surprised in the least as we came through the door. She didn't even lift her head as she asked, "Did you find what you were looking for?"

"There's a scroll missing from your collection," Joen said.

That got the librarian's attention. "Missing?"

"Missing. Not present. It ain't where it's supposed to be, you know?"

The librarian looked shocked. "All the documents in this library are magically marked," she said. "They can't be removed, or I'd know about it!"

But Joen had already pulled me past her. It was then that I realized Joen wasn't carrying the scroll case anymore.

"Oi," Joen said as we rushed to the door, "if you say so!"

"But . . .," the librarian sputtered, "you wait now."

Joen, still running, let go of me to push the doors open with both hands, and we were out in the bright spring sunshine. Sunshine? I thought. How long had we been in there?

I followed her down the steps at a run while a loud clamor of gongs and bells sounded behind us.

"Do you still have that scroll case?" I asked Joen as we ran out into the street.

Joen shot me a mischievous glance and tore off into a shadowy alley.

"I can't believe you just did that," I said as we crouched in a narrow alley next to a pile of old wash buckets. We had spent most of the day crisscrossing the city, barely ahead of one group of city watchmen after another.

"That's not all," Joen replied, pulling a small object from her pocket. She flipped the magical lens into the air, caught it, and pocketed it again.

"You are a pirate after all," I said. "They're going to track us down for that, if not for the map."

"We'll be long gone before she even bothers to check on it," Joen answered.

"Will we?"

"Anauroch isn't that far from here, you know? A month, at the worst."

"To Twinspire?" I asked. "That's where the gods chose the Sentinels, right? Maybe we can find their names there."

"Oi, to Twinspire!" Joen said happily.

"Not so fast," said a man standing in the shadows nearby. "Twinspire is long buried, and the world is better off because of it."

CHAPTER 73

CHRYSAOR EMERGED FROM THE SHADOWS, HIS BLUE SKIN SHINING IN THE SUN, HIS HAIR a bit longer than I remembered.

"You've been following us all this time?" Joen asked.

Chrysaor shrugged. "I didn't have to follow you. I simply waited for you to take the next logical step on your journey and to come here."

"You wasted a year just waiting?" I asked.

"A year spent in Silverymoon is hardly wasted," Chrysaor countered. "Trust me, my boy, I have my own ways of keeping busy."

"Well, you should spend another here, then," Joen said. "You ain't coming with us."

"You shouldn't be going at all, young lady," he replied. "It's far too dangerous, especially for you."

"I can handle myself."

"I've no doubt you can fight. But it's still unwise."

"And for me? Is it too dangerous for me?" I asked.

Chrysaor laughed. "You forget my purpose, boy. If you go to Twinspire, perhaps you further your quest to destroy the stone, or perhaps you fall and the artifact is lost for a time. Either way, I gain."

"If killing me would benefit you, why haven't you tried it yet?"

Chrysaor shrugged and threw me a crooked smile.

"I'm with Joen on this one," I said. "You stay here, we leave, we never see you again."

"If you so wish," he said. "But you'll never find Twinspire without me."

"Oi, that tune's getting old."

I patted the map on my hip. "We'll find it."

"How old is that map?" he asked. "And how detailed? The world is not static, you know. Things changed over the eons. Twinspire is long since gone. And besides, you know there are beings with a vested interest in the stones not being destroyed."

"You mean the Sentinels," I answered.

Chrysaor nodded. "Powerful beings, those Sentinels. Ages old. And you want to kill them."

"No," I said. "I just want to be rid of the stone."

"Which will kill them, which they do not want. So you think they'd let you get any closer to your goal? Even now, they surely have eyes upon you."

Of course I knew he was right, that cultists of Beshaba at least had already confronted us, were spying on us.

"Oi, don't listen to him," Joen said, turning to me. "And don't trust him."

"I don't," I replied. "And I don't believe him, that we can't find it. But I also don't see the harm in taking him."

"He just said he wants you dead, didn't he?"

"But he's had plenty of opportunities and never tried to kill me," I answered.

"The boy speaks wisely," Chrysaor cut in.

"Quiet," Joen and I both answered at the same time.

"Oi, it's your quest, it's your decision," Joen said.

I pondered a moment, then said to Chrysaor, "As before, you walk ahead, you don't share our camp, and you don't share our food."

"Of course," the blue pirate said with a bow.

"Then let's fetch our horse and be off."

"To Twinspire," Chrysaor said, and I thought I caught a hint of excitement in his voice.

"To Twinspire," Joen echoed, her tone remarkably similar to that of her most hated enemy.

"I wonder whose campsite this is," Joen said, stirring some ash with one of her daggers.

Chrysaor started to say, "It probably belongs to—"

"Oi, I wasn't talkin' to you, eh?" Joen interrupted.

The pirate smiled. "Of course not," he said. He bowed low, turned, and walked out of the campsite. But he took only a few steps—just a token gesture—before he stopped and turned to face us again. He still wore that smug, knowing grin. I rolled my eyes. The genasi fully expected we'd be asking his opinion, and soon.

This abandoned campsite was the first sign of life we'd seen since we entered the desert two days ago. And it was hardly a sign: blowing sand had covered most of it. Any bedroll that had been here was long since gone. The only evidence that anyone had ever been there was the simple fire pit lined with small stones and filled with ash.

"Oi, Maimun. I asked you a question, eh?"

"I have no idea," I replied.

"The ash is still warm," she said, touching the surface with her hand. "I'd say that's a good sign, you know."

"Or it's just the sun," I said.

Our journey had taken us only nine days, and another three after we'd reached the desert, but in those twelve days it seemed the season had shifted. It was still spring, technically, but summer was a mere month away. And here in the desert, the warm season seemed to start sooner.

I walked a quick perimeter. The campsite lay in a low trough between two towering dunes of sand, so I wanted to get a good view of the surrounding land from the crest of those dunes. There were wicked things in wild areas like Anauroch, and we'd be easy ambush targets here should anything be hunting.

"You shouldn't worry," Chrysaor said, seeing me walking my path. "Desert hunters rest in the day and hunt at night. You've another seven hours or so before you need to worry."

"We, you mean," I said.

"But I'm not part of this little troupe, am I?"

"No, but I doubt a desert hunter will know that—or care either."

Chrysaor laughed. "How many times must I escape from you before you realize I'm in no danger?" he said.

"As I recall," I answered, "I escaped from you first."

Chrysaor's smile did not diminish. "You did at that. Correct me if I'm wrong, but didn't a particular spellcaster come to your rescue, though? And tell me, where is your wizard friend now, and how will he rescue you out here?"

"Correct me if I'm wrong," I replied, "but didn't you escape by jumping in the water and swimming away? I mean, you are a creature of elemental water, aren't you? So tell me, where is your ocean now, and how will it help you escape out here?"

"Oi," Joen called from the fire pit. "I think I found something!"

Chrysaor and I dropped our little argument and trotted over to join her. "What is it?" the genasi asked.

Joen scowled at him and didn't answer.

I rolled my eyes, exaggerating the motion, making sure she'd see it clearly. "What is it?" I asked.

She held up her hand—and in it lay a piece of crumpled, charred parchment. "It looks like the same parchment as the ones in the library," she said. "Maybe the missing scroll?"

"Well now," the genasi said with a mischievous twinkle in his eye, "wouldn't that be a marvelous coincidence, happening upon something like that way out here, just by virtue of luck?"

Ignoring the genasi, I took the parchment from Joen and fumbled open my pack, withdrawing the map we'd taken from Silverymoon. I held up the two pieces together.

"Doesn't look the same," I said.

"Well, one's all burned, the other ain't," Joen replied.

Chrysaor coughed loudly and cleared his throat. We ignored him and continued to examine the maps, but he continued to clear his throat and fidget.

"What?" Joen and I both said at the same time.

Chrysaor said nothing, just pointed to the ground at his feet. He made a brushing motion, then dropped his foot to the ground. Unexpectedly, it landed with a loud *clomp*.

"So you found a rock," Joen said, her voice tinged with anger. She didn't budge as I moved to investigate.

"It's not a rock," I said, reaching Chrysaor.

The stone beneath his feet was solid. I dropped to my knees and began to clear sand, soon finding the edges, about three feet apart in any direction. The stone was a rough square.

"It's a paving stone," Chrysaor said, "set by some ancient hand."

"Oi, if it's a road, where're the other stones?" Joen asked.

I scraped my hand out a foot or so from the side of this first stone and hit something solid. "Right here," I said.

I stood, clomping my boots against the ground as I walked. They were softer than Chrysaor's, so the sound was far less satisfying, but I could definitely feel the solid surface beneath my feet.

"Looks like it heads this way," I said, walking along the trough between the sand dunes. With each step, I stomped my foot down, and each time I felt it connect with stone.

The wind picked up, swirling the sand around. The sand obscured my vision, but somehow, with everything slightly hazy, the stones became clearer, the path more obvious. I broke into a light jog, following the path as it cut a wide turn around a great mound of sand.

Then, in the distance, I saw something strange—it was part of the landscape, but not natural. It was some sort of rock formation, I supposed, a column reaching up from the desert. Though it was largely obscured by the blowing sand, it looked even more out of focus, like it wouldn't be seen clearly even on the clearest day.

I quickened my pace, covering the last hundred yards at a dead sprint. At that speed, I couldn't feel the paving stones beneath my feet, but somehow I knew my path followed the ancient road. Joen and Chrysaor couldn't keep up, and I could hear Joen calling out from behind me, though I couldn't make out the words.

When at last I reached the object, I understood why I couldn't clearly make out its shape. It was not, as I had thought, a pillar of stone. It was two pillars, side by side. From the angle I approached them from, they were lined up one after the other so they seemed to shift relative to each other. That, combined with the wind-driven sand . . .

"What happened to the sand?" I asked no one in particular.

As suddenly as it had appeared, the sandstorm vanished. Once again, the afternoon sun beat down on my head and shoulders, hot and oppressive. I tried to recall where in my run the wind had died. I was sure it had happened before I'd reached the pillars, but I couldn't quite remember. I hadn't been paying attention to anything except my goal during that sprint.

"Oi, you're standing on it," Joen said, finally catching up to me. She was a bit out of breath. Chrysaor soon followed, jogging lightly.

"You know what I meant," I said. I walked around the first pillar, studying it closely. It was a simple column, perhaps eight feet tall and two feet across, carved, obviously ancient, but not eroded in the least. Runes and sigils traced over the perfectly smooth white surface, some carved, some written in a deep red ink that also had not faded despite the apparent age of the structure.

"Ah," Chrysaor said from behind me, "here we are, drawn as if by the power of the Goddess of Luck herself—oh, ah, yes . . ." He ended with a smug chuckle and I could feel Joen staring daggers at him.

I looked at the second pillar. It appeared nearly identical to the first, though the runes were different. And unlike the first, the second column had a rope tied around it. The rope stretched away from the pillar at a steep angle, diving into the sand below, completely taut, as if it were attached to the ground—or attached to something buried beneath the ground.

"Oi, what are you doing?" Joen said, staring at me curiously.

I pointed to the rope. "I wonder where that goes," I said.

Joen's eyes widened in surprise. She ran over to the rope and reached out with trembling hands, not daring to touch it.

"What's wrong?" I asked, joining her at the second pillar.

"Have you seen anything like this?" she asked, breathless.

"What, like a rope? Yes, I have, on more than one occasion."

She gave me a sour look. "You know what I meant," she said.

"I really don't," I replied, but she ignored me.

She swept her hand in an arc, about even with the noose of the rope, where it was tied around the pillar. She struck the pillar and she withdrew her hand, nearly falling over backward.

"It's tied to something!" she said.

"Yeah," I said. "It's tied to that big pillar."

"What pillar?" she asked.

"You can see it?" Chrysaor asked me. "Interesting, though not unexpected."

"What do you mean?" I asked. "Why wouldn't I be able to see it?"

"She what?" asked Joen.

"Obviously not for the reason she can't see it," he said.

"Please, be more vague."

"There are usually only four beings on this plane of existence who can see the pillars at the gate to Twinspire," he said.

"Usually?"

"Well, certain creatures who aren't from this plane could see it, I'm sure—demons, devils, archons, beings of that nature—but only four who are native."

"Oi, the bearers and the Sentinels, eh?" Joen asked.

Chrysaor nodded.

"So what do the carvings say?" I asked.

"I don't know," Chrysaor answered. "I can't see it." His answer seemed disingenuous. I figured he was lying.

Joen pulled a small object from one of her many pockets. "I'm still not sure what you two are talking about, but I suppose you'll just have to read it yourself, then," she said. She held up the small glass lens she'd taken from the library at Silverymoon.

"Resourceful," Chrysaor said as Joen handed me the lens.

"Thank you," Joen said, beaming. Then she apparently realized who gave her the compliment, and her face dropped into a scowl.

I held the lens up to my eye, peering at the carving. " 'Tymora, guide my way, guide my feet, that I may find fortune even when I stumble,' " I read aloud. "It's a prayer to Tymora, all of it."

"All of it?" Chrysaor said. "All to Tymora, none to Beshaba? This place is sacred for both of them."

"Oh, right," I said, turning around. "There's another pillar."

"Nice of you to share that information," Chrysaor said with a grimace.

"Oi, get off your high horse," Joen said. "You knew about this place, eh? And you didn't show it to us, did you?"

"I offered, and you told me to be quiet," the genasi reminded her.

Joen scoffed, waving her hand dismissively at him.

"It's a prayer to Beshaba, all right," I cut in. "Really harsh too. 'May the road of my enemies be forever full of pitfalls, and spikes, and fire, and pain, and blood, and—' "

"Oi, that's enough," Joen said. "We get the picture, you know."

"There's more," I said.

"We don't want to hear it," she answered.

"No, I mean there's something else entirely. The prayers are carved in, but there's some kind of writing in ink as well. But the lens isn't translating it."

"What does it read?" Chrysaor said. "It could be magical text, unable to be magically translated. But I am quite versed in the various languages of the land."

Something about the pirate made me nervous just then—more than normally around that unpredictable genasi. He always seemed so detached, as though he didn't really ever take anything seriously, but now he seemed a bit too keen to know what was written on a pillar consecrated in the name of an evil goddess.

"It reads, *'Sirlar, geri sekilekegini golgeler,'*" I said, slowly and carefully enunciating each syllable, though I had a nagging feeling I shouldn't have.

As soon as I finished, the ground began to violently shake. I fell, and Joen only managed to hold her balance by grabbing the rope. Chrysaor seemed somehow unaffected, swaying as a tree in a windstorm, but in complete control of his body and his balance. I was not surprised.

But I was a bit startled when the ground fell away beneath us.

CHAPTER 74

A SINGLE SHAFT OF LIGHT PENETRATED THE DARKNESS—DIFFUSE, LOST IN THE swirl of sand, dust, and pulverized stone. The shaft angled in—it was midafternoon above—and cast a dully glowing circle of light on a great wall of stone. Crystals lined the wall, sparkling in the light and reflecting it out into the massive cavern beyond.

It took my eyes many heartbeats to adjust to the dim light, and it took the dust at least as long to settle. I stood on a rough stone floor lightly coated in the dust of ages. As I gained my bearings, it became clear I was in some sort of natural cavern. Three sides made a semicircle more than a hundred feet across, and on the fourth side the floor sloped down into impenetrable blackness.

"We should . . .," I started to say. But I realized that I stood alone.

That I stood at all was itself a minor miracle. The hole above, where the ground had fallen out beneath us, was at least fifty feet up. I ran my thumb across the one ring I wore, an enchanted ring I'd been given by my mentor long ago, one of three magical treasures I'd inherited from him. Its magic had slowed my descent and saved my life.

But Joen had no such ring.

"Joen!" I called out in the peculiar voice of terror that comes when sudden relief becomes even more sudden dread.

The only response I heard was my own voice echoing back at me, at once muffled by the sand and somehow amplified by the cavern.

I scrambled around, low to the ground, looking for any sign that she'd fallen in with me. But the cavern was too uneven, the light too dim, and I could make out only the many juts and gullies of the water-carved floor—and one unnatural object.

It was a rope, one end coiled neatly around a stone, the other reaching heavenward.

"She grabbed the rope," I whispered to myself. "Right before we fell, she grabbed the rope." I looked up to the ceiling, to the hole. Sure enough, there was a form there, humanoid, descending slowly. "Joen!" I called again.

"Not quite," Chrysaor answered, coming into view. He beat his wings—his *wings?*—a few times, circling as he dropped, landing gracefully right beside me. "You are surprising," he said. "I thought my journey ended, yet you live."

"Where's Joen?" I demanded.

"No, that's not the question you want to ask," he said. "There is a much more obvious and more important one."

"What, about those ugly wings?" I was, of course lying. His arms had turned to beautifully feathered white wings, the wings of a great eagle, perhaps. But at that moment, nothing about him could have been beautiful to me. "I don't care. Where is she?"

Chrysaor laughed at me. "Of course not the wings," he said. "They're trivial, if convenient." He clapped his hands together—or, rather, his wing tips—and the magic faded, the feathered appendages again replaced by blue-skinned arms, sleeveless, with nondescript white leather cords around each wrist. His hands dropped to his hips, and he assumed a pose I was more familiar with in Joen: defiant, even petulant, ready to fight if he didn't get his way.

I dropped my own hand to the hilt of my sword. "What have you done?" I said.

"The question you should have asked—," he began.

"Where is she?" I said, interrupting him. I drew my sword slowly from its sheath.

"The question is," the pirate went on, "did I know what the spell was going to do? Did I lead you into this trap? Is it my fault you're down here?" He drew his own fine, thin blade from its sheath.

"Tell me where Joen is," I demanded, advancing a step.

"The answer, of course, is yes, I knew." He brought his blade up just as I lunged forward. Metal rang against metal, and the genasi skipped back a step, keeping distance between him and me. "Yes, of course it was a trap. And yes, of course it's all my fault."

I set myself in an aggressive posture. It was much like the fencer's stance I'd learned long ago from Perrault, but informed by my training at the Tower of Twilight. This time, I set my right foot—usually my trailing foot—a half step ahead of my left, rather than a half step behind. Still I kept it horizontal to my body while my left foot I kept vertical, facing directly at my enemy. I gripped my blade in both hands, hilt held near my left shoulder, blade extending across my body. If Chrysaor attacked me while I was in this stance, I would be well able to defend, but my mobility would be side-to-side, rather than a retreat. So I would be more able to exploit any holes he left in his own defenses.

But he didn't attack. He simply stood five or so feet from me, his own blade vertical in front of him, his posture relaxed. "I knew, you see, because I lied," he said.

"You like hearing the sound of your own voice, don't you?"

"Yes, I find it rather pleasant." He chuckled.

I planted all my weight on my forward foot, dropped my right hand from the hilt of my saber, and lunged at him. My right arm swung down behind me and my left foot leaped out ahead, knee bent, with my right leg locked behind me. My sword darted forward, as fast as a lightning bolt, covering those five feet in the blink of an eye. The tip dived straight for Chrysaor's heart.

His sword flashed across, but he was late on his parry, as I knew he'd be. For the first time, he seemed caught off guard, surprised by the suddenness and viciousness of my attack. He fell back, bending at the waist, back, back, until he was doubled over. My sword grazed along his chest, cutting a few straps on his tunic. His parry finally reached my blade, but with no strength behind it.

I finished my lunge, not trying to redirect my thrust at all. I simply let my graceful movement play itself out, coming to a rest at full extension, my sword pressed firmly against Chrysaor's chest. He, to his credit, held his balance despite the extraordinarily awkward angle he was bent at. That is, he held his balance until I pressed downward with some force.

Chrysaor, the blue pirate, who had always seemed so in control, fell unceremoniously to the dirt, landing flat on his back.

I stepped up, bringing the tip of my sword down to the hollow of his chest. I stepped on his hand for good measure, and he released his sword, useless at that angle anyway.

"Where," I repeated, "is Joen?"

"You don't want—," he began.

I kicked him in the ribs. Hard. He winced in pain.

"Where?" I asked again.

"She's still up above," he said.

"Alive?"

"Unharmed. But trust me—"

I kicked him again. "Never again," I said.

"You don't want her to come down here," he finished anyway.

"She was right about you all along." I retracted my sword, sheathed it, and collected Chrysaor's fallen blade. It was not curved like my saber, but was of much finer make, light and balanced. It was far from ideal, surely, but it would do. I lamented briefly the loss of my old sword, the sword Perrault had left me, the magical saber that could burst into flame on command.

"Curious," Chrysaor said.

"What is?"

"That." He pointed into the darkness, to where a small point of light shone, a bluish glow. "It seems your way is marked. That, I did not expect."

"My way may be marked," I confirmed, "but as I said, I will never trust you again."

I moved to take the rope, planning to climb to the surface and check on Joen. I slipped Chrysaor's sword through a loop on my belt, took the rope in both hands, and started to climb.

I'd only gone a few yards, though, when something about the feel of the rope changed. It was suddenly less balanced, less than a perfect line to the surface, to where it was tied off. It swayed a bit, not dangerously, but completely out of my control.

I peered upward through the still-sandy air to the surface. I thought I could make out something moving up there. It was a person climbing down the rope with some speed. Her hair shone golden in the slanting rays of the sun.

"Joen!" I called.

"Oi!" she called back as I started shimmying back down the rope.

"What took you so long?" I asked.

"That blue son of a wharf rat did something to me, eh?" she called. "Tied me up or something."

I hopped down the last few feet to the stone floor and glared at Chrysaor, who had risen to his feet. "She was bound, magically but gently," he said in response to my angry look. "And for her own good."

"Her own good is not for you to decide," I said.

"Nor you," he countered.

Joen slid down to join us. "Well, let's ask me then, eh?" she said. As soon as her feet hit solid ground, her daggers left their sheaths.

"Don't kill him," I said.

"Oi, why not?"

I struggled for a good answer. A moment ago, I could have killed him myself, but that was because I thought he'd hurt Joen. She took my hesitation as an invitation, advancing on the genasi.

"Because," I said at last, "he didn't kill us."

"He tied me up," she reminded.

"He could have killed you."

"Maybe next time he will, eh?" she asked.

"No," Chrysaor said, "there won't be a next time."

"Because you'll be dead already," Joen said, advancing another step.

"Because my task is complete."

"Could you be more vague?" I asked. "If you're working for Elbeth, maybe I could understand why you would bring us to Malchor Harpell, and why you would bring us here. But why would you send me down here and tie Joen up on the surface? Why separate us? Why not just tell us what you really want with me, with the stone, with this place . . . with whatever it is you really want?"

He laughed. "All that would take some effort. Now, my sword, if you please?"

"I do not please," I answered. "Consider it the price of your life."

"Very well," he said. He bowed low, first to me, then to Joen, who looked as if she were about to charge the last few feet and stab him midbow. Then he clapped his hands together three times in rapid succession. With a dazzling white flash, his arms turned into wings.

"You should have stayed above," he said to Joen. "I'm very sorry, my dear, for what is to come."

He leaped skyward, beating his wings a few times, pulling himself up and out of the tunnel.

Joen looked after him with a mix of anger and disappointment. "Well, that was interesting, eh?" she said.

"Something like that."

"Where do we go from—?"

The rope started coiling up at our feet, and we both stepped back, staring as it gathered in a mess on the stone floor.

"Oh," Joen said, "no, he didn't."

I closed my eyes and took a deep breath. I thought I heard Chrysaor's laugh echoing down from above, but maybe I just imagined it.

"Yeah," Joen said, "he sure did."

"I don't . . ." I hesitated, feeling stupid. "I don't kill people."

Joen looked at me and didn't have to say, "Yeah, all right, but maybe just that once." Her eyes said it all.

"Our path is marked," I said, changing the subject and turning toward the darkness.

In the distance, the blue light flickered then went out completely.

CHAPTER 75

D O YOU KNOW WHAT AN UMBER HULK IS?" I ASKED, TRYING TO BREAK THROUGH JOEN'S stony silence.

She carried a torch we'd found in the magical pack Malchor had given us. I wasn't sure whether the magical pack had conjured it in the manner it created food when we needed it, or if the wise and forward-thinking wizard had simply stashed a torch in there for us, just in case.

"It's a creature that lives in the deep, dark places of Faerûn," I went on. "It stands eight or nine feet high, and it's wider than you are tall. And its whole body is covered by thick plates of chitinous armor, like an ant's shell but much thicker. And it has—"

"Oi, is there one about to bite your head off right this exact moment?" Joen interrupted.

"Yeah, no. Sorry. It's just, this place made me think of them. 'Umber' means 'shadow,' you know, and there are a lot of shadows down here."

"Please just stop talking."

"Sorry." I wasn't wrong about the shadows, though. The torchlight seemed puny in the massive cavern, a tiny pinprick of light in a vast, empty, black nothing. But it was enough to illuminate the numerous stalagmites stretching up from the ground that cast long, deep shadows stretching to the distant walls. We could faintly see the walls, and as in the place we'd initially fallen into, they were flecked with some reflective crystals that caught what meager trace of our light reached them and threw it back at us, a faint twinkle in the distance.

A rustle, a hint of motion just beyond our light, made Joen jump.

"Don't worry," I said quietly. "It's not an umber hulk. They're very adept at stealth. You'd never hear it—"

"Shut up about umber hulks!" she said in a harsh whisper. She shifted her torch to her left hand and drew a dagger with her right. The rustle came again, and Joen, apparently honing in on its location, let fly.

Her dagger darted through the air, torchlight seeming to shimmer as it reflected off the perfect blade. It struck the ground just beyond the circle of our torchlight, throwing a brilliant spark. It ricocheted like a stone skipping off a pond, bouncing with a *clang, clang . . . splash.*

Joen's eyes went wide at the sound of her treasured weapon hitting water. She rushed forward, sputtering, having apparently forgotten that some potential danger lurked directly in her path. And she brought the torch with her, leaving me standing, shocked, in near-total darkness.

I recovered my senses and ran after her, catching her about twenty paces ahead, at the edge of a still pool of black water. Joen's arms were elbow deep in it as she sifted around. Tears around her eyes and on her cheeks glistened in the flickering torchlight.

"Oi," she said. "Oi, I didn't mean to . . . I didn't . . . oi, please . . ." She withdrew one of her arms to wipe away her tears, but her arm was just as wet.

I dropped to my knees beside her. "It's all right," I said. "We'll find it."

I rolled up my sleeves, intending to help her search, though the water looked really deep and I didn't expect to find anything.

But something caught my eye: a glint, a reflection, under the otherwise-unmarred surface of the pool. Tentatively, I reached in for it. The water was lukewarm and not unpleasant. As my hand approached the shining object, that object seemed to approach my hand as well. When my fist closed around a small, scaly something, I pulled my arm out, and with it a small creature. It was an ugly thing with a pale brow, chitinous body, four spindly legs, two long antennae, and a spiked tail it started twirling like a maple seed.

And in its mouth it held a sparkling dagger.

"Uh, Joen," I whispered. When she didn't respond, I gently nudged her. She turned to look and saw the fish and the dagger.

She gasped in horror. "What is that . . . thing?" she asked.

"It looks like a baby rust monster," I said, remembering Master Sage Hix Loiren's *Corrosive Animals of the Heartlands* from Malchor's library.

"A . . . rust . . .," she stammered.

"Yeah, a rust monster. They live in caves and eat metal: ore, crafted, doesn't matter. They especially like magical metal."

She gasped again and snatched the dagger from the rust monster's mouth. In a single fluid motion, she grabbed the scaly little thing by the tail and flung it back into the water.

"Hey," I said, "it was helping you!"

"It was trying to *eat* my dagger!" she answered. She peered intently at her blade, running her finger along its edge, searching for any imperfections.

"At least it brought your dagger back to you."

"It's not damaged," she said, obviously relieved.

We both stood up and looked around. It took us a few moments to reorient ourselves, but we were soon on our way in the only direction we had left to go: deep into the cave. The pool of water emptied into a slow-running stream, which in turn emptied into a larger pool. A faint, nondescript echo soon grew into an almost deafening roar as we walked along the edge of an increasingly fast-moving river, the black water turning white around jagged stalagmites studded with crystals whose razor-sharp edges glinted in our torchlight.

We walked along the river, moving with the flow, for only twenty yards or so before our route became clear. Two bridges, narrow constructions of stone, arched over the water near the wall of the cavern. Below them, the river raged more violently than ever, narrowing and descending as it disappeared beneath an overhanging ledge.

Joen moved to the nearest bridge.

"Wait," I said. "I have a bad feeling about this."

"What, another umber hulk gonna jump out and attack us?" she asked.

"Har har," I said. I pulled a coin from my pocket and flipped it onto the bridge. The coin bounced along once, twice, skipping off the stone. My throw had been perfect, and the coin slid perfectly along the bridge's arc.

But as soon as the coin touched the center of the bridge, the stone structure simply disappeared. One moment there was a solid if narrow arch, the next, the coin dropped into the raging torrent below, swept out of sight. Then, as quickly as it had vanished, the bridge reappeared.

We tried the same trick again on the second bridge, with the same result.

"So," Joen said, "we find another way across, yeah?"

"There is no other way," I said. "Why would someone build a matching pair of magical bridges if we could just go around them? But there may be something more to it." I looked around and soon confirmed my suspicions.

Seven white candles sat in a line on a small, flat stone beside the river, directly between the two bridges. I moved to take a closer look.

"I've seen this before," I said. "In the Lady's Hall in Baldur's Gate. It's part of a prayer to Tymora. See how the wicks are very long?" I motioned Joen closer, and she approached hesitantly. "We light the candle on Tymora's end, and the wick will fall toward or away from the next." I took Joen's torch and moved to light the rightmost candle.

"How do you know which end it is, eh?" she asked. "I mean, what if you light Beshaba's candle instead? Won't that be bad luck?"

I shrugged and brought my hand to my chest, to the magical stone blessed by Tymora, to my curse. "Somehow, I don't think that's going to happen," I said.

Joen rolled her eyes at me. Even in the flickering, dim light I saw the motion clearly. But she didn't object as I brought the torch down to the candle.

But it wouldn't light.

"See?" she said.

I frowned and moved the torch to the leftmost candle. It wouldn't light either.

"Odd," I said.

"You think?" Joen crouched down beside me. "Oi, there's something written here." She pointed to the stone beside the candles, where, indeed, the otherwise-smooth surface revealed a beautifully flowing, carved script.

I pulled the magical lens from my pocket. "It says, 'Let Tymora's luck guide your path.' Great, that's useful. I mean, isn't that exactly what I've been trying to do? But the candles won't light."

Joen wasn't paying attention. As I rambled on, she took up the torch and set it to the center candle. After a few heartbeats, the wick fell to the left, lighting the next candle, and that one soon followed, and again. And as the fourth and final candle lit, the one all the way to the left, that bridge began to glow with a faint white light.

I looked at Joen with some amazement. "How did you know to do that?" I asked.

She shrugged and walked to the bridge.

"Wait a moment," I called. "You don't know it's safe."

"Learn to fly in the last few hours?" she asked me over her shoulder. She knew I hadn't, and we both knew we couldn't get back out the way we came. She shrugged and kept walking, taking the torch with her. I followed so as not to be left in darkness.

"So how much farther do you think it is, anyway?" she asked when I joined her on the other side. "To whatever it is we're looking for here, that is?"

"I don't know. I saw a light down this way, but it was far off and I couldn't really judge the distance."

"What kind of light? Was it that bridge, then?"

"No," I said. "It was a blue flicker, like a magical torch."

As I finished my thought, a blue light sprung up in the darkness, not a hundred yards from us, and maybe thirty feet off the cave floor. I stared at it a moment and would have liked to look a bit longer. I thought, though I couldn't be sure until my eyes better adjusted, that it was, indeed, in the shape of a flaming blade.

But as soon as the light sprung up, Joen gasped, and off she went again at a swift walk, then a light jog, and soon a dead sprint. With the magical boots I'd stolen from Sali Dalib, I had no trouble keeping up with her. But I wasn't sure I wanted to be going that direction so fast, so unprepared.

The blue light blinked out again, not as if it had been put out, but rather hidden from view. Joen slowed as we neared the spot where it had been, and we approached cautiously.

Two massive obelisks rose out of the cavern floor. Each stretched heavenward, to the darkened ceiling, coming to a point far above us. The torchlight caught on their surfaces, each of white marble, perfectly smooth except for runes carved around the thick stones, starting at the bottom and winding their way upward. The surfaces shone brightly, without a speck of dust on them despite the untold centuries they'd spent here undisturbed. They caught Joen's torchlight and threw it back at us, seemingly brighter than before.

My eyes traced the runes, following their parallel paths toward the ceiling. It took me only moments to be sure that, as I'd suspected, they were perfect mirror images of each other.

Joen's gaze, though, fell to the cavern floor between the spires.

"Oi," she said quietly. "Get on your guard, eh?" She gently set down her torch and drew her daggers.

I followed her gaze to the ground, to the object lying there, which she approached. Four feet across, perhaps, oddly shaped . . .

"It's a body," Joen said, kneeling beside it. "A dwarf. Doesn't look too old either."

"Not too old? A young dwarf?"

"Not too long lying here, I meant," Joen explained. "Dwarf's old, though, gray beard . . . and what's this?" She stood up, holding something that glittered in the light. As I sorted the object out, an empty feeling hit me in the stomach.

"Spectacles," I whispered. "Big nose?" I asked, moving slowly toward her.

"Big nose," she said, even as I finally saw the dead dwarf's face. "And he's holding something."

"His name is Alviss," I said, bending solemnly to regard him. I don't know why I did that, but I felt the need to look at him closely, to confirm his death, as if I were letting his spirit know that someone cared he was gone. I'd lost a lot of friends, I realized then, and many closer to me than Alviss had been, but I did care. I had to care, as I had to hope that someone might care if it were me lying there. It seemed obvious, and somehow I knew it anyway, that Alviss had died alone, in this dark and empty place. No one should die like that.

"He's a friend," I said.

Joen gently pried open his fingers to get at the object he held.

"Any wounds on him?" I asked.

"Don't see any," Joen said. "Look at this, though." She grasped some object and pulled it from his hand.

The still air was suddenly filled with wind, a powerful, swirling gale. Dust flew everywhere, obscuring everything. The two pillars glowed ever more brightly until they were unbearable to look at. I saw Joen stagger and fall, but I couldn't move to help her. A low hum resonated throughout the area, echoing off the distant cavern walls. Then, as suddenly as it started, the wind died away.

And all the light from the obelisks and from our torch died with it.

I drew my sword and looked around, listening for any potential danger.

"Joen," I whispered harshly, but got no response.

I tried to remember exactly where Joen had fallen, but the storm had been so disorienting. I moved slowly, feeling my way across the ground until I bumped into an object lying motionless. But it was Alviss, not Joen.

"Joen," I said again, more loudly.

I heard a shuffling noise to my side, much like the one we'd heard earlier when Joen had nearly lost her dagger. We'd never actually found out what had made that noise, I remembered. I could only hope that this noise was different, that this noise was my fallen companion.

I moved toward it, leading with my sword, flat side down so as not to accidentally cut Joen.

Something brushed past my shoulder and I spun, sword sweeping across.

Someone caught the blade and held it fast.

"Calm now," she said, but it wasn't Joen's voice, it was Jaide's.

"You've been following me, following us," I said.

"No," she replied. "I got here first."

"You knew where this place was? How to find it?"

"I do."

"How?"

"That should be obvious by now, child," she said somberly.

Only the darkness prevented Jaide from seeing the shocked expression on my face—eyes wide, jaw slack. "You're a Sentinel," I said. "Tymora's Sentinel."

"Take this," she said, forcing something into my open hand—the hilt of a sword. The hilt of my sword, my old magical blade that I'd thought lost. "How . . .?" I started to ask, at the same time bringing the sword's magical blue flame out. But as the area was bathed in a soft blue glow, my question caught in my throat.

On the ground, beside poor, dead Alviss, Joen lay motionless.

CHAPTER 76

JOEN!" I GRASPED HER SHOULDERS AND SHOOK HER, BUT SHE DIDN'T STIR.
"She's . . . is she . . .?" I stammered.

Jaide put a hand on my shoulder and grasped Joen's hand with the other. She closed her eyes, concentrating for a moment. "No," the elf said. "She isn't dead, just unconscious."

I breathed a long sigh of relief, then wrapped Joen in a great hug.

Suddenly the air around me felt different, denser somehow, and I became acutely aware of Jaide's hand. It had grown impossibly hot. The light from my sword flickered then died. The air seemed almost solid, and I found breathing impossible. Then I was bathed in bright light and breathed freely. It took my eyes a few moments to adjust. Jaide took her hand from my shoulder. The wind rustled my hair.

The wind.

I was outside, kneeling in the sand beneath a beautiful desert night sky, a few hundred yards from the cavernous hole that formed the entrance to the ruins of Twinspire.

And the girl wrapped in my arms was awake.

"Oi!" Joen said. "It's just me, eh? Relax!"

"I thought you were dead," I said, breathless.

She looked around. "I ain't dead? Well, that's a relief, eh?"

"What you picked up," I said, "is it the size of a fist? Perfectly round and black, heavier than it looks?"

She nodded. "Black pearl, right? Yeah. Why, what is it?"

"The Stone of Beshaba, I think," I said.

"Oi, I should probably put it back, then."

"I don't think you can," I said, but hesitated to say the rest. "I think it's bound to you now."

Joen's face fell as she ran through a stream of confused emotions. She started breathing in gasps.

"But we needed both to destroy both," I reminded her.

"Oi, but this is not good, eh?" she said, managing to catch her breath. "Now where do we go, and how fast can we get there?"

"We'll ask Jaide," I said, turning to the elf.

"We'll ask—?" Joen sputtered.

Jaide stood a few yards away, patting Haze gently on the neck, offering the mare a drink from one of the waterskins tied to her saddle. The mare was obviously happy to see the priestess.

"Oi, what are you doing here?" Joen said, rising to a sitting position. "Come to get your horse back?"

"First," Jaide said, "we have to be out of this desert."

I took Joen's arm, helping her to her feet. She rose unsteadily, but once she was standing she found her balance.

Perhaps it was the light—though the moon was full and the stars shone brightly, it was still dim—or perhaps the dust, but Haze's coat of striking white hair seemed somehow more lustrous than normal. Jaide, though, seemed somehow diminished from the last time I'd seen her. Her porcelain skin looked dull, wrinkles framed her eyes, and even a streak of gray laced her black hair. As usual, she wore her hair pulled over one ear, but the point of the other had a notch in it.

She saw me looking, and brought her hand up to her ear. "Shark bite," she said, "while I was recovering that fine sword of yours."

"Oi, do tell us how you managed that," Joen said. Anger tinged her voice, as it always seemed to when Jaide was around.

"Magic, mostly," Jaide answered. "Besides being one of the Sentinels, I am also a priestess of some power."

While I blinked and shook my head at that matter-of-fact admission, Joen seemed entirely unfazed.

"But how'd you know he lost it, eh?" she asked.

I piped in, "Sentinels watch their bearers, don't they?"

"Indeed," Jaide answered.

"So you were watching me when I fought Asbeel on the island."

"When *we* fought him," Joen said.

Jaide nodded.

"So you came out after me, what, to check on me? To give me Haze? To find my sword?"

Jaide nodded again. "Yes, and in that order," she said. "But also for another task." She turned to look at Joen, staring intently, as if she meant to drill a hole through the girl with her eyes.

Joen matched her intensity, even took a step toward Jaide. For a long time their eyes locked on each other until finally, Jaide blinked and turned away.

"I also came to ask your good Captain Deudermont to arrest and detain the pirates he had on board, and not to honor his word to them." She said it so simply, it took me a good moment to register her meaning.

"You told him to lock them up?" I said, unbelieving. "Even Joen?"

"Especially Joen," she answered.

Two sounds stuck me in rapid succession: the airy burst of Joen's horrified gasp and the soft sound of steel on leather as her daggers slid from their sheaths.

"Oi, you wanted me . . . killed?" Joen said with difficulty. She advanced another step, her pose threatening. I moved forward to intervene, but Jaide spoke first.

"Never that," she said. "I simply wished to keep you away from this place." Joen approached another step, but Jaide stood her ground, arms out wide, unthreatening.

"Keep me away, eh?" Joen snarled. "By whatever means?"

"Obviously not," Jaide answered. "I could have killed you any number of times or had you forcibly held in Silverymoon, or in the Tower of Twilight, or captured on the road. You have no idea the influence I could wield should I so desire."

"So why didn't you, then?" Joen pressed.

"I wanted him to come here." Jaide motioned to me. "I just hoped he would come alone."

Joen shook her head, either unsure or unbelieving.

I had it figured out, though. "You wanted me to take the stone because it wouldn't be bound to me," I said. "The Stone of Tymora is already bound to me, so the Stone of Beshaba would have no power over me. But now it's bound to Joen."

Jaide nodded. "After what I witnessed on that island, I knew she would follow you to the ends of the world if you should ask," she said.

I recalled my first experience with clairvoyance, the magic of distant seeing, also called scrying. I had sat in a darkened room in the back of an inn, watching through a crystal ball as Perrault, my mentor, had retrieved the Stone of Tymora from this very same elf. I should have known right from then that she was one of the Sentinels. Who else, after all, would be protecting the sacred stone? And my guide for that magical journey had been . . .

"What happened to Alviss?" I asked.

Jaide's gaze dropped to the floor. "He tried to take the stone, but it was not meant for him," she said, a great sadness filling her voice. "That is why I wanted to keep you away, Joen. Not only because I feared it would bind to you but because I feared the stone may well kill you."

Joen's stance had slackened some. She no longer seemed ready to pounce at Jaide. She even sheathed her daggers, though she kept her hands near their hilts.

"None of this answers my question, though," I said. "Where do we go from here? I suppose you know who and where the other Sentinel is?"

"I do," Jaide answered. "But it is not in my power to tell you."

"Not in your power?"

She smiled, a sad smile if I'd ever seen one. "The goddesses put many blessings upon the Sentinels, but also many curses. We are not allowed to interfere with you, only to watch and to ensure the stones pass as they should. We cannot tell you of the other bearers, past or present, or of the other Sentinel."

"Oi, can't or won't?" Joen asked.

"There is no 'or,'" the elf replied. "There is no choice. You seem to forget, both of you, the nature of the goddess I have sworn to serve for all eternity. Tymora is not the goddess of quests or processes. She rules the sphere of fortune, and as such, she impels us all to seek our own fates, to make our own ways. What I can tell you, though, is that you already know the name of the other Sentinel."

Joen and I looked at each other and it was obvious she wanted me to say something, but all I could do was shrug. What was I to do, tell a priestess she was wrong in the way she'd served her goddess for centuries? She was right, and no matter how unfair it felt, I knew she wouldn't tell me. But that didn't mean I had any idea who the other Sentinel was, or why she thought I should know.

"Now come, dawn is not far off," Jaide said. "We should camp and rest, and set out in the morning."

"Set out for where?" Joen asked. "Oh, wait, don't tell me, you—"

"Pick a place," I cut in, thinking maybe I was finally starting to understand the nature of the goddess of luck. "Anywhere, anywhere at all."

We thought a moment.

"The Tower of Twilight," I said at last. "We should inform Malchor of what's happened, and we can stay there a while before we move on."

Joen smiled, skipped over, and gave me a hug. She and Jaide moved—together, and not in anger—to Haze to unpack and set our camp.

But I wasn't sure we were much better off with Jaide than we had been with Chrysaor.

PART IX

"I was wond'ring," the pirate captain said, "when ye'd mention this."

The sun peeked over the eastern horizon, illuminating the beach. The pirates' torches had long since burned out. I'd been speaking in the darkness since, but neither my audience nor I seemed to mind much.

"Mention what?" I turned to face him, to find him holding a small metal object. My stiletto.

I growled slightly. "That doesn't belong to you," I said. "You don't deserve to hold it."

"No, I don't," he agreed, tossing it lightly to me. I was so stunned, I almost failed to catch the dagger.

"You'd return my weapon so easily?"

"Ye're already armed," he said. "Ye're outnumbered fifty ter one. Do ye think the weapon ye hold when we kill ye much matters?"

"So you do intend to kill me."

He laughed. "Yer story's nearly done, ain't it?"

"That's yet to be seen," I said, twirling my dagger about. "But tell me, what comes after that?"

He laughed again.

"Haven't ye already figured that out?"

"Well, then, I think this is where the story ends."

His eyes widened a bit. "Haven't we been over this?"

"If I don't tell you the story, it dies with me," I said. "Well, I think the rest of the story I'd rather let die."

For once, the pirate captain wasn't laughing. "Now, boy—," he started.

"Don't call me 'boy,'" I said. "The last one to call me that got run through." I flicked my wrist, and the magical blade in my hand rippled and extended, stretching into a fine saber.

"Young man, then," he said. "I'm not sure ye know what ye think ye know."

"I know what pirates do to their prisoners."

"Do they arm their prisoners?" he asked, leading.

"Apparently so."

"No, and ye know it," he said. "We don't be meaning te kill ye, or ye'd already be dead."

"You want to hear my story, or I'd already be dead."

"Aye, a fine story it be. But, ye see, there be a shortage o' fine sailors on the seas these days."

"And you fear I might kill one of your fine sailors?"

"I think ye might be one o' them," he said.

"What do you mean?" I asked. "I might be one of who?"

"One o' our crew," he said. "If ye be wanting the job. We could use someone who knows the sea, with the eyes fer the crow's nest."

"I . . .I," I stuttered. "I don't know what you're talking about."

"Join our crew," he said. "Tha' plain enough fer ye?"

"Yes," I said. "I mean, no. I mean, I get it, but I don't want it."

"Well, that be yer choice," he said. "But ye don't need fear us any longer."

"So you'll let me go?"

"Well, not jus' yet. We want ter hear the rest o' the story first."

"And when I finish, I can go? Why should I trust you?"

He did not smile, he did not laugh. He simply said, "The offer's good, young man. I got no grudge against ye, and nothing ter fear by letting ye go. Though I'd rather be adding ye to the crew."

"I think I've had enough of the sea," I said.

"And the story?"

"I've had enough of that too. But you asked, so here it is."

CHAPTER 77

UR JOURNEY BACK TO THE TOWER OF TWILIGHT HADN'T BEEN ESPECIALLY DIFFICULT. The days were warming, and summer was nearly upon us by the time we arrived.

"What is she, anyway?" Joen asked, patting Haze's lush mane in Malchor Harpell's stable.

"She's a horse, stupid," I said.

Joen pulled back from Haze, and the horse nickered softly, shaking her head. Walking around the mare to where I stood, still brushing absently at the pristine mane, Joen punched me in the shoulder. Hard.

"Ow," I said, recoiling. "What was that for?"

"Calling me stupid," she said.

"If the shoe fits," I said.

She kicked me in the shin. "Oi, what about shoes?" she said, winding up for another kick.

"Hey, hey, stop already," I said, retreating a few steps. "You're not stupid. I'm sorry I said you were." I laughed a little, and Joen joined in.

"Oi, but really," she said. "A horse doesn't walk on water, you know? So what is she?"

I shrugged. I'd never heard nor read of any creature like Haze, and it never occurred to me to ask someone who might have the answer. "Malchor or Jaide would probably know better," I replied.

"I think she's an elemental," Joen said.

"Or maybe half-elemental. Like Chrysaor. Haze's great-great-grandmother was a sea horse or something."

"No," Joen said. "She's more pure than that. She's not touched by the elements, you know? She walks on the water like it's just . . . natural, like she was born to it."

"The water walking actually tires her out," I said. "She can only do it for a short while."

"Well, if she's an elemental, she'd be from another plane, right?" Joen asked. "Like, from a place that's just water everywhere?"

"Maybe."

"So maybe she's just not used to this plane, or her magic doesn't work as well here or something like that."

I thought for a moment, then said, "No, I don't think that's it. If she were from a place that's just pure water, wouldn't she swim? And she's fine on land too. And there's that mist that rises from her hooves when she wants it to."

"Oi, I haven't seen that," Joen said, a bit of excitement in her voice. "Mist, eh?"

"Yeah," I said. "She can bring up a whole lot of it too. Like a big cloud rolling across the ground."

"Well, maybe she's all about the air, then," Joen thought aloud.

"Then she'd be able to fly."

Joen held her arms out to her sides like mock wings. "I'd love to fly," she said, closing her eyes and leaning forward as if into a strong wind.

I shrugged and said, "The land and the sea are enough for me."

"Enough?" she laughed. "You'd rather be tethered to the ground than free to fly?"

"To fly and to fall," I countered. "At least on land you know where you are."

"If I could fly, I wouldn't fall, eh?"

"Everything falls. Everything that climbs into the sky has to come back to the land. But all that flying, all that *freedom*"—I stressed the word sarcastically—"just means when you get back down, you don't have a place to call your own."

"Birds build nests, though," Joen said.

I laughed. "If you could fly, would you build a nest?"

Joen thought for a moment then shook her head.

"See, that's the problem with the freedom you want. You haven't got a place to keep the things you need, the people you love. You haven't got a home."

"Oi, I'd rather take those things and people with me. Then wherever I am, that's my home, eh?"

It was my turn to shake my head.

Before I could answer, the door to the stable swung open and Malchor Harpell walked in. "It's both," he said. "Haze is a creature of both air and water. And very astute of you two to figure that out, if I may say."

He'd been meeting with Jaide in private while Joen and I had tended to Haze.

"Both?" I asked. "Air and water? Then where is she from?"

"She is from right here, on our very own Prime Material Plane," Malchor said. "She was created of the elements of air and water and bound here by powerful magic."

"Oi, if she's made of magic, can she die?"

"She can be killed, certainly," Malchor said.

"But could she just . . . die of old age?" I asked.

Malchor shrugged. "It depends how she was created. But I doubt anyone powerful enough to bind her would want that. I'd rather expect that over time, her magic could simply fade away."

"When?" Joen asked. "Why? What would make her fade away?"

"Could be she's bound to a specific person or a specific thing. When that person or object is no more, the magic unravels. But if that were so, well, she wouldn't still be here." He stepped up to the horse and ran his hand along her flank.

We stood in silence for a good while, each admiring the beauty of Haze, each hoping she'd be with us for a good while longer. It occurred to me that she was my oldest friend. I'd met her when I was just an infant, when Perrault had taken me from my parents' ruined house and delivered me to Elbeth in the High Forest. The thought of her not being around any longer disturbed me greatly.

"Well, enough of all that," Malchor said at last. "I have guest rooms all ready for you, if you'd like to take some rest. How long do you plan to stay? My tower is open to you for as long as you'd like."

Joen shrugged, and I answered, "Not long."

"Very well, then. I'll show you to your rooms. You can get washed up, and we'll have a meal in an hour."

"Wait, Malchor," Joen said. "Are our old quarters open?"

"Yes, they are," he answered.

"Could we just take those instead of your guest rooms?"

Malchor smiled at her. "Of course, of course. You'll find all the doors unlocked. I'll see you in the great hall in an hour's time."

He bowed and left, and we walked in silence, following the old familiar path through the strange tower that had been our home for a year. As we approached the final door, the entry to the circular training hall, Joen hooked her arm through mine.

"I know who Haze is bound to," she said softly.

"She's not bound to me," I said. "She's older than I am."

"Of course," Joen said. "She's bound to Perrault."

That thought had crossed my mind, but I'd dismissed it. "You heard Malchor. If whoever she's bound to dies, she'd fade away. And Perrault is dead."

Joen stopped walking, pulling me to a halt beside her. "No he isn't," she said. She put her hand up to my chest.

"What, the stone?" I asked, skeptical.

She rolled her eyes, that familiar gesture of mock disdain I'd come to know so well. "No, stupid," she said. "Under the stone. He's alive in your heart, eh?"

I stared at her for a long time, then unhooked my arm from hers. I tried to say something, but couldn't push the words past the lump in my throat.

So instead, I punched her in the shoulder. Hard. "I'm not stupid," I said. I tried to say it casually, but my voice cracked somewhere in the simple statement.

Joen chuckled and rolled her eyes again, and pushed past me and into the room. She skipped off to her quarters, and I followed suit, heading to my old room to wash off the dirt of the road and the single tear I couldn't hold back.

"Oi, are you going back to Baldur's Gate?" Joen asked of Jaide, who sat across from her at the table. Malchor's great hall looked much the same as when we'd first arrived here more than a year ago. A feast of magnificent proportions covered the massive table. Malchor and Jaide sat side by side, with Joen and me opposite them.

"No," Jaide answered. "My duties there are at an end."

"What were those duties, anyway?" I asked.

Jaide hesitated. "It is the task of the Sentinels to watch the bearers of the stones, usually from afar," she said. "Not to interfere, but to ensure that the stones pass on as their wielders die."

"Oi, that's a bit morbid," Joen said.

Jaide laughed. "I held the Stone of Tymora for you," she said, motioning toward me, "until such time as you were ready. And I have now witnessed the Stone of Beshaba's passing as well. So until one or both of you pass on, I have no task but to watch."

"But you can watch from Baldur's Gate," I said.

"Or I can watch from up close," she answered. "Usually the Sentinels keep their identities hidden from the bearers, but since you both know me . . ." She let the thought trail off with a shrug.

"And not to interfere?" I said suspiciously.

Again, she just shrugged.

I let the subject drop, and the conversation soon shifted to the future. Joen still pressed for a return to the sea, and Jaide thought that a fine idea. I joined the discussion only halfheartedly. I knew exactly where I wanted to be going next and exactly what I had to do. I couldn't believe that Tymora's Sentinel would allow me to destroy the stone, but I couldn't escape the feeling that only Jaide could lead me to the magic I would need to do just that. Having her along would give me time to try to convince her, or trick her, into pointing me in the right direction.

After the meal, as we exited the great hall, Malchor put his hand on my shoulder, holding me back. Jaide and Joen paid little heed—they chatted like old friends, wandering off to wherever. The change from when they'd first met, on the deck of *Sea Sprite*, was remarkable. Then, Joen had taken a dislike to Jaide for no good reason and with no real explanation. But not long after Jaide teleported us out of the cavern, they had become as thick as thieves. In fact, I found myself a little jealous.

"You seem disinterested, my friend," Malchor said as the two disappeared around a corner.

"Disinterested in what?" I asked.

"In the future. Joen is excited, and even your elf friend is interested in where you'll go next. But you . . ." He let the thought trail off.

I shrugged. "They're acting as if it's all over," I said. I put my hand to my chest, to the sash cradling the stone against my heart. I said nothing, but Malchor understood the gesture.

"You still intend to destroy it," he said.

"I do," I answered. "But Joen has no past with the stones. The grief they bring, the destruction. She wasn't there when Perrault died, or when Asbeel burned the forest around me and Elbeth, or when my parents—"

"Her parents are dead as well," Malchor said sagely. "They have been since she was young, just like your own. Ill fortune falls on all of us from time to time, not just those who carry magical stones."

"It just falls on some more often than others," I said.

"Wise words. But will destroying the stones necessarily change that?"

"Yes," I answered. "I never wanted this. It's just by bad luck that I came to have it. If I can destroy it, I can take control of my own fortune."

Malchor was shaking his head before I'd even finished. "It will not change what has already happened."

"But it will prevent it from happening again, to me or to someone else."

Malchor blew a long sigh. "I'm not going to deter you from this, am I?"

"No."

"Well, then I may as well help direct your path."

"You have information?" I asked, a bit shocked. "Did Jaide tell you where the other Sentinel is?"

"No and no," he answered. "But I can find out with a magical ritual. It will require three things, though."

"Another test? I have to prove I'm worthy of your information again?"

"No, nothing like that." Malchor laughed, a strained sound void of mirth. "You've long since proven your worth. I simply require some components for the ritual. First, I need a lock of hair from the one Sentinel. Second, I need Joen's blood. Just a drop will do."

"And third?" I asked.

He paused a long moment before answering. "I need a name," he said.

"But I don't know the name."

"Jaide indicated to me that you've met the other Sentinel."

"Yeah, she told me the same thing."

"Well, think hard, then. Meet me in my quarters just before the midnight hour with the required components, and I'll help guide your path." He took his hand from my shoulder and walked away, leaving me to think.

I've met the other Sentinel, I thought. But who?

CHAPTER 78

MY HAIR?" JAIDE ASKED SKEPTICALLY.

I nodded, standing uncomfortably in Jaide's austere bedchamber.

"You intend to do some magic, don't you?"

I nodded again.

Jaide studied me for a long time. "I'm surprised, I must admit," she said. "I expected you to engage in some attempt to steal a lock of my hair. I certainly didn't think you'd just come right out and ask."

I shrugged.

"Why didn't you?" she asked, unfastening the tie that held her hair to one side, and pulling a small razor from the shelf beside her. She had taken one of Malchor's finest guest rooms, complete with a washroom and a full kit of grooming supplies.

You can read my mind, I thought but didn't say. *How can I sneak up on you if you can hear me coming?*

Jaide smiled and didn't answer. She brought the razor to her hair, cleanly severed a lock, and handed the hair to me.

But how will you get the other components? I heard her voice ask in my head. *The girl will not likely give you her blood so easily.*

Surprised, I asked aloud, "How do you know what else I need?"

"I gave our host the ritual," she answered.

I blinked a few times. "But you, the Sentinel of Tymora of all people, have known all along that I mean to destroy your goddess's artifact. And for all your talk about just watching, not being able to help us, you've helped us all along."

It was Jaide's turn to shrug. She turned away from me to the mirror on the wall.

I considered pressing her, but I figured she'd been as forthcoming as I could have hoped for, and far more than I'd expected.

"I need a name," I couldn't resist saying. "Who is the other Sentinel?"

"I've told you before," she said. "I can't fight your battles. That is for you to do."

"But you can give Malchor the ritual that will tell me who the Sentinel is?"

Jaide laughed. "I don't make the rules," she said.

No, I thought, not caring that she could hear, *you just bend them.*

She moved slowly, fluidly, each twist the natural extension of the previous, each setting up the next. The glint of metal from her hands, the daggers weaving and cutting, only amplified the mesmerizing effect of her dance. Forward, back, high, now low, she attacked, her blades striking the various arms of the practice dummy with perfect precision.

The room was much as we'd known it for a year. In the center of the circular chamber the oddly shaped, segmented, many-armed pillar stood impassively, accepting of its role as the victim of Joen's deadly dance.

Her tempo increased. The grace of her movements didn't suffer with speed. If anything, she seemed more fluid, more hypnotic. I stood in the doorway in a state of awe at how fine a fighter she'd become.

And I wondered how it would affect my plan.

I watched for a while as Joen went through her routines. She practiced with her daggers each night before bed while we were on the road, but only simple, slow attack and defense routines to keep her muscles in shape, to keep her memory sharp. She seemed grateful to once again have the dummy to spar with, to have a focal point for her energy. And she seemed grateful too, to have the full run of the room. She circled constantly, a slow waltz punctuated by occasional sharp sidesteps, usually followed by a devastating attack.

But not always. That was the beauty of her dance. Her moves flowed so well together, but not predictably. Anything she did, she could follow with a number of other moves—forward or back, attack or defense, it all blurred together.

Again she upped the tempo, her daggers a blur, her arms weaving together so quickly I was surprised she didn't tie herself into knots. But she remained precise, and the dull thump of steel on wood echoed through the room. She stepped to her left and stabbed out hard. She cut back to the right, and brought her daggers across in a quick cut. She stepped back then skipped forward, one blade high, the other low. Then, with a flourish, she spun a full circle, dizzyingly fast—and her foot slipped on the wood floor, sending her sprawling painfully to the floor. I gasped and she grunted. Her dagger came out of her grip and skidded across the floor, almost cutting her. She closed her eyes and groaned as she rolled over onto her back, gingerly touching bruises and pulled muscles.

"Are you all right?" I asked.

She didn't answer or even look at me at first. Instead she drew the deep black stone from her belt pouch and was about to throw it against the wall, but something made her stop herself. She looked down at it and I thought she was going to cry, but she sniffed and wiped her nose on the back of her hand, and put the stone back into the pouch. She looked up at me finally and said, "It'll kill me eventually."

I nodded.

"Dummy's all yours if you wanna spar, eh?" she said. "Maybe get familiar with your new—your old blade, you know?"

"It's all right," I said. "And I do want to spar. But not with the dummy."

She looked at me curiously, then turned her gaze to a rack set against a wall in the back of the room. The rack held fake weapons carved of wood that were magically enchanted to hold the same balance as their real counterparts. A saber and several daggers rested among the collection, along with many others.

"You'll have an advantage," she said. "I'm tired, you know?"

"So will that be your excuse when I beat you, or the whole bad luck thing?"

She grinned slightly, gave an exaggerated roll of her eyes, and scrambled to her feet and headed for the weapon rack. I followed her. She walked with confidence, even anticipation, but my knees shook.

Joen pulled a pair of daggers from the rack, twirling them to test their weight and balance. Apparently satisfied with her choices, she walked to the middle of the room. "So what are the rules, then?" she asked as I approached the collection of weapons. "First blood?"

Hopefully, I thought. "Until one or the other yields," I said. I took the only saber from the weapon rack. It was balanced to match my previous blade, so it was a bit heavier than the magical sword I once again carried. But it was familiar, at least.

Our first passes resembled her dance with the pillar. She stepped to her left and I matched her, keeping her in front of me. She moved back to the right and I moved with her. We rotated around each other in a slow dance, sizing each other up.

She darted forward, right arm extended, left tucked in close to her body. I stepped back, bringing my blade up to defend myself. Her straightforward thrust wasn't difficult to parry. My blade connected from below with hers, and the sharp crack of wood on wood echoed in the large chamber. I forced her blade up and out, her blade swishing harmlessly through the air near my head. I stepped to my left with the motion of the parry, keeping her body between me and her other dagger. But she didn't press the attack, instead withdrawing her extended arm.

I followed suit, bringing my saber back into a defensive position. I could have attacked, but her footing was good and her daggers still in place to deflect anything I could throw at her.

She stepped back and I stepped back, and we began our circling dance again.

"Thought I could end it quick, you know?" she said. "I want to get to bed soon."

"Don't worry," I answered. "It'll be over before you know what hit you."

"Oi, 'cause nothing's gonna hit me, eh?"

I lunged forward before she finished her taunt. The tip of my sword leaped at her face pulling my whole body out into a single line in perfect balance. My weapon covered the four feet to her in an instant. If she'd been distracted at all, as I'd hoped, she may not have been able to react to such a sudden attack.

But she was not distracted. She bent backward at the waist, taking advantage of my high angle of attack. Both her daggers came up in front of her, crossed, and braced against her forearms. Her blades, like mine before, defeated the attack from below, forcing my blade up and away from her body.

She continued to bend backward, sliding one foot out behind her to maintain her balance. She rolled one dagger under my blade, the other over. She then shifted her weight onto her back leg, sliding her forward leg out to the left, turning her body with it, so her side was to me.

If I'd had control of my blade, I could have taken advantage of her position. But I discovered that I couldn't move it at all against her surprisingly effective lock. Instead, I found my sword moving with her, across my body. She would disarm me soon, I knew.

I couldn't attack her, nor could I retreat to my defensive posture, and she knew it. I could see the confident smile creeping onto her face.

I couldn't move backward, so I moved forward instead. I pushed, lowering my right shoulder and slamming hard into her.

Joen, surprised by my move and stunned by the impact, tumbled away. She managed to turn her rough landing into a barrel roll, absorbing much of the impact. But she lost a dagger in the process. She came to her feet, looking a bit shocked and possibly even angry.

"Oi, so that's how it's gonna be, eh?" she said sharply. "I thought we were gonna be civil."

I grimaced. I didn't want to upset Joen, but neither could I accomplish my plan without causing her some injury.

"I'll be civil," I said quietly. "I'll even let you get your other dagger."

"How gracious," she said.

She retrieved her lost blade and set herself again in a defensive stance. Again our dance resumed.

This time, though, was a bit different. Our pace was faster. Step right, step right, step forward. We each launched a few short attacks, though nothing as ambitious as our first exchanges. Wood struck wood, and feet scuffed on the stone floor.

As we settled into a give-and-take routine, two things became obvious to me: First, Joen wasn't really very tired from her sparring with the dummy. And second, she was the superior fighter. It was only a matter of time before I made a mistake and she took advantage. This would all be for nothing, and I'd need a whole new plan.

I moved forward, chopping my blade down diagonally from the right. Joen had previously deflected that simple attack, but this time, she simply sidestepped it, moving out to her left.

She darted forward, a mirror image of her first attack. Her left-hand dagger led the way. Her right, she kept close to her body.

I halted the momentum of my sword easily, around my left hip, and reversed it. I put my right hand flat against the blade to balance it, turning my right elbow in low, pointed at Joen. I rolled my left hip forward as well, sliding my right foot back behind me. The hilt of my sword stayed against my hip, but the blade came around, turning with me, striking her dagger just before it would have stabbed my shoulder.

I extended my left arm, but left the sword's tip in place. The pommel of the weapon was farther from my body than the tip, and the whole length of the blade pointed at Joen.

I snapped the tip toward her, the blade cutting the air. But her right-hand dagger, still close to her body, was perfectly aligned, and she picked the attack off cleanly.

She brought her left hand back in toward me, her deflected dagger once again diving for my side. I had no choice but to slide to my left, away from the attack.

Though my body was out of her reach, she continued the motion, bringing her left dagger up beside the right, against my blade. With both hands and good leverage, she shoved my blade up and out. I tried to retreat but she mirrored my every move, pulling her body in close to mine. I tried in vain to maneuver my sword, to bring the blade in between us, to somehow break the clinch.

She pressed in tighter, one dagger holding tight to my blade, the other sliding down toward my chest. I could see the fire in her emerald eyes as her face came in close. I could feel her breath against my skin, her long hair brushing gently against my face.

She brought her dagger in against my chest, and her mouth a mere inch from my ear. "Yield," she whispered.

Every part of me wished to do so. She had beaten me, and I knew it. Were we real foes with real weapons, I would have been dead. I would have yielded, but I had other plans. I grasped the hilt of my sword in both hands, and tugged mightily on the pommel. I couldn't overpower her parry, but I didn't have to. I didn't need the blade of my saber. Either end of a sword hurts.

Joen's eyes widened in disbelief as the pommel of my wooden weapon rushed in, crashing against her face, knocking her off her feet.

She landed hard. Her two wooden daggers, suddenly free of her grip, clattered against the floor. Both hands covered her face, and she rolled around for a few moments in apparent agony.

Then she stopped, opened a space between her hands, and looked at me.

I expected anger, even rage. I thought she might get up and attack me. But behind those hands, her eyes were moist with tears. Behind the tears, her look was one of disappointment, of betrayal, not of rage.

I could hardly bear to look at her. I averted my eyes, backing slowly, expecting but not getting some harsh words from her, about how I'd cheated, how I should have yielded, how I was a terrible person.

But when she managed to sit up, all she said was, "Got that blood you came looking for?"

"I'm sorry," I whispered. "Jaide?"

She forced a smile and nodded.

Feeling like a fool, I turned and left, walking out of the room still holding the wooden sword—with the blood from Joen's broken nose on the pommel.

CHAPTER 79

MIDNIGHT COULD NOT COME SOON ENOUGH. I ARRIVED AT MALCHOR'S STUDY EARLY— I couldn't return to my room, so close to Joen's, so soon—but found the door locked. So I sat and waited, with a lock of Jaide's hair in one hand and the bloody practice saber in the other.

I couldn't stand to look at the weapon, to think about the awful thing I'd done to Joen, the crunching sound her nose made when it broke.

I tried to divert my mind, to focus on the third object, the one I had not yet found: the name of the other Sentinel.

It was someone I knew, Jaide had said. I knew a good many people—the crew of *Sea Sprite*, the various folk I'd met on my previous travels with Perrault, even a few interesting folk from Memnon and Calimport who'd helped or hindered my journeys. But I seriously doubted the Sentinel could be Sali Dalib, the merchant I'd stolen my magical boots from; or Dondon, the halfling disguised as a street orphan; or the nameless seer in the market in Memnon.

I also knew the Sentinel still lived, so that ruled out Perrault and Alviss, and a few others. So who, then?

My first thought ran to Captain Deudermont and the crew of *Sea Sprite*. I'd met them soon after the stone had come into my possession—actually, almost immediately after I'd lost Perrault. They had taken me in, protected me, though I was a stowaway on their vessel.

But my meeting them had been due to my actions, not theirs. I'd taken shelter from the demon Asbeel and hidden in the hold for days, only to be discovered after a battle with pirate raiders in which I was wounded. The Sentinels know where the stones are at all times, Jaide had revealed to me. If any on board had sensed the stone, they surely did not show it.

But maybe the Sentinel wouldn't have wanted to reach out to me then. As Jaide said, the Sentinels were meant to be observers in all this. But still, someone could have come to my aid during the fight instead of letting me battle a nasty troll all alone—and nearly die.

And, of course, I was still angry with Deudermont for what he'd done to Joen as we approached Waterdeep.

No, I decided, it was no one on board *Sea Sprite* when I'd arrived. Not Lucky or Tonnid or McCanty or Tasso. Not Deudermont. And that also meant it was neither Drizzt nor Wulfgar, who had also been on board at the time.

I was a bit disheartened at the realization that it couldn't be Drizzt Do'Urden. Our fates seemed somehow connected. For the past few years, we'd run into each other on several occasions. Always we were heading in the same direction, be it south to Calimshan or north to Silverymoon.

And besides, I thought the world of the dark elf. He always had words of encouragement or advice for me, sometimes even some real aid to my cause.

But I had confronted him about a connection to the Stone of Tymora, which had been suggested by the seer in Memnon. And he'd told me, honestly I believe, that he didn't know of what I spoke.

The midnight hour had arrived, but still Malchor did not appear. I thought about knocking at his door, but decided to wait a little longer.

I was missing something. Jaide thought I knew enough to figure out who the Sentinel was. She wanted me to continue my journey, for whatever reason.

Drizzt wasn't the Sentinel, but what of his friends? Bruenor Battlehammer, the dwarf warrior and now King of Mithral Hall, had arrived during the fight with the pirates. He'd ridden in on a flying chariot of fire, along with his adopted human daughter, Catti-brie. How had they found us, exactly? Of course, considering their means of transport it wasn't unreasonable to assume magical aid, but what if Bruenor knew exactly where I was? Or, more precisely, exactly where the stone I carried was.

I considered their arrival in a whole new light. I'd always assumed they'd been searching for Drizzt. But what if they had been actually searching for me?

Bruenor had never interacted with me much. He'd been cordial, though not especially polite—but of course, dwarven politeness is a contradiction. Catti-brie, though . . . When I lay wounded among the injured from the fight, when the ship's surgeon—or the sailor taking on that role—had used burning tar to seal my wound so that I wouldn't bleed out, it had been her angelic face that had watched over me, her hand that held mine.

And she was indeed beautiful. Malchor had said the goddesses had chosen two persons of exceeding grace as the Sentinels. Jaide surely fit the description. And Catti-brie would as well.

No, I realized. I was remembering what Malchor said incorrectly. Not "persons" of exceeding grace, but "elves" of exceeding grace. And Catti-brie was human. She was less than a decade older than I. She couldn't be the Sentinel.

Frustrated, I pounded the door, hard. My toe stung from the blow, but the sharp pain gave me something to focus my mind on. I didn't know many elves—only one, really—and I already knew she was a Sentinel. It couldn't be Elbeth, my next possibility, or any member of her Circle, or any of the people I'd met in my travels in Calimshan, or Chrysaor the genasi—

I stopped. I didn't actually know for sure that Chrysaor was a genasi. Robillard, the wizard, had told me so. In fact, not everything I knew about genasi necessarily fit with what I knew of Chrysaor.

A genasi is of elemental heritage, and I'd always assumed Chrysaor was descended from a creature of elemental water. As Robillard had said, somewhere in his lineage there was a water nymph, or something of that nature. The physical characteristics of the genasi were determined by that heritage. Chrysaor's skin and hair color seemed to fit, as did his seafaring tendencies.

But he also could breathe underwater and swim extraordinarily fast. He was more at home beneath the sea than on land. And this would not be true of a genasi.

On the other hand, there was a race of elves who lived beneath the seas, with pale blue skin and hair that ranged in color from green to white, including the sea-foam coloring of Chrysaor. Malchor had not specifically labeled the Sentinels as moon elves like Jaide, or even surface elves. An aquatic elf would not be out of the question, surely.

And I considered Chrysaor's actions too. We'd first met in the brig of the old *Sea Sprite*, in Memnon harbor. He'd been among the pirates who had attacked us. He had tried to kidnap me—had even succeeded in taking me off the ship, underwater into the harbor, and may have escaped cleanly had not Robillard come to my rescue.

Each time I'd met him after that, he'd not tried to kill me, but had actually aided my journey. He led me to the stone, guiding me to the isle where the Circle held it. He had helped Joen and me get to Malchor's tower. He'd then led us to the Stone of Beshaba, buried beneath the sands of Anauroch. His every action seemed to be about bringing the bearers, current and future, to the stones.

Yes, it all made sense. Chrysaor was the other Sentinel.

Malchor's door swung open. The wizard stood in fine ceremonial robes, a censer in hand, a grave look on his face.

"Are you ready?" he asked.

I nodded. But something nagged at me, something Jaide had said. But I couldn't quite place it.

I winced as the knife sliced my finger, but I made no noise, as Malchor had instructed. The study was dark except for a single candle set on the table in the center of the room. Scented smoke from the censer filled the small, round chamber. Two bowls also sat on the table, one in front of each of us. In mine, there was only crystal clear water. In Malchor's was the lock of Jaide's hair and a few scrapings of the stains of Joen's blood. As I held my hand across the table, a few drops of my blood joined the mix.

Malchor chanted, his voice low. I could barely make out individual words in the chant, and couldn't understand those I could distinguish—he spoke in some arcane language. He would chant for some time, he'd told me, and when he finished, the light would go out. And at that moment and that moment only, I would say the name of the other Sentinel. If I was correct, his image would appear in the water of my bowl, hopefully with some way of describing his location.

Why we had to go through all this elaborate ritual, I was not sure. I'd seen scrying magic used nearly two years ago, when Alviss had helped me spy on Perrault and Jaide. But that spying was directed at Perrault, not Jaide. Maybe it was more difficult to use such magic to find a Sentinel. I had no idea.

I trained my thoughts on Chrysaor, tried to convince myself that I was certain. He always seemed able to find me, he knew where Twinspire was, he actively wanted us to find the Stone of Beshaba. He was the perfect candidate.

But still a doubt tugged on my mind.

Why had he led me to the Circle, the druids who were determined to keep me and the Stone of Tymora hidden forever, in order to restore balance to the world? And when that plan had failed, why would he have helped us seek the Stone of Beshaba?

And when that was achieved, when we entered the cavern at Twinspire, he left.

Twinspire. Where we'd met Jaide. She'd said something . . .

Shark bite.

Jaide had a nick on her ear. She had been wearing her hair to cover it since, and the excuse was unconvincing. A shark had bitten her, she'd said. Wouldn't a nick from a sword be more likely?

I tried to visualize the nick and found it remarkably ready in my mind's eye. And it was not clean, not a cut like a fine sword or a dagger would make. It was the sort of thing a serrated blade might make as it pulled past her head and caught her ear.

And there was something she'd said when I asked for a name. "That is for you to do," she'd told me. It was the second time she'd used that phrase.

The first had been when I'd asked her to kill—

Malchor's chant rose to a crescendo and the candlelight disappeared, snuffed in a blink. It was time for me to say the name.

Chrysaor, my brain yelled. It must be. It can't be who you think it is. He's dead. He's gone. He's not the Sentinel.

But I knew it in my heart, and couldn't stop myself from saying it aloud.

"Asbeel."

CHAPTER 80

I'M NOT GOING WITH YOU." JOEN PUT HER HAND ON THE STRAP OF HAZE'S SADDLE AS I was tightening it.

"You'll be cursed with bad luck for the rest of your life unless we destroy these stones," I said, pushing her hand away and continuing my work. "You have to come with me."

She punched me in the shoulder, but not very hard. "You're dumb, you know? Do you even have a plan?"

"Asbeel is in Baldur's Gate. He's the other Sentinel."

"That ain't a plan."

"I'll make him destroy the stones."

"Oi, make him? Make him how?"

"I've beaten him before."

"We," she corrected me. "We beat him before—with help from Robillard. And just barely, eh?"

I shrugged. "I've learned a lot since then."

"Not enough, though. He'll kill you!" She let out a sort of half gasp, half sob, then brought her hand to cover her mouth.

I stopped what I was doing and stared at her. Tears rimmed her emerald eyes. She brought an arm up to wipe the tears away, but that only made her crying more obvious. She tried in vain to keep her sobs down, to keep a straight, tough face.

"I have a say in this," Joen said, her voice barely a whisper. "We should just move on, you know? We can live with this. We can be free."

"No," I answered. "We can't be free. These stones, these curses, will always be there to bind us unless we do something about it. Unless *I* do something about it."

She was shaking her head before I finished. "There's always something, eh? If it ain't the stones, something else will make bad things happen. It's just life."

"Then we need to make something good happen instead."

"I'm not coming with you," Joen said again.

"Fine, then," I said, turning back to my work. "I'll just have to do this alone." Joen turned and bolted for the door. She meant her exit to be dramatic, I knew, but it didn't go so well. Her ankle tangled in one of the straps of Haze's bridle that was lying on the floor beside the mare, and Joen stumbled and nearly fell headlong into the door. She, graceful Joen, would have slammed her face into the wood, already-broken nose leading the way, if the door hadn't opened.

Instead, she crashed into Jaide's ankles, nearly bringing the elf tumbling down beside her.

I trotted over as Jaide helped Joen back to her feet. The girl brought her hand to her face in a futile attempt to stem the trickle of blood from her nose.

"See?" I said. "Would you have fallen like that if not for the cursed stone you carry?"

"Yeth," she said, her voice slurred under the gushing blood. "You bwoke my nothe, with ow without the thtone."

"Yeah, and you're so clumsy, you always trip over lines and fall into doors. Nothing new there."

She punched me again.

"I am sorry about the nose, though," I said. "I had to do it to—"

"Thneak off without me and pewfowm a thecwet witual to find out whewe Athbeel ith, I know," Joen finished for me.

I stared blankly at her for a few moments.

"She said," Jaide spoke up, "you snuck off without her to perform a secret ritual to find out where Asbeel is."

"I know what she said," I lied. I turned to face Joen. "Does that mean you accept my apology?"

Joen looked at me for a long time in silence. The blood stopped flowing, and she took her hand away from her face, grabbing a rag to wipe up the last of the liquid. Finally, she nodded her assent.

"Good," I said. "Now, I have work to do." I went back to Haze, fitting her saddle tightly. There was strength in the horse's eyes, and she offered no complaint as I prepared her for the road. She would carry me to the Gate and help me avenge Perrault once and for all.

"Maimun," Jaide said from the door. "There is something we must discuss."

"Can it wait?" I said, not looking at her.

"I'm coming with you," she said.

"No," I answered. "I'll join you after I've finished with Asbeel."

"You don't make the rules," she said.

"My horse won't carry us both. I plan to go very fast."

"However fast you can go, I can go faster."

"And then what?" I asked. "You intend to help me fight Asbeel? I thought you couldn't fight my battles."

"I can't. But you're forgetting you need both Sentinels to perform the ritual and destroy the stones. And both stones too. I have to come."

"Joen's already decided not to come," I said. "So I'll have to just capture Asbeel, I suppose, and bring him back to you. You and Joen can go to Waterdeep. I'll meet you there with the demon."

"Oi," Joen said. "Don't be stupid. I'm going to come with you too so you don't get killed, you know?"

I smiled at her, but she didn't smile back. She turned on her heel and walked out of the stable.

We reached Baldur's Gate on Midsummer's Eve, just as the sun set. We approached from the east as the sun descended just behind the city, lighting up the towers and spires as if they were beautiful golden candles. The temple district, up on the hill and full of grand structures of marble and stone, looked especially wondrous.

"Where is Asbeel?" I asked Jaide. "You can sense him, right?"

"No, I cannot," she answered.

"I thought the Sentinels could always sense each other."

"Not when we're under the protection of one of the goddesses," she said, "the blessed sanctum of a temple dedicated to Tymora or Beshaba. When we seek shelter there, the connection is lost."

"Ah, so that's why you needed me to do the ritual," I said. "You knew he was hiding at a temple, but you didn't know which one."

"Oi," Joen cut in, "you mean the ritual where he had to break my nose?" There was an edge to her tone, though I couldn't tell if it was anger or simply sarcasm.

Jaide laughed lightly, apparently thinking it was the latter. "Yes, that one. Though he didn't have to break your nose, he just needed some of your blood."

I shrugged. "If I'd asked nicely, would you have helped me?"

Joen didn't answer and I cringed at the thought that I'd hurt her for no reason.

"It's also why," Jaide said, "I have for so long stayed here, in the Lady's Hall in Baldur's Gate."

"And why you kept the Stone of Tymora there," I reasoned. "Until you thought I was ready to take it."

She nodded.

"Oi, does Baldur's Gate have a temple to Beshaba?" Joen asked.

"No," Jaide said. "Few cities have organized temples to the Lady of Ill Fate."

"Well, then we know where he is, eh?"

"We should probably find lodgings for the night," I said. "We're tired from the journey, after all."

"Asbeel knows where we are," Jaide said. "I cannot sense him, but he can sense me and both stones. He knows we've come, and he won't give us a night to rest."

"We should at least put Haze up," I said.

"The temple can lodge her," Jaide answered. "Come, I'll lead the way."

CHAPTER 81

THE TREMENDOUS DOUBLE DOORS SWUNG OPEN SILENTLY WITH EASE AND GRACE THAT belied their massive size. The chamber beyond was equally massive, its walls and ceiling barely visible in the dim light of our torch and the dimmer light of the single candle resting on the altar at the far end of the room. The floor was pristine marble, white as snow, with swirls of pink and blue dancing across it in no discernable pattern. A single figure wrapped in a white cloak, hood pulled over his head, knelt before the altar.

This scene seemed so familiar, yet so foreign. I'd last looked upon this room two years ago this very night. Then, it had been Jaide kneeling at the altar and Perrault walking through the door. I'd only seen the room through Alviss's magical crystal ball, and how grand it had appeared. This time, though, from this angle, it seemed far larger and far less grand.

Joen and I stood frozen in the doorway, but Jaide walked confidently, her footsteps echoing in the cavernous room.

"Come," she whispered to us, and we each took a step forward.

"Yes," said the figure at the altar, his voice low and imposing. "Do come. It has been so long since I've seen you."

He rose to his feet, shrugged off the white cloak, and turned to face us. He was a mere silhouette against the candlelight behind him, but I knew the shape well enough: bald head, sharp features, pointed ears.

Asbeel.

"Not long enough," I practically shouted. "You should be dead."

"Yes, I should," he answered. "But so should you, many times over. We each have Tymora to thank for our lives." He walked out from the altar, and the light seemed to follow him—no, to grow with him. The walls, the floor, the ceiling all glowed with a dim white light that only grew as he approached. The light revealed the whole expanse of the room, the white columns lining the walls, and the alcoves with smaller altars and carvings and etchings of words, poems or prayers, I could not tell.

It also revealed the speaker—not Asbeel's red-tinted skin, sharp-toothed mouth, and twisted face. It revealed the pale skin of a moon elf, one of Jaide's kin.

I had long wondered what type of creature Asbeel really was. His demonic appearance had certainly suggested he was a being of the lower planes, but he didn't fit exactly with any of the types I knew about. Could it have been that his demon form was but an illusion? That he was truly an elf?

"Dear sister," the elf who was Asbeel continued. "At long last you've brought them both to me."

"She didn't bring us," I said.

"Oi, we've both faced you before," Joen added.

"Not you, fools," he said, his voice smooth and calm. "You are not relevant. I was speaking of the blessed stones."

"The bearers brought the stones of their own free will," Jaide said.

"Whatever helps you sleep, sister," Asbeel answered.

"We did," I said. "We brought them, and we're going to make you destroy them."

"Nothing would please me more."

"What's that supposed to mean?"

Asbeel laughed, a hearty laugh filled with mirth, something completely foreign to my experience of him. Always before, his laugh had been a horrid, grating thing.

"Have you truly learned so much and yet so little?" he said. "Next you'll tell me she hasn't even revealed how the ritual occurs!"

Jaide spoke before I could answer. "One of the bearers must kill one of the Sentinels, the Sentinel who watches his specific stone."

"Not a problem, then," Joen said, drawing her daggers and moving toward Asbeel. Jaide reached out an arm and held her back.

"Not here," she said softly.

"And why would you care that it not be here, sister?" Asbeel asked. "This is not the home of your Lady, after all."

"What's that supposed to mean, eh?" Joen asked.

Again Asbeel laughed that mirthful laugh, which I found somehow more unsettling than the wretched chortle I was used to. "It's worse than even I suspected!" he said. "My dear sister never even told you which goddess she serves? Oh, how cruel!"

My gut clenched tight. I did my best to keep a straight face, to not let Asbeel know his words had surprised me. But they surprised me all right, and the fact that one corner of Jaide's lips curled up in a touch of a smile, and that she didn't refute Asbeel's claim, made the blood run cold in my veins. I was so wrong, for so long, in so many ways. I was wrong about Perrault, then too, wasn't I? Wasn't it he who had put me in contact with Jaide, a servant of an evil goddess? Could he have known? Why would he have done that?

"You've all been manipulating me," I said, my voice tight in my throat. "You've lied to me over and over again, cursed me, pushed me around, put me in harm's way, led me here against my will. So she serves Beshaba, and you serve Tymora. That changes nothing."

"It changes everything!" he said, his manner maddeningly jovial.

"All it changes is who gets the pleasure of killing you," I said, drawing my magical stiletto—the stiletto I'd inherited from Perrault.

"Not here," Jaide said again, more forcefully.

"She's masked the truth from you, my dear sister has, and overstepped her bounds as much as I have."

"Why do you keep calling her sister?" Joen asked.

"Because," Jaide answered, "he is my brother by birth."

"Twins, you see," Asbeel continued. "The goddesses chose twins to bear their blessing."

"It is a curse," Jaide said.

"You no more believe that than I do."

"Oi, why not just stop, then?" Joen asked. "Just ignore your goddesses, you know?"

"Oh, he did," Jaide said. "That's why his appearance is so twisted beyond these walls. That's the punishment he suffers."

"You should suffer as I do," Asbeel said, his voice low and menacing, all traces of mirth gone from it. "You betrayed the charge as thoroughly as I did. More so, even."

"You seek the bearers of your sacred stone so that you may kill them," Jaide said, revulsion obvious in her tone.

"To facilitate the passage of the stones to their rightful bearers, this is our divine task. You, though, you tried to stop it entirely."

"Stop it?" I asked.

Jaide sighed. "I suppose it's time you knew everything. You see, your parents were my dear friends—as was Perrault, Alviss, and Elbeth. We adventured together—many years ago. And then one day your mother found the Stone of Tymora. And everything changed. Asbeel killed your mother, and your father when he tried to defend her, to facilitate the passage of the stone to someone of his choosing. But the stone bound to you before Asbeel could stop it. Asbeel was furious. And I was horrified. You were so young. Too young. When I heard what had happened, I had Perrault deliver the stone to me and hide you away. When you turned twelve, he felt you were ready to bear the stone and let the goddess's will reign. I feared the stone's power would be too much for you, but I felt it could not be lost. I had a responsibility to bear, and I had hoped Asbeel would relent. But then Perrault died." Jaide glared at Asbeel. "And I no longer wanted to take part in the havoc the stones wreck on their bearers' lives. Elbeth convinced me she could help, she and the Circle would take the stone back and protect you, but when that didn't work, and you escaped the island with the stone, I came to find you, to push you on your way. If this was to end, the ritual was the only way. But you had to discover it for yourself."

I swallowed. I had longed for answers for so long, but this was almost too much to bear. And there was still one thing that didn't make sense to me. "What about Chrysaor? Was he working for you all along?"

Jaide shrugged. "Chrysaor was helping both Elbeth and me to push you on your way, when we couldn't risk revealing ourselves to you."

Joen held out the black stone in her hand. "How does this thing fit into all this?"

"Not long after Perrault died, the last bearer of the Stone of Beshaba passed away, of natural causes, and so I hid it away," Jaide said. "In the one place in all the world where it could not seek a new soul."

"Twinspire," Asbeel growled. "I should have known it was there."

"The place where the goddesses first bound the stones to mortals, and the two of us to the stones," Jaide continued. "But Alviss discovered it. After Perrault died, I confided my plans to him. I shouldn't have trusted him. He insisted we should not meddle with Beshaba's will, and he spent the next year and a half searching for the Stone of Beshaba, aided by Beshaba's cultists."

I glanced at Joen and whispered, "The goblins! And those spies in the library."

Jaide nodded. "He had much help. He and his friends tried to stop you in your quest. And he found the stone first. I'm sorry for what had to happen to him."

I gasped. "You killed him?"

"It was the only way. My motives were the purest."

"And that's why you don't look like a demon—like Asbeel," I added.

"Wrong!" Asbeel shouted, his yell echoing in the cavernous temple. "She is not corrupted because she hides away in the sanctuaries of Tymora! Look at her closely in the wider world, boy, you'll see. She's turning. She's changing. She's becoming just like me."

"Enough of this talk," I said.

"Yes, enough indeed," Asbeel answered. "I tire of you, boy. If the ritual is the only way I can be done with you, then so be it. That is what you want, isn't it, dear sister? In full knowledge of the consequences?"

Jaide nodded solemnly. "I know now I cannot stand in the goddess' way."

"Then let it begin," Asbeel said. Asbeel walked through the doors. As soon as he crossed the threshold, his features changed. His face became twisted, his skin took on a red hue, and great black wings sprouted from his back.

"Oi, what consequences?" Joen asked, falling into step behind him, daggers still in hand.

"Our fates," Jaide said, "are tied to the stones. If Maimun succeeds in the ritual, he will destroy the stones and Asbeel and me along with it."

"All these years trying to hide the stones away," Asbeel said, "and only now you choose oblivion?"

"I choose freedom," she replied.

We walked through the city in silence and darkness. The only light was the occasional torch from a guard patrol on the walls, or a candle in the window of a shop or home of a night owl. The only sound was the soft clap of our feet against the cobblestone roads.

Our path wound through the middle of the city, though I was certain it would have been faster to skirt the edges. I assumed at first that Asbeel simply wanted to avoid any potential guard patrols—after all, he was wearing his demonic visage openly, though from past experience I knew he could hide it if he so desired. But he walked with a confident swagger, and he led us with purpose.

So when he came to a stop outside a nondescript building in a nondescript part of town, I was somewhat surprised.

"I thought you said the docks," I said. "Or would you rather die here?"

Asbeel laughed. "Don't you recognize this place, boy?" he said.

I looked around for a moment, taking in the scenery. Then it hit me.

"There should be a sign above that door," I said. "This is the Empty Flagon, Alviss's tavern."

"It was indeed," the demon said with a laugh.

"So you brought me here, why? To show me that even the places you burn down are rebuilt?"

"I didn't burn it down," he said.

"Then who did?"

"I don't care one bit about that. I brought you here to remind you where your dear mentor died. If he cannot best me, what makes you think you can?"

My stiletto was out of its sheath before I fully registered his statement. With a flick of my wrist, I triggered the dagger's magic, extending it into a fine saber, thin and balanced and just slightly curved. And ever so sharp.

Asbeel laughed again, more loudly. "Not here, boy, and not yet."

"I say right here," I growled. "Right now." I advanced a step.

"Stop." His voice was forceful, and there was magic behind it as well. I felt the waves of mental energy roll through my brain, commanding my limbs to hold fast, demanding that I obey.

Something seemed to shift in my mind. It flooded down through my body like a shower of warm water. All at once I could feel a series of connections taking shape in my mind and body. Throughout the thirteen months at the Tower of Twilight, I was fed subtle lessons—fragments only—hidden in the exercises and books. I never saw them as connected before, never saw the whole. Never knew I was learning to resist, to make my own choices. To be my own man.

With a silent thanks to Malchor Harpell, I took another step forward, defiant.

"You do not know the ritual," the demon said, a note of respect in his voice for the first time.

"I don't care," I answered. I gripped my sword in both hands, rushed forward, and swung with all my might.

Asbeel brought his empty hand up to block, but it wasn't empty. His own wicked sword—a huge piece of twisted metal, curved and serrated and burning with red flame—appeared from nowhere to intercept my swing.

I put all my weight behind that blow, all my strength. Metal clashed against metal. Asbeel's sword, held in one hand, moved barely an inch.

Undeterred, I chopped again, a mighty overhead swing. My defenses were nonexistent. If the demon took a swing at me, I would be helpless.

But he didn't have time to swing. He could only maneuver his much larger blade up above his head to catch my sword. Again, the ring of steel filled the air. Again, I withdrew my blade, my attack defeated.

Blue flame, I thought, and my sword responded. A thin blue fire traced along the sharp edge of the sword, a mirror to Asbeel's red. I brought my sword up beside my ear, set my feet a half step apart. I moved my right hand from the hilt to the blade, resting my palm against the flat of the sword, just above the hilt. I let that hilt rest beside my ear.

"Come, then," I said. "Do your ritual, and let me kill you."

"The ritual," Jaide said, "is simply combat. A bearer fights a Sentinel, the hands of fate—Tymora and Beshaba—choose the victor, and either the bearer dies and the stone passes on, or the Sentinel dies and the stone is no more." Jaide looked to me. "I assume you choose to fight Asbeel."

"Gladly," I gripped the hilt of my sword tighter and glared at the demon.

"Oi, then why do you need all four of us here?" Joen asked.

"Proximity," Jaide said. "The stones must be together to be destroyed."

Asbeel flashed a wicked grin. "It is as I told you, children," he said. "But I choose the time and the place."

I rushed forward, lunging for his heart, but he retreated a few steps. His wings beating mightily, he lifted off the ground.

"The docks," he said. "There we will finish this. Look for my flame." He beat those horrid, batlike wings again, ascending into the night sky.

"Why did he bring you here if he wanted to fight at the docks?" Joen asked.

"He thought he could intimidate me," I said. "But he was wrong. This place doesn't remind me of where Perrault died. Perrault died at the docks when Asbeel struck him. This place is something else, was always something else."

"This is where you brought Perrault when he was injured, right?" Joen said.

"And it's where his dearest friend lived," Jaide added.

I nodded, feeling a new strength surge inside of me. "This was not his death. It was his home," I said.

CHAPTER 82

IF I HAD ANY DOUBT WHAT ASBEEL MEANT WHEN HE TOLD ME TO SEEK HIS FLAME, IT WAS made ever so clear when we reached the docks. A single boat, perhaps thirty feet long with a single sail, sat at the end of one short pier in a nearly empty section of the harbor.

The sail was, incidentally, ablaze.

A small group of people had gathered on the shore nearby to watch. Mostly they were the vagrants of the area, those who would still be awake at this late hour. We pushed through them, and they gave way willingly.

Asbeel awaited our arrival on the boat. He stood directly below the flaming mast.

"Whose ship is this?" I said, stepping to the end of the short pier.

"Ours now," he said. "You've learned much since last we met."

"I have. Have you?"

He laughed. "You have much yet to learn, though."

"We shall see."

"Indeed." He set his feet wide apart, brought his sword up, its jagged, twisted hilt near his forehead. "Come on, then."

I stepped onto the ship, set my feet and my blade, and again called up the sword's blue flame. Joen moved to follow, but I motioned her back.

"I have to do this alone," I said.

Asbeel heard me and laughed.

Joen shook her head. "You ain't alone, though," she said. "I'm here."

"No," I said. "He's mine. Mine alone."

Joen looked hurt. I turned away from her so I wouldn't have to see that expression, so I wouldn't lose my focus on the task at hand.

"You never did get Malchor's lesson, did you?" she asked in a whisper. "He told you to release your arrogance, but you're cocky as ever. And you don't kill."

I heard her, but the words barely registered. I approached Asbeel, weapon at the ready. Joen didn't follow.

I circled to my left, as I had in my spar with Joen, intending to take stock of the demon. He stood impassive, his sword held high, his back to the mast. He didn't even turn his head to follow me. Did he want me to kill him, to be done with it all?

No, I thought, that would be too easy.

I moved all the way around to his right side. Any farther and I would have to contend with the mast itself should I attack. So I had a choice: attack now, or reverse my circle.

The latter would reveal weakness in my approach, so I chose the former.

I stepped forward, bringing the sword in a tight circle over my head, dropping my right hand to the hilt as it swept past my ear. The momentum of the quick motion brought my arms out and my blade whipping around, fast and true, at Asbeel's midsection.

He didn't move at all. My blade sliced right through him—or rather, through the air, through the illusion of the demon. I noticed a bit too late. I couldn't stop my swing. My fine sword bit deeply into the ship's mast.

I heard a rush of air behind me. On the pier, Joen shrieked. The demon swept over the far rail of the ship where he'd been hidden from my view.

I couldn't release my sword. I couldn't block his attack. All I could do was let go of my blade and dive forward, tucking into a roll as I went.

I felt the rush of air, the heat of the demonic flame as his sword swept across just inches above me.

I rolled to my feet, skittering away from the demon. He advanced, smiling wickedly.

"You didn't fight fair!" I yelled.

"Those aren't the rules," he said. "I don't need to fight fair. I just need to win."

As if to enhance his point, he grabbed my stuck sword, pulled it from the wood, and flung it aside. It should have fallen into the water, but at the last moment it hit a guide rope and spun around it, momentum lost, so that the sword fell instead on the deck, though farther away from me.

Asbeel advanced slowly, tracing his finger along the edge of his horrible sword. He seemed to be savoring the moment. I retreated as far as I could, to the stern rail of the ship.

I was out of options. I needed to take a chance. He approached, barely five feet from me, still grinning wickedly. Distracted, maybe?

I dived to the side, to his left, away from his sword hand. I tucked into a roll, meaning to tumble right past the surprised demon. It was a good plan.

Except, of course, he was not surprised. He kicked out his muscled leg, catching me square in the forehead, and sending me skidding across the deck.

"And so it ends," he said somberly, raising his sword for the killing blow.

I struggled to stand, but my head throbbed, my ears rang. I couldn't find my feet. All I could see was that horrid sword, the blade that had killed Perrault, that had taken so much from me.

I heard a scream, but it didn't register. I saw a flash out of the corner of my eye, but it could not take my focus. All I could think of was my impending death.

But then Asbeel withdrew, howling in anger and pain. He turned to face the pier.

Something small, something metal, fell to the deck. It was one of Joen's daggers, its blade wet with Asbeel's blood. She'd thrown it and obviously, she'd hit the mark.

I scrambled forward and grabbed the dagger. He seemed not to take note. I thrust the blade upward, as high as I could reach from my prone position.

It dug deep into Asbeel's thigh, and his scream amplified tenfold.

He brought his sword down, pommel first, driving it into my back. This was not much better than the blade would have been, though. It was that jagged, twisted hilt that had struck Perrault two years ago, that had caused the poisoned wound that had eventually killed him.

The wicked metal cut through my cloak, the once-magical cloak I'd inherited from Perrault, as if it were paper. It dug deep into . . .

Not my back. Surprised, I pulled away, scrambling toward the rail, still holding Joen's bloody dagger. Asbeel didn't pursue, instead falling back several steps.

I climbed to my feet, still amazed that I wasn't even wounded. But as I rose, something heavy fell out of my shirt.

The sash that held the stone had taken the blow, and had been severed in the process.

"This is not how it goes!" the demon roared.

"As if you make that choice," I said. I flipped Joen's dagger to her and scooped up my own sword. Together, we advanced on the wounded demon.

A column of light, narrow and small but brighter than any torch, appeared in front of Joen, then another and another, quickly encircling her. She tried to move forward, but the light was like a steel cage.

"He is correct," Jaide said, stepping onto the ship. No longer were her hands empty. She held a staff, itself also appearing as if it were made of light. I'd seen her fight with that staff one time, against Asbeel. "Joen should not interfere, and she will not again. This fight is for you alone."

"It is already tainted," Asbeel spat. "The wench has already defiled the battle."

"Then Jaide should release her," I said. "And we'll just kill you, ritual be damned." I scooped up the severed sash, held it high. "I'm starting to think I like this thing after all."

Asbeel growled, but had no answer.

I settled into my attack stance again, and the demon set his guard high, as his illusion had done earlier. But he clearly favored his uninjured right leg. Blood poured out of the wound in his left.

I decided to change tactics and abandoned the Eastern-influenced stance I'd adopted at Malchor's tower.

I set my trailing foot behind me, angled left to right, and my forward foot I set under me, pointing straight at my foe. I let my right hand trail behind me, curled up like the tail of a scorpion. I brought my sword to my forehead in mock salute, sweeping it out to the side then back to my defensive posture.

"So you regress," the demon said snidely. "You fall back on Perrault's style, the one that got him killed."

I didn't bother answering the demon. I shuffled ahead a few steps and lunged, dropping my trailing arm and leg to full extension, the tip of my sword leaping for his heart, my whole body a perfectly balanced, perfectly smooth line.

Asbeel brought his sword across and picked off my attack, but the motion clearly pained him. I withdrew. The length of my retreat, a full three feet plus the length of my blade, put me out of even his considerable reach, should he wish to counterattack. I lunged again, this time angling my sword to my right and down, directly at his wounded leg.

He brought his sword down, but not quite quickly enough. My blade grazed along the already bleeding limb, opening a fresh gash.

Asbeel howled and swung his sword, aiming for my head, but I had already withdrawn and reset, and his blade whistled past harmlessly short.

As soon as the sword passed, I lunged, again aiming for his wounded leg. He could not possibly defend with his blade, so he instead tried to move the leg. But it was slow, and he was off balance, and I scored another solid hit.

Asbeel tried to retreat, but I paced him, stabbing at his leg repeatedly, sometimes hitting, sometimes just missing, but always keeping him on the defensive, on the retreat. I drove him all the way back to the far rail of the ship, and lined up one final lunge.

He was wounded, he was tired, he was off balance. There was no way he could stop my attack. I lunged for the demon's foul heart.

As I started my motion, the deck before me burst into flames. Immensely hot, they rocketed ten feet into the sky, a wall of red fire. I only barely managed to stop myself from diving headfirst into the blaze. My arm sunk in to the elbow.

In searing pain, I withdrew. Only by Tymora's cursed luck was I still holding my sword. I couldn't feel my arm at all. I fell to the deck, writhing in agony, trying in vain to regain some composure before the demon dropped upon me.

He emerged from the fire limping heavily, barely able to put any weight on his many-times-wounded leg. But he would not have to in order to kill me, I knew. My mind screamed at my body to stand, to mount some defense, but my muscles would not heed the call. All I could manage was a crawl toward the pier, a futile attempt to escape.

It became even more futile as another wall of flame leaped up from that rail. I heard the lines tying the ship to the dock snap. We were drifting in the current of the great river Chionthar, headed for the open sea.

Asbeel laughed at me. "I don't even need to do anything, do I?" he said. "The fire alone will kill you and the girl." Within the cage, Joen was crying and mouthing words, but the magic apparently also blocked sound. I heard nothing.

I was about to die, and I just wanted to hear her voice. I looked at her, into her beautiful emerald eyes. At least these two beings could not steal that from me, that last look.

Asbeel approached, albeit slowly, and raised his sword.

I brought my own blade up in my right hand, my left tucked uselessly against my chest. It would offer a feeble defense, I knew.

Asbeel's sword started its descent.

Then it flew away, along with the demon.

Haze had plowed in hard, driving her head into Asbeel's chest, launching him across the deck. She stood over me as I shakily rose to my feet, still clutching the sword in my good hand.

The demon roared, rising to his feet, every bit as shaky as I was.

There it was, at last, I knew. The truth of what Malchor had told me. I had to lay aside my arrogance, else I would face the demon alone. And had I been alone—truly alone, as I insisted moments earlier—I would be dead already.

Above, I heard one of the crossbeams holding the sail snap, then the other. The flaming canvas dropped to the deck.

"Well, I said it already," Asbeel said, his voice once again confident. "I can just let the fire kill you."

I leaned heavily against Haze, the heat of the inferno sapping my strength. I could hardly argue. Even Haze seemed somehow less substantial in the fire.

And less, and less. A thick fog rolled out from the mare even as her physical form seemed to fade. Soon, the boat was blanketed in a thick cloud of cool fog. It didn't last long, fading after mere moments, and when it was gone, Haze was nowhere to be seen.

Neither was the fire, though. The fog had quenched it completely.

"And so another one dies," Asbeel taunted.

"You know what the difference is between you and me?" I asked.

"There are oh so many! Age, prowess, wisdom, take your pick."

"It's much simpler than that," I said. "I can walk."

I rushed forward in a suicidal charge, swinging my sword wildly.

Asbeel blocked my first swing and my second, but on my third, he missed the parry.

Perrault's magical saber dug deep into his shoulder. I pressed with all my might, forcing the demon and his weakened leg over backward. He fell hard to the deck, his sword slipping from his grasp, over the rail, and into the water below.

I withdrew my blade, lining up the killing blow. Asbeel grabbed it with his bare hands, wincing in agony as the blue flame burned his flesh.

"What do you fear the most, child?" he whispered.

"Not you."

"No. You fear the loss of something."

I glanced at Joen, only for a heartbeat, but Asbeel saw it.

"Exactly," he said, and he let go.

My sword drove into his chest, through his heart, and out his back.

The demon gasped in pain. "She lied to you," he whispered.

"You've all done nothing but lie to me," I spat.

"My sister. She lied. The ritual is in two parts. If one bearer kills his Sentinel . . ."

I twisted the blade, and Asbeel writhed. "Done," I said.

"Then, the other Sentinel kills . . ." His words trailed off, his eyes went dark.

It took me a moment to register his words—a moment I didn't have.

"Joen!" I cried, turning to face her. The magical cage had fallen away, and she was smiling at me.

Jaide's magical staff was swinging for the back of her head.

And Joen had no idea.

The staff struck her hard, the dull crack echoing across the water. Joen fell limp, tumbling over the rail into the rushing river.

I ran across the deck to the rail, still holding my bloody sword. But the water was pitch black, and I could see nothing.

"Joen!" I called. "Where are you! Answer me, please!"

"She's gone," Jaide said softly.

I turned on her, bringing my sword up. "You lied to me," I snarled.

She nodded.

I rushed in to attack and she didn't defend herself. With hardly a thought, I plunged my sword into her chest. As with Asbeel, I drove Perrault's sword through her heart and out her back.

Asbeel had been Perrault's sworn enemy, had killed the great bard. Jaide had been his friend, had helped protect him—and me.

But she was a liar and a murderer. I withdrew my sword, and she tumbled to the deck. I drove it in again.

"I am sorry," she whispered. "But you are free now."

Her eyes closed for the last time.

I slumped to the deck beside her. The stone, still in its sash, rolled across the deck to me.

Free, yes. But broken too.

EPILOGUE

A terrible woe that be," the pirate captain said. "And I see why ye didn't want ter tell us tha' end. But tell me, young man, aren't ye glad ye got it off yer chest?"

I managed a smile past the moisture in my eyes. Yes, it had hurt, but it had felt good too.

"How long has it been since?" he asked.

"Two long years," I said. "And until you took it from me when you took me captive, I carried the stone still.

To remind me of what I lost."

The pirate captain nodded. "So, will ye reconsider me offer?" he said.

I shook my head no.

"Aye, I thought not. But either way, ye'll be needing this back." He held out his arm, extending the torn leather sash that still cradled the Stone of Tymora.

"No," I said through the lump in my throat. "I won't. It's not magical anymore."

"Funny," he said. "I got me a couple wizards on me crew, an' they looked at it good, an' they tell me it still be powerful magic."

I shrugged and said, "Maybe some residual . . ."

"See, they also say this one's magic too." He withdrew a small black object from his pocket and rolled it to me.

The Stone of Beshaba.

"Where did you get that?" I asked.

A female voice spoke up from behind me, from the entrance to the cave. "He got it from me."

I turned to face her. Her blonde hair, freshly cut, bounced across her shoulders, and her broad smile lit the beach around her. Her emerald eyes, wet around the rims, bored into me.

Joen.

I rose unsteadily to my feet as she approached, slowly at first, then all in a rush. She wrapped her arms around me in a great bear hug.

"How . . . I thought . . .," I stammered, searching for something to say.

She brought her finger to my lips to silence me. I stopped talking, stopped even trying, and just looked at her.

She leaned in close, moved her finger out of the way just long enough to plant a quick kiss on my lips. Then she tipped her head, indicating the pirates behind me.

I turned to look and saw that the pirates were kneeling before her.

"A good yarn indeed," the pirate captain said to Joen. "You were right as a'ways, me queen."

"You're qu—?" I started.

"That's a whole other story," Joen said. "It'll take a while in the telling."

I looked around at the gathered pirates, the island beach, the predawn light breaking over the horizon. I laughed at the thought that this, here, was home—a home that Joen had brought me to.

"I've got time," I said. "And freedom."

ABOUT THE AUTHORS

R.A. Salvatore is the author of forty novels and more than a dozen *New York Times* best sellers, including *The Pirate King* which debuted at #3 on *The New York Times* best seller list.

Geno Salvatore has collaborated on several R.A. Salvatore projects including Fast Forward Games' *R.A. Salvatore's The DemonWars Campaign Setting* and *R.A. Salvatore's The DemonWars Player's Guide.* He co-authored R.A. Salvatore's DemonWars *Prologue,* a DemonWars short story that appeared in the comic book published by Devil's Due Publishing. He is a graduate of Boston University and lives in Massachusetts.